# Cassandra's Conflict

# Cassandra's Conflict

FREDRICA ALLEYN

First published in 1993 by
Black Lace
332 Ladbroke Grove
London W10 5AH

Copyright © Fredrica Alleyn 1993

Typeset by CentraCet, Cambridge
Printed and bound by Cox & Wyman Ltd, Reading,
Berks

ISBN 0 352 32859 2

# Chapter One

$A$s the taxi sped through the streets of Hampstead, Cassandra Williams tried not to get too optimistic. Certainly the job sounded ideal, and the woman at the preliminary interview had seemed to think that she was highly suitable, but as always at times like this, her ex-husband's parting words came back to haunt her.

'You're hopeless, Cassie!' he'd shouted, throwing his clothes into a suitcase. 'I should have left you years ago. Most men would have given up after the first six months.'

'I don't know what you mean,' she'd cried, but deep down she did. She'd always known, right from the wedding night, she just hadn't wanted to hear him say it.

'You're frigid!' His voice echoed round their small flat, and even Paul had the grace to try and soften the accusation once he saw the look in her eyes. 'It's probably not your fault,' he conceded. 'Your parents were old enough to be your grandparents, and they never let you out of their sight long enough for you to learn what life was really about, but I'm not wasting the rest of *my* life trying to show you.'

For a moment Cassandra had considered suggesting that his clumsy fumblings and lack of experience hadn't helped her either, but in the end she kept quiet. After all, Louise obviously found him exciting or she wouldn't have bothered to entice him away.

When he reached the front door she made one final appeal to him. 'But what shall I do, Paul? I've never worked. I came straight from home to this flat. How am I going to live?'

'I've no idea, but don't try going on the streets, you'll starve to death,' he said cuttingly, and that had been the end of her marriage.

'Here we are, Miss,' the driver said. Cassandra came back to the present with a start and climbed slowly out onto the pavement. The taxi had stopped in front of a pair of wrought-iron gates at least eight feet high. Behind them she could see a long gravel drive curving away out of sight behind some tall trees.

'Seven pounds fifty,' the driver said impatiently.

Cassandra handed him a ten pound note and he promptly drove off without even offering her the change. It didn't seem a good omen.

The gates were locked, but there was no sign of a bell. Glancing up, Cassandra saw a tiny surveillance camera pointing down at her, its glowing red light indicating that she was being filmed. As she remained staring at the camera in surprise, the gates swung silently open. Swallowing hard, she began to walk up the drive.

Once round the bend and out of sight of the road, it straightened again, ending in front of a low-built, Georgian-style house. There were numerous windows, most of them with continental shutters on the outside, and as Cassandra stared about her she thought how very quiet it was after the bustle of central London. She might almost have been in the middle of the country. Distracted by the silence, she failed to notice the young woman looking down at her from one of the top floor windows.

Before she had time to ring the bell, the front door was opened by a very pretty young maid in a smart grey and white striped uniform. Cassandra held out the letter of introduction that the woman had given her. 'My name's Cassandra Williams,' she explained. 'I have an appointment with Baron von Ritter at eleven o'clock.'

The maid smiled but still didn't speak, she merely gestured for Cassandra to follow her across the rather dark hall with its highly polished parquet flooring and into a small ante-room. She sat slowly down on one of the two winged chairs set on each side of an ornate marble fireplace.

After the maid had gone there was the sound of a door opening and a woman in a navy and white uniform walked briskly past Cassandra's line of vision and out of the front door. Cassandra guessed she was another applicant and thought despondently that the woman looked far more qualified to be a nanny to the baron's two small daughters than she was.

As she continued to wait she realised that the house was amazingly silent. There were no sounds of children's laughter, no footsteps to indicate that people were moving around anywhere, and no sounds of conversation. If she hadn't seen the young maid and the woman leaving she could have imagined herself entirely alone, and yet she knew from the first interview in the Kensington office that the baron had a fiancée, two young daughters and what the interviewer had called 'a full complement of staff'.

Cassandra began to feel a little uneasy. Apart from the woman in Kensington, no one knew of her connection with this house. If anything were to happen to her, no one would realise. Both her parents were dead now, and she never heard from Paul. Fear tightened her throat and she started to get out of the chair. Suddenly her instinct was telling her to go, and go quickly.

'Mrs Williams?' asked a low, cultured voice.

Cassandra turned. The man in the doorway was about six feet tall. He was tanned a golden brown and his fair hair was parted at the side to flop untidily down over his right eye. His face was round, almost cherubic, but his eyes didn't match it. They were a dark brown, large and widely spaced with arched eyebrows that made him look as though he were about to ask a question. They were unusual eyes, and wise in ways that Cassandra couldn't even begin to imagine. A pulse in her neck started to throb and she felt strangely excited.

He was studying her carefully, his eyes taking in the pleated grey skirt, the high-necked cream blouse and the shining dark hair pulled back off her face in a loose ponytail. He also noticed the full lower lip and the fact that his presence had caused her breathing to quicken.

'You are Mrs Williams?' he repeated, and this time she could detect a trace of accent in the voice. The woman in Kensington had told her that he was from Austria.

'I'm sorry, yes I am. You took me by surprise. I was just wondering if there was anyone else in the house and . . .'

He nodded thoughtfully to himself, his expression grave, and then suddenly he smiled and a tiny dimple appeared in his left cheek while his eyes crinkled at the corners. It was a dazzling smile, and Cassandra felt her solar plexus take on a life of its own as it seemed to rise up into her chest and constrict her breathing. Her legs also felt inexplicably weak. She wondered if she was ill.

'I'm sorry to have kept you waiting,' he said smoothly. 'You know how it is.'

She didn't, but she nodded. 'Yes of course. Anyway, I think I was probably early.'

'No, you were on time. Please, follow me.'

Wondering how he knew she'd been on time, Cassandra followed him across the hall into a large, sun-filled drawing room. Surprisingly heavy dark red drapes hung at the windows and the deep wool carpet was also red with an oriental-style black pattern on it. Despite the sun she felt suddenly cool and shivered.

The baron seated himself in one of the easy chairs, then indicated that Cassandra should sit in a ladder-backed chair directly opposite him. She sat well back on the seat and folded her hands in her lap. Unseen by her, the baron's eyes gleamed with appreciation.

'You sit well,' he said softly. 'I believe in good deportment, and good manners also. Whoever has the care of my daughters must have old-fashioned values. I do not approve of modern methods of child care. Discipline is a necessary part of life, and if we do not teach it to our children how will they learn to discipline themselves in later life?'

Cassandra nodded. 'That's absolutely true. My parents were very strict.'

'And that has helped you in your adult life?'

She hesitated. Considering what a mess she'd made of everything it would hardly be truthful to say yes. 'Well, I'm not sure. I mean, I'm certain they were right but . . .'

'Perhaps you didn't learn the lessons well enough?' He smiled, but there was an intensity to the question that she didn't understand, and his constant scrutiny unsettled her. She tried to be honest.

'Maybe not,' she conceded. 'I suppose I rebelled against them a bit. All children do, don't they? And I thought they were old-fashioned and out of date. That's probably why I married Paul, because I knew they disapproved. Now he's run off with a wealthy older woman, so obviously they were right all along.'

'Have you admitted this to them?'

'I can't,' Cassandra said quietly. 'They're both dead now.'

He leant forward in his chair. 'But you have brothers and sisters?'

Cassandra shook her head. 'No, I'm all alone.' Her voice was forlorn.

He leant back again so that his face was partly in shadow, but she could see him nod to himself and he said something in a quietly satisfied tone.

'I'm sorry, I didn't catch what you said,' she apologised.

5

'I said that you were quite perfect.'

Cassandra's eyes widened in surprise. 'But you haven't asked me about my qualifications. I mean, I've never actually had any experience with children. I like them of course, but . . .'

'Why of course?' he interrupted.

'Well, everyone likes children don't they?'

'No, they do not. Katya,' he hesitated, glanced at Cassandra's innocent face and then continued smoothly, 'she's my fiancée, she most certainly does not like children. This is why I need someone young enough to be like a mother to them as well as strict enough to teach them the rules that I believe are necessary in the nursery.'

Cassandra remembered her own childhood and although she badly wanted the job she knew that she had to speak out. 'I think that love is just as important as discipline,' she said resolutely.

The baron's eyes fixed themselves intently on hers and although his face was grave a trick of the light made it appear to Cassandra that they were dancing with amusement. 'I absolutely agree,' he said quietly. 'Love and discipline together make the perfect combination.'

Cassandra was delighted that she'd found the courage to speak out, because far from antagonising the baron, her statement seemed to have confirmed his feeling that she was perfect for the job. Within minutes he was instructing his secretary to draw up a contract and asking Cassandra when she'd be free to start. She was dazed by her success.

'As soon as you like really. I only rent my flat by the week and at the moment I'm unemployed.'

'Then you will return and gather together your possessions and in the morning I will send a car to collect you, yes?'

Cassandra nodded. 'That would be wonderful.'

'Good.' He put out a hand and his surprisingly long fingers touched the back of her wrist. 'I hope you will stay with us for a long time. Change is not good for children.' Her flesh seemed to burn beneath his touch, and yet she was still cold. She had great difficulty in wrenching her eyes away from his, which seemed to hold some kind of message for her.

'Don't worry, I don't like change either,' she said at last, her voice unsteady. 'One of the things that attracted me to the job was the fact that you avoid the public eye. I know it's unusual these days, but I've always lived a protected life and it's wonderful here. I mean, you're almost in a world of your own, aren't you?'

'Yes, we are,' he said slowly. 'I think you'll fit in here very well indeed, Cassandra. The outside world is never allowed to intrude into this house. We are very self-contained.'

Cassandra realised she didn't even want to go and collect her things. All she wanted to do was stay in this house with this strangely charismatic man and his family. 'When do I get to meet the children?' she asked, suddenly realising she should have mentioned them earlier.

For a moment the baron looked surprised, as though he'd entirely forgotten their existence. 'Ah yes, the girls. I suppose you should see them now, before you commit yourself to anything!'

He stood up and pressed a bell by the mantelpiece. Within a few minutes there was a light tap on the door and a statuesque redhead ushered two tiny blonde-haired girls into the room. The baron glanced briefly at the redhead. 'Thank you, Abigail. I'm pleased to say that we have found a replacement for you. This evening you can return once again to the pleasures of the outside world.'

The girl averted her red-rimmed eyes, her porcelain skin flushing a delicate shade of pink.

'Abigail is unfortunately not a believer in discipline,' continued the baron. 'She has therefore decided to leave us. She has been a great disappointment, I'm afraid.'

Feeling awkward, Cassandra turned to smile sympathetically at the girl, only to find Abigail's eyes were full of tears as she stood in front of her employer waiting uncertainly for his instructions. 'That will be all,' he said sharply and she hurried from the room. There was a brief, uneasy silence.

The two girls stood in front of their father looking up at him through thickly-lashed blue eyes and Cassandra was relieved to see that they looked happy and relaxed in his company. He put a hand on the head of the taller of the two girls. 'This is Helena, who is four, and this little one, who looks so misleadingly angelic, is Christina; she is two. Girls, this is Cassandra, who is to be your new companion as long as you don't frighten her away.'

The girls giggled, covering their faces with their hands and peeping out at Cassandra as they did so. The baron shrugged. 'I understand that all little girls giggle. It's irritating but harmless, I suppose.'

'I expect they're shy.'

He frowned. 'I hope not. I don't allow shyness in this house.'

Cassandra didn't know if he was joking or not but she noticed that the girls quickly uncovered their faces. 'I'm quite shy,' she confessed.

The baron looked thoughtfully at her. 'That we will cure. Now children, off you go. I'm sure lunch is ready for you in the upstairs nursery. You will see Cassandra again tomorrow.'

They both gave tiny little curtsies before walking decorously out of the room. Cassandra quite expected to hear them giggling once the door closed behind them but she couldn't even hear their footsteps in the hall.

'Now you have met them, do you still wish to come?' the baron asked.

'Of course. They're wonderful, and so beautiful!'

'They look like their mother.' He didn't sound as though that pleased him. After a brief silence he glanced at the clock. 'I'll have someone drive you home.'

Cassandra couldn't believe how much she wanted to stay, and wondered what it was about the house and its owner that attracted her so strongly. 'A taxi will be fine,' she assured the baron.

'I prefer to use my own driver. I dislike strangers around the house. Peter will drive you.' He picked up the telephone, spoke a few words in French and then replaced the receiver. 'The car will be round the front in a few minutes. I will walk you to the door and we look forward to you joining our household tomorrow.'

'About the contract,' Cassandra said hesitantly. 'The woman in Kensington explained about the money but she was a little vague about other details.'

'The terms are generous,' he said abruptly, as though annoyed she should doubt it. 'You also become a member of the family, but you do have to agree to abide by the rules of the house, which is not unreasonable. Apart from that there is just the secrecy clause.'

Cassandra, who'd always longed to belong to a family, looked at him in surprise. 'Secrecy clause?'

He shrugged. 'I'm rich and famous. When people leave my employment I don't wish them to go talking to the press about their life here. Like you, I desire privacy and seclusion.'

'I'd never talk to the press about you!' Cassandra said in horror.

'I'm sure that is true, but if it is in a signed document then you cannot, whatever the temptation. If people leave with an imagined grudge or . . .'

Up above them a door opened and what sounded like a cry of distress floated down into the hallway.

'I knew you would understand,' the baron concluded abruptly. He then turned on his heel and walked quickly away from her, up the wide staircase to the galleried landing above.

Slowly, Cassandra walked out of the front door to the waiting car.

* * *

9

The baron stood by the lead-paned window of the master bedroom and watched young Peter, his valet for the past year, drive Cassandra down the driveway on the way back to the tiny flat, the location of which his inquiries had already unearthed. It was in a decaying area, full of people caught up in the downward spiral of debt and unemployment. He'd known that she would take the job if it was offered, but never in his wildest dreams had he expected her to be so perfect. A small smile of anticipation played around his mouth and he let out his breath in a tiny sigh.

The petite blonde woman lying naked on the huge circular bed heard the sigh and laughed. 'She should have come giftwrapped; she must be the most exciting present you've had in years.'

Katya was excited too, but her voice had the bored tone of a woman who in ten years of jet-setting had seen and done everything so that life was now empty.

With her long, tousled silver-blonde hair and petite bone structure she looked misleadingly innocent. From a distance she could have been mistaken for an adolescent, but she was twenty-nine and without makeup the years showed. Not that she ever let the baron see her without makeup. She had no desire to be ejected from his life. Marietta's death had ensured her continuing presence in this house and now she was safely ensconced in Dieter's household she wasn't going to make way for anyone else.

'Did you see it all, Katya?' he asked her.

'Of course. I adore our in-house movies. Her expression when you told her that love and discipline were the perfect combination was wonderful. She quite obviously had no idea what you meant.'

'We must keep the tape. Before long she will know only too well. Once the game is over I shall enjoy letting her see herself as she was.'

Katya stretched lazily, running her hands over her breasts and wishing that Dieter would turn his attention to her. 'When does Abigail leave?' she asked.

He kept his back to her, but she saw the fingers of his left hand begin tapping lightly on the window ledge, a sure sign that she had his interest. 'Tonight; her contract terminates at six o'clock.'

'Don't you think she should keep working until then?'

There was no mistaking the cruelty behind the words and the baron's pulse quickened. Nevertheless, he played for time. It was his policy to keep his women on edge, uncertain as to what he did or didn't want. Besides, Katya's enjoyment of Abigail would be greater than his. He had already tired of the redhead who had never grasped the rules of the game and was far too easily reduced to tears. He didn't mind Katya having her pleasure, but it wouldn't hurt her to have to work for it a little.

'I think I'd prefer to wait for Cassandra,' he replied.

Katya's mouth tightened. She hated it when he was difficult, but still couldn't find the key to manipulating him. 'I just thought you might like to give her a farewell present, a bonus if you like,' she said lightly.

'She hasn't earned it,' he said shortly.

'Come and sit on the bed,' Katya coaxed. 'I've been lonely up here all the morning.' She used her little-girl voice, although she was slowly coming to realise that unlike most men, the baron wasn't affected by it.

'Lonely!' He turned to face her at last. 'I don't believe you were exactly alone my darling. Peter certainly wasn't in his quarters when I rang for him, and I distinctly heard Abigail weeping a few moments ago. I only hope young Cassandra didn't realise what the noise was. We don't want to alarm her yet.'

'When I say lonely, I mean without you. Peter's just a boy and Abigail's becoming tiresome.'

The baron laughed. 'Peter's a very well-built nineteen-year-old.'

'And Abigail's a well-built twenty-year-old. If she hasn't earned a bonus, perhaps she should have a final punishment?'

'For what?' Despite himself, Dieter was intrigued by the lengths his mistress would go to, to get her own way.

'For failing to complete the game?'

'Very good! Yes, I think that would be fair. It's important to be fair, otherwise the entire game is pointless, but a penalty for not finishing it is an excellent idea. Ring for her then.'

Katya smiled and kissed the side of his neck. 'I will. She's already distressed, which will make it even more enjoyable. You're so good to me, darling.'

'It's nice to know you appreciate me.'

A small warning bell sounded inside Katya's head. She mustn't push him; she had to seem independent but never bossy. He didn't want a clinging woman – Marietta had clung – but neither did he want an overbearing one. Sometimes she didn't think he wanted a woman permanently at all. He wanted the excitement of the game and nothing more. Love, closeness, emotional ties, they were all anathema to Dieter; and yet Katya was sure he was searching for something more. If only she could discover what it was.

Summoned by the buzzer in her suite of rooms that was soon to belong to Cassandra, Abigail tapped on the door and entered at the sound of the baron's voice. He was sitting on the side of the bed and she looked nervously at him. Despite all that had happened over the past few months she could still feel the impact of his masculinity, and the overwhelming sexuality of him that had given her such pleasure at the beginning. It had all been good then; it was only the woman who had spoilt it.

The baron watched Abigail's grey eyes turn towards the middle of the bed where Katya was sitting in the lotus position, her small firm breasts erect, and he saw the fear on Abigail's face. She had never learnt to share, never learnt to accept Katya's pleasures as well as his. It was a pity, because now she would never know what

12

she might have become if she had played his game for longer.

'Katya's upset that you're leaving us,' he explained, walking behind Abigail to lock the bedroom door. 'She's especially upset that you and she have never managed to get on better, and she feels that it must be her fault.'

Abigail watched the baron as he moved round the room but she didn't attempt to answer him. She knew that the words he was saying were meaningless, the truth was always something else, something she'd never learnt to work out quickly enough to please him and now she chose silence because if she was silent she couldn't break a rule.

'Do you think it was her fault, Abigail?' he continued, putting a hand beneath her chin and tilting her head.

Abigail managed to whisper, 'No.'

'Good, because neither do I. I think it was your fault. Basically you're an intelligent girl, but you never really tried to understand us, or the way we like to run our household. You broke the rules, but refused to accept punishment. You were like a small child who shuts its mind to all learning. So, you were to blame and you spoilt the game for all of us. Because of this we have had to abandon the game and start a new one. Such an inconvenience calls, I think, for a penalty payment. A small fine before you leave us for ever.'

Abigail's breath quickened and the baron watched the rise and fall of her breasts beneath her clinging summer dress. Slowly he reached out and slid the straps from her shoulders so that her arms were pinned to her sides, then he undid the two buttons above her waist and slid his hand up to cup one of her bare breasts. As his fingers moved in tiny circles around the nipple it sprang to life and she swallowed hard.

'Come to bed.' His voice was smooth, reassuring, but she took no comfort from that because Katya was still there, crouched naked at the foot of the bed with her green eyes shining like a cat's. Abigail hated her. Hated

13

her innate cruelty, and uncanny knowledge of how Abigail's body responded.

'Come!' He put his free hand round her waist and pulled her to the edge of the bed, then pushed her so that she fell backwards onto the goosedown duvet.

Only her legs were free, but they felt heavy with fear and in any case she knew there was no point in fighting the pair of them, they always won and she had never known pleasure like the baron could give her; it was just that she couldn't bear to have his mistress there as well. Fear was not an aphrodisiac for Abigail, and that seemed to be considered a failing in this terrifying household. Despite that, she still hoped that this time the baron would give her the pleasure he had at the beginning. She always hoped.

The baron watched the conflicting emotions play across her face and felt a spark of excitement. It was always a pleasure to watch someone fight against their own sensuality, and even if this lush redhead was too obviously sexual it was still exciting to know that her greatest moment of ecstasy yet would be ruined by Katya. The piquancy of the situation was enough to make it worth letting Katya have her way.

He turned to his eager mistress. 'Fetch the cords.'

'No!' Abigail shouted, but the baron laid a finger lightly on her lips. 'Of course we must have the cords. It increases the pleasure. You learnt that early on, remember?'

'Not with her here. I don't want her here when I'm tied down. Please!'

'My dear Abigail, this is a penalty. You're not here for your pleasure but for ours.'

Abigail fell silent, but she wished desperately that she'd been able to use her bathroom before she came. Her bladder was uncomfortably full.

With a speed born of practice, Katya brought the soft silk cords from the ottoman beneath the window, wound them round Abigail's ankles, then spread the girl's long legs wide as she slipped the cords through

14

the metal loops that were concealed all round the edge of the circular bed.

Once that was done, Dieter took off his own clothes and then sat beside Abigail on the bed, slowly unfastening the remaining buttons of her dress until it fell away from her, revealing the heavy, dark nippled breasts that so fascinated his mistress.

With a glance at the silent girl lying there rigidly, he took hold of her arms and Katya moved round the bed to fasten Abigail's wrists in the same fashion as her ankles.

The baron's eyes slid down the creamy body. She was far too lush for his taste he realised. Katya had chosen her while he had been in the Loire overseeing the renovation of the château. She would never have been his choice, and mentally he filed that away as an error by Katya.

Also, whilst unwilling to lose herself in the game that had been set up, she had been far from inexperienced and offered very little resistance to anything that the baron had done. But for her constant battle against Katya's teachings he would have tired of her long ago. When he compared her full-blown body with the slim figure of Cassandra Williams he could hardly be bothered to continue with this final act, but he supposed Katya deserved it.

Bending his head he kissed Abigail's closed eyelids and temples, at the same time letting a hand wander over her shoulder and down the inside of her arm before straying across her hip and stomach. He lowered his head and inserted a nipple into his mouth, flicking at it with his tongue as his roving hand continued down over her stomach until the heel came to rest on her pubic bone.

Briefly he exerted gentle pressure, and she gasped and tried to push herself down into the bed. He heard Katya laugh. 'Her bathroom door's been locked all morning,' she purred from the shadows. The baron smiled at Abigail whose eyes had opened wide with fear and discomfort. 'That should increase your pleasure,' he murmured.

Abigail knew better. 'No, please,' she gasped, but his quick fingers pressed against her aching bladder and despite herself she gave a whimper of discomfort and fear. Immediately Katya moved forward, bent down and closed her tiny sharp teeth sharply over the imprisoned girl's nipple, already swollen from the baron's ministrations.

Pain shot through Abigail's breast like a tongue of flame but this time she bit her lip and kept silent. The baron watched her closely, waiting for the effects of the bite to die away. Then he spread the palm of his hand flat against her lower stomach and massaged her carefully, increasing and decreasing the pressure according to the expression in the girl's eyes. The torment she was suffering excited him, and he felt himself growing hard so that the head of his manhood brushed against Abigail's hipbone.

For endless minutes he continued to press and release until Abigail was quite certain that she was going to lose all control and flood the bed. It had happened to her once before, when she'd been alone with Katya, and the punishment had been so terrible that she didn't think she could bear it again.

Her eyes pleaded with the baron, but he was impervious, and then just as she felt that she must cry out, the tension and pressure began to send different signals to her brain, tiny sparks like electric shocks that made the lower part of her abdomen tense and her hips lifted slightly off the bed.

'Keep still,' the baron ordered. 'Haven't you learnt anything here?'

She groaned, trying to muffle the sound behind clenched teeth, and knew that she must keep still and endure everything because at least this was the last time. A drop of moisture fell from the tip of the baron's engorged penis and Abigail's nerve endings were so tightly stretched that even that made her jump. The baron laughed and abruptly pressed his hand harder against her. This time it was unbearable, but he seemed to know that because his hand quickly moved and his fingers parted her silky outer lips and fluttered delicately along the damp flesh beneath her clitoris.

Abigail felt her bud of pleasure begin to swell. The baron hadn't touched her himself for over two weeks and her treacherous body had missed him. Now the pressure of her full bladder and her screaming nerve ends were desperate for the release he used to give her.

Slowly he trailed his tongue down between her breasts, moving over her stomach and then descending to her thighs. She was frantic now for him to suck on the tiny button, to put his tongue deep inside her and move it in that unique way of his that drove her out of her mind with pleasure, but he lingered between her thighs and she could only wait for him to choose his moment.

Half mad with longing and pleasure she suddenly felt a tiny hand insert itself beneath the plump cheeks of her bottom and she struggled against the long-nailed fingers scratching lightly at the delicate skin round her second entrance, but Katya could never be denied and the pain distracted Abigail from the pleasure of the baron's attentions.

Suddenly the baron decided to move, and the delicate point of his tongue darted between her inner lips and inserted itself inside her, just as she'd wanted and if anything it was even better than she'd remembered. The initial pain of Katya's fingers began to fade, a heavy fullness seemed to fill her bowels and bladder and the baron's hands continued to work at her breasts, gripping them harder now until the pressure was too great, but his tongue was still doing incredible things to her and her whole body began to tremble on the brink of a huge orgasmic spasm.

For what seemed an eternity she was suspended on the verge, and then he quickly moved his tongue from her inner warmth and swirled it round her swollen clitoris. There was a flash of red light behind her eyes, her body jerked up off the bed, stretching the silken cords to their limits and just at the moment that her body was shaken to the core by her orgasm, Katya pushed three fingers into her tight anus while the baron's fingers dug hard into the soft flesh above her pubic bone.

Abigail lost all control of herself as her body thrashed in ecstasy against the constricting cords and her bladder finally emptied itself of its own volition. Realising with horror what had happened, she screamed her feelings of hatred and degradation aloud in a long agonised sobbing wail.

Katya's busy fingers ceased for a moment as she turned to smile at Dieter, who had now drawn back from the writhing girl and was looking from one woman to the other, his face entirely expressionless.

As the last shudders of Abigail's climax died away, Katya bent her head and began to lick the girl clean between her thighs. Abigail shut her eyes against the indignity, but Katya was in her element.

The baron put out a hand. 'It's enough. Untie her.' Reluctantly, Katya obeyed him. 'Look at me,' the baron said softly to the weeping girl.

Experience had taught her that it was best to obey while his voice was still gentle and slowly she lifted her eyelids. He stared at her, and she wanted to hate him, but she couldn't.

'You see,' he told her. 'It was good for you. If only you had been willing to play the game properly I think there is much you would have learned about yourself. Who knows, perhaps there would even have been a permanent place here for you.'

Abigail couldn't bear to think that she might have missed the chance of spending her life with the baron. 'You mean I could have stayed with you?' she whispered, imagining life here without the hated Katya.

He brushed a strand of auburn hair off her sweat-soaked brow. 'Of course not with me! I think there could have been a place here for you with Katya.'

'But she's perverted!' Abigail sobbed. 'Can't you understand that love doesn't have to be like this.'

'It's such a waste, all this talk of perversion and normality. Pleasure is all that matters, but you never understood that, did you? It wasn't your fault; Katya chose badly. As for love . . .' His voice tailed off in amusement.

Still sitting between Abigail's limply spread legs, Katya had been casually caressing the younger woman's reluctant flesh, but at the baron's words her head lifted as she felt a premonition of danger.

'It wasn't my fault!' she protested.

'You sound like one of the children.' His words were light, but the rebuke was clear enough. She must not use her little-girl voice any more and she must accept responsibility for her own mistakes. Except that the redhead hadn't been a mistake, not really. If only Dieter had given the girl more time, but he was bored and so they had to move on to a new game. Abigail hadn't given him enough excitement. At least if Cassandra failed to titillate his jaded palate, it would be his own fault.

'I don't want to leave you,' Abigail suddenly exclaimed, sitting up and kicking out at Katya who jumped off the bed. 'I know I could make you happy. You could do anything you liked to me. You could . . .'

'Go away.' His voice was colder than she'd ever heard it. 'You are beginning to annoy me. Don't you realise that what you are saying is the worst thing imaginable to me? I don't want a woman who will let me do anything. Where's the excitement in that?'

'But . . .'

'Get out! Peter will drive you to a hotel as soon as he gets back. And remember the contract you signed – absolute discretion. You've been amply compensated financially, although I'm sure I can trust you anyway.

After all, you'd hardly want people to know how you've been living for the past few months would you?'

Abigail glanced at the huge TV consul set in the corner of the bedroom and then up at the ever active camera high in the corner of the room. 'No,' she whispered, her head drooping.

'I thought not. Now go.'

After she'd left, Katya put her arms round the baron, pressing her naked breasts against his broad back. 'Let's watch a replay of that on TV,' she suggested. 'It should be exciting. She was out of her mind there for a moment.'

The baron reached round behind him and pulled Katya onto his lap, running a hand absent-mindedly over the nape of her neck as she took his still erect penis in her mouth and sucked lightly on it. 'I don't think so. I have other things to attend to now. Besides, there is tomorrow to look forward to.'

'But I want you inside me,' Katya murmured, lifting her head for a moment. 'I want you to . . .' He pushed her off him, hard enough to make her tumble back onto the floor and she felt another flash of unease. He wasn't only bored, he was irritable as well. If this next game failed to please him she might well lose her place here.

'Then perhaps you'd send Peter up this afternoon,' she suggested, picking herself up from the floor. 'I'm sure he'd like to see it.'

The baron nodded, hardly glancing at her as he began to dress. Katya wanted to scream at him to be jealous, to protest, or at the very least to say he'd stay and watch with them, but that wasn't his way.

'I think Cassandra Williams will give us a lot of fun,' she assured him.

At last the baron's bored expression lifted and he nodded. 'So do I. Already she's constantly in my mind. It's rare to find such innocence these days. I doubt if her husband gave her one moment of pleasure in their dull marital bed, and later on Rupert will be enchanted.'

'Perhaps she's frigid,' Katya teased.

She was delighted when Dieter laughed. 'Have I ever been wrong about a woman before?' Katya shook her head. 'Of course not. She's a deeply sensual young woman who daren't admit it to herself. To force her to face the truth, and to pit her intelligence against mine in the game will be a source of great pleasure.'

'I'm looking forward to it too,' Katya agreed.

'There is one difference to the game this time,' the baron said as he pulled on a lightweight jacket. Katya listened attentively; his games were always so complicated. 'It will add a little excitement for you as well I think.'

'What is it?' she asked eagerly.

'This time there can only be one winner.'

'One winner?' She didn't understand him.

The baron nodded. 'Either you or Cassandra, my darling.'

Katya swallowed nervously. 'What happens to the loser?'

He shrugged. 'I'm not sure. Perhaps the loser goes to Rupert, or perhaps she just disappears.'

'You mean if I lose I'll have to go away for a time?'

'I mean that if you lose I don't ever want to see you again.'

Panic welled up in Katya. Only through Dieter could she fulfil all the complexities of her sexual makeup. Her cruelty, her love/hate relationship with other women, her increasing desire for young men, none of this bothered the baron. Where else would she find a lover so understanding and willing to indulge her.

'But I need you!' she blurted out, and then wished she could bite her tongue off. Dieter couldn't bear to be needed.

'I know that, which is why you'll try all the harder to win.'

'What are the rules this time?'

The baron moved towards the door. 'This time, Katya, even you won't know the rules. However, since

21

you've played so many games before I think you still have a distinct advantage over Cassandra, don't you?'

Shocked, Katya stared at him. She wanted to cry with despair. First of all he hadn't laid a finger on her the entire day, and now he was telling her that there was a chance she might be banished from his house for ever.

'It's not fair,' she said faintly.

He frowned, and reaching out a hand caught hold of her right nipple, pinching it very hard between his thumb and forefinger. 'I decide what's fair, remember?'

She squirmed. He was hurting her. Normally she liked that and he knew it, but this time it was different and she wanted him to stop. 'Remember?' he repeated. Katya nodded.

His whole hand closed round her breast and he squeezed it brutally, at the same time bending over her and kissing her fiercely, his tongue thrusting into her mouth angrily, while his fingers continued to tighten their hold until at last the pain in her breast and the force of the kiss combined to give her a brief orgasm. As soon as he felt her body jerking he released her breast, removed his mouth from hers and walked out of the room. It wasn't enough, and Katya knew he knew that too, but for now it would have to do.

From tomorrow there would be much more and already her self-confidence was reasserting itself. After all, she knew Dieter intimately. Knew all the secrets of his dark soul. How could an innocent like Cassandra Williams possibly win any game devised by the baron? She couldn't. Dieter had only said that to make her uneasy, but she would make sure she played the game well.

Dieter's world of dark, bizarre eroticism was the only world she'd ever felt at home in. She doubted if she could exist outside the house in Hampstead.

# Chapter Two

Cassandra was both excited and nervous as she watched the young driver take her two shabby suitcases out of the boot of the sleek black Daimler and carry them in through the front door of the baron's house. It was wonderful to feel needed, to know that someone actually wanted her to work for them, but it was also frightening to cut herself off from everything that she'd ever known before. She knew it was ridiculous, but in some ways this house in Hampstead seemed like a foreign country, and she had never had the courage to travel abroad.

At last she took a deep breath and followed Peter inside. There was no one in the hall. Her two cases had vanished; she assumed they'd been taken upstairs, and once again everywhere was silent. After a few seconds she heard light footsteps on the upstairs landing, and briefly remembered the strange cry that had come from that direction just as she was leaving after the interview. At the time she'd thought it was one of the children, but later, with time for her imagination to run riot, she'd convinced herself it was more like an adult's cry of pain and the thought had worried away at her like an intermittent toothache.

'I thought I heard the car!' a woman's voice

exclaimed, and Cassandra looked up to see a young woman with a mass of silver-blonde hair that fell to her shoulders in a cascade of curls, coming down the stairs.

She was tiny, only a little over five feet tall, with delicate bones and her face glowed with a golden tan which accentuated her startling green eyes. To Cassandra she was like some wonderful exotic bird and the clinging minidress that she wore outlined the kind of figure that usually indicated hours of aerobics and swimming and a dedication to perfection that Cassandra always found unbelievable when she read about it in papers or magazines. However, looking at this young woman and guessing that she was the baron's fiancée, she couldn't help but realise that for women with enough time and money it undoubtedly made sense. A man like Baron von Ritter would only be drawn to beautiful things, and this young woman was definitely beautiful. It was the first time Cassandra had ever studied another woman's body so objectively, and as she realised what she was doing she quickly averted her eyes as she felt a blush spreading up her neck.

Katya had spent a considerable amount of time that morning getting ready for her meeting with this woman who, without knowing it, was her adversary in the game that was about to begin, and she felt a glow of satisfaction as she saw Cassandra's blush. She smoothed her hands down over her hips, as though straightening out some invisible wrinkles in the dress but actually emphasising her curves, and then held out her right hand in greeting.

'You must be Cassandra Williams. I'm Katya Guez, I live here with the baron and his adorable little daughters. They're such fun, but far too energetic for me I'm afraid. I'm a night owl, and they're a couple of larks. Now that you're here at least I'll get my beauty sleep again!'

She gave a girlish giggle, and Cassandra smiled back, totally unaware that Katya had never got out of her bed to see to either of the girls in her life, and that if she had her way they'd both be sent off to boarding school as soon as they were eight.

'I'm quite good in the mornings,' Cassandra responded.

'But not at night?' asked Katya, her voice suddenly soft.

'I'm usually in bed by ten,' Cassandra admitted. 'My parents always said you couldn't burn the candle at both ends.'

'How boring they sound. My parents hardly ever found time to sleep. They couldn't bear to waste a minute of their lives.'

'Do they live in England?' Cassandra asked.

Katya's eyes filled with tears – the baron could have told Cassandra that she cried crocodile tears more easily than any woman he'd ever met – and her voice dropped to a whisper. 'They died in an aeroplane crash three years ago,' she confided.

'How dreadful!' Remembering the death of her own parents, Cassandra's easy compassion was instantly aroused.

Katya, who'd never known who her father was and whose mother had died from venereal disease shortly after she'd finished educating her twelve-year-old daughter in all the ways it was possible to please a man, let her mouth droop for a moment and then gave a brave smile. 'Well, we mustn't dwell on the past. Everyone has sadnesses in their lives. Let me take you upstairs and show you your room. It's been thoroughly spring-cleaned since Abigail left yesterday and we've changed all the curtains and bed coverings so that it fits your personality better. Dieter didn't think you and Abigail would share the same taste in interior design.'

'I really didn't expect . . .' Cassandra's voice tailed off. She found it hard to imagine a man who was interested enough in his employees to change the decor of his rooms for their convenience.

'But the bedroom's so important to a woman isn't it?' Katya said, putting one small hand lightly on Cassandra's elbow as she guided her up the stairs and round to the right along the landing. 'I think it's so important to have the right kind of bedroom. Of course you've got your own little living room and bathroom, but I expect you'll be with us a lot of the time. Abigail was. She was such a success at our little dinner parties. After a few drinks she became very vivacious!'

Cassandra felt her stomach tighten a little. 'I'm afraid I'm not a dinner-party kind of person. Besides, I'm here for the children. I'm sure the baron won't want me mixing with his friends.'

'You're one of the family now,' Katya insisted. 'Don't look so nervous, dinner parties are one of the highlights of life here. Dieter knows such interesting people.'

Cassandra wished that the other woman would take her hand away from her elbow. She realised she was only trying to be friendly but the effect was rather overpowering. She felt relieved when they stopped in front of one of the heavy oak doors and Katya pushed it open. 'Here we are, your bedroom.'

Cassandra stared about her in astonishment. The bedroom was larger than the whole flat she'd just left, and it was dominated by a huge four-poster bed with apricot-coloured curtains pulled back and fastened to the posts with large oak rings. There was no quilt but instead an embroidered tapestry bedcover in gold and beige shot through with threads of the same apricot colour as the curtains. The floor was covered by a beige wool carpet so deep that you sank into it as you walked and the heavy drapes at the windows, similar in texture to those she'd seen in the drawing-room during her interview, picked up the gold thread of the bedspread. The luxurious beauty of it all distracted her from the fact that the windows were covered by heavy vertical iron bars.

Katya watched the way Cassandra's eyes lit up at the sight of the room, and she remembered that Abigail had been totally disinterested in it the day she'd arrived. Of course the colours had been different, vibrant and more obviously opulent, but her indifference should have told Katya something. As a sensualist herself she knew how important the right surroundings were, how much easier it was to be sensual in a room that pleased the eye. She had a feeling that Cassandra's slim body would also appreciate the pure silk sheets that would be changed every day, and she felt a moment's excitement as she pictured the almost boyishly slender figure sliding into bed, brushing the innocent flesh against the caresses of soft, arousing material.

'It's really lovely!' Cassandra enthused turning to Katya. She was a little surprised to find her hostess somewhat distracted and breathing unevenly, but realised that the room was hot.

'I think I'll open a window,' Cassandra said quickly.

'They don't open,' Katya interjected.

Cassandra frowned. 'Why not?'

'Well, Dieter's obsessed with the girls' safety. He's always worrying that they're going to fall off their ponies or out of windows, so most of the windows in the house are shuttered and barred. There's a fan above the bed. It works very well, we've got one in our room too, and there's also air conditioning but I'm afraid we don't use ours much. It seems to dry your throat out after a while.'

'But it's stuffy in here,' Cassandra persisted.

For a moment Katya's eyes flashed angrily, then she gave a quick smile and putting out a hand tugged gently on what Cassandra had taken to be an out-of-date bell pull. At once a huge wooden fan in the ceiling started to rotate silently, and cool air moved around them.

'See! I told you it was marvellous. When I'm hot I often lie on the bed quite naked and let it cool me down that way. You can't imagine how good it feels.'

Cassandra, who was hot and sticky by now, could imagine it very well. She found that she could also imagine Katya without her clinging micro-dress lying spreadeagled on the bed, and this made her so uncomfortable that she didn't know what to say.

Katya watched the younger woman and smiled to herself. This wasn't even going to be a contest. There were no depths to Cassandra. She was simply a surprisingly naive and as yet unawakened young woman, but there was nothing in her that would hold the baron's attention for very long. After all, it could only take a certain amount of time to spoil the innocence, and after that she couldn't imagine he'd find anything of interest in her. No, she, Katya would be the winner of this game, and she should never have lain awake half the night worrying about her opponent. From now on if she stayed awake at night it would be to plan the girl's degradation and downfall, then when the game was over she'd persuade Dieter to hand Cassandra over to Rupert for safekeeping. That way Katya would know the degradation would continue and could even, if she found a lot of pleasure in her over the next few weeks, pay the occasional visit herself. Rupert wouldn't mind.

'I'm so glad you like it,' she said brightly. 'Lucy will be up to unpack your cases in a minute. The baron will be home shortly after lunch and he'll explain what your duties are for the rest of the day. If I were you I'd have a little rest before you come down for lunch. The bathroom's through that door there; be careful, there are a couple of steps it's easy to miss.'

'Where do I go for lunch?' Cassandra asked.

'When it's nice like today we usually eat out on the back terrace. The children will join us. Their manners don't matter in the garden!'

'I thought their manners were amazing,' Cassandra protested. 'They were the politest little girls I've ever met.'

'How sweet you are.' Katya smiled again, but only with her mouth, and Cassandra took a small step away from the other woman. Suddenly she had the feeling that Katya didn't really like her, but she knew she must be mistaken because she'd been chattering away like an old friend until then and anyway Katya didn't have any reason to dislike her.

'Thank you,' Cassandra murmured.

'Oh, I didn't mean it as a compliment,' Katya replied, but before Cassandra could reply Katya had turned and left the room, letting the heavy oak door swing shut behind her.

The baron was sprawled face down on the bed, resting his chin in his hands as he kept his eyes glued to the TV set in the corner of the room. When Katya came in he didn't even acknowledge her presence, and although piqued she knew better than to try and force him to speak.

The silence in the room grew heavy with anticipation as they watched the unsuspecting Cassandra begin her exploration of the bathroom with its sunken whirlpool bath, and the baron smiled as she looked in astonishment at the wall behind the bath which was totally covered by a vast mirror. He watched as she studied herself in it, leaning forward to remove some speck of dust from her face, which was entirely free of makeup. The movement brought her so close to the concealed camera that she seemed to be looking straight into the baron's eyes and his lips parted slightly at the tranquil innocence of her gaze.

'Surely she'll take a bath,' Katya said urgently.

'Be quiet!' the baron hissed furiously. He didn't mind if Cassandra did or didn't use the bath; the very fact that only she could decide what they would see was half the excitement and Katya's voice was an unwelcome intrusion into his thoughts.

Cassandra buried her face in her hands for a moment, as though weary, and then straightened her back and stared critically at herself in the mirror. After a brief hesitation she removed the band holding her thick dark hair back off her face and shook her head. As her hair fell in a dark curtain the baron let out a tiny breath while Katya, sitting on the window seat in sullen silence, began to nibble on a carefully nurtured fingernail, a sure sign that she was agitated.

29

Again there was a pause, this time while Cassandra examined the taps and tried to work out how the various combination of jets worked, and then she lifted her hands and started to unbutton her safari-style cotton dress. Once the buttons were undone she shrugged it off her shoulders and let it fall to the ground behind her, then bent forward to unclasp the soft cotton bra. She then extended her arms at an angle so that this time the garment fell in front of her, leaving the secret watchers with a perfect view of her tiny breasts, their creamy pallor emphasised by the rose-coloured nipples, small tight buds more like a child's than a woman's.

The baron swallowed hard and gave a sigh of satisfaction. Katya yawned. 'She's almost flat-chested, Dieter! How boring.'

'I admit she isn't as over-ripe as your Abigail, but I'd scarcely call her flat-chested. Besides, look at that tiny waist, and her stomach. So inviting! I can just picture you with her, Katya. You'll certainly be the first woman she's ever made love with. Don't you find that exciting?'

She did, but she didn't like the look in Dieter's eyes as he stared at the screen. Abigail had never had that effect on him, and Cassandra looked so young for her twenty-three years while Katya was well aware that she looked old for her twenty-nine.

At last Cassandra stepped out of her touchingly childish white cotton panties and stepped into the bath. As she lifted her right leg, Dieter and his mistress gained their first sight of her most secret place and this time they were equally hypnotised by the screen. She had an abundance of very dark pubic hair, while the outer lips of her sex were small and tight, so that they only caught the briefest glimpse of the soft pinkness within before she sank down into the water and laid her head back against the edge of the tub.

'Do you think she'll play with herself?' Katya asked excitedly, remembering how Abigail had delighted them on her arrival.

'I would be most disappointed if she did,' the baron

replied. 'This is no Abigail, my dear. Compared to your redheaded house wine this girl is a dark and mysterious claret. A rare wine and one to be savoured slowly. No, we'll get nothing more from this.' He switched off the set by remote control.

'I hadn't finished watching,' Katya exclaimed.

'Of course you had. Enjoy your lunch with her my darling, and make sure the children behave. At dinner tonight wear the sapphire blue dress with the plunging neckline, and nothing beneath it.'

'We aren't having guests are we? What does it matter what I wear?'

'The game has begun, Katya; you lose points for asking questions.'

Anger flared in Katya, but she forced it down. If Dieter thought he was annoying her he'd be delighted, and make the game more complicated. Her earlier certainty that Cassandra was no threat had vanished as they'd watched the screen. She hadn't seen such hungry desire on Dieter's face for a very long time, not since he'd first set eyes on Marietta at that wretched ball in Venice, and it had taken five long years for Marietta to vanish from the scene. Five years and her death. She had no intention of letting Cassandra stay around that long.

'You'd better get down to lunch,' the baron reminded her. Katya watched him roll onto his back, and her eyes moved down so that she could see for herself the visible sign of how Cassandra had aroused him. She moved towards the bed, watching him carefully for any sign of irritation or boredom, but there was none, simply an expression of amused tolerance.

'You really want her, don't you?' she asked quietly, sitting herself on the edge of the bed.

'Of course I do! Why else would I have employed her?'

'Tell me what you want to do to her.'

He shook his head. 'That would give too much away. Remember, this is a competition for you as well.'

'But you want to spoil her, don't you? Admit that at least. You want to change her, turn her inside out until she doesn't even recognise herself.'

The baron shrugged. 'If you say so.'

Katya ran a hand up his trouser leg and let her fingers move softly over the bulge at his crotch. 'This tells me you do.'

It was a mistake. He took her hand tightly in his and moved it away, crushing her fingers painfully together as he did so. 'Leave me alone and go down to lunch. I have to see Lucy.'

'Why?' Katya demanded.

'She and I have some unfinished business to attend to. Run along, Katya. I dislike it when you keep asking questions.' She had no choice but to leave.

Katya was in a very bad mood when Cassandra finally came into the garden to join her and the girls for lunch. She tried to disguise it, well aware that Peter, who was helping to serve the lunch, would report everything to the baron, but it was difficult to smile at the younger woman as she approached.

'I'm afraid I'm a few minutes late,' Cassandra apologised. 'I got lost and ended up in the library.'

'It doesn't matter to me, but the baron's obsessed with punctuality. You should remember that in future,' Katya said, signalling for the maid to pass round the plates.

'Of course. I expect I'll soon find my way around. The trouble was, there wasn't anyone to ask. Where do the staff hide away? I never see anyone!'

'They keep to their quarters. Helena, sit up straight and put your plate on your knees. Didn't Abigail teach you anything?'

The four-year-old glanced at Katya from beneath lowered lids. 'Not much,' she said quietly. 'She was always disappearing into your room.'

Katya turned to Cassandra. 'I'm afraid Abigail was rather taken with my clothes and makeup. I often

32

caught her in the bedroom on some flimsy pretext or other. I suppose you have to feel sorry for someone like that but it wasn't nice. That's why she had to go.'

Cassandra's eyes widened. 'Really? The baron said something about her not being keen enough on discipline.'

'Well, there was that too, but really she was thoroughly untrustworthy. The agency chose her for us. This time the baron insisted on doing the interviewing himself. So much wiser I think.'

Cassandra nodded. 'You do need to meet people before you can . . .' She stopped as a strange cry pierced the air. It wasn't like the one she'd heard on her previous visit; there was no suggestion of pain in the sound, but it disturbed Cassandra. She glanced at Katya to see if she'd heard it. The other woman's face had gone very white and for a second she was quite motionless, but then her hands busied themselves with her food and her colour returned.

'Yes, I agree,' she continued smoothly. 'It's always better to meet people face to face. You can learn so much from expressions, don't you think?' Her green eyes stared straight into Cassandra's. The effect was hypnotic. The younger woman felt unable to look away, and as she stared at Katya she began to feel strange. Her limbs started to feel heavy, and as her shoulders relaxed she felt a peculiar sensation in the pit of her stomach. Katya leant towards her, putting out a tiny, multi-ringed hand and moving it towards Cassandra's knee. 'You know, Cassandra, there are things I . . .'

Helena, staring at her father's mistress in fascination, let her legs slip to one side and the plate fell from her knees and shattered on the patio. The crash of breaking china jolted Cassandra back into the present, and Katya leapt to her feet in a fury.

'You stupid, stupid child! Look what you've done. You wait until I tell your papa about this. He'll be very angry and you'll be punished, won't she Cassandra?

33

I'm quite sure Cassandra knows the right punishment for careless, clumsy, ugly little girls like you.'

Helena's big blue eyes filled with tears and she clasped her hands together in her lap. 'I didn't mean to,' she whispered. 'It was an accident.'

Christina, apparently unperturbed by her older sister's tears, looked up at the word accident. 'Mama's dead,' she said clearly. 'It was an accident.'

'Be quiet, Christina!' Katya's voice was lower now, but unmistakably menacing and Christina shrank away from her.

'I didn't mean to,' Helena repeated, her bottom lip trembling as she looked at Cassandra.

'Don't worry,' Cassandra said quickly. 'We all have accidents from time to time.'

'Goodness me, I'm afraid you won't last long,' Katya said, her anger suddenly draining away. 'Dieter wouldn't approve of that sentiment at all.'

'But she's only four!' Cassandra said, longing to put her arms round the little girl but not sure if she should. 'It isn't as though she threw it deliberately.'

'I want her punished,' Katya said flatly. 'That's all there is to it. She spoilt the lunch.'

'Good afternoon ladies! Is there some kind of problem?' asked a masculine voice, and the baron walked lightly up the steps from the french windows to the patio.

'That clumsy daughter of yours has just broken a piece of the dinner service,' Katya said spitefully. 'She didn't like it because I was talking to Cassandra and she wanted some attention.'

Shocked, Cassandra opened her mouth to protest but then closed it again. She'd only just arrived. She couldn't possibly contradict the baron's fiancée in front of him, and yet it was all so ridiculous and unfair and she knew it was her job to put across the child's point of view. She tried to think how she could tell the baron the truth without appearing to contradict Katya.

'Helena, is this true?' the baron asked his daughter.

Helena hung her head and fiddled with her fingers.

'Answer me, is it true?'

'It was an accident,' his daughter whispered.

Christina tugged at her father's jacket. 'Mama's dead,' she reminded him. His eyes moved quickly from the tiny two-year-old to the watching Cassandra, and suddenly he smiled. 'It's too nice a day to spoil with an argument. I think we'll forget it this time. Peter, clear the mess up. Katya, your masseur's arrived. Lucy will take the children upstairs for a nap while I have a talk with Cassandra here.'

As the girls scampered away and Peter began to sweep up the broken china, Cassandra glanced at Katya and saw that she was absolutely furious. Her eyes were glinting with anger and her mouth was a thin, tight line while two vivid spots of colour stood out on her cheeks.

'Katya, your masseur,' the baron reminded her.

'I wanted her punished,' Katya said icily. 'She spoilt . . .'

'I know exactly what she spoilt,' he said. His voice was low and didn't carry to Katya. 'You had no business to try and seduce her over lunch. I am not pleased with you.' He raised his voice again. 'Hurry up, darling. You know how Pierre hates to be kept waiting.'

'That's just too bad,' Katya snapped, and she walked slowly back towards the house, emphasising the fact that she intended to keep him waiting.

Cassandra stood up and waited for the baron to speak. She'd thought about him a lot since the interview, and now that she was facing him again her heart was beating rather too fast and she felt ridiculously pleased to see him. He smiled at her, almost as though he was equally pleased to see her.

'Katya always makes a terrible drama out of everything. Now you can see why she would not make a good mother substitute.'

'I expect it's difficult to take on two little girls,' Cassandra said.

'Ah, you play the diplomat! Very good, my dear. But

35

tell me, what was the truth of it all? Did Helena want attention or was it an accident?'

Cassandra took some steadying breaths and looked straight at her employer, determined to be truthful with him from the start. 'I thought it was an accident. It isn't easy to balance plates on knees even when you're an adult.'

'Good!'

'Also, she was very upset. Usually when children want attention they make scenes, but they don't shed real tears, just tears of fury.'

'So Katya lied?' he asked softly.

'No, I'm sure she thought it was deliberate.'

'Are you?'

Cassandra was confused. Actually she wasn't sure. It had seemed to her that Katya had been furious about something else and had taken it out on the little girl, at the same time taking a perverse pleasure in the child's distress, but she knew she couldn't possibly say that. 'Perhaps there are undercurrents between the two of them that I don't know about,' she said at last.

The baron nodded his approval. 'Well said. Perhaps there are many complexities of emotion in this house that you have yet to learn about, but that will all be part of your education won't it? You plainly have an abundance of commonsense as well as all the other more obvious virtues.'

His eyes travelled down her body and then back up again, quite slowly and without any attempt to disguise his appraisal. Cassandra was amazed to find that she didn't mind, that she even stood slightly straighter beneath his gaze. When he looked into her eyes again his expression was neutral. 'I think you will do very well,' he commented, almost to himself, then he put out a hand, touched her lightly on the cheek and turned back to the house. 'There is a timetable in your room. Study it and then commence your duties. You will dine with us at nine tonight. The children should be asleep by then, and if they do wake one of the nursery staff will see to them. Dress is formal.'

Left alone in the garden, Cassandra felt totally confused. She'd expected a long talk with the baron while he outlined the way in which he wanted her to structure his daughters' days; instead, he'd spent no more than five minutes with her in which nothing had really been said and yet she felt strangely changed.

Now that he'd gone she could still feel the gentle touch of his fingers on her cheek, and recall the way his eyes had scrutinised her, and how her body had tightened beneath his gaze in a way it had never tightened when Paul had looked at her.

Even now her nipples felt hard against the fabric of her bra, and she was more aware of her body than she'd ever been. The long skirt that she was wearing seemed to be brushing insistently against her legs and without realising what she was doing she moved her hands down over her hips and thighs, just as Katya had done when she came down the stairs towards her that morning. It felt good, and she lifted her face to the sky and let the sun's rays touch her face, warming it until the glow began to spread down her throat as well.

From an upstairs window, Dieter von Ritter watched the tall, slim young woman as for the first time she began to be aware of her body as something that needed more than food and clothing and his own body stirred. When he'd let his eyes travel over her he'd been picturing her as she'd been on the screen, her unawakened body pale and slim and, best of all, unaware of what was to come.

That had been all he'd expected to get from the examination, a quick frisson of pleasure, but it had become much more. She'd seemed to come alive beneath his very gaze. He'd seen how the pulse beneath her ear had started to quicken and he'd known then that this was going to be a very special game. It was going to take every ounce of his self-discipline not to hurry her through the tests, but he knew that the savouring of each moment should be extended to give them all the maximum amount of pleasure possible. And pain too of course, but to him they were the same thing, and they would be to Cassandra, he was sure of that now. There would be no repetition of the tears and pathetic whimperings of Abigail. No, this girl would understand and rise to the challenge. It was a long time since he had felt such excitement.

The door to the upstairs study opened and Pierre, the masseur, stood in the doorway. 'Do you wish to join us, Baron? Madam is ready now.'

The baron blinked and looked away from Cassandra. 'Yes, I wish to join you,' he said sharply. 'Tell Katya to fetch Peter as well.'

Katya was pleased when Pierre told her that the baron wished to join her. Lately he'd seemed less interested in her body, and even the fact that Peter was to join them didn't spoil her pleasure. Peter always added to their pleasure.

It was only when the baron came into the tiny but well-equipped gym that Katya's pleasure began to fade. He looked thoroughly irritated. Not angry, that could often be stimulating, but as though she was spoiling something for him and that hadn't happened for a long time. At the beginning it had been part of her learning programme, but it was something she'd left behind a long time ago and she had no wish to experience it again.

'Darling, how lovely!' she said brightly. 'Pierre's wonderful, but only as an hors-d'oeuvre.'

'Why did you try to seduce Cassandra outside?' he asked, totally ignoring her remark.

'Seduce? All I did was chat to her! I thought she should think of me as a friend, to make it more interesting later on.'

He frowned. 'I saw you from the window. You were trying to seduce her. If Helena hadn't dropped her plate when she did, you were actually going to touch her weren't you?'

'Of course not!' Katya gave a small laugh, that was quickly cut off as the baron put a hand to her throat and tightened his fingers.

'You're lying to me. I told you not to touch her before tonight and you were deliberately going to disobey me. That's cheating, and I don't play with cheats. Perhaps I should replace you before we begin.'

Katya struggled to free herself from his grip, coughing and spluttering while an impassive Pierre looked on. Suddenly he let her go and she drew in her breath with a rasping sound and swallowed, only to feel a sharp pain from the bruised tissue of her throat.

She wished she wasn't lying naked on the table where she'd been given the massage. Dieter was in a strong position standing over her, and there was no way she could get off the table if he didn't want to let her.

For a moment he stared down at her, and his dark eyes were heavy with annoyance. He lifted his head as Peter came into the room. 'Peter! Excellent. Fetch my small riding crop and the black leather two-piece for Madam.'

Katya pushed herself upright on the couch. 'No, Dieter! That's not for me, not any more. It's for . . .'

'It's for anyone I choose, my dear, unless you don't want to play, of course?'

'Has the game begun?' she whispered.

He smiled unpleasantly. 'It began yesterday. I must have forgotten to tell you.'

Yesterday. Her mind raced, trying to remember what had happened yesterday apart from the scene with Abigail, but she couldn't recall anything of consequence, although if she hadn't thought Dieter was busy with Lucy she would never have attempted to lay a finger on Cassandra in the garden. Now she realised that he must have deliberately made Lucy simulate sounds of passion in order to mislead her, and she'd fallen for it.

Peter quickly came back into the room and handed over a wooden box to the baron. Slowly he removed the contents. A tiny riding crop, which Katya knew he could handle with more accuracy than anyone would believe possible, a thick black band of velvet, and what appeared at first to be an ordinary black bikini, but made out of rubber.

Katya tried to quell her fear. 'Darling, isn't this rather dated?'

'No more than some other things in the house,' he said cuttingly. 'Put on the blindfold.'

'No! I like to see what you're doing. I enjoy . . .'

'This is for my enjoyment, not yours. Put it on.'

She knew that if she didn't he'd only get Peter to do it for him and so she took the piece of velvet material in her hands and slipped it down over her head until her eyes were covered and her world was nothing but darkness.

'Now lie on your back,' the baron instructed her. She started to turn over but her body missed the edge of the couch and she began to fall. Her lack of vision had affected her balance and she couldn't pull herself back, but she knew that Dieter was standing right by her. To her horror he didn't try to save her, and with a tiny scream of fright she fell from the couch onto the floor, hitting her right hip sharply. She bit back a moan of pain.

'Get back on, my dear. This is wasting time.'

She got unsteadily to her feet, her hands reaching out blindly for the couch and then with great difficulty pulled herself up again, terrified that she'd fall off the other side. By the time she was finally lying flat on her back, her body was bathed in sweat, and her hair was plastered round her face in tiny tendrils.

'Put the bikini on her, Peter,' the baron instructed.

Katya felt Peter's large hands threading her legs through the openings in the bikini bottom, and then he was struggling to pull the thick rubber over her damp flesh. It pulled and tugged at her, pinching and nipping her skin, dragging heavily all the way and she lifted her hips from the couch to try and help him, although she hated the indignity of it and of what was to come.

'Keep still,' Dieter said coldly. 'Let Peter manage alone.'

Katya's breathing was uneven now and the baron watched the rise and fall of her breasts with amusement. He'd known she'd hate this and was satisfied with his choice of punishment.

The rubber bikini bottom was finally in place, and Katya suddenly felt Peter's long fingers carefully pulling her outer sex lips through the opening between the legs; he knew that her sex must be fully exposed, the tightness of the rubber distending it to make an easy target for the baron's crop. As he manipulated her into place, Peter let one of his fingers brush around the delicate flesh surrounding the clitoris and she flinched at the unexpected touch, but at the same time she felt a trickle of moisture begin to seep out from her rapidly moistening opening. The baron pushed Peter to one side and looked down at her. 'Whore,' he said with a soft laugh and she felt the tip of the riding crop move lightly up her left leg for a moment before he removed it.

'Sit up!' he said after a short silence. She obeyed, but swayed as she did so, hating the heavy blackness that surrounded her. Peter lifted her arms, quickly pulled the bands of the bikini top onto her shoulders and then fastened it at the back with the heavy metal clip. There were holes cut in the front of the cups, but this time it was the baron who pushed them into place, sucking hard on each of her nipples in turn, and as her breasts swelled so the rubber clung more tightly to her, forcing the nipples and surrounding areoles to stand out as yet another target for him.

'Wonderful! Lie down flat again and lift your hips for a moment.' His shallow breathing was audible to her, but his voice was even, with no trace of the excitement she knew he was feeling. As she lifted her hips she felt cool air between the cheeks of her bottom and suddenly remembered that there was a second hole in the bottom half of the bikini, a hole that allowed her to be penetrated there as well. The baron's probing hand found the hole and he inserted his finger for a moment, to make sure that everything was correctly aligned. He let it stray between the tight cheeks of her bottom, his fingernail grazing the tensed flesh. 'I think it fits a little more tightly than when we first used it on you, Katya. Perhaps you've put on some weight,' he remarked as he withdrew his finger. 'Lower your hips now. We're ready to begin.'

Katya lay silently on the couch. She knew that Pierre was still standing in the corner of the room, and that thought excited her because as far as she knew all his sexual experiences so far had been with men. Peter was by her side, she could smell the tang of his aftershave and almost feel his excitement, but she had no idea where the baron was standing. The silence was as deep as the darkness and she could do nothing but wait. As she waited her fear and arousal both increased, the fear stimulating her sexual desire.

Peter, entirely naked, looked across the tightly encased body of his employer's mistress and felt his cock pressing against his stomach. His testicles were already tight, but he knew that he would not be allowed relief yet. He glanced at the baron, awaiting his signal. When it came he reached out and moved his hand in soft circles around the exposed flesh of her upper stomach, just above the cruelly tight top of the bikini bottom. Katya gave a tiny sigh and despite herself she knew that she moved very slightly up towards the source of pleasure. It was a mistake. With a quick flick of his hand, the baron brought his riding crop down across one of the protruding nipples, leaving a bright red line in its wake. Katya drew in her breath so sharply that it made a wheezing sound and she bit on her lip as the pain increased for a few seconds before dying away. Peter's hand returned to her stomach, and this time she lay unmoving, but her flesh began to swell with the

42

pleasurable sensations he was arousing and as it did so, the rubber garment tightened its grip on her and her breasts felt as though they'd burst under the constriction.

At another sign from the baron, Peter bent his head and took the reddened nipple in his mouth, letting his saliva moisten the livid mark and then gently tonguing the whole of the exposed area until finally he couldn't help but take the whole of the nipple and surrounding flesh into his mouth.

Katya, with her sense of sight removed, found the sensations Peter was arousing even greater than usual and as he sucked on her painfully engorged breast she felt a tugging sensation begin at the base of her stomach, sending thrills of pleasure up through her until they became one with the pleasure on her breast.

The baron watched as her legs fell limply apart during Peter's attentions. He positioned himself at the foot of the couch and watched for the moment when her upper torso began to arch. He didn't have long to wait. Katya was desperate to make some sound of pleasure, to move her hands and clutch hold of Peter's head, but she knew better. However, finally she couldn't help but push her shoulders down into the couch to force her nipple more firmly into Peter's mouth and at once the moist warmth was withdrawn and almost before the air had begun to chill her damp skin, the baron lifted his hand and the riding crop came down again with remarkable precision, leaving a second red line that cut straight across the middle of the already scarlet nipple. The pain on top of the cessation of pleasure was too much, and Katya yelped.

'Hush!' the baron whispered, and his gentle tone made her excited body tremble. 'Pierre,' he continued smoothly. 'Hold her ankles apart please, we must have no movement now. Peter, you hold her shoulders, and take this. You'll need it later.'

Alone in the dark world that Dieter had created for her, Katya longed to know what it was he was handing to Peter, and yet she didn't dare ask. Blindness seemed to strip her of her strength of character; she was afraid to do anything that might make her position worse, partly because she knew that this was an important move in the game, and having played this part before it should be her chance to score well, but only if the rules were the same. Briefly she understood something of the confusion Abigail had felt, but it was quickly forgotten and followed by a desire to make sure Cassandra suffered more intensely than any previous competition before the game was over.

Her thoughts were interrupted by the touch of a tongue between her thighs. Since Peter was holding her shoulders and Pierre her ankles she knew it must belong to Dieter, but it was different from the way he usually used his mouth on her there, more delicate, almost like a tender lover might begin his ministrations.

She could feel the blood pounding round her body. The tightness of the rubber bikini emphasised everything that was happening to her, and while Peter continued to hold her shoulders he also licked her neck and ear lobes while between her thighs the baron's tongue slowly inserted itself between her outer lips and ran with calculated precision up and down the flesh below the shaft of her rapidly swelling bud of pleasure that was throbbing with a life of its own.

She could feel her juices flooding out of her, and heard a soft murmur of appreciation from the baron as he licked them away, but at the same time as his tongue was working her so well, she felt the light touch of the crop trailing a path up the outside of her right leg. It came to a halt at her bare waist as he laid it gently across her, but she knew that he still had one hand firmly on the handle.

Peter's tongue went into her ear, jabbing hard and swirling in a way he knew she liked and her hips twitched involuntarily. 'Be careful,' the baron said quietly. Katya was terribly aware of her swollen sex

44

lips, of the vulnerability of the exposed inner flesh and she tried desperately to remain quiescent.

After what seemed an eternity of lips and tongue the baron finally moved a hand between her thighs and very carefully he pulled back the protective hood of the clitoris so that the jangling nerve ends were fully exposed and entirely unprotected. She felt the light crop begin to move, slithering over her stomach and then down her side until it disappeared altogether.

The baron now pushed the top of the cleft between her outer lips upwards so that her clitoris remained exposed. She felt as though the whole area must be visibly pulsating with desire so desperate was she for a climax after all the ministrations. Peter, at a further signal from the baron, quickly moved his mouth and this time took the undamaged nipple into it, grazing it with his teeth until it formed a hard little point in his mouth. At the same time he put a large hand round the breast that had twice been marked with the crop and tightened his fingers until he forced a whimper of pain through Katya's tightly closed mouth.

Watching his mistress closely, the baron slid a hand beneath the tight rubber waistband and down until his fingers were in her soft pubic hair. Then he rotated the palm of his hand, pulling the restricted flesh so that it snagged against the rubber, leaving her even more exposed between the opening in the crotch. Pierre pulled her ankles as far apart as he could and waited, his eyes glittering with an excitement he'd never felt before.

Returning to her sex lips the baron pushed two fingers into her wet entrance and moved them quickly from side to side, watching as her head began to twist and turn at the far end of the couch. Then he withdrew them sharply, but as her head began to slow pushed them back, this time with a third finger added. The three fingers moved in circles, touching the inner walls of her vagina until he finally let one flick against the elusive G-spot that he could locate so unerringly in her.

45

For Katya it was all too much. Peter was sucking and squeezing her desperately aching breasts so fiercely that they felt as though they would tear the rubber apart if they swelled any more, the heavy pressure in her lower abdomen had spread upwards until her whole belly felt as tight as a drum and wave after wave of pleasure was building up inside her until her body could bear no more. She knew that her clitoris was fully exposed, knew what would happen if she climaxed but she had no choice.

'Please?' she whispered once, hoping that permission might still be given.

'No.' The baron's voice was uncompromising.

'I must, I must!' She sounded frantic, and despised herself for it.

'No,' he repeated calmly, and again his finger flicked the G-spot.

Her body tightened, nerve endings stretched to their limit, her belly arched and her breasts rose as the pleasure expanded into a huge ball of pressure that would tear her apart if it didn't find some release. She tried desperately to distract herself but it was hopeless, the wave reached its peak and with a scream of despair she gave in, and felt her whole body jerk off the bed as the mind-blowing ecstasy finally tore through her.

It only lasted a moment, because at the height of the pleasure the baron's crop struck. It flicked against her hideously vulnerable clitoris causing pain such as she'd never known and as she tried to twist away from the agony Peter reached for her hips, turned her roughly onto her side, pulled her to him and thrust himself through the second hole in the bikini bottom, forcing the swollen glans of his penis through the cheeks of her bottom, still tightly clenched against the agony of the baron's crop. She cried out in pain, and then as she felt the warmth of his ejaculation begin to flood through her, the pain changed into a dark, red-hot pleasure that tightened her stomach muscles again and the baron watched with amusement as her thighs stiffened and her now free heels drummed against the bottom of the couch.

Peter groaned with relief as he was finally able to relieve the aching pressure in his testicles, and he gave no thought at all to the blindfolded, thrashing woman he was using other than to mentally thank the baron for his permission finally to use her.

After he'd withdrawn the boy watched as his employer pulled off his trousers and revealed his own erection, the purple tip glistening with moisture. For a few moments he let it brush against the wounded, scarlet opening of Katya's sex, and he smiled as the flesh jumped and jerked beneath the velvety touch of the soft skin. He was pleased that Katya, her body rigid with fear and rearoused sexual tension, made no sound this time.

After that he climbed lithely onto the couch and crouched above her, pushing his erection down so that it could caress the still red and swollen nipples that were protruding so invitingly through the thick rubber cups. Katya gritted her teeth. She adored the feel of his manhood on her breasts, gloried in the velvet softness of the touch, but both her breasts and between her thighs still ached with the torture he'd inflicted on them and she knew better than to think he'd finished yet.

For minutes he continued to tantalise the nipples, watching the puckered skin smooth and expand as he rubbed the ridge of the glans against them, leaving a trail of clear liquid behind him. Then the baron took hold of her upper body, twisting it round so that her head was no longer supported by the couch and hung limply back, exposing her throat as she tried frantically to swallow.

He remembered how much she'd always hated what he was about to do and it increased his pleasure. Katya remembered too, and began to thrash her head from side to side but Peter was quickly there, gripping her tightly at the temples while his fingers dug into her scalp until her eyes watered beneath the blind.

'Open your mouth,' the baron said harshly. She did as she was told. If she didn't it would only prolong her torment. 'Good girl!' Her body shivered, and then he was forcing his way into her mouth, pushing his erection down between her teeth and into her throat, moving backwards and forwards, thrusting ferociously in and out until she felt that she would choke. His cock had never seemed so large before. She was terrified that she'd suffocate or choke to death before he'd finished, and in the darkness there was nothing but the feel of him sliding down her throat, filling her airway. She tried to relax the throat muscles, as he'd taught her long ago, but her fear made it impossible and then, when her heart was racing as though it would burst and her throat felt raw from the violence of his movements, he finally climaxed and the hot, sticky liquid erupted from him and flooded her mouth and throat until she began to choke.

The baron withdrew immediately, his eyes totally without expression. Peter started to release his grip, but the baron frowned in displeasure. 'Keep hold of her. She must swallow it all.' Katya swallowed again and again. The back of her neck ached where it had been crushed against the edge of the couch and her whole body was bruised and battered by what had happened. She wanted to cry, with furious humiliation, something that hadn't happened to her for many, many years, but she didn't dare. If she cried then she would have lost before the game had even started properly, before Cassandra had faced a single test, and that thought helped her keep control.

At last, when he was satisfied that she had swallowed every drop of him, the baron let Peter release her head and he himself pulled her back into position. He looked down at her thoughtfully for a moment, then reached out and removed the blindfold.

Katya's eyes stared up at him, still sightless for a few seconds, then she blinked and began to adjust to the light again, but he knew that for once he'd managed to put a flicker of genuine fear into those green depths and he raised his eyebrows at her in amusement.

'Perhaps next time you'll wait until you're invited before you touch, yes?'

Katya wanted to promise him that she'd wait, to swear that she'd never disobey him again; it was what he'd always demanded in the early years, but some sixth sense told her that now the rules were different. 'Perhaps,' she replied coolly, and was rewarded with a look of appreciation before he moved out of her line of vision.

'Get her out of that costume and into a bath,' he told Peter curtly. 'She needs to rest before dinner.'

'I can do it myself,' Katya said fiercely as Peter approached, and the boy backed off, looking to the baron for instructions.

The baron shrugged indifferently. 'Just as she likes. Pierre, it's time you were gone. I hope you aren't expecting extra payment for overtime?'

The masseur shook his head, hardly able to believe what he'd seen and thinking excitedly of what a story he'd have to tell his friends when they met up later that night. 'Good,' the baron continued pleasantly. 'And naturally I don't expect a word of this to pass your lips.'

'Of course not!' Pierre lied fervently.

The baron smiled, watched him leave the room and promptly picked up the telephone. 'Make sure the masseur does not arrive home tonight,' he said softly into the mouthpiece.

When Katya had finally managed to take off the rubber suit and was at last sitting in her deep, shell-shaped bath, she ran her hands down over her bruised breasts, touched herself between her thighs where the flesh was so exquisitely tender and with a shiver of delight recalled all that had just happened and anticipated the dinner that was to come. This time it would be Cassandra's turn to be tested. The beginning of her own, particular kind of torture, the wonderful destruction of innocence.

49

# Chapter Three

*T*he first thing that Cassandra noticed as she walked into the oak-panelled dining room was the heat. It had been a very warm day for late May, and she'd been grateful for the ceiling fan in her room when she changed for dinner. She knew from Katya that the house had air conditioning and had been anticipating a cool evening meal with relief. In fact the room was stiflingly hot; thick moss-green curtains covered the windows trapping the heat of the day and preventing any chance of some fresher night air entering. Crossing the room to the long mahogany table, she realised with astonishment that a wood fire was burning in the fireplace.

Katya was already seated at the table. She was wearing a blue velvet dress with a plunging neckline while round her throat a diamond and sapphire necklace glinted in the light from the candles set in the silver candelabra in the middle of the table. Her blonde hair had been piled on top of her head and her skin glowed a soft golden brown, making Cassandra acutely aware of her own pallor.

'What a pretty dress,' Katya said sweetly.

Cassandra had thought it pretty once; it was a pale pink strapless chiffon creation that clung tightly round her breasts before falling in gentle folds to mid-calf, but compared to Katya's sophisticated creation it was pathetic and she felt certain she must look like an overgrown child in a party frock.

'The colour's cute,' Katya continued. 'Pink's adorable, and it gives you a little more colour too.'

'It's very warm in here,' Cassandra ventured.

Katya showed her perfect little teeth in a delighted smile. 'I know! Dieter loves to do things like this.'

'Like what?' Cassandra asked in confusion.

'Unexpected things. When it's hot he lights a fire, when it's cold he opens the windows and turns off the heating. It's all part of his obsession with people learning to discipline their bodies. He thinks that the mind can control everything. Tonight we must think cool and then we'll feel cool. Don't you think that's brilliant?'

'Not really. I mean, it isn't cool is it? It's hot.'

'Perhaps I haven't explained it very well. I'm afraid I'm really very stupid, not at all cerebral; not that Dieter minds!' She gave a ripple of laughter.

'Does it matter where I sit?' Cassandra asked.

'You're over there, opposite the fire.'

Cassandra took her seat and felt the heat from the flames across the table. She took a tissue from her clutch bag and dabbed at the perspiration on her top lip. It was all becoming a nightmare.

'Haven't you offered Cassandra a drink?' the baron asked as he strode into the room, pulling at the frilled cuffs of his dress shirt. 'What a poor hostess she must think you, Katya.'

As Katya hurried across to the drinks cabinet, the baron lifted Cassandra's left hand to his mouth and brushed it with his lips. It was the lightest of touches, but a small shock of pleasure darted up her arm and she almost snatched her hand away in surprise.

'How were the children?' he continued smoothly. 'No trouble I trust?'

'They were fine. Helena didn't want to eat her rice

51

pudding, she seemed to expect blackcurrant sorbet, but apart from that . . .'

'Now and again I change the menu,' the baron explained, watching Katya hand Cassandra a goblet of wine. 'I think it's so much more interesting if life holds surprises.'

'Only if they're pleasant ones,' Cassandra remarked dryly, gulping her wine far too quickly because she was so thirsty.

The baron watched her tilt her head back and visualised the liquid flowing down her throat. His eyes narrowed and his fingers began to tap lightly against the table top. Katya reached across and covered his hand with hers, stilling the telltale sign of his excitement.

'But life holds so many unpleasant surprises it's better for children to learn to face disappointment early on, don't you agree?' he asked.

'Not really. Childhood's precious; life will be hard later on as you say, but if you've had a secure start it's much easier to cope with life once you're older.'

The baron leant across the table and refilled her glass. 'Ring for Lucy to start serving, Katya. I'm afraid I don't agree with you, Cassandra, but then that's part of the pleasure of meeting new people, isn't it? Teaching them that there are different ways of looking at life.'

'Do I teach you or do you teach me?' Cassandra asked, astonished at her own courage and realising that she must drink her wine more slowly.

'My dear girl, we teach each other! Soup, Lucy, how perfect.'

Cassandra had been hoping for melon or a mousse of some kind. The bowl of steaming thick vegetable soup was the last thing she felt like eating and she glanced around the table for some water.

'Salt?' Katya asked, pushing the silver cruet towards her.

'Actually I was wondering if there was any water.'

'No,' the baron said shortly. 'Lucy, bring more wine.'

The candles on the table were scented, and the combination of the wine, the heat from the fire, the sweetness of the candles and the hot soup were nearly too much for Cassandra. She felt her eyelids begin to droop and a small trickle of sweat ran down her back. In the end she gave up and pushed the soup bowl away from her. The baron looked down the table at his mistress and they smiled at each other.

The soup was followed by roast beef, and the beef by a thick crusted apple pie served with clotted cream but while Cassandra simply picked languidly at the food Katya ate everything that was put in front of her with apparent relish. All Cassandra seemed able to do was drink, and since she never saw when the baron refilled her glass it was impossible for her to know how much she'd drunk.

At last, when she was so lightheaded with the heat that she felt sure she was going to faint, the baron pushed back his chair. 'We'll take coffee in the drawing room, Lucy. You may put out the fire now.'

Cassandra got to her feet and swayed. At once the baron was at her side, a hand firmly beneath her elbow. 'Come along, Cassandra. The drawing room's cool, you'll feel better there.' She leant against him, her legs suddenly turning weak as she tried to walk. Katya came to assist the baron but he waved her away with a dismissive flick of his hand.

In the drawing room the curtains were again drawn, but the air conditioning was on and Cassandra took deep breaths of the cool air then sank gratefully into one of the deep armchairs. Before coming down to dinner she'd pulled her hair back into a loose chignon, but the heat of the dining room had made it damp and strands had escaped and now clung to the back of her neck in rich brown swirls that made the baron long to reach out and lift them from the creamy flesh. He desisted. That would come later.

As Lucy entered, bringing the coffee on a tray, the baron withdrew to a chair in the far corner of the room, stretching his legs out in front of him. As soon as Lucy had gone Katya, who was sitting opposite Cassandra, leant forward in her chair. 'Did you try and think cool thoughts?' she enquired gently. 'You looked so hot all the time, and it really would have helped you know. I used to find it difficult, but in time you can learn to master your body in almost every situation.'

'I couldn't think of anything except how hot I was!' Cassandra confessed. Her head was still spinning and she was finding it hard to concentrate on what Katya was saying.

'Drink some of your coffee,' Katya urged her.

'I'd really rather have some water. I feel a little faint,' Cassandra confessed, horribly aware that her dress was beginning to stick to her like a second skin.

'The coffee will clear your head,' the baron remarked. 'Besides, how can you teach my daughters to discipline their bodies if you can't control your own? It all comes from here.' He tapped the side of his head. 'Pain, pleasure, comfort, discomfort, we can control it all, can't we my darling?' As he was speaking he got up from his chair and moved to stand behind his mistress.

Cassandra watched over the rim of her coffee cup as his hands reached across the back of Katya's chair and slid onto her shoulders. She took a quick gulp of coffee. It was strong and a little too bitter for her taste, but at least it wasn't alcohol. When her cup was empty she replaced it on the small side table and leant her head back against the back of her chair. The room seemed to be expanding, and the figures of the baron and his mistress were expanding with it until they seemed to be almost on top of her. She realised that the coffee hadn't helped at all, in fact, it had made her feel even more peculiar.

Katya's eyes gleamed across the room at her and Cassandra quickly sat up straighter in her chair. The baron's hands were moving over Katya's upper arms now, small circular movements that were hypnotically soothing. Cassandra's own skin tingled as though he were touching her.

Slowly, very slowly, his hands moved back up and the long fingers caressed the sides of Katya's neck before moving inexorably down to where the V of the dress exposed the gentle swell of her breasts. Cassandra's breath caught in her throat. She wanted to look away, and yet she couldn't. Despite the air conditioning she was hotter now than in the dining room, and her mouth was dry.

For a long time his fingers lingered there, moving gently and insistently and Cassandra could see the top of Katya's breasts swelling and the dress tightening round the concealed lower half. The baron's head had been bent, but suddenly he lifted it and stared directly into Cassandra's eyes for a moment before leaning down until his head touched the top of Katya's and then his left hand slid right inside the deep V of the neckline and Cassandra watched incredulously as he tenderly lifted one round globe free of the dress. He then put his palm flat against Katya's ribcage and pushed upwards until he could take the hard peak of her nipple into his mouth.

Cassandra's heart was beating loudly in her ears and her own breasts were aching, longing for his knowing fingers to touch them just as they were touching Katya. No one had ever touched Cassandra that way. Paul's fumblings had borne no resemblance to the delicate way the baron was playing with Katya and even through the drugged mists of her mind she knew that this was what her body wanted, needed, and that if she couldn't have it she would die.

Small whimpering sounds of pleasure were coming from Katya's mouth, and from time to time the baron would take his lips from her breast and press them against her mouth to silence the sounds before returning to the rapidly darkening nipple.

After a time Katya's hips began to move in the chair and she reached up for the baron's free hand, bringing it down to her stomach so that he could press his fingers against her there, rotating his hand in time to the rotations of his tongue round her exposed breast.

Cassandra could hear her own breathing now, harsh and laboured, and Katya was making tiny mewing sounds of pleasure that increased in volume as the baron took the nipple and surrounding area into his mouth and began to suck hard on it, like a child at the breast.

Cassandra's thighs were tense and trembling, there was a dull ache in the pit of her stomach and her breasts felt as swollen as Katya's looked. Her entire body felt strange, so sensitive that even the touch of the chiffon skirt against the soft skin at the back of her knees was almost unbearable and without realising it her hands crept slowly upwards to cup her own breasts.

All at once, Katya's mewing sounds changed to breathless gasps, her hips moved more urgently, the baron's hand slid lower down her stomach and its movements became less gentle and then the petite, silver-blonde woman's whole body bucked violently in the chair and Cassandra stared at the scene despairingly, heavy-eyed and tense as the other woman found release; release which Cassandra unknowingly needed herself.

When Katya's body was finally still, the baron released her and walked towards Cassandra, his eyes going to her breasts where without realising it she was caressing herself through the tight folds of the chiffon. He crouched down in front of her, noting the slack mouth, the feverish brightness of the eyes, and the taut tension of the body. 'You see,' he whispered. 'There are always ways of distracting yourself from discomfort. Katya was just as hot as you in the dining room. She didn't want the food any more than you did, but she knew that if she ate it she'd be rewarded. Wouldn't you like a reward?'

Cassandra stared back at him, trying to will his hands to reach out and comfort her, fondle her aching breasts.

The thought horrified her, she knew it was lewd and wrong, but at that moment it was all that mattered.

'Please,' she whispered.

'What?' He smiled his most charming smile and smoothed a strand of hair back off her face.

'Touch me,' she implored him.

'Where?' He was still smiling indulgently.

She couldn't say it; even drunk and semi-drugged she couldn't bring herself to say it and shook her head helplessly.

'Tell me what you want,' he said softly. 'How can I help you if I don't know what you need?'

'I want . . .' She swallowed hard. Her breasts were still tight aching knots, the nipples painful against the bodice of the dress, but nothing on earth could make her express her need.

'Yes?'

Tears filled Cassandra's eyes. 'I can't tell you,' she whimpered.

'Silly girl! Here, drink a little more wine.'

She tried to push the glass away, but he persisted, holding the rim of the crystal goblet against her lips until she finally opened her mouth and tipped her head back, letting him dribble the wine down between her teeth and feeling its coolness as it slid down the back of her throat.

'There, that will help. In a few minutes we'll try again.' He got to his feet. 'Katya,' the voice was less gentle now. 'You can leave us.'

Katya stood frozen with astonishment in the middle of the room. 'No! I stay, that's always the way it's been.'

He turned away from Cassandra, his face twisted with temper. 'This is a different game, remember? You've done well tonight, but one wrong move can set you back several places!'

'You bastard!' She was furious with him.

He dropped his voice. 'Don't worry, I won't seduce her tonight. This is just to get her started.'

'This is just for you,' Katya snarled.

'You're free to drop out of the game,' the baron reminded her, and now his eyes were cool. 'Is that what you want?'

'Of course not.'

'Then go; you can always have Peter for the night. I may join you later.'

As a furious Katya left the room, the baron turned back to the heavy-eyed Cassandra lying semi-sprawled in the chair. 'Now my dear, one more sip of the wine and then we'll try again, yes?'

Cassandra was beyond protest. This time she reached towards him almost greedily as he put the goblet to her mouth, but before he let her drink he dipped his finger in the liquid and carefully inserted it between her lips, running it round the velvet softness of her warm moist mouth and mentally comparing it to the other lips, the other entrance, that would one day be his too.

For a moment she was taken by surprise, but then she found herself sucking on the finger, delighting in the feel of her tongue round the wine soaked smooth skin. She heard him give a sigh, then the finger was withdrawn and the glass was there again.

'Drink deeply, Cassandra,' he urged her. 'Open your throat wide, take it all.' He poured the liquid slowly at first, but as he saw the muscles of her throat relax he tipped the glass more sharply and Cassandra felt the wine flooding her until she began to choke. 'Relax, savour it, the taste, the feel, all the sensations should be appreciated,' he whispered. His voice calmed her so that she was able to swallow it all, and when it was gone she felt a sense of loss.

Slowly she lifted her head again and found that the baron was sitting on the arm of her chair, his wide brown eyes softer than usual as he nodded his approval. 'That was good. So good that I'd like to give you a reward, but the rules must be obeyed.'

'Rules?'

He laughed. 'You have to ask for what you want, remember?'

Cassandra nodded, and her eyes went to the baron's hands resting lightly on his knees. He followed the direction of her gaze. 'Say it,' he urged her. 'Tell me what you want me to do.'

'I want you to do what you did to Katya.'

He shook his head. 'That's not enough.'

Cassandra's breasts were so painful that she couldn't bear it any longer.

'I want you to touch my breasts,' she gasped. 'Please, please do it now.'

He didn't smile any more, his expression was almost grave. 'You see, it wasn't so hard was it? But how can I touch them while you're in that ridiculous dress?'

Cassandra stared at him, her brain dulled by the wine and the sexual frustration of the evening. 'I don't . . . I hadn't thought.'

'Take it off.'

Her eyes filled with tears. 'I can't! Katya didn't have to take hers off.'

The baron put out a hand and let his fingers brush lightly against the material encasing her. Her skin leapt at the touch. 'It isn't the same like that, is it?' he asked quizzically.

Cassandra shook her head. 'No, but . . .'

'Lean forward,' he told her quietly. Almost collapsing with relief that she did not have to do it herself, Cassandra did as he instructed. She felt his hand tug at the top of the zip that ran the length of the dress, then he put his hands under her arms and pulled her to her feet so that the dress slithered to the floor, leaving her standing in front of him wearing only a pair of cream French knickers. He caught his breath with excitement.

Gently he pulled the pins out of her carefully arranged chignon until her hair tumbled freely about her face and down past her shoulders, then he stepped back to look at her more carefully.

Cassandra watched him, her breasts rising and falling, her tiny nipples standing erect and pink and hardening even more beneath his gaze. She followed

59

his eyes as they swept down her, and was proud of her small waist and narrow hips but she wished that her legs weren't trembling so much.

The baron felt a hard lump of emotion in his throat, something he couldn't identify but which he knew he'd experienced long ago, before life had become so boring, and suddenly he didn't want Katya to see what was going to follow. This slim, unawakened girl in front of him would never take pleasure in the kind of scene he and Katya had played out that afternoon, and suddenly his own part in that sickened him.

In his temper he'd only pandered to Katya's deep-rooted masochism, and it had been a mistake. Well, if she was masochistic enough to enjoy being deprived of seeing what was about to happen he'd be astonished, and it was with great delight that he turned and flicked the switch on the tiny remote control box set beneath the coffee table. Now they were truly alone.

Cassandra had begun to shiver. She had never wanted a man's hands on her before, never had any desire for Paul to touch her or even kiss her, and yet now, virtually naked in front of a man she'd only just met she was almost frantic with longing while he stood there totally calm, simply watching her.

The baron saw the indecision on her face and moved towards her. 'Lie down on the rug,' he said quietly, and his hands pushed on her shoulders. She sank down gratefully, at least now he wouldn't be able to see the way her legs were shaking. He sat down next to her and reached for the opened bottle of wine. Automatically, Cassandra opened her mouth.

'Not again, greedy one!' She stared up at him as he tipped the bottle slowly and let chilled wine splash onto her breasts, making her gasp as it landed on her hot, aching flesh.

Almost idly he ran a finger round both nipples, spreading the wine over the whole surface area of the breasts. Cassandra wanted more, and pushed up towards him. 'No, lie still. You must always lie still during pleasuring. If you move, I have to stop.'

'Why?' she whimpered.

He shrugged. 'It's more fun that way. Now, I shall drink some wine myself.' She watched his head descend to her breasts and as his warm tongue lapped at the liquid where it was spilling from her breasts and down to her ribs she groaned with pleasure. The tongue was feather light, almost as though he were a kitten licking a saucer of cream. After a time he cupped her breasts with his hands, pushing them upwards and closed his whole mouth over each of the breasts in turn, sucking very carefully to begin with, but then increasing the force until the tugging became almost painful.

Cassandra's head began to move from side to side with excitement. In some strange way the baron's sucking and tonguing seemed to be making things worse rather than better, so that her whole body was screaming for attention, but Cassandra knew instinctively that it wouldn't receive it. Whatever it was she needed, she would have to ask, and at the moment she didn't have the words and besides she didn't want him to leave her exquisitely sensitive nipples.

The darts of pleasure grew and turned to flames. She felt as though her upper body was on fire and without realising it her legs began to move restlessly against the thick pile of the rug and the touch of the material helped her. Automatically, she began to move as much of herself as she could so that nearly all of her bare back and legs were being caressed by the long strands of the rug, heightening her senses so that her body was more alive than ever before.

The baron knew what was happening, but it was only when she began to move her hips that he put a restraining hand across her stomach. 'No, not tonight, Cassandra. Keep still now,' he murmured, lifting his head from her engorged creamy globes. Noticing the flush of sexual excitement on her neck and chest, he knew that he could bring her to a climax within a few seconds.

Cassandra felt his hand on her bare waist and her hips stopped moving, but the effort needed to keep still was tremendous and it was only because she so desperately wanted to please him that she was able to do as he ordered.

He looked at the delicate buds that topped her breasts, and marvelled at the childlike innocence they seemed to represent, but there was nothing innocent in the glazed look in her eyes or the ragged way she was breathing.

He drew back from her for a moment to touch a bell set in the control panel and then he put a hand down, took her left nipple between a finger and thumb and began to pinch it. At first the pinch was so light she couldn't feel it, but then the pressure increased until it began to hurt, and she gave a small cry.

'Hush!' he said soothingly. 'Wait, trust me, Cassandra. This will be good for you.'

Cassandra moaned fretfully. The unattended breast longed for his mouth while the pain in the other was distracting her from the pleasures of the past half hour. Then, suddenly, the quality of the pain changed and it turned into a different kind of pleasure from before, a red-hot pleasure sharper than anything that had preceded it and her head went back hard against the floor.

Seeing this, the baron quickly bent his head and took the other nipple into his mouth, grazing it lightly with his teeth before clamping his lips firmly round the glorious hard roundness of her and sucking with all the force he could muster while at the same time the fingers of the hand holding her other nipple closed together hard.

The sensations flooded through Cassandra. She closed her eyes and flashes of colour exploded behind her lids, the tightness in her abdomen increased and it was only his restraining hand that kept her hips still, then suddenly her whole body was rocked by an explosion that sent electric currents tearing through her so that she actually screamed aloud as sweat poured from her body and a trickle of liquid escaped from between her thighs wetting the fabric of her French knickers.

The baron sat back and watched Cassandra as her eyes opened and she stared at him in bewilderment. Her breasts no longer ached, they were tender and slightly sore but the dreadful pressure had gone, and her whole body felt limp as though she'd swum thirty lengths of a pool or gone for a long run.

'I take it I did it right?' the baron said sardonically, and his change of expression, the lack of tenderness in his eyes, made her feel terrible. Her head was clear now. She was no longer dizzy or disorientated and she couldn't believe what she'd let him – no, asked him – to do.

She was about to speak, to apologise or something, anything to help her through the moment, when she realised with a shock that there was someone else in the room. She gave a gasp and put her arms across her breasts, but the baron moved them firmly away.

'It's only Lucy. Servants don't count.'

'You rang, sir?' Lucy said politely.

'I believe I did. A pot of tea, China I think, with lemon.'

'Very good, sir.'

There was nothing on Lucy's face to indicate that she was seeing anything unusual. Cassandra was horrified. She felt humiliated and betrayed and tried to scramble up. The baron reached out a hand and caught hold of her elbow.

'There's nothing to be ashamed about. You were sexually aroused and wanted me to give you an orgasm. I obliged. If you were hungry, I'd feed you. There's no difference.'

Cassandra opened her mouth to tell him that she would never have let him touch her if she hadn't been given too much to drink, but the words wouldn't come out.

'Have you ever had an orgasm before?' he asked intently. She tried to wrench herself free of his grip but she wasn't strong enough. 'Tell me,' he insisted, 'and don't lie. I'll know if you lie.'

Cassandra's head dropped. 'No,' she said miserably. 'I never have.'

'What a clod your husband must have been,' said the baron dispassionately. 'You're made for sex, Cassandra. I knew it when I first saw you, and what happened tonight was nothing, nothing at all. There's so much for you to learn, so much to experience, and you'll love it all.' His eyes began to shine with excited anticipation.

'I want to leave,' Cassandra said quietly.

The baron merely laughed. 'Of course you don't want to leave. How could you leave me now, when your body's just starting to come alive.' He put out a hand and slid it up the leg of her French knickers, trailing a finger through her moistness. 'Don't you want to know what it's like to be kissed there? To be touched all over your body?'

As he talked he kept his eyes fixed on hers, and to her shame Cassandra felt the liquid begin to escape from her again, and saw him smile as his fingers felt it too. 'You're special, Cassandra, very special. You can't leave now. You need someone like me, someone to teach you what your body can do, and how to discipline it.'

The last words made her shiver with a strange excitement that she couldn't explain and she was still staring at him when Lucy re-entered the room with the tea tray.

'Put it on the table, Lucy. Don't you think Cassandra's got a beautiful body?' he added casually.

Lucy smiled cheerfully at Cassandra. 'Very beautiful, sir. I wish I was tall and slim.'

He laughed. 'I think you do very well as you are. Run

64

along now. You can go to bed, you won't be needed any more tonight.'

Cassandra stared at him. 'Why do you want to humiliate me even more?' she asked, and to his surprise he felt almost moved by the distress in her eyes.

'I'm not humiliating you, Cassandra. I'm showing you that there's nothing to be ashamed of in sex. Later on, you'll understand more about sharing, now is probably too soon.'

Cassandra wished he'd take his hand away from between her thighs. It agitated her, making her flesh feel hot and tense. He saw the signs of fresh arousal beginning on her face and suddenly realised why. At once he withdrew his hand. She'd had enough for tonight, and normally he would have sent her up to her room by now but there was something about her that fascinated him. Once he knew what it was, her spell would be broken, but until then she was more intriguing than any woman had been in a long time.

'Go to bed,' he said and his voice was so kind that Katya would never have recognised it. 'In the morning all this will seem like a dream.'

She sat up, looked around for her dress then began to try and struggle into it. The baron shook his head, helped her to her feet and then slid it down over her body himself, smoothing it carefully over her hips and small tight bottom until he felt the flesh leaping in response.

'I don't understand,' Cassandra muttered, her eyes suddenly beginning to close as exhaustion, drugs and alcohol began to catch up with her. 'I thought . . .'

He tipped her chin up and looked intently at her. 'What did you think?'

'I thought you had to love people before you could . . .'

'There's no such thing as love, Cassandra,' he told her quietly. 'It's a myth; a fable; a fairy story that allows women to stop feeling guilty about their sexuality. Sensuality, lust, eroticism, those are real, but not love.'

Cassandra clasped her arms round her body. He was wrong, she knew that, but after what had happened she was in no position to argue with him. 'How can you let me look after your children after this?' she asked as she began to walk away from him.

'I knew all about you when I chose you. This has nothing to do with my children. Now get some sleep. I'm away all day tomorrow, but I'll be back for dinner. If it's fine we'll dine out of doors, so much cooler for us all!' He was laughing when she closed the door behind her.

It was nearly four a.m. before the baron climbed into his circular bed, but Katya was still wide awake, staring hot-eyed into the darkness. She hadn't been able to believe it when the closed-circuit television screen went blank. At first she'd had Peter rushing round trying to mend it, and when he'd told her that it had been turned off by Dieter she'd screamed like a fishwife at him. Nothing like that had ever happened before and she felt very frightened.

'Still awake, Katya?' the baron asked softly.

'Yes.'

'Did you and Peter have a nice time?'

'Probably not as nice as you and Cassandra.'

He laughed. 'Probably not.' He put out an arm and pinioned Katya on her back. 'I hope you're not thinking of making a scene. That would be a big mistake.'

'Why should I make a scene?'

His arm relaxed. 'Quite so! I was thinking that soon we should be ready for a visit from Rupert and Françoise. Perhaps you would arrange that.'

Katya's spirits lifted. Even if Cassandra coped with Dieter and the rest of the household, she'd never cope with Rupert and Françoise. No one ever could, except for her, which was why she was still there while even pathetic Marietta was gone. Marietta, who'd made the mistake of falling in love with her debauched husband

and then committed the even greater folly of telling him so.

'Don't you think Helena's growing more like Marietta every day?' she murmured as she turned over to sleep.

The baron smiled to himself. Katya was obviously badly rattled. 'Perhaps, but that's better than growing more like me! As a matter of interest, Katya, did you enjoy yourself in the gym this afternoon?'

This was one area in which Katya knew she could score. 'Yes,' she said proudly. 'The pain was unimaginably glorious. Even I have never experienced such satisfaction. It was sublime.'

Feeling slightly sick the baron turned over and went to sleep while Katya, certain that this had put her one move ahead, finally slept too.

# Chapter Four

Cassandra awoke the next morning with an aching head and dry mouth. She fumbled for the alarm clock, her fingers thick and heavy, and by the time she'd turned it off her heart was racing madly. For a few minutes she lay there wondering if she was ill, but then memories of the previous evening flashed through her mind like slides on a screen and her body went hot. 'It must have been a dream,' she murmured to herself, but when her hands moved to her breasts the tenderness of the nipples and surrounding skin told her only too clearly that she was wrong.

She stumbled out of bed and into her bathroom, then ran an extra hot bath before climbing into the sunken tub. Through the haze of oil-scented steam she was able to study herself. There were tiny red marks and the beginnings of bruises showing clearly on her small white breasts. Cassandra couldn't believe it, and yet even while she was trying to understand how it could have happened, her body was remembering the pleasures and her legs moved lazily apart beneath the water, allowing one of the jets to play between them.

The shock of the sensation it aroused brought her to her senses. Quickly she washed all over then stepped out, wrapped herself in one of the huge, soft towels and rubbed her body harshly until she was dry. Fleetingly she felt a brief moment of panic at the thought of facing the baron over breakfast, but then she remembered that he'd said he'd be away all day and she relaxed again. She just wished she could remember how Katya had come to leave them alone after dinner. There was also a vague memory of another person in the room, a watcher in the shadows, but this was confused and might, she thought, have been part of a dream rather than reality.

As soon as she'd dressed in what she thought of as a regulation dark skirt and white cotton blouse, she took out the baron's list of instructions and checked through them. After breakfast each day he wanted the girls to have some form of exercise – she decided that today they'd make use of the indoor pool tucked away in a separate building at the back of the house. Mid-morning they had a drink and then 'something educational' was meant to take them up to lunch. In the afternoons there was a rest period, and then a trip out; museums, cinemas, zoos or parks were suggestions Abigail had put in, although Cassandra felt that Christina was far too young for anything more than a zoo or park. This was followed by time to themselves, tea at five o'clock, a story and game, bath then bed by six-thirty.

Two things on the list surprised her. One was the fact that the times the children were to use the bathroom were set down, almost as though the girls wouldn't know when they needed to use it themselves, and the other was the instruction: 'You have to maintain total control of the girls at all times. Any disobedience or failure to keep to the programme must be punished immediately.'

Try as she might, Cassandra couldn't work out how two small girls could fail to keep to the programme when they were entirely dependent on her to take them anywhere. Some time, she thought, she'd question him about it, but most certainly not tonight.

The girls were awake when she went in, and they

looked at her in surprise. 'You came from your own room,' said Helena, quickly pulling off her nightdress and pulling on a red and white checked dress with smocking on the chest.

'Where else would I come from?' Cassandra asked.

Helena shrugged in a gesture very like her father's. 'Papa's room, or Katya's,' she added, pulling the corners of her mouth down. 'That's where Abigail usually spent the night. She only used her own room when she'd been naughty.'

Cassandra felt uneasy. 'What do you mean, naughty?'

'Don't know. Perhaps she didn't eat her food or something. What are we doing today?'

'I thought we'd go swimming this morning, and this afternoon we could go for a walk on Hampstead Heath.'

Helena shook her head. 'No, we can't, not unless we take bodyguards and you have to arrange them the day before. Don't you know anything?'

'Not really. You'll have to help me learn,' Cassandra smiled.

Helena stared at her. 'I'm not helping you. If you get punished we won't. Hurry up, Christy, or you'll be late and that's a penalty point.'

Cassandra took the smaller girl on her knees and began to help her with her clothes. 'I don't believe in penalty points myself. That must have been Abigail's way of doing things.'

Helena deftly fastened her sandals. 'No, it's Papa's. You shouldn't help her so much, she'll never learn anything if you spoon-feed her. Papa says spoilt children disgust him. There, I'm ready.'

Cassandra looked at the beautiful little face and noted the unusually determined set of the mouth. 'You're very quick and efficient, Helena, but somehow I don't think Christina is quite as clever. She'll need help to be as self-sufficient as you.'

'She's like Mama,' Helena said witheringly. 'Mama couldn't do anything for herself either.'

At that moment a gong sounded downstairs. 'Quick!' Helena's face flushed. 'We've only got three minutes. Come on, Christy, hurry!'

'You haven't used the bathroom,' Cassandra said.

'We have. We use it at six forty-five and then after breakfast at eight-thirty, silly. Now, come on!'

'We're the only ones eating,' Cassandra pointed out. 'If we're a few minutes late no one will ever know.'

'Lucy will know, and she'll tell. It's her job to tell. Come on, Christy!'

Cassandra followed them as they dashed along the landing and down the stairs and she felt deeply troubled. Helena wasn't behaving like a four-year-old should, and Christina seemed in a world of her own, carried along on the tide of her sister's instructions. As for Lucy caring whether they were all late for breakfast or not she couldn't imagine how Helena had become so paranoid but decided that Abigail must have lied to them in order to try and get their obedience. Well, she'd do it by love.

It was two minutes past eight when they sat down at the dining table for breakfast. The heavy curtains that had been so tightly closed the night before were tied back and the windows were all wide open, letting the morning air into the room. When Cassandra glanced at the fireplace there was no trace of any fire, and she began to wonder if the nightmare scene of the heat and heavy food had all been part of a disturbed night. They could be she knew, but the marks on her breasts were all too real.

The day passed quickly. The girls were happy and at ease in the pool, and it was so warm that although Cassandra wasn't a strong swimmer she was able to spend two hours there without getting chilled. As Helena had predicted there was no one who could take them to Hampstead Heath, so instead they went on a nature walk round the wooded area of the grounds while Cassandra taught them the names of flowers and birds.

71

After tea they played in the nursery with a giant floor jigsaw, its pieces large enough for Christina to handle, and then in no time they were bathed and she read them a piece from *Alice in Wonderland*, taking up from where Abigail had left the bookmark.

'I like Alice's adventures,' Helena said sleepily as Cassandra kissed her goodnight. 'She lived in a confused sort of place too, didn't she?'

'She didn't live in it, she just thought she did. It was really all a dream,' Cassandra explained.

'Was it? How do you know?'

'Because the author tells us that at the end of the book.'

'We're not in a dream are we?'

Cassandra, remembering her own feelings when she woke that morning, could understand her confusion. 'No, you're not. This is all real.'

'I thought it was, only so many people come and go since Mama died. Will you stay long or will you cry a lot and disappear?'

Shocked, Cassandra stared at Helena, remembering that cry of pain on the day of her interview.

'Well?' Helena demanded.

Cassandra put out a hand and touched the anxious little girl gently on the forehead. 'No, I won't go,' she promised. 'I'll stay here for as long as you want me.'

'Good!'

Helena seemed satisfied, but Cassandra was very disturbed and began to wish that she had someone outside the house who knew where she was and would worry if she too 'disappeared'. But then she gave herself a mental shake. Probably Helena thought that Abigail had disappeared, when all that had happened was that she'd been dismissed. Children were so powerless that it made them fearful, that was all.

At seven forty-five, just as stipulated on the timetable, she went downstairs and out through the French windows into the garden, remembering that the baron had said they'd be eating outside that evening.

She had taken some time deciding what to wear, embarrassment over the night before making her even more self-conscious than usual. When Katya, dressed in a minute multi-coloured bikini with matching knee length see-through shirt over the top, saw Cassandra's wide-strapped, square-necked cotton sundress with its full, fifties-style skirt, she smiled to herself. Whatever had happened last night it obviously hadn't encouraged Cassandra to take any pride in displaying her body.

'Do have a drink, Cassie. May I call you Cassie?' she added as an afterthought.

'I prefer Cassandra. My ex-husband used to call me Cassie, I always thought it made me sound like a spaniel.'

'Perhaps you reminded him of one! Try this fruit punch; it's delicious.'

Cassandra took the drink from the other woman's beautifully manicured hand and wished she could stop biting her own nails.

Katya stretched sensuously on the sunbed and gave a sigh of pleasure. 'I adore this hot weather. I'm always trying to get Dieter to spend more time abroad but he won't. He seems to like this horrible country. He shouldn't be long now, he was changing a few moments ago. How were the girls?'

'I think they've enjoyed themselves today. I certainly did.'

'I don't think enjoyment is of primary importance, is it? Dieter certainly never gave Abigail the impression that their life was meant to be one long holiday. I think you're probably too soft-hearted, which won't do them any good. I shall tell Dieter that as well.'

'We did educational things,' Cassandra said evenly. 'Learning can be fun too, and they're very young.'

At that moment the baron came up the patio steps towards them. He was wearing perfectly tailored dark blue slacks and a short-sleeved white silk shirt with blue and gold stripes in it. His fair hair looked as though it had just been washed and was falling into his eyes so that he had to keep brushing it back with his fingers. He seemed to be in a very good mood because his eyes were bright and there was a half-smile on his lips as he sat down in a reclining chair next to Katya's sunbed.

'Peter's bringing out the food, my darling. Do you intend to lie flat on your back to eat as well as for everything else today?' he asked with amusement.

Katya laughed and sat up, wrapping her arms round her tanned knees. As the shirt fell open Cassandra couldn't help but see where the bikini bottom rode up between Katya's thighs, clinging so tightly to her that her sex was clearly outlined. Embarrassed she averted her eyes.

When Peter arrived with a large tray of salads and cold meats, his eyes went straight to Katya as well, and Cassandra saw that his hands were shaking when he put the tray down on the ornate metal table. The baron watched Peter closely, and his lips curved upwards for a moment when Katya, in apparent unawareness, swung herself round to the side of the sunbed and put her feet to the ground, knees spread well apart causing the material to cling even more tightly while concealing the actual outline of her sex. It also had the effect of bringing her breasts forward, and from where Peter was standing it was possible to see the top of Katya's nipples. He glanced at the baron, but there was nothing in his employer's eyes but merriment and so, disappointed, the lad withdrew from the garden.

Cassandra, who had been very aware of what was going on, felt the same tightness in her chest that she'd experienced the previous evening, only this time it wasn't caused by lack of air.

'So, what have you done today, Cassandra?' the baron asked her abruptly.

'They've had an enjoyable day!' Katya said with a harsh laugh. 'I don't think Cassandra understands . . .'

'I don't believe I spoke to you,' the baron said, keeping his dark eyes fixed on Cassandra. Katya flushed and fell silent.

74

'I took the girls swimming, Christina managed without a float, and this afternoon we had a nature walk in the woods.'

'Good. I understand that you wanted to go to Hampstead Heath.'

'Yes, but it seems I have to give advance notice of outings, so I've arranged that for tomorrow instead.'

'Fine. I understand also that you were all late for breakfast.'

Katya brought her knees together tightly with an air of excited anticipation. Cassandra looked at him in surprise. 'Only three minutes!'

'Three minutes or three hours, late is late. I remember making my thoughts on punctuality very clear to you from the beginning, is that not so?'

'Yes, but . . .'

'Then you know that you failed to keep to the timetable. The girls were late for breakfast, and there must be a punishment.'

'It wasn't their fault,' Cassandra protested. 'It's up to me to make sure they're on time.'

He smiled gently at her, and the dimple that had intrigued her at her interview appeared again. 'But of course. I was talking about a punishment for you.'

Katya put her hands together in a tiny clapping motion and sighed with satisfaction. Bemused, Cassandra turned towards the other woman. 'I don't understand.'

'Of course you don't!'

There was no help to be had from that direction, and so Cassandra turned back to where the baron sat in his chair, watching her calmly. 'Have some more punch,' he suggested, refilling her glass, and all at once she remembered how he'd poured wine over her the night before and the memory of the cool wine on her heated nipples made her blush and she sat there helpless to stop the flow of colour as it spread from her neck up over her face.

'Isn't she adorable,' Katya said, her voice honeyed. 'I've never seen anyone blush so sweetly before!'

Cassandra grabbed the glass of punch and drank from it thirstily. It had a strong fruit flavour and she had vague memories of fruit punch being served by her parents at Christmas so she felt quite safe, certain that it couldn't be too alcoholic.

She was just about to take her first mouthful of salad when the baron spoke again. 'I think we'll swim before we eat. Come!' He reached out a hand and pulled Katya to her feet. She smiled up at him. 'Cassandra, you will have to help Katya, she isn't a very proficient swimmer yet, although like Christina she can manage a few strokes without a float.'

Taken by surprise, and relieved that the matter of punishment seemed to have been dropped, Cassandra quickly stood up. 'I'll go and get my costume.'

The baron reached out and caught hold of her wrist. 'No, no costume. That's what makes adult swimming parties so much more fun than children's.'

She tried to pull away but his hand was strong and his fingers tightened painfully on her wrist. 'Come along, Cassandra, don't be difficult. There could have been many worse punishments you know,' he added quietly.

'I don't understand.'

'This is your . . . penalty is perhaps a better word, for being late for breakfast. We'll eat later, Peter,' he called over his shoulder and then pulled the protesting Cassandra down the paved path that led to the pool while Katya hurried on ahead, her rounded buttocks swaying provocatively in the tight bikini.

Inside the pool room the air was warm and humid. The dark ferns that grew in huge pots at each end of the room seemed more sinister in the evening, casting shadows over the marbled sides and out into the water. There were lights beneath the water now as well, shining up to illuminate any swimmers and as Katya stood at the side and stripped off her bikini top,

76

Cassandra twisted free of the baron and pushed at the heavy rubber doors, but to her surprise they didn't move.

'They're sealed I'm afraid, Cassandra. You can't leave until I release them,' he said slowly. 'Now don't be difficult. You enjoyed the pool this morning, didn't you?'

The punch must have been stronger than she'd realised because once again she felt heavy and lethargic, and it was difficult to keep her mind alert.

'That was different!' she protested. 'Look, I'm sorry about this morning, and you can deduct something from my pay if you like, but I don't want to swim without a costume and . . .'

'You don't *want* to swim without a costume! But of course you don't, that's the whole point of punishments or penalties. If you want to do something then it's a reward. Although, Cassandra, by the end of tonight I hope you will think of this as a reward,' he added quietly.

She shivered, then jumped as Katya dived into the water with a loud splash. 'She looks a very competent swimmer,' Cassandra pointed out.

'Perhaps she'll help you then. Now, take off that terrible dress. I can't imagine why you put it on in the first place.'

Below them, Katya trod water and looked up fascinated by the frozen expression in Cassandra's eyes. There was a look of desperate hopelessness in them that excited the baron's mistress, but also the beginnings of desire, and that was unexpected at this stage.

The baron put out a hand and slid one of the wide straps off Cassandra's shoulder, only to find that there was a bra underneath it. He laughed. 'Not a chastity belt too, I hope! Turn round.'

'No,' Cassandra said, wishing that her voice sounded firmer, and that her body wasn't already tightening with unwanted desire for the touch of his hands again.

He flicked two fingers lightly against her cheek. They

stung, and she took a step back in surprise. 'Do as you're told, Cassandra. Remember, you must learn to discipline yourself if you're to stay with my children.'

Cassandra remembered her promise to Helena, and wondered if the baron had somehow learnt about that too. Slowly she turned, and felt him unbutton the back of the sundress and then the clasp on her bra was released and he peeled dress and bra from her at the same time, letting them fall to the damp mosaic at her feet.

She was breathing quickly now, her nipples already distended and her small breasts beginning to swell just at the touch of his fingers on her naked back and shoulders. His hands slid lower and he hooked his thumbs into the sides of her panties, then crouched down and slid them down her legs while Katya stared up at her from the water, her green eyes inspecting every inch of Cassandra's body as it was revealed to her.

'Step out of them,' he murmured, and she obeyed like a sleepwalker, the drugged punch already taking effect and making her more malleable. But the baron had made sure that she wasn't too heavily drugged. He didn't want her initiation to be something she couldn't remember. By the time he actually possessed her the drug would have worn off, and in future it wouldn't be used at all. He had to conquer her himself, without subduing her artificially, or there was little point in the exercise.

Behind her, Cassandra could hear the baron taking off his own clothes, and when he was finally naked he took hold of her hand and led her to the steps that led down into the shallow end. There he moved in front of her and turned to face her, putting out both hands to lead her down into the water.

As he backed in ahead of her she noticed the heavy thickness of the dark brown hair on his chest and the way it gathered into a straight line from his waist down to where his erect penis jutted out of his lighter, springy pubic hair. She saw too the hard muscles of his upper arms and chest and the tight, firm thighs, also covered in hair. She wondered what it would feel like to have her naked body pressed against his from head to toe, and then pushed the thought away in shame. As the warm water edged up her legs she shivered, knowing that in a moment it would touch her exposed sex and aware that Katya and the baron were watching for her reaction when it did.

She wished that her pubic hair wasn't so thick and dark. Katya had a fair light blonde triangle that hid nothing while Cassandra's was like a forest, covering everything.

'Come! Come!' the baron urged, pulling her down inch by inch, and as the water touched her outer lips she drew in a quick breath and he laughed at her, moving his hands up to her waist as he swung her off the steps and into the water. Then he put her down on her feet, bending his knees slightly so that they were face to face. At her waist his fingers splayed out, caressing her hips and upper abdomen for a moment, until without warning he pulled her sharply towards him so that her legs went from under her and slid between his until she was lying on her back in the water, her breasts exposed.

'Come and see, Katya,' he called.

Cassandra struggled to find her feet. 'No!' she protested, but he only shook his head in reprimand. 'Be still, Cassandra. Feel the warmth of the water. Feel it cradling your body, touching you, enveloping you. Isn't it a good feeling? I have a theory about water. Because we spend our formative months in liquid I think we have a natural affinity with it; our bodies want to be in water but evolution has made it impossible for us to spend our lives this way. Never mind, we will make the best of it in the privacy of our pool, yes?'

His voice was always so quiet when he spoke to her that Cassandra couldn't help but relax with him, and her legs floated up to the surface behind him so that only his hands on her waist were supporting her, but those hands were firm now and even when he manoeuvred himself round to her head he didn't relax his grip at all.

Katya swam quickly and swiftly over to them, and then stood beside the prone Cassandra, looking down on the girl's immature but obviously aroused breasts with fascination. The baron nodded at her, and with delight she bent her head and sucked tenderly on one nipple, noticing at the same time that there were tiny bruises round it showing only too well that the baron had enjoyed them the previous evening.

Cassandra lay in a daze, floating in the warm water, her body relaxed and yet more alive than she could ever remember it, and although she knew it was Katya's mouth on her breast she didn't mind because it was the baron's hands holding her body, and the feelings of pleasure Katya's mouth were giving her were almost as intense as those he had aroused the night before.

'Isn't she glorious,' the baron said. 'Suck a little harder. She likes that, don't you, Cassandra?'

Cassandra swallowed hard. She didn't like it when he spoke to her, it made everything too real; she preferred to drift in a dream-like state, pretending she had no control over the situation.

'Tell Katya that you'd like her to suck harder,' he repeated more harshly, but Cassandra closed her eyes and kept silent.

'That's very naughty,' he reproved her, and at a signal from her lover Katya closed her tiny teeth sharply round the delicate nipple and as Cassandra jerked with shock the baron removed his hands and such was her surprise that she disappeared below the water for a few seconds before emerging coughing and spluttering with water in her mouth, eyes and ears.

The baron didn't give her any time to recover, but quickly turned her onto her back again and with his hands under her armpits swam into the deep end with her while Katya swam alongside, letting her hands trail along the young woman's legs as they went.

Once they were out of their depth, Cassandra was pushed and pulled to the side of the pool and her back was pressed against the bar at the side. 'Put your arms on the rest, and let your legs float in front of you,' the baron instructed, his voice hard.

This time Cassandra did as she was told.

'Good!' He rested one arm on the bar next to her and put his left hand beneath her buttocks, pushing the lower half of her body up until it was half out of the water. 'Keep her like that,' he told Katya and then swam round until he was treading water between Cassandra's legs.

'Keep your eyes open and watch me,' he told her as her eyelids began to droop. He was pleased when they snapped open immediately. There was a spotlight directly below them on the pool floor and it outlined the girl's long trembling limbs and dark pubic triangle of hair, exciting him far more than he'd expected.

Her mouth was tightly closed, but when he began to gently massage her calf muscles and ankles he saw it slacken slightly so that he could just see her front teeth between her pale lips. 'Push her up more,' he told Katya, and when Cassandra's flat stomach finally broke the surface of the water he bent his head and covered it with featherlight kisses while his hands strayed beneath the cheeks of her bottom which he massaged firmly, the movement pressing her abdomen more tightly against his mouth.

Cassandra felt her legs growing heavy and once again her heart was beating loudly in her ears. The skin of her stomach seemed to be stretched too tightly, and she had an ache at the base which the constant ripples of the water caused by the baron's movements only aggravated.

'Keep your legs up, Cassandra,' he told her quietly.

'They're heavy!' she whimpered.

He smiled. 'You must still keep them up. Would you

like Katya to lick your nipples again?' The thought was almost unbearably exciting, and Cassandra looked beseechingly at him. 'Then ask her,' he instructed.

Cassandra turned her heavy head to the waiting woman. 'Please, lick me again,' she begged. Katya smiled, and did as she was asked.

The baron stared into Cassandra's dark eyes, watching them clouding with desire and sensuality and his own excitement was almost painful. He couldn't remember when his testicles had last felt so tight and his cock was throbbing impatiently, but he was too well disciplined to allow himself to be hurried.

For nearly half an hour he and Katya continued to caress and stimulate Cassandra as she lay in the warm water, her head resting against the side of the pool. They concentrated on her breasts, neck, ears, feet, ankles and stomach but they remained well away from the throbbing area between her thighs, an area that they both knew with keen pleasure must be desperate for attention. Although she managed to obey the baron's constant commands to keep her legs up in the water, Cassandra couldn't help but move them round more and more as their cunning fingers and mouths tantalised her awakening body.

Eventually the baron's expert eyes, taking in her flushed face and despairing frustrated expression as well as the telltale movements of her body, told him that it was time to progress. He and Katya lifted Cassandra from the water and onto the mosaic.

She was so shocked by her removal from the blissful warmth of the pool and the abrupt cessation of caresses that she cried out, but the baron was quickly beside her, wrapping her in a towelling robe. He then picked her up and carried her through a small door set at the side of the pool and into a warm, well-lit room with a low king-sized bed in the middle of it, its mattress covered only by a huge white Persian rug. Cassandra was tipped from the towel onto the sensual bed covering. 'Now,' said the baron with satisfaction, 'we can really begin.'

He sat down at Cassandra's feet and carefully spread her legs apart, letting his fingers drift up her inner calves as he did so. She felt the pressure of the rug rub against her aching flesh, just below her secret opening, and pressed herself down against it, grateful for any kind of contact there.

'No!' The baron's voice broke through the pleasure and she quickly relaxed her hips again. 'That's better; it's always better to wait, my dear, although we can understand your impatience, can't we Katya?'

At his words, Cassandra twisted her head and stared across the room to where Katya was watching them both, her own hands moving automatically over her tightening breasts with their large nipples.

'I don't like her here,' she whispered. The baron smiled. 'Does she have to stay?' she continued.

Katya watched her lover, alert and tense in case he dismissed her again as he had done the previous night. If he tried she'd fight it this time. She was too aroused herself to leave now, and she knew that he would expect her to oppose any dismissal but after a brief moment of thought he nodded at Cassandra. 'Of course she stays. This is not for your pleasure, remember?'

Cassandra didn't remember; if this wasn't pleasure she didn't know what it was and she looked at him in bewilderment.

'Think,' he urged her, his hand creeping further up her leg and brushing against her pubic hair. 'Tell me why you're here.'

His teasing fingers were driving her out of her mind; all her senses seemed to be concentrated between her thighs, all she wanted was for something, anything to touch her there where her body was inflamed with unsatisfied excitement. She tried desperately to think of the answer he wanted, and as she was thinking, his hands spread her more widely and he lowered his mouth to kiss the inside of her trembling thighs while his fingers continued to brush her thick dark pubic hair like a soft breeze.

'It's a punishment!' she gasped, suddenly remember-ing. 'I was late for breakfast and this is my punishment.'

'Good! Good!'

Very carefully he parted her outer lips, and for the first time saw the delicate light pink of the inner lips that he would tantalise and inflame until she could bear it no longer. A small slick of moisture was escaping from the narrow opening but her clitoris was still buried and she was so tense that he realised it would take longer than he'd imagined in the pool.

'Relax, Cassandra,' he murmured soothingly. 'Just lie still now, and let me teach you what a man can do for a woman.'

Cassandra wanted to relax, wanted him to do some-thing, anything, about the tight aching flesh he was touching with his slim, cool fingers but she couldn't help remembering Paul and how his impatient hands had always left her sore and frustrated so that there had never been anything in their lovemaking for her except a disappointment and a sense of failure, and she didn't want to fail this fascinating man leaning over her body so possessively.

'It won't be any good.' Her voice was so low he had to strain to hear the words.

'Of course it will be good,' he assured her. 'Trust me now.' He glanced at his mistress who quickly reached up to a small chill cabinet on the wall behind her and brought him a tall aerosol can. He took it from her, squirted a small ball of foam into the palm of one hand, then dipped his fingers in it and began to spread it lightly up and down the channels of Cassandra's revealed flesh.

She jumped at the unexpected coolness and tried to sit up. 'No, lie still; it's only cream, just to help us on our way a little.' With great care he smoothed the mousse-like mixture all around her, working it over every piece of flesh and swirling it round her increas-ingly damp entrance before bending down and flicking it away with his tongue, making her jolt up off the bed in shocked surprise.

Although she knew the movement was involuntary, Katya fully expected the baron to reprimand Cassandra, but instead he gave a tiny secret smile and when he saw her struggle to regain her previous immobility he nodded in delight. 'Excellent, my dear. You're a quick learner.' Katya frowned, and waited for those boyish hips to start twitching, a movement she wouldn't be able to control and which would certainly bring her punishment.

Cassandra stared up at the white-tiled ceiling and wondered how what she and Paul did together in their marriage bed could in any way be related to what was happening to her now. Her breasts were so sensitive they even responded to the movement of air from the fan above her, her spine and the backs of her legs were tingling from the touch of the Persian rug and the tight heaviness of her belly reached down to where the baron's cunning hands were persecuting her tormented flesh until she felt like she was going to melt with the sensations he was eliciting.

As the baron licked the cream from her he let his tongue flick round the entrance to her inner passage and she was so over-stimulated there that she tried to draw away, but his hands gripped her thighs and kept her still. When all the cream had gone he brought Katya round to his side and got her to hold the girl carefully open while he concentrated on finding and arousing that tiny hub of pleasure that would finally push her over the edge into her long delayed climax.

Katya was excited too; he could hear it from the way she was breathing and see it in her heaving breasts and the moisture that trickled down between them. His eyes warned her not to speak as he tenderly inserted one long, narrow finger inside Cassandra and moved it almost imperceptibly from side to side, waiting for the dampness to surround it.

Very quickly now her juices began to flow more

easily, and at last as Katya held back her outer lips, Cassandra's clitoris was finally revealed to them, still covered by the protective hood but swelling with excitement at the baron's skilful ministrations.

He moved a hand to the base of her tense, trembling abdomen and rotated his hand, watching as the pulling motion of the surrounding skin indirectly stimulated the clitoris as well and now, at last, Cassandra's hips began to twitch and she gave a quickly stifled moan. 'Touch yourself, Cassandra,' he told her tenderly. 'Put your hands on your breasts, squeeze your nipples, rub them as you'd like me to rub them. Do it, do it now.'

His words excited her so much that she didn't hesitate. Her hands went gratefully to her burgeoning breasts and she grasped them eagerly, like a child reaching for its bottle. He was thrilled by her obedience, and by the obvious pleasure she got from her own, unskilled hands.

Carefully, cunningly he continued to move the centre of her pleasure by indirect manipulation and her hips twitched more and more until they were raising themselves up off the bed as her abdomen tightened so much that it was visible even to him. The taut skin added an edge to his own and Katya's arousal and he felt Katya's hands move towards his pulsating erection. Furiously he turned to face her, and when she saw his expression she quickly removed her hand.

'Keep still, Cassandra,' he remarked at last, but there was a gentleness in his voice that Katya had never heard before at this stage in any game and she looked sharply at him. The girl tried, they could both see that, but it was too much to ask of her untried body and her nerve endings couldn't be controlled.

The baron gave a soft laugh and released the pressure against her pubic bone, quickly sliding his hand lower until finally he was able to run his finger around the outside of the soaking clitoris, barely touching the flesh but driving her insane with the delicacy of the movement. She needed more, and groaned in her ecstatic torment.

'Silence!' Katya shivered with delight at the harsh note that had finally entered his voice. This was how she liked the game to be played. Without needing to be asked she handed him the final implement, a long, pointed feather, which he carefully twirled in the hot liquid at the mouth of her entrance; then he trailed up the jumping, teased and over-excited flesh, making Cassandra thrash her head even more frantically around, at one stage burying it in the rug in a frantic attempt to silence her moans of bliss.

At the clitoris itself he hesitated, and Katya expelled her pent-up breath as she watched and waited. His hand was steady, but inside the baron too was stimulated almost to breaking point, knowing that the girl on the bed was fighting so desperately to obey his rules, trying to discipline a body beside itself with new and all-consuming sensations, and that in a moment he would plunge her into an abyss of bliss she had never imagined even in her wildest dreams.

Katya pulled the outer lips wider apart, exposing the clitoris more. As he expected, at the peak of its excitement the clitoris tried to withdraw and he bent his head closer to the quivering body spread-eagled on the bed. 'Bear down, Cassandra, push down hard, show yourself to me.'

She could feel her flesh withdrawing tightly into itself, feel the bunching of the nerve ends, the gathering tightness that was like cords inside her body, but she struggled to do as he said and he saw with appreciation that her obedience had been total as the clitoris was forced out again, utterly exposed to the merciless feather.

Swiftly and deftly he let it brush against the centre of all Cassandra's sensations, encircling the swollen bud and then covering the top. Her body reacted as though she'd been electrocuted.

Katya, knowing what to expect, threw herself across

Cassandra's knees, but the previously unawakened girl's upper body thrashed from side to side, her hips lifted themselves high off the bed while her mouth opened and she screamed deliriously, almost losing consciousness with the intensity of her climax as all the over-stretched and diabolically tortured nerve endings were finally permitted their release.

The baron watched her body as it continued to twist and twitch, and he wouldn't allow her to close her thighs against the relentless arousal of the feather even when she wanted to. Instead he kept up the stimulation until her last cries died away and the pleasure began to turn to discomfort. Then, and only then, he ceased.

As Cassandra lay there, drenched with sweat, her eyes closed and her hair clinging limply to her head, Katya turned sweetly to him. 'She moved,' she said with satisfaction. 'What's the punishment for that?'

He looked at her with considerable interest. 'I rather thought you'd say that, my dear Katya. Unfortunately you seem to have forgotten that you were meant to keep silent, and the punishment for speaking is banishment. Leave us now.'

Katya flushed scarlet. Now was the best time. Now was when he would let her begin to rearouse the trembling girl, long before her screaming and defenceless nerve ends really wanted it and she always loved their second, reluctant and spine-shattering orgasm which often made them weep because it brought as much pain as pleasure.

'No, please!'

'Don't beg, Katya, it disgusts me. Leave at once!'

'Shall I send Peter in instead?'

He raised an eyebrow. 'Do you think I need help? How unflattering.'

'But Dieter . . .'

On the bed, Cassandra stirred and moaned and the baron quickly looked at her with his appraising eyes. There was no doubt she was exhausted, but she would welcome him, he was sure of it and he had no intention of letting Katya be there for that. He reached out and cupped a hand round Katya's soaking vulva, gripping her so tightly that her nipples hardened with the pain.

'Get out of here, now,' he said irritably. With a cry of frustration she went, leaving him alone with Cassandra.

Dieter von Ritter slid onto the bed and positioned himself above the exhausted girl, now staring up at him with tranquil eyes. 'Lift your hips,' he said urgently, and as she obeyed he slid a small pillow beneath them. 'That's good, now wind your legs round my waist, quickly!' She thought it an impossible order, her legs felt too heavy to move, but to her surprise she was able to do as he said, and as her small ankles crossed behind his back he lowered himself onto his elbows, hesitated for a second and then thrust the distended head of his cock into the tight warmth of her.

Cassandra's body had been winding down, but at this intrusion the nerve endings began to come alive again, and she felt sparks of pleasure radiating upwards towards her navel. He waited a moment, rotating his hips so that he was stimulating the area just inside the entrance, where her G-spot should be, but he was too close to climaxing to be able to wait and find the tiny swollen gland on the inner wall and although he could tell from her widening eyes that he had been close he couldn't wait any longer and suddenly gave himself up entirely to his own pleasure. He thrust harder and harder, feeling her body jolt with each movement and enjoying her gasps of protest at the force of his thrusting until at last the almost unbearable tightness in his testicles burst free and he felt the warmth of his ejaculation rush through him until it exploded into the bucking, gasping body of the girl beneath.

It was the most intense orgasm he'd had for several years, shaking his whole body from head to foot, and he was surprised to hear himself groan with relief as his sperm gushed into her, freeing him from the tension just as he'd freed her minutes earlier.

Beneath him, Cassandra pressed her hips hard

against his, caught in another swirling vortex of pleasure that made even her fingers and toes tingle and when he collapsed on top of her she had no idea that all he usually did after a climax was withdraw and walk away.

He was heavy, but she didn't mind, she simply lay there and enjoyed the feel of his male body covering hers.

When the baron finally came to his senses he was amazed to find himself lying on the girl and quickly rolled off her, turning his back and trying to gather his senses. 'Next time,' he said as his breathing became more even, 'you will learn to share your pleasure.'

Cassandra heard the words, but didn't fully understand the meaning. 'Share?' she asked.

'But of course; you've a natural sensuality, my darling girl, and it would be selfish in the extreme to deprive others of an opportunity to take pleasure from this. Also, we must develop your self-control. You did well today, but in future some of the mistakes you make will have to be punished.'

All Cassandra really took in were the words darling girl. She didn't much care about the rest of it, that endearment was enough for her. She'd heard him speak to Katya, and to her during their evening's sexual pleasure, but it was the first time he'd used that particular expression and she was quite certain that it was special, and equally certain that she could become special to him. She had to learn to become special, because he was like an addictive drug and she knew she would never have such pleasure from any other man. She also realised that Katya must feel the same, and there wouldn't be room for both of them in his life.

'Why do you make your children use the bathroom at set times?' she asked sleepily, and the change of subject took him by surprise.

'They must be able to control their bodies. If I take them to the theatre or the ballet I don't want them fidgeting around demanding that I take them to the cloakroom. Their bladder and their bowels must be mastered early. It's all a question of training.'

'Well I don't think I could do it all the time. Suppose you've had a lot extra to drink or something? What happens then?'

The baron remembered Abigail and smiled to himself. 'Then, my dear Cassandra, it all becomes an incredible challenge and can have very stimulating results, as you will discover in time.' He turned to face her and pressed his hand hard against her stomach. 'What you felt here, today, can be made twice as arousing, twice as explosive; you will find yourself driven hysterical with the sensations that can be aroused in such situations, Cassandra, and teaching you will be one of the greatest pleasures in my life so far.'

Cassandra shivered and sat up. She didn't know if she could take anything more intense than the experiences she'd had tonight. He saw the doubt in her eyes. 'We are still at the beginning, my dear. There is a long, delightful road ahead of us – if you want to stay with my daughters that is?'

Cassandra looked into his dark brown eyes and felt her blood begin to course through her veins again. 'Yes, I want to stay with your daughters,' she said calmly and as he climbed from the bed and left her he looked at her sitting in her vulnerable nakedness, her body still shining with the afterglow of sexual satisfaction, and he admired her for her self-control.

'I was right,' he murmured approvingly. 'You are a great asset to our household. Goodnight, Cassandra. If you're hungry a meal will be sent up to your room. We must dine outside some other time!'

Alone in the middle of the bed, Cassandra felt the baron's seed seeping out from between her thighs and knew that whatever happened to her here she would never willingly leave him. In just two days she had already learnt more about herself than she would ever have believed possible, although she sensed that the longer she stayed the more unacceptable she might find the facts she faced about herself. But she didn't mind. And she was anxious to learn everything he wanted to teach her. She had been disciplined by her parents all through her childhood. The baron was exactly the kind of man she needed to fulfil herself, and she wouldn't ever leave him willingly.

# Chapter Five

*I*t was not yet six o'clock, and the baron stood quietly in the corner of Cassandra's bedroom, watching her sleep. Her long dark hair was spread out on the pillow, her arms rested on top of the duvet, placed neatly on each side of her. His pulse quickened and he stepped towards the bed, glancing at the small red light glowing faintly above the curtain rail. He knew that Katya was watching and that she would have a good view. He only wished that, like her, he could be in the house all day, but in some ways having to wait until midnight before he could watch Cassandra play out the next stage of the game was a good thing. He knew that he was too greedy for the pleasures she was bringing him.

As he brushed his hand across her cheek, Cassandra stirred and muttered to herself. 'Cassandra, wake up,' he whispered urgently. Her eyes struggled to open. He knew only too well how exhausted she must be after all that had taken place in the swimming pool. He shook her shoulder. 'Quickly, wake up!'

Struggling through the heavy mists of sleep, Cassandra managed to open her eyes and pushed herself upright. 'What's the matter? Is it the children?'

'The children are fine. I have to be away until late

tonight, and there is something you must have before I go.'

She rubbed sleepily at her eyes and wondered how he could look so fresh and spruce after their hours of lovemaking. The thought brought back all the memories and realising that he was staring down the neck of her nightdress her breathing began to quicken.

'What is it?' she asked, unable to think of anything that Katya couldn't have given her at a more sensible hour.

With a quick movement that took her by surprise the baron pulled the duvet off her, and she gasped in surprise. 'Pull your nightdress up to your waist,' he instructed her. She still wasn't properly awake and anyway obedience to his orders was becoming automatic. Her hands moved to her sides and she pulled at the silken material, feeling it slip up her long legs and over her stomach, leaving her revealed to him from the waist down.

He switched on her bedside lamp so that he could see her better. 'Now turn round, lie sideways across the bed and spread your legs wide.' This he knew would give the hidden camera its best view.

Already Cassandra's stomach was twisting with excitement, but between her legs her flesh felt sore from his attentions the night before and she wasn't sure she could bear another prolonged session of such delicious torment.

She needn't have worried. As he knelt on the floor between her feet he was already glancing at his watch, worried in case he was going to be late for his meeting. He reached up between her thighs and she heard a strange clicking sound. Alarmed she pushed herself up and tried to see what he was doing.

The baron opened his hand and nestled in the palm she saw two small balls joined together by a piece of thin cord with a long loop extending from the second one. She tried to pull her thighs together but his hands pushed them roughly apart again. 'Don't be foolish;

these are love balls, designed to give you constant sexual stimulation while I'm away.'

'I don't want constant sexual stimulation!' she protested. 'I have to look after the children and . . .'

'I want you stimulated today. Now spread your legs for me and stop arguing. If you persist in being difficult I shall have to ask Katya to discipline you for me when I'm gone. That, I think, you would not enjoy at all.'

Cassandra knew only too well that Katya would relish the opportunity to discipline her and she shook her head, then lay down without any further resistance. In their bedroom, Katya bit her bottom lip, furious that the girl hadn't persisted in crossing Dieter. She was longing to be given her for a day.

Back in the bedroom the baron squeezed a little lubricating jelly onto his fingers and moved them carefully around the entrance to Cassandra's love tunnel. He knew the flesh would be sore and had no wish to aggravate it further until that night. The jelly was cool and soothing, and Cassandra felt herself opening to him. He waited for a few minutes, his fingers sliding on the tender young flesh for a little longer than was strictly necessary, then he pulled on the sides and opened the mouth of her vagina wider so that he could insert the balls.

As the cool metal slid inside her, Cassandra gasped with shock and instinctively tightened her muscles, pulling them deeper into her. 'These will strengthen the muscles of your pelvic floor, my dear,' said the baron softly, reluctantly releasing her. 'They will widen your love channel which will make that tiny, sensitive little bud of yours press against its hood as you move about. I am also leaving you some special underwear, tight little panties that will press against you to increase the pleasure. Now stand up, let me see how you manage with them.'

She swung her legs from the bed and stood in front of him, but as she stood the nightdress fell about her again, concealing everything, and with a sound of irritation he put his hand in the neckline and ripped it from her in one quick jerk.

'Now walk around the room, Cassandra.' She did as he said, and felt the love balls lying heavily against her opening. She was terrified that they would fall out. 'Bend over and touch your toes,' he said softly. She did, and instantly felt a tug on the flesh between her thighs. 'Good. Finally, sit on the floor, cross your legs and rock backwards and forwards.' Her mouth dry and her stomach taut she did as he said, and almost at once the pressure began to build up inside her. Her breath caught in her throat.

The baron watched as tiny beads of perspiration broke out on her upper lip. 'Enough! Stand up again. Good! As you can already see, they are effective, all the more so when you bend or rock. However, on their own they should not be enough to cause you to climax, and I do not expect to learn that you have found the ultimate satisfaction with them or I shall be displeased.'

Cassandra looked at him beseechingly. 'When I'm standing like this they feel as though they're going to fall out. Suppose they do?'

'If they fall out you will suffer a penalty, but there is no reason to fear. You must simply contract your pelvic floor muscles against them at such times. It will feel good and keep them safe. These are very light, in time we will progress to heavier ones. One word of caution, be careful they are not released when emptying your bladder. That calls for a little more skill, but you will manage I am sure.'

She stood in front of him, her skin prickling with a mixture of desire and fear, and then he handed her a minuscule pair of briefs that she pulled on. As he'd told her, they were very tight, and the combination of the pressure from the panties against a clitoris already extended by the love balls excited her so much that she felt a bead of moisture gathering at the mouth of her vagina.

The baron knew very well how excited her flesh

would be all day. He had anticipated her body's response, and the sight of her flushed face and heaving breasts gave him a sublime pleasure. Now he could imagine her all day, poised on the edge of an orgasm that wouldn't come, constantly aroused and unable to satisfy the craving of her newly educated flesh.

'Enjoy your day my dear,' he said tenderly, and then he was gone and poor Cassandra was left with her already pulsating flesh, aware that she couldn't possibly go back to sleep but must instead try and distract herself from the sensations inflaming her.

At seven o'clock she went in to look at the children. In her mind she had already planned a quiet day for them all. They had a play area in the grounds with a climbing frame, slide and swings where she thought they could spend the morning, and then in the afternoon she'd arranged for Peter to drive them to the shops so that the children could have a milk shake and choose a birthday present for their grandmother in Austria, who was seventy the next week.

Everything was turned upside down by the sight that greeted her when she went into their bedroom. Christina's bed had been stripped and she was sitting in her dressing gown playing with her dolls on the table by the window, while Helena was sitting up in bed, her eyes bright with excitement.

'Christy wet the bed!' she told Cassandra gleefully. 'Papa was really cross and Lucy has to stay in her room all day.'

'Most children of two wet the bed from time to time,' said Cassandra reassuringly, but neither Helena nor Christina seemed bothered by the incident. 'Lucy let her have an extra drink, so it's her fault,' Helena explained. 'Papa said she should have known better after all the training she's had. She cried and cried but he was very mad with her.'

'Did you ask her for an extra drink, Christina?' Cassandra queried.

Christina looked up from her dolls. 'Mama gave me

drinks,' she said with a breathtaking smile. 'Mama kissed lots.'

Helena's eyes were fixed on Cassandra's face. 'Would you have given her an extra drink?' she asked accusingly.

'If she was thirsty I probably would have done.'

'Then you'd have been shut in your room all day and you'd have missed the riding, wouldn't you?'

'Riding?' Cassandra sat on the edge of Helena's bed and felt the smooth love balls move inside her, spreading her outwards and pulling on the nerve endings that were directly connected to the clitoris. She tensed her inner muscles, and to her shock a ripple of pleasure ran up the middle of her belly, teetering on the edge of a tiny climax. She pulled her knees together and tried to will the feeling away.

'Yes, riding,' Helena continued. 'Papa says me and Christy can ride our ponies today and there's a horse for you as well. Peter will be there to make sure we don't fall off. He thought you'd like a ride.'

The almost diabolical cruelty of the baron shattered Cassandra. He must know only too well what the effect of horseriding would be on her body and yet he'd made it clear to her that there must be no climax to ease her arousal. It was unbearable, and for a moment she wanted to cry.

'Won't that be fun?' Helena persisted.

'Yes,' Cassandra said brightly. 'It will be lovely. I can hardly wait. Now, we'd better hurry. We don't want to be late for breakfast.'

'It doesn't really matter today. Lucy can't tell because she's got to stay in her room. I think I'll wear my denims. It's allowed on riding days.'

'I'm not sure you can put them on yet. If we're riding this afternoon then we'd better go and get your grandmother's present this morning, and your Papa wouldn't want you wearing jeans to the shops.'

'We can't shop this morning, we're going to Imogen's house. She's a friend. Her mama was friends with our

98

mama, and Papa told us we were going this morning. We can wear jeans there; it's all playing in the garden and stuff like that.'

Cassandra knew that Helena didn't realise that her day had been arranged with the specific purpose of leaving Cassandra in the worst possible situation, but just the same for a moment she found herself close to disliking the self-possessed four-year-old who had her father's air of utter confidence.

'Your Papa's certainly put himself out for you this time,' she said and Helena's sharp ears recognised the sarcasm.

'I'll tell him what you said,' she announced as she began to pull on the coveted jeans. 'I used to tell on Abigail.'

'I'm surprised he listened to you. Telling tales isn't a nice thing for young ladies to do.'

'Oh I used to get punished, but it was worth it because so did she and that made her cry and cry. We both hated Abigail a lot. Not as much as we hate Katya, but nearly.'

'You don't know what you're talking about,' Cassandra said, shocked by the vehemence of the little girl's tone. 'Hating is a very strong word.'

'I know, I know. Mama used to say it was wrong to hate anyone, but look what happened to her. I'm going to hate as much as I want. Papa does.'

'Well, it's different for men, and anyway he's an adult. Now hurry up. Christina, put the dolls away there's a good girl.'

Christina did as she was told. 'Mama killed,' she said sweetly as she sat on the stripped bed and stretched out a foot for Cassandra to put on a sock.

Startled, Cassandra's hand stopped in mid-air. 'She wasn't killed, Christy, she died.'

'Come on!' Helena said loudly. 'I want my breakfast.'

As soon as the meal was over a chauffeur who was new to Cassandra whisked the girls off to their friend's house, and within minutes Katya had come into the room. This morning she was wearing tight denim slacks and a bright yellow halter top that emphasised her full breasts.

'I'm afraid Lucy's being punished today,' she said sweetly to Cassandra. 'It's such a bore when one of the staff are absent, but Dieter was adamant. Do you think you could remake Christina's bed for once? I do realise it's not what you're here for but . . .'

'Of course,' Cassandra said quickly. 'It's no trouble.'

'Lovely, and then we'll take Lucy a drink or something. I hate to think of her lying in her room all alone without even a glass of water or anything.'

Cassandra was amazed that Katya should have a normal feeling about anyone but she liked Lucy and nodded in agreement. 'That would be kind. Besides, I'm sure the baron didn't mean she couldn't have anything to eat or drink.'

'Are you? How quaint!'

It was only when Cassandra began to make up Christina's bed with the clean sheets that she realised how much bending and stretching was involved, and every time she bent the love balls moved inside her, titillating her nerve endings and making her lower abdomen jump and go taut. The pressure from the clinging panties only emphasised her response to the pressure of the balls, but even at its most acute the arousal never reached a point where it could crescendo into the release that was needed, and by the time the bed was made Cassandra was nearly in tears with frustration.

Katya, who knew from Cassandra's trembling hands and over-bright eyes how well the balls were doing their insidious work, gave her a cheerful smile and handed her a tray with a pitcher of iced water and cut glass tumbler on it. 'There, let's take this to poor Lucy. Peter, do you have the key?'

Peter, wearing tight-fitting jeans and with his torso bare, emerged silently from behind Katya, a small Yale key in his hand. 'Yes, Madam.'

'Lovely! Off we go then. She'll be pleased to see us!'

Cassandra felt that Katya was rather overdoing Lucy's plight. After all, the rooms in the house were large and comfortable and at least this was giving Lucy a day off. But when they'd climbed to the top floor of the house, where it was much darker than the floor where Cassandra slept, and Peter turned the key in the door so that they could walk into the gloomy room, she began to feel more nervous, and Katya's obvious excitement was worrying.

With the shutters closed and locked against the outside world it was difficult to make out the bed, but gradually Cassandra's eyes adjusted to the gloom and she finally saw the outline of a narrow, high bed with iron bedposts set beneath the window and on it, lying spread-eagled face down, was Lucy.

'Guess what, Lucy,' Katya said, dropping her voice to a silky whisper. 'We've brought you something to drink.'

Cassandra walked across the uncarpeted floor, which contrasted starkly with the luxury of her own room, and placed the tray carefully on the small table beside the bed. A ray of light pierced the heavy wooden shutters, and with a cry Cassandra realised that not only was Lucy naked but also her wrists and ankles were fastened to the four posts by handcuffs, while across the middle of her back there was a thick leather strap, pressing cruelly into her flesh, and this strap was fastened at the sides by buckles at the edge of the bedframe.

The young maid's hips and buttocks were raised up despite the strap, and when Peter finally turned on the dim bulb that hung unshaded from the socket in the ceiling she realised that beneath Lucy's stomach was a small, hard velvet cushion. Lucy stared up at Cassandra with scared eyes. 'I don't want a drink,' she whispered. 'Please don't let her give me one.'

'Now then, Lucy, it's very kind of us to come and see you,' Katya said in honeyed tones and she moved quickly to the bed to stare down at the tightly imprisoned girl. 'Let's see how you're doing, shall we?' she continued, and Cassandra watched as the older woman slid one tiny hand beneath Lucy's stomach, inserting it between the cushion and the girl's shrinking flesh, pushing her fingers deeply into the soft area above Lucy's pubic bone.

Lucy gave a cry of pain, but she couldn't arch away because the strap allowed her no movement at all.

'How full you feel,' Katya murmured, her eyes glittering as she lifted Lucy's head by her hair. 'Now, drink this water. Do as I say or the baron will be angry. Cassandra, put the straw in the glass, poor Lucy can't lift her head very well. Now suck, Lucy, suck hard and empty the glass.'

At first the young maid refused, her eyes dull with misery she simply let the straw rest between her teeth and refused to drink, but then Peter crossed the room and when he came to the small basin where Lucy washed in the mornings he turned on one of the taps and the sound of the water trickling down the plug galvanised the girl into action. Frantically she sucked on the liquid, drinking so fast that she nearly choked, and Katya kept her hold on her hair so that her neck was taut and they could all watch the water making its way down towards her already full bladder. Only when the glass was empty did Peter turn off the tap and the torturing sounds stopped.

'She needs to pee,' Katya explained to a stunned Cassandra. 'Because she let Christina wet the bed she has to go all day without using the bathroom. The strap keeps her bladder pressed against the cushion so that she can't find any respite from the discomfort. Every time she drinks the pressure increases, as she knows very well. By the end of the day making her drink will be very difficult indeed, but we'll manage. Peter has done this before.'

'But that's wicked!' Cassandra said, feeling sick. 'It

wasn't her fault that Christina wet the bed. All small children do. Besides, how can you . . .'

'She must learn to discipline herself and then she can discipline others. You remember Dieter told you that! Anyway, after a time there's an indescribable pleasure to be gained from this. Lucy knows that, she remembers Abigail I'm sure, don't you darling?' And once again the tiny hand insinuated itself beneath the body that was straining against its bonds. For a moment Katya's fingers stayed still before pressing with knowing cruelty into the flinching belly of the tortured maid.

As Lucy cried out, begging for release from the wicked strap that was forcing her against the unrelenting velvet cushion, Cassandra realised that she was getting terrible sick excitement from seeing the frantic helpless girl, particularly from the sight of the tightly fastened legs trembling in their attempts to lift the body slightly so that the back of her thigh muscles shook with the strain.

Cassandra's own muscles tightened, and the love balls moved within her, rolling together with an audible click that made Katya stare sharply at her and then a knowing smile parted her delicate mouth. 'You see,' she said gleefully. 'I told you it was exciting, and it is. You can feel it too, can't you?'

Cassandra was so over-stimulated by the pressure of the heavy globes within her and the sight of the imprisoned girl that her stomach felt as though it had a tiny snake within it, coiling and slithering around inside her, shifting the heavy ache from one part of her abdomen to another.

'Touch her,' Katya urged her. 'Feel Lucy for yourself. Feel how tight she is, and she's aroused. The cushion's damp with her love juices. See for yourself.'

Cassandra hesitated, but then she saw the amusement in Katya's eyes and knew that the other woman didn't expect her to obey. Ignoring poor Lucy's pleas, she eased her hand beneath the girl, and when Lucy's flesh leapt and jerked Cassandra's middle finger accidentally brushed where the girl's swollen clitoris was pressing against the cushion and Lucy gave a cry of protest.

'No! No, please! I can't hold back if you do that. Please, please don't touch me there.'

Katya's eyes were dark with anger, but she could do nothing because of the ever-present camera. Her fury could only be taken out on the hapless Lucy, and so she poured another half tumbler of water and told Peter to force it down the maid before he left, then signalled for Cassandra to follow her out of the room. The last sounds Cassandra heard were the young maid's cries of anguish as Peter carried out his orders.

It was impossible for Cassandra to get the thought of Lucy out of her head. She'd never touched a woman intimately before, and the memory of her finger trailing across the wretched girl's protruding, damp clitoris and the frantic response of the debased tissue gave her the strangest feeling of both power and pleasure. Every time she remembered it, her own inner muscles tightened, and at once the love balls would press against the sides of her extended vagina until she could scarcely breathe from the rising pressure within her.

Before she and the girls went riding that afternoon, Cassandra finally had to visit the bathroom, unable to postpone relieving her own bladder any longer. As she sat down the balls rolled towards the front of her inner passage, and frissons of delight rippled upwards through her body. It was almost impossible to relax her muscles enough to pass water, and she sat there for what seemed an eternity, breathing slowly through her open mouth until some of the rigidity of pent-up passion dissolved and then at last she was able to relieve the dull ache that had been increasing all the morning. As she felt the hot urine spurting from her she thought of Lucy and shivered as she suddenly realised that one day the baron might punish her in a similar way.

When she followed the excited girls down to the

paddock she knew that Peter was watching her closely, and for one terrible moment it occurred to her that he knew about the fiendish love balls the baron had left inside her, but she quickly dismissed the idea. 'How's Lucy?' she asked quietly.

Peter glanced over his shoulder to see if Katya was anywhere near. 'She's almost hysterical. I've just been in with some coffee, and she knew that was an irritant. I had dreadful trouble getting her to swallow it.'

'How long will she stay like that?'

'Not much longer now. We'll probably set her free after the ride.'

Cassandra swallowed hard, her mouth dry. She was ashamed to realise that she wanted to be there to see Lucy when she was released, although she didn't fully understand why.

Helena and Christina were obviously at home on their ponies, and although Peter walked at the head of Christina's pony, holding it firmly by the leading rein, she actually seemed more secure in the saddle than Helena, who occasionally slipped sideways before grabbing at the pommel on the sadle for safety.

Cassandra's horse was a light chestnut, with gentle eyes and a placid disposition but as soon as she was in the saddle and the horse began to move the love balls pressed so hard against her that she nearly flew off the leather and it was only the knowledge that Peter was watching her that kept her in her seat. Her tightening nub of pleasure was forced down against the leather, bumping against it and then lifting as the horse began to trot slowly round the paddock.

Moisture seeped out of Cassandra's secret opening, as she made despairing efforts not to climax while the relentless, arousing movements of the horse and the love balls forced the tight panties past her outer lips until they were sticking to the damp flesh that ran from her front opening to the other hole between her tight buttocks. There the material stuck fast in the moisture her own excited body had produced and every centimetre of the flesh between her thighs felt as though it was distending as the pressure grew and grew.

She was unaware of how her face was changing during this cruelly tantalising exercise the baron had devised, but Peter saw the flush rising in her normally pale cheeks, saw the pulse at the base of her throat beating wildly and watched as her legs gripped the horse's sides with trembling determination. Her breasts, encased today in a tight fitting camisole top, rose and fell with the horse's movements and as her excitement grew, her nipples distended until they were plainly visible to the lad through the sweat-damp, now semi-transparent material.

All at once Cassandra felt a change in her body. The many tongues of excited pleasure began to melt into one and the snake in her tense stomach began to uncurl. She realised with horror that if she didn't do something she would come, and there was no doubt in her mind that the baron with his uncanny skills would know and punish her accordingly. With the picture of Lucy so clear in her mind she couldn't let it happen and she pulled sharply on the reins, bringing the horse to an abrupt halt.

With the cessation of movement the snake settled down again. Her wickedly stimulated flesh had a brief respite and the jangled nerve ends began to settle. Ignoring the startled expression on Peter's face and the shouts of the girls, Cassandra stayed quite still until she was sure that it was safe to move and then slowly dismounted. As she crossed the paddock she met Katya coming towards her.

'How clever you are,' Katya said, who had been leaning over the narrow fence watching the girl struggle with herself. 'And I was so looking forward to being allowed to punish you myself. Ah well, it will come in time. Now, I think the children should have their tea and we will go and release Lucy from her confinement. I think you'll enjoy that, Cassandra.'

Cassandra's body was shaking with frustration, but

106

she felt a keen sense of pride in foiling the other woman's expectations. As soon as the children had been passed to the nursery nurse for tea she went up the next flight of stairs and met Katya and Peter on the top landing.

The three of them went into the still dark room. Lucy had been moaning softly into her pillow, but fell silent at the sound of the door opening. 'Turn on the tap,' said Katya, and Peter obediently did so. Lucy buried her face deeper in the bed and as Cassandra moved closer she saw how the girl had tried so hard to pull up off the cushion that the leather strap across her back was buried deep in her soft flesh.

'It's nearly over, Lucy,' she told her, but Lucy only lifted her head for a moment and stared silently at Cassandra while tears rolled down her face.

Katya saw them and laughed. 'Tears, how divine! Poor, poor Lucy. But have you been good? That's the question.'

'Yes, yes!' Lucy said quickly.

'I must see for myself,' said Katya, and she knelt on the bed between the girl's parted legs and delicately brushed the fingers of one hand round the plump cheeks of the girl's bottom before slipping the hand palm uppermost under her and up onto the velvet cushion, her fingers probing into Lucy's bursting abdomen as she went.

Lucy cried out, pulling away so hard that the bed posts to which her ankles were fastened creaked in protest, but the manacles held firm and there was no escape.

'Yes, quite dry,' Katya said with apparent satisfaction. 'Now then Lucy, think about how lucky you are. In a moment you'll be able to relieve yourself, to let your bladder relax and feel that hot, burning liquid flow freely. What rapture, Lucy. How wonderful it will feel, and we'll be here to watch you spend yourself. We'll see the relief on your face, and watch your swollen little tummy relax as it releases its burden. I expect it will sound like the water you can hear now in the basin, don't you?'

All the time she was talking, her fingers were moving expertly across the girl's lower stomach and digging into her pubic mound, pulling down so that the over-loaded bladder pressed against her hand. 'How much longer can you wait, Lucy? Five minutes? Fifteen minutes?'

'I can't wait! I can't wait!' the girl cried, her tears flowing faster. 'Turn the tap off, please. Oh God, help me!'

'Then just two minutes, Lucy, and in those two minutes I'll pleasure you, to make up for all this, yes?'

'No!' Lucy screamed, but Katya simply smiled up at Cassandra whose own face was hot and whose flesh was jumping almost as much as the wretched servant girl's. She watched as Katya's spare hand opened the cheeks of Lucy's bottom, and then one tiny finger was inserted into the puckered opening and almost imper-ceptibly moved from side to side while the hand beneath the trapped girl shifted lower to touch the clitoris which had been pressed against the velvet cushion for most of the day and throbbed beneath Katya's touch.

Katya kept both hands still for a moment, just long enough for Lucy to raise her head in expectation of release, and then with calculated cunning she moved all her fingers and the clitoris was stroked at the same time as Lucy's tight little anus was stimulated by the knowing finger and just as Katya had known she would be, Lucy was lost.

Cassandra watched with a dry mouth as the young girl's body was racked by an organsm almost too intense to be pleasurable. The tight bonding holding her to the bed prevented her from enjoying the climax to its full while at the same time increasing the pressure on her bladder so that, like Abigail before her, after struggling all day, she lost control of her tortured bladder and her urine flooded from her in a hot stream, running down over the cushion that had wreaked such havoc on her body all day, then soaking the mattress as she lay sobbing with a mixture of intense orgasmic pleasure and the bitter knowledge of defeat.

'Turn her over,' Katya said harshly. Cassandra took a step back. She couldn't believe what she'd just seen, and knew that she ought to run away, get out of this house where such things seemed everyday occurrences, but she couldn't move because her breasts were full, desire was raging in her and she knew she was no different from the other two in the room.

Peter quickly undid the manacles and leather strap and turned the debased and humiliated girl onto her back where she lay silently, her legs still spread apart and her body slack after the shattering explosions that had just torn her apart.

'You failed, and for that you get flogged,' Katya said with relish. Lucy moaned but didn't attempt to move from the bed. Peter handed the baron's mistress a small piece of cord, split at the end into a miniature cat-o-nine-tails but without the lead at the ends. Katya raised her arm and brought the lash down over the young girl's unprotected and distended breasts. Cassandra's own breath drew in sharply at the sight of it falling on the lush body, and then she swallowed hard at the vivid red lines it left across the previously white globe.

Katya continued to punish Lucy, working her way across each breast, down her stomach and then across the inner thighs before she finally stopped, threw the lash away and crouched over the hapless girl. 'Now for the sweetness, my darling little Lucy,' she whispered and Cassandra was amazed to see a smile cross Lucy's lips as Katya bent her head and let her golden curls brush against Lucy's sex, moving her head from side to side until Lucy began to groan and press upwards whereupon Katya pressed the plump thighs apart and inserted her tongue into Lucy's pussy, darting it in and out in a quick, steady rhythm that within seconds had the servant girl's body convulsing in another orgasm and this time her body was free to arch and twist and she screamed with pleasure, all previous torture forgotten.

'There,' Katya said with satisfaction, cupping the girl's sex with her tiny hand and squeezing gently. 'Wasn't that good?'

'Yes, yes!' Lucy said eagerly.

'Would you like one more? From Peter this time?' Lucy nodded shyly, but as Peter began to strip off his denims and move towards the bed, Cassandra turned and fled. She'd seen enough. Her body was crawling with unsatisfied desire and the dark perverse pleasure that had invaded her earlier seemed only to have added an extra dimension to her need. It was a need for relief, but also a need for the baron. It had to be him. She couldn't imagine herself lying like Lucy, defiled, debased and then being satisfied by Katya and Peter. Without the baron there was no point in satisfaction. But with him there she knew now that anything was possible. Or she thought she knew that, because the truth was that she still had no idea what anything meant to a man like Dieter von Ritter.

# Chapter Six

*T*he baron watched the screen closely, his eyes fixed on Cassandra as she suddenly turned and ran from the room where Peter was about to pleasure Lucy. 'You see,' Katya said triumphantly. 'She ran away.'

'Yes.'

'I admit I thought she was going to stay, but in the end she lost her nerve.'

'She stayed to watch you,' the baron pointed out. 'I wonder why it was Peter who drove her out?'

Katya shrugged. Motives didn't bother her, only results, and at last Cassandra had made a mistake.

'Has she touched herself today?' he asked languidly. 'Given herself relief?' Although the question was casual his eyes were sharp with interest.

'No,' Katya conceded reluctantly. 'We've watched her all the time, or had the cameras on her. She's been close once or twice, but she never came.'

'How wonderfully restrained, and what a fever pitch she must be in now,' he said with satisfaction. 'Where is she?'

'Waiting in her room. I told her that you would want to see her when you got home.'

He looked at his watch. 'It's now midnight. The love balls have been in for eighteen hours, and she's been

111

horseriding and watched Lucy's agony and ecstasy. She must be more than ready for us. Come, it's time. Bring Peter too, but wait outside until I call you.'

'I thought she was never going to make a mistake,' Katya admitted, running a hand over the bulge in his slacks that she'd seen appearing as he'd watched the monitor.

'Mistake? Who says she's made one now? Perhaps I didn't want her to stay and watch Peter.'

'It was a step in her education,' Katya protested.

'No, it was a step in mine,' the baron corrected her. 'Remember, my darling, the rules are not the same this time. I'm looking for a different kind of winner. There, now you've had a hint, which is most unfair on Cassandra but after all we've known each other a long time.' He smiled smoothly at her, but she ignored that. Dieter's smiles meant no more than his kind words or his occasional moments of tenderness. The real Dieter was buried too deep for her or any other woman to find, but that didn't mean she was going to give him up. She just wondered what he meant by a different kind of winner.

Cassandra was lying flat on her back on the bed wearing only a robe when the baron entered her room. He didn't knock, but she hadn't expected him to. Quickly she sat up, her still innocent eyes looking questioningly at him.

'So, how did you enjoy the little toy?' he asked, sitting down next to her and opening her robe so that he could run his hands down her quivering body.

'I . . . It was almost too much to bear,' she confessed. 'I kept wanting . . .'

'Release?'

'No! I mean, yes, but not just any release. I wanted . . .'

'Tell me,' he urged, and surprisingly he bent and kissed her gently on the lips.

'I wanted to feel your hands there,' she admitted, blushing scarlet.

'My hands? Well, that's good to hear! However, I think that tonight we must let someone else's hands enjoy you. I told you that you would become one of the family, and families mustn't be selfish. However much I treasure you, I have to let them share from time to time.'

He could see from the pain in her eyes how much he'd hurt her, but she didn't protest, simply continued to stare at him as though seeking some kind of answer in his eyes.

'First, I will remove the love balls,' he said reassuringly. 'I think they've tormented you long enough. Spread your thighs darling girl.' As soon as he used those words again, Cassandra relaxed. She lay back and spread her legs so that he could hook a finger through the dangling loop of thread and then he pulled. He pulled slowly and steadily so that she felt them moving through her hot, moist channel and as they moved her arousal began afresh and she had a job not to pull away and get them removed quickly so that she didn't disgrace herself by climaxing at this last moment.

The baron watched her carefully, saw the tension in her and the way she parted her lips to breathe more steadily and he was pleased. As the second ball popped out, covered in the milky fluid she'd been secreting for so many hours, he lifted it to his mouth and sucked greedily on it, the taste of her exciting him more than he'd have believed possible after so many women.

'There, that's over for today!' He gave her swollen mons a tender squeeze and then forced himself to take his hands away. Tonight the other two would pleasure her while he gave instructions and watched.

He coughed, and immediately Katya and Peter entered. Cassandra sat up and watched them approach her. Peter was already naked and semi-aroused. The baron guessed that Katya had been fondling him outside the door and mentally deducted a point from her score. Peter, aware that he shouldn't be aroused at this stage, wouldn't meet his master's eye.

'Lie on your stomach, Cassandra,' the baron said quietly. She tensed, remembering Lucy and also feeling more vulnerable when she couldn't see what was happening. 'Quickly!' His voice had lost its caressing tone, and she obeyed. 'Good. Now, lift your hips a moment while I slide this pillow beneath you. Excellent.'

The three of them looked down at Cassandra's tight, upthrust buttocks and Peter's erection was so urgent that the baron looked at him in amusement. 'Where's your self-control, tonight?' he asked mildly, and at a sign from him, Katya reached out and pinched Peter's testicles hard. The pain made him gasp and his erection diminished with great speed. The baron laughed. 'That's better. Now, here are some Thai beads. I want you to put them in her, Peter.'

Cassandra turned her head to look over her shoulder at the baron. 'What are Thai beads?' she asked nervously. He held up a rod covered with plastic beads. 'Look, they're tiny compared with the love balls.' She relaxed again and Katya nearly laughed at the girl's ignorance.

'I think we should tie her legs,' Katya said. 'She may resist.'

The baron ran a hand idly up the back of Cassandra's left leg. 'I think not, she'll need to move her legs about in order to accommodate the beads. You won't give us any trouble, will you, Cassandra?'

Cassandra's over-heated body was so busy taking pleasure from the feel of the silk sheets against it that she had missed what they'd been saying. 'No, of course not,' she replied calmly, hoping that whatever they were going to do it would finally release her from the day's frustration.

Peter took the lid off a jar of vaseline and dipped his index finger in it. The baron studied Cassandra for a moment. 'I think perhaps we will have you on your side with the pillow beneath your hips. Turn please.' She obeyed and then felt him pushing at her legs. 'Draw your knees up to your chest. Further than that, pull them up with your arms until you are almost in a ball. Good! Excellent!'

As she drew up her legs the tight coil of excitement within her began to unfold again, triggered by the pressure on her abdomen. 'Peter is going to put the beads inside you now,' the baron said calmly. 'I will stand in front of you and you must keep your eyes on me all the time. Do you understand?'

'Yes,' she whispered, but she didn't at all, not until Peter's finger, well lubricated by the vaseline, began to tickle the entrance to her rectum did she fully understand and immediately she gasped in protest.

'Be still,' the baron murmured. 'Trust me, this will be wonderful again. It's what you need after the love beads. A different, more total climax to ease the suffering you have endured for me. Still now.'

She tried to obey him, but Peter's finger felt thick and the skin round her rear entrance contracted against the invasion. No one had ever touched her there, and she was terrified at the thought of the pain that must come.

'Cassandra, this is not good enough!' The baron was plainly irritated. 'Let him proceed or we will be here all night.'

'Please, I don't want it!' she said.

His eyes clouded with disgust and he looked at her as though he hardly knew her. 'How can you say that when you haven't ever tried it? Now don't be such a baby. I am trying to reward you and all you can do is whimper. If you don't keep still, Katya will truss you like a chicken and I shall leave.'

'No!'

He nodded in satisfaction. He understood her need for him, and it was useful. Slowly Peter's finger moved in circles around the entrance, pushed in a fraction, rested until her churning bowels adjusted to the sensation and then pushed in a fraction more. She had a terrible cramping sensation in her lower abdomen and was terrified of emptying her bowels in front of them all so great was the feeling of pressure that the finger caused.

Gradually though her body adjusted, and then the finger was withdrawn and the whole process repeated with two fingers, and again the cramping spasm passed although this time it brought tears to her eyes, but they were tears she kept silent.

'Keep looking at me,' the baron reminded her, and when he saw the tears excitement sparked in the depths of his gaze. Excitement and a kind of pride that helped her endure.

'Is she ready for the beads?' he asked at last. Peter nodded, took the flexible rod in his hand and slowly began to insert it, twisting it every time a bead reached the tightly puckered mouth.

'I can't!' Cassandra gasped. 'I need the bathroom. I can't take it.'

The baron put out a hand and to Katya's fury stroked the heaving breasts. 'Of course you can, and in a moment the pleasure will start. Relax your muscles, let it in more easily.'

She couldn't relax, but once the rod was in place and Peter started to carefully rotate it her body began to be aroused as tingles of excitement spread through her. The baron knew how sensitive the virginal walls of her rectum would be and when Peter tugged softly on the rod so that he could push and pull it back and forth Cassandra's eyes widened with surprise as the darts of pleasure became so intense all pain was banished.

Now that the rod was in, the baron got Cassandra to turn and crouch on all fours with Peter behind her manipulating the rod. Then she was made to lower her upper body with her weight on her forearms and then Katya slid beneath her, lying flat on her back and reaching up to where Cassandra's sex lips were tightly closed beneath the lush of dark hair.

The baron moved to the head of the bed so that he could still watch Cassandra's face, and she kept her eyes determinedly on him, while Katya's deft hands

116

parted her outer lips. The flesh beneath was very damp, the love beads had done their work well and her state of arousal was still intense despite their removal. Katya swirled her little finger round the mouth of the love channel, then drew the moisture up and over the frantically protruding clitoris that had been trapped all day against the tight panties the baron had made her wear.

As soon as Katya's finger touched the clitoris, Cassandra jerked with pleasure and Peter quickly turned the rod, twisting the beads so that the walls of the rectum were also stimulated. Cassandra's mouth opened as she gasped, feeling the snake uncoiling rapidly inside her while her drum-tight abdomen expanded like an over-ripe fruit about to explode.

'Not yet,' the baron said quietly.

Cassandra gasped. She didn't think she could hold herself back. The sensations were too many and too overwhelming. Her self-control had been stretched beyond endurance all day, and now he was ordering her to wait even longer. Katya, looking up at the rigid abdomen and watching the play of the skin rippling over the frantically struggling muscles, knew that they had very little time left. Quickly she moved her other hand and inserted the tiny vibrator into Cassandra's soaking pussy.

It was a totally unexpected movement, and with the vibrator whirring inside her front opening and Peter playing so skilfully with the Thai beads inside her violated rectum, Cassandra was nearly driven out of her mind. She kept her eyes on the baron, but the snake was slithering around inside her now, totally out of control as wave after wave of pleasure began to build. 'Wait one second,' he ordered her, and she tried to dull the sensations, but it was no good.

Finally he took pity on her. Reaching down between her arms he closed his hands round her throbbing and neglected breasts and tightened his fingers round them, catching the nipples between the gaps in his fingers until the nerve endings shrieked and the blissful, agonising stabs of pleasure-pain shot through her to join the other incredible sensations. At last, with a cry of submission, Cassandra gave in to the demands of her body as a giant convulsion caused her to arch her torso into the air and thrash wildly around, only just giving Peter time to hurriedly pull the Thai beads out of her before the walls of her back passage clenched themselves together as the orgasm racked her body.

She would not have believed it possible to feel anything so intensely. The waves that had been gathering together seemed to crash down on her and she heard herself screaming in a frenzy of excitement as her body was finally freed after nearly twenty hours of unsatisfied stimulation.

The baron, having released her breasts, watched as she thrashed around the bed in her throes of passion and his own erection was so hard it was painful. Quickly he undid his flies and it sprang free, its head purple and glistening. Roughly he reached for Katya, pushing her down on the bed next to where Cassandra was finally still, and turned the familiar body to face him pulling her hard onto his cock, moving her body back and forth so that her breasts kept being squashed against his chest and with every movement Katya's flesh was pulled tight and her pubic bone pressed against the baron's thigh each time he brought her towards him so that when he exploded into her she too toppled over the edge and threw her head back with a cry of satisfaction.

As soon as he'd finished emptying himself into her, the baron pushed Katya making her tumble to the floor. His sperm was still dripping from the end of his cock and he turned to the supine figure next to him and carefully brushed the last few drops off across her now detumescent nipples.

Cassandra started with surprise and opened her eyes to see what he was doing. He stared at her, almost as though she was providing him with a puzzle he couldn't answer, and she smiled back at him, content at last.

He bit thoughtfully on his lower lip, then turned away from the girl and got off the bed. Katya, excited by his roughness and the fall, was waiting expectantly. He glanced at Peter, whose balls were drawn up in what was obviously an agony of tightness, and nodded at him. 'Take her how you like. From behind if possible. I shall watch it later.'

As Peter fell gratefully to the carpet and began to separate Katya's rounded buttocks, Cassandra fell asleep and the baron, strangely disquieted, went to his own, private bedroom where no woman ever joined him.

When Cassandra and the girls went down to breakfast the next morning, the baron was already there. Normally, unless he was needed at a business meeting, he never rose until mid-morning, but this particular morning he was dressed casually and Cassandra wondered what had brought him down so early. He greeted the girls with kisses and smiles, but although he spoke politely to Cassandra there was a coolness in his eyes that disappointed her and she became aware that he was watching her very closely all the time, as though searching for something that she was keeping hidden.

'The children are going to Austria tomorrow,' he announced abruptly. Both girls began to shout with excitement. 'My relatives like to see them from time to time. They will be away three weeks.'

Cassandra frowned. 'Three weeks? They'll need a lot of clothes. It doesn't give me much time to get ready.'

'They have clothes there, and you will remain here so no work is involved.'

Helena looked momentarily dispirited. 'Why can't Cassandra come too?' she asked.

'Because I don't pay her to go off having holidays the moment she arrives! Your aunt would be most upset if

119

I sent a nanny with you, Helena. She loves giving you all her attention.'

'But we like Cassandra. What will she do without us?'

The baron's enigmatic eyes met Cassandra's. 'What indeed? I'm sure Katya and I can find things to keep her busy. Would you agree, Cassandra?'

A tingle of excitement stirred in Cassandra and her mouth went dry. 'It's a large house, there's always plenty to do,' she agreed.

'But you're not a servant!' Helena protested. 'You can't wash and . . .' Her voice trailed off as she stared at the bowl of porridge Lucy was placing in front of her. 'I don't like porridge!' she wailed.

'Me does,' Christina said, picking up her spoon and beginning to eat. The baron watched as his elder daughter continued to stare at the bowl in disgust.

'If you don't eat it you can't go to Austria,' he said pleasantly.

Helena's eyes filled with tears and she looked appealingly at Cassandra. 'It makes me sick,' she whispered.

Cassandra glanced at the baron who was now watching her rather than his daughter. 'If she doesn't like it, it doesn't seem fair to give it to her,' she pointed out.

'Fair? Whoever said life was fair?' He smiled suddenly. 'My dear Cassandra, you're in charge of them, surely you can get a small bowl of porridge down a four-year-old. Whatever happened to the old fashioned discipline we discussed at your interview?'

'Just try a little, Helena,' Cassandra said coaxingly, but she knew already that the child wasn't going to eat it, and knew that the baron was aware of this as well. He had known right from the moment they came into the dining room what was going to happen, and it didn't really concern his daughter at all, but as yet Cassandra couldn't work out how it was going to affect her.

For half an hour she tried to persuade the increasingly truculent Helena to eat the porridge, but by this time it was so cold and unappetising that even Christina was staring at it in disgust. Finally Cassandra gave up. 'Leave it then,' she said shortly.

'But I want to go to Austria!' Helena wailed. 'I want to see Aunt Marguerite and my cousins. I want to! I want to!'

The baron's face went white. 'Be quiet, Helena. Your manners are disgraceful. Cassandra has obviously been spoiling you. As for Austria, we'll make a bargain. As long as Cassandra eats everything she's given today then you'll still have your holiday. Now go to your room and tidy your toys. I don't want to see you again until bedtime. Badly behaved children make me feel ill.'

Both the children slipped from their chairs and sidled past their father. Helena stopped by Cassandra's side. 'You will eat everything, won't you?' she asked urgently.

Cassandra could feel the baron's eyes on her. 'Yes, of course,' she promised, although she knew that if she were given a plate of tripe and onions then Helena would just have to miss Austria, but somehow she didn't think that was quite what the baron would have in mind.

Once the children had gone he stared at her. 'You intrigue me, Cassandra. You have built such a protective shell about yourself that I wonder if it's possible to reach your centre, and yet at the same time you're as vulnerable as the girls. It's an intoxicating mixture. Last night I couldn't sleep,' he added, and it was obvious that for him this was a new experience.

'I'm sorry,' she said automatically.

He tilted his head to one side and examined her searchingly. 'Yes, and so you should be because it was your fault.'

'My fault?'

'Last night, for a moment . . .' He stopped. 'It's of no importance. You enjoyed last night, didn't you?'

She remembered the Thai beads, and the moment when Katya had inserted the vibrator inside her so that

121

her body had gone into a spasm of ecstasy and her cheeks went pink. 'Yes,' she murmured.

Now he laughed, and the tension that had previously been apparent in him vanished. 'Yes indeed! Lunch is formal today. One o'clock in the dining room. The girls will eat in the nursery.'

Although the morning was busy as the girls tidied their toys and argued about what ones to take on the plane with them, Cassandra found herself continually glancing at her watch. She knew that the lunch was going to be special, and that it was here that she would be expected to eat whatever the baron and Katya chose to put in front of her so that Helena could still go to Austria. Fear and excitement kept her in a constant state of dread mixed with anticipation.

At exactly one o'clock she went into the dining room. Katya was already there, drinking a glass of sherry and smiling far too widely for Cassandra's comfort. 'Isn't this fun!' she exclaimed, filling another glass and handing it to Cassandra. 'I hope you're hungry!'

Cassandra drained the sherry in one go and held out the glass for a refill. Whatever lay ahead she had the feeling that alcohol would help.

'One is sufficient,' the baron said, coming in quickly from a door at the back of the room and taking the glass from her. 'We want you to be fully in control of yourself for Peter's sake!'

Cassandra looked from the baron's smiling face to Katya's bright eyes and she swallowed hard. 'Peter's sake?'

'Of course. He's your main course, my dear. How experienced are you in matters of oral sex?'

Cassandra's eyes widened and she felt slightly sick. Once or twice Paul had tried to get her to experiment, but she'd always ended up retching violently and even at the memory her stomach began to lurch. The baron saw her expression and sighed. 'Dear me, I do hope poor Helena isn't going to be disappointed after all. Ah, Peter, come in please and lock the door behind you.'

Cassandra watched Peter cross the room toward them. He was a tall, fair-haired lad and well built for nineteen. The thought of taking him in her mouth made Cassandra back away as he advanced.

The baron pointed to a winged chair. 'Sit there, Peter.' The lad obeyed. Now the baron turned back to Cassandra. 'Take off your dress, my dear, and the bra too I think. It's more exciting to see your breasts free.'

'I don't want to do this,' Cassandra said nervously.

'Of course you don't. If you did the whole exercise would be pointless. You're the substitute for Helena. Since you couldn't make her eat her porridge you have to eat Peter. In olden days it was called finding a whipping boy!' Katya laughed and smiled at her lover.

'Kneel down between his legs,' the baron said. Cassandra thought of Helena and obeyed. Her legs were trembling as she settled herself on the carpet, and she was grateful for the protection of the lace edged panties that she'd been allowed to keep on.

Peter's hands were gripping the sides of the chair and he was staring straight ahead, not daring to get too excited at this stage. He was still wearing his jeans, but Cassandra could see the telltale bulge as his cock strained against the zipped-up fly.

'Undo him,' the baron said impatiently. With shaking hands she fumbled with the zip. He had nothing on beneath the jeans and as soon as the zip was lowered his erect penis sprang out and up until it was almost flat against his stomach.

'You'll have to kneel higher,' Katya said, laughing at Cassandra's expression. 'Poor Peter won't want you pulling it down, that might spoil the pleasure for him.'

The baron was watching Peter. 'Be careful,' he warned the lad. 'I'm relying on you to control yourself. God knows, you've had enough lessons from Katya.'

'I think he finds Cassandra rather more exciting,' Katya remarked, noticing the beads of sweat on Peter's upper lip. 'It must be her innocence!'

Cassandra knelt upright, her eyes fixed on the thick,

blood filled shaft in front of her, topped by the purple swollen head with the tiny slit that already had a bead of clear moisture in it. She had no idea how to start or what to do that wouldn't make her feel even worse than she did at this moment.

The baron moved in behind her and put a hand on her bare shoulder, letting his fingers move gently round in small circles while he pushed her long hair forward so that strands of it brushed against Peter's erection making him catch his breath in excitement.

'Learn well, Cassandra,' he murmured. 'Once you've discovered the joys of giving pleasure in this way, you can pleasure me. I can hardly wait to feel your warm, moist mouth enclose me and to see you swallow my seed. Learn it for me.'

She shivered as his hand wandered down her exposed spine, lingering every now and again to play over separate vertebrae while her nipples hardened at his touch. 'Lean forward,' he said quietly. 'Lick the moisture from the tip, and let your tongue go into the slit as you do so.' Katya moved to stand behind the chair, so that she could look down on Peter's straining cock and the slim, dark haired girl's first, amateurish attempts to fellate a man.

Cassandra knew that she had to obey, and very slowly she put out the tip of her tongue and lapped at the tiny clear bead of moisture. It tasted salty on her tongue, but just as she was about to pull away she felt the baron's hand on her head and remembered to flick the point of her tongue into the split. Peter gave a soft moan and the head of his penis swelled even more.

'Go round the outside ridge,' said the baron calmly. 'Lick at it as though it were an ice cream, and put a hand at the base so that he can feel your fingers gripping him there.'

Cassandra obeyed, and as she worked, Katya reached down and undid the belt on Peter's jeans so that they could be spread open exposing his stomach to the gentle caress of Cassandra's hair.

Once the jeans were opened up Peter was instructed to lift slightly and the baron pulled on the legs of the jeans until the tightly bunched testicles were also within Cassandra's reach. Soon she was being instructed to lick them as well, and although she didn't like the feel of the skin there, she was excited by the way they rippled and tightened, and also by Peter's ragged breathing.

After a time the baron decided that she must now take the straining cock into her mouth, but this time he met with more resistance from Cassandra who pushed back against his guiding hand and began to panic. Katya smiled to herself. It was obvious Cassandra wasn't getting enough pleasure from this, and as it would become an integral part of the girl's life from now on, she would lose points regularly. Personally, Katya couldn't imagine why any woman wouldn't be excited by the power of giving a man oral sex. It was one of her favourite occupations and she had often spent whole afternoons bringing Peter to ejaculation more times than he wanted in her enthusiasm.

Cassandra's resistance excited the baron, but he also wanted the lesson to go well and so he released her for a moment and went away, only to return with a small pot of yoghurt which he handed to Katya. His mistress quickly pushed the younger girl out of her way and carefully spread it over Peter's throbbing penis. She longed to suck some of it off herself, but Dieter was right there and she didn't dare, so she contented herself with giving the lad an almost fatal flick of her finger on the delicate skin of his perineum as she stepped away.

Peter gasped, his penis strained, but he caught his employer's eye and managed to contain himself. The baron waited until the erection began to diminish slightly before pushing Cassandra back towards him. 'There, now perhaps you won't be so silly. Take him in your mouth and suck off the yoghurt.' Cassandra opened her mouth, hesitated for a brief second and then took her courage in both hands and dipped her head. Her lips encountered the cool yoghurt and as the baron continued to give instructions she obediently sucked at the dripping liquid, almost unaware of the effect she was having on the lad in the chair.

The baron and Katya watched as Cassandra unknowingly began to warm to her task. Her fingers moved delicately round the base of Peter's shaft as she found her rhythm and her head moved steadily up and down as she sucked hard, at the same time flicking her tongue around the head.

Peter's almost uncontrollable excitement communicated itself to Cassandra as his flesh leapt and throbbed inside her mouth. She rose higher on her knees and bent lower, so that her hair brushed all over his belly adding yet another stimulation. He felt so hard that it was painful, and he looked to his employer for permission to ejaculate but the baron shook his head.

Peter's testicles were bunched tightly against his body and his stomach muscles were rigid with his efforts not to shoot his sperm into the warm and innocently wicked mouth. 'Put your free hand under him,' the baron whispered against Cassandra's ear. 'Let your fingers caress his buttocks, and inside the crease.'

Peter heard and knew that once she did that it would all be over for him. Cassandra heard too, and almost in a trance she obeyed. All her earlier fears had vanished as she'd experienced the sense of power that so appealed to Katya, and now the feel of Peter's pulsating flesh in her mouth was an aphrodisiac and her whole body felt as excited as if someone had been arousing her.

Her slim hand worked its way between the jeans and Peter's flesh, and on round to the crease between his hard buttocks. The light, inexpert touch was even more arousing than Katya's knowing fingers, and as Cassandra's mouth continued to suck deeply and her tongue flicked round the head the final intrusion of a finger into the sensitive skin of the opening to his rectum triggered Peter's ejaculation and he didn't have a chance to look to his employer for permission as his sperm was finally released and spurted into Cassandra's mouth.

At that moment she did try to draw away, but the baron's hands held her head firmly in place and he instructed her to keep sucking and swallowing until the lad's body had finally stopped jerking in the chair because Cassandra had milked him dry. When her head was released, Cassandra felt a pang of loss and she tried to give Peter one last, appreciative lick but he almost screamed with discomfort and the baron laughed deep in his throat as he tenderly moved her away from the prone lad.

'You'll hurt him if you don't let him rest. Unfortunately men aren't like women. One is all we get at a time! How well you did, my darling. Wasn't she clever, Katya? I've rarely seen Peter so excited.'

'She was better than I'd expected,' Katya admitted. 'Well done, Cassie,' she added with an attempt at a smile.

Cassandra pushed her hair back over her naked shoulders in an unselfconscious gesture that greatly excited the baron. 'Please don't call me Cassie, Katya. I'm sure I asked you not to once before.'

Katya's eyes blazed. 'We employ you, Cassie. I think you'd do well to remember that.'

'I employ her,' the baron said calmly. 'If she wishes to be called Cassandra then that's what she shall be called. Stand up my dear, let me look at you.'

Cassandra stood in front of him, her cheeks flushed from bending over Peter, her nipples erect from the excitement of the whole experience and a look of triumph in her eyes because now Helena could go to Austria and she would be here alone with this man who was beginning to dominate her every waking moment. Unlike Abigail she was not afraid of Katya, because Katya had very little authority unless the baron allowed it.

The baron saw the triumph in her eyes and savoured it. It had been a difficult challenge but she'd come through it well; as she took each advancing step she enabled him to broaden the scope of the game. Now that she was well grounded in the basics he could increase the degree of sophistication, which was why he was sending the children away.

Tomorrow, when the girls had gone, Rupert and Françoise Piccard would arrive and the pace and manner of the game would change dramatically. He always enjoyed their visits. He and Rupert had grown up together, had their first sexual experiences at the same time and knew each other's deepest, darkest secrets.

Cassandra was still standing in front of the baron. Idly he reached out and let his hands move down the sides of her, tightening their grip at her narrow waist. He put one hand in the small of her back and pushed so that her flat abdomen was forced forward. Bending his head he flicked his tongue into her navel, swirling it round just as she had swirled her tongue round Peter's swollen glans. She moaned softly and he let his free hand wander between her thighs, pressing his fingers against the crotch of her panties where they encountered immediate evidence of her own sexual excitement.

For a moment he let his fingers play against the damp cloth, fingering her through the material and feeling her lips beginning to swell and part, but when she tried to move against his hand he stopped, stood up straight again and then pulled the pants down by hooking his fingers in each side of the waistband.

'I'm sure Katya's thirsty after all the excitement,' he said casually. 'Come and drink from Cassandra, darling, while Peter here gets dressed and finds us all some lunch.'

Katya came quickly to his side and then knelt in front of Cassandra, pushing at the inside of the girl's thighs until she spread her legs a little wider giving Katya better access. Carefully, Katya spread the outer lips and began to lick at the moist channel, letting her tongue dip now and again into the vaginal entrance before

128

spreading the milky secretion up the inner lips but she was careful not to touch the slowly protruding bud of pleasure directly, only swirling her tongue around it so that the hood drew back leaving the tight mass of nerve endings begging for a caress.

Cassandra's legs began to shake with sexual tension and she tried to move her hips so that Katya's tongue would touch that part of her that was aching and tightening more and more as the clever tongue continued to swirl around all the rest of her.

'Keep still and look into my eyes,' the baron said. Cassandra did as he said, and his eyes seemed to draw her out of herself and into him so that she felt as though she didn't exist except as a part of him, and the life he was creating for her.

Katya slipped her tongue inside Cassandra's damp opening and curled it up against the front wall, pressing as hard as she could against the G-spot. Cassandra's toes began to curl and she whimpered without knowing it because her eyes were still locked on the baron's and she was almost drowning in the warm depth of his gaze.

Her lips parted, her breasts rose and fell, the neglected nipples rigid and dark with desire and while the baron never released Cassandra's eyes his right hand made a small gesture to Katya who swiftly removed her tongue, moved it up the slippery sides of the inner lips and then flicked rapidly against the underside of the desperate clitoris with three lightning-fast, feather-like movements.

It was the trigger for Cassandra's release and she gasped, rising up on her toes and almost falling so that the baron had to reach out and pull her naked body against him as she shivered and trembled in his arms, continuing to jerk long after Katya's tongue had been withdrawn. Finally she was still and the baron bent and lowered her to the carpet. 'Well, time for our next course I think. Peter, why aren't you dressed yet?'

Katya and Dieter both looked at the lad, whose state

of semi-arousal was obvious to them both. 'Not yet I'm afraid,' the baron said shortly. 'Katya seems to be making you greedy. Perhaps you should have a few days starvation!'

Katya made a face. 'I only use him because you're away or busy so much.'

'You sound like a complaining wife,' he said shortly. 'Cassandra, get dressed. And tidy your hair, you look like a cheap whore lying there like that. I can hardly believe you're the same girl I interviewed such a short time ago.'

Although he sounded annoyed he smiled at Katya who smiled back at him as they remembered the video they had of Cassandra's first visit to the house. Poor Cassandra, still shaken by the violence of her own orgasm and the experience with Peter, quickly got to her feet and pulled on her clothes.

Suddenly she felt like a whore, and yet only moments before she'd been certain that there was something special between her and the baron, something that he and Katya didn't share and which would keep them together for a long time. Now it seemed that she'd imagined it all and only pride kept her from weeping, but as she passed the baron to go and tidy herself up he reached out, squeezed her round the waist and gave her one of his rare but enchanting smiles. Since Katya didn't see it, it meant that both she and Cassandra ended up feeling well pleased with their unusual lunch.

As to what the baron really felt, only he knew; and he never told anyone anything.

# Chapter Seven

'You'll like Rupert,' the baron said as the front door bell rang. 'I'm not so sure about Françoise; Katya and she are great friends but . . .' He shrugged, as though to indicate that he didn't necessarily expect Cassandra would share the friendship.

'I've heard of him,' Cassandra replied. 'Paul used to love watching the skiing on Sunday afternoons, and he was world champion for a time wasn't he?'

'Indeed. However, the training is hard, the discipline continuous and Rupert likes to enjoy life, so he retired and married Françoise.'

'Is she French?'

The baron shook his head. 'Brazilian, I think. She was a model but she comes from the slums and you know what they say about that. You can take the child out of the slums but you cannot take the slums out of the child. Françoise is living proof of the truth of this! Amusing of course, but not quite what one would have expected of Rupert, except that she is the unexpected!'

There was the sound of voices in the hallway, and a baby cried. 'There are also now twin boys, not yet a year old as I recall.'

'Will I be looking after them?' Cassandra queried.

'Of course not. You will be looking after us! No, they

131

have brought their own nannies, and probably a paedia-trician, too. Rupert is terrified of losing one of his heirs! Come and meet them all. We will have great fun over the next few days I think.'

His eyes were glowing and his face livelier than she had ever seen it, yet Cassandra felt very uneasy. She was just about managing to cope with the baron, Katya, Lucy and Peter; the thought of becoming involved with yet more people was a terrifying one, but she knew that if she wanted to stay in the baron's house – and she did – then she must learn to cope with his friends, whatever they might be like.

Like most women her first impression of Rupert Piccard was that he was stunningly handsome. He had rather long, blue-black hair, piercing blue eyes with black lashes and a darkly tanned face with gleaming white teeth. The teeth were very slightly crooked, a small imperfection that was fortunate because it added character to features that would otherwise have been too perfect. He was taller than the baron by about two inches, but much slimmer than Cassandra had expected. She supposed it was because whenever she'd seen him he'd been well padded out in ski clothes.

Rupert smiled warmly when the baron introduced Cassandra, but he seemed a little surprised by her. 'I thought you said she was a redhead, Dieter?'

'That was Abigail. She is no longer here. She disap-pointed me.'

'Right! I see. Well, Cassandra doesn't look in the least disappointing. English women are so wonderfully unsophisticated. I can understand why you choose to live here, Dieter! Cassandra meet Françoise, my wife.'

Françoise, who'd been deep in conversation with Katya, turned to look at Cassandra through her slanting dark eyes. She was tall, at least five feet nine inches, and very slim with a golden brown skin and her black hair with copper highlights fell to her shoulders in natural curls. She was wearing a tight multi-coloured silk dress with a sash tied round her non-existent hips

132

and seemed like some exotic bird that had strayed into the wrong country by mistake.

Cassandra held out her hand again, and knew that Françoise didn't like her any more than Katya did. The handshake was brief, the smile never touched the eyes and she sounded bored as she murmured a greeting.

The baron watched from the shadows and smiled to himself. He'd known that Katya would quickly get Françoise onto her side, just as he'd known that Rupert would find Cassandra as fascinating as he did, and so far everything was going very well.

Behind the two women stood a short, slightly over-weight girl with heavy-lidded eyes and a sulky mouth. She was holding a chubby baby in each arm, but paid them very little attention as they waved their hands around in the air and yelled for food.

At last the noise seemed to penetrate Françoise's brain and she turned to the adolescent girl. 'Why don't you keep them quiet, Clara?' she demanded, her voice deep and authoritative. 'If I'd known how stupid you were I would never have agreed to take you into our household. Your poor stepfather has been very unlucky.'

The hapless Clara went bright red but she didn't attempt to defend herself, and at that moment a much older woman in nanny's uniform came through the front door, took the babies from the girl and turned to Rupert. 'Where is the nursery?' she asked crisply, and Cassandra realised with some surprise that the woman was Scottish.

'On the second floor, you have three rooms adjoining,' the baron replied, his gaze on the overweight adolescent now standing alone with her tight dress sticking to her ample breasts and thighs.

'Look at her!' Rupert laughed. 'I mentioned her in my letter didn't I, Dieter? She's Claud Brunswick's step-daughter. Her father died last year, and apparently until then she'd been kept at home all her life. Governesses, nannies, private dancing lessons but absolutely no contact with the outside world. Claud felt Françoise and I could widen her horizons while he and her mama are on their honeymoon cruise. We're doing our best, in fact Françoise has hardly left her alone during the journey, but we've kept her intact for you.'

He laughed and so did Katya and Françoise, but Cassandra could only look at the girl with pity. She was probably about eighteen, and if she could shed some of her puppy fat would have been quite good looking, but her painful silence and unfortunate sullen expression made her presence among these glittering people ridiculous.

Françoise reached out and took hold of one of Clara's large breasts, clearly visible through the dress. She squeezed it for a moment, then let it rest in her hand. 'I adore her breasts,' she informed Katya. 'Sometimes I go to her room in the night, wake her up and just lie there licking and nibbling on them for hours. I wish I could have breasts like that.'

'You'd look ridiculous!' Rupert exclaimed with a laugh. The baron still kept his eyes fixed on the girl, assessing her reactions to Françoise's touch and casual talk.

Françoise went across to the baron. 'How are you, darling Dieter? You look as fit as ever. Is he fit?' she enquired of Cassandra.

'I've no idea,' Cassandra said calmly. 'I look after the children.'

'In that case why aren't you in Austria?'

'Perhaps I thought some of our visitors were still children,' the baron said with a lopsided smile.

Françoise didn't seem certain how to deal with his remark and looked to her husband for assistance, but Rupert only laughed again. 'Well said, Dieter. You're right of course, Françoise hasn't grown up at all, that's why she treats Clara like a toy.'

'She looks very exciting,' Katya said softly. Françoise nodded vigorously. 'She is! Let me show you. Clara, come with us. Are we in our usual room, Dieter?'

'Of course.'

'Good. Come along, Clara, and Katya too. You men can talk about the usual boring sport for a time.' She hesitated. 'What about her?' she asked Katya, pointing to Cassandra.

'Cassandra works for me,' the baron said coldly. 'I decide where Cassandra goes, not Katya.'

Françoise pulled a face. 'Where is your sense of humour, Dieter?'

'Stored away with your brain, Françoise.'

Françoise glared at him and flounced upstairs, pushing the heavy-breasted Clara ahead of her. Cassandra found herself alone with the two men. 'Perhaps you could make us some coffee, Cassandra?' the baron suggested, and she was grateful for a chance to get away on her own.

After the men had been served coffee, Cassandra went up to her own room to change for dinner. On the landing she paused, hearing the sound of soft sobs coming from one of the guest rooms, but she quickly hurried on. What happened to Clara was none of her business, and since her stepfather knew Rupert she told herself that it couldn't be anything too terrible; all the same, the girl's heavy eyes and sullen docility disturbed her.

After she'd bathed she was just pulling on her silk stockings when there was a brief tap on her door and the baron entered. 'I hope I'm in time, my dear. I want you to have these again tonight.' He held out his hand, and nestling in the palm were some more Japanese love balls, but these were larger than the first ones she'd had and she could vividly imagine the effect they'd have on her.

'Lie on the bed,' he said softly. 'I'll put them in for you.'

'Why tonight?' she asked.

'To add to the stimulation of what promises to be an excellent evening. Wear the tight panties as well, I want to know that every time you sit or bend the pressure is

135

there for you, arousing you, but of course there must be no release!' He laughed, as though such a thought was ridiculous.

'Why are they bigger?'

'Because you're more advanced, you can stand greater stimulation.'

He pressed her back against the bedcover and she spread her legs for him, but when he put a hand between the join of her thighs she was dry. He quickly pushed up the camisole top she'd just put on and began to suck on her nipples. He sucked very slowly, gradually increasing the pressure and drawing his head slightly away so that the nipples were elongated by the movement at the same time as they became excited. The two small breasts themselves started to swell and he reached out and rubbed her stomach, his palm flat against the taut skin. He pressed quite firmly and she felt a glow building up inside her, pleasantly warm at first and then more urgent and all the time he continued sucking on her nipples and tugging them as though milking her.

It was bliss for several minutes, but then she realised that she needed to use the bathroom and wished he'd hurry up and insert the love balls so that she could relieve herself. The baron saw the change of expression in her eyes and wished he had the time to exploit the new sensation, but he didn't.

'Keep still,' he murmured, then moved away, releasing her breasts and stomach as he checked that she was now moist between her thighs. She was, and although she found the first ball difficult to take, he coaxed and encouraged her until all three were in, then got her to stand up and walk round the room, the string hanging between her outer lips and sticking to her secretions. Finally he pulled her down onto his knee and rocked her to and fro. The balls moved within her, the hood of her clitoris pulled slightly, pressure began to build within her and moisture seeped out between her distended lips and onto the thick dark curls of pubic hair.

The baron laughed and pushed her gently off him. 'Excellent! A good start to the evening. Now go and use the bathroom, finish your dressing and join us in the study for drinks. Wear the turquoise silk that I bought you. Oh yes, and no stockings. The silk will feel better against naked thighs.'

He left and as the door closed Cassandra felt a frantic desire to dash after him and implore him to let her have just one climax before dinner, some relief from the steady aching need that he'd deliberately started within her and which would, she knew, increase all through the evening, but there was no point, she simply had to bear it.

When she was finally ready she was just leaving her room when Françoise came down the landing. 'There you are! Dieter told me to make sure and catch you before you went down. You are to come and see Clara. She's in our room at the moment.'

Cassandra followed Françoise, now dressed in an equally exotic silk trouser suit, into the large bedroom and then stopped in amazement. In the middle of the king-size bed lay a naked Clara. Her large, unconstrained breasts were being stroked by Katya, whose hands were encased in sheepskin covered mittens which were obviously driving Clara to distraction. Her nipples were so tight they looked ready to burst, and just as Cassandra came into the room Katya took off a mitten and flicked one of the nipples hard with her middle finger. Clara cried out and the nipple reddened. Katya smiled, flicked at it twice more, and then replaced the mitten and began stroking the damaged flesh with the insidiously soft sheepskin again.

It was obvious that this treatment had been going on for a long time. Clara's hands were tied through rings above her head which forced her breasts upright to make them an easier target, while Lucy was crouched at the foot of the bed holding the girl's ankles apart.

Françoise looked over her shoulder at Cassandra. 'Clara adores this, just watch. It's one of the first things

I ever taught her to like. Until then I don't think she'd even touched herself below the waist!' From the foot of the bed Françoise picked up a small feather duster, similar to ones used for lampshades or ornaments, and she ran this tenderly up the girl's thighs, moving it round in tiny circles and making Lucy push Clara's ankles up the bed so that she could 'dust' behind her knees before she moved higher to work on the inner thighs.

Poor Clara groaned and cried, obviously in despair because she hadn't yet been allowed an orgasm and her plump abdomen seemed to be swelling even more under the cunning attentions of the two women who were obviously thrilled with their new toy. Eventually the duster moved to the abdomen itself and Clara cried out with pleasure, the skin tensing as the nerve endings flashed signals of delight into her brain.

'She'll have to come soon,' Cassandra said, seeing how Clara's head was thrashing from side to side.

'Come? But no. There has not yet been an orgasm for Clara. She has had to keep waiting until tonight. She is our present to Dieter. He will give her her first climax after dinner. Won't that be nice, Clara?' she added, letting the duster slip between the thighs for a brief second but quickly removing it when the over-excited flesh leapt in response.

'You mean you've been treating her like this and never let her come?' Cassandra asked, unable to keep her eyes away from the plump, uninitiated body on the bed, so skilfully trained and yet so miserably unfulfilled.

'Of course. Rupert has sometimes joined me too, but he uses his tongue on her, doesn't he Clara? She likes that, although she doesn't think she should because her mother has brought her up to be a silly prude. Now, we must tie her feet before we go down to dinner, and you must keep her stimulated, Lucy, but only a little. Keep her aroused, but not too close to release or Dieter will be cross with us all.'

Lucy smiled and nodded, and Cassandra was amazed

138

that despite her own humiliations the girl didn't mind participating in Clara's. But then she realised that if Lucy had been unhappy she would have left the household. It seemed that she enjoyed the house in Hampstead as much as the other occupants.

Clara's feet were quickly fastened through loops, and then the three women left her with Lucy licking the sweat from the other girl's breasts and beneath her armpits, an exercise that only seemed to cause her to sweat even more.

Inside Cassandra the love balls moved heavily, and she had to tighten her muscles against them. At once there was an ominous tugging sensation at the base of her stomach and she had to breathe quickly through her mouth to avoid even the smallest orgasm. The walk downstairs made them yet more intrusive and small shivers of pleasure darted round her belly before she reached the bottom and the safety of level ground.

Dinner that evening was served by a maid Cassandra had never seen before. She was quick, efficient and took no notice of the conversation going on around her.

Rupert was telling Dieter about a live sex show that he and Françoise had been to in Germany where a girl had taken a snake inside her. 'I can't imagine how she got it all in,' he commented. 'I know they coil up small but I still don't think it's possible. Somehow or other they faked it. I did think of buying a python and trying it out on Françoise, but for once she refused me.'

'Only because they can kill you!' Françoise protested. 'I think I'd like a large snake inside me for once, but not a python!'

Katya laughed. 'Dieter put a tiny beetle inside Abigail. She went absolutely hysterical. If she hadn't been tied down I think she'd have thrown herself out of the window.'

Françoise licked her lips. 'A beetle? How stimulating.'

Cassandra tried not to listen to them. None of this had anything to do with the way she felt when the baron was with her. Snakes, beetles and live sex shows weren't the reason she was so tied to this house, and she wished Rupert and Françoise had never come. And yet, there was Clara. Every time she thought of Clara upstairs, with Lucy making sure that every part of Clara was stimulated and aroused, her own stomach tightened and the love balls pressed against her vaginal walls so that she had to try and lift some of her weight off her chair to ease the pressure.

The baron watched Cassandra during the dinner. The silk dress was semi-transparent and he could see her increasing arousal as the fiendish love balls did their work and he knew that when they finally went upstairs and he deflowered Clara, Cassandra's excitement would be almost unbearable for her. To his surprise, the thought of this made his manhood stir and he decided to distract himself.

'Cassandra is using some Japanese love balls tonight,' he told them all. 'I find that very arousing. I wish you'd done the same Katya my dear, that would have given me twice the pleasure!'

Katya felt a surge of anger. She hadn't known what was happening because she'd been caught up in playing with the plump little virgin Françoise had spent so many weeks training. She cursed herself for being too easily distracted but smiled contritely at Dieter.

'My darling, I am so sorry, but I don't need love balls. I'm always excited when you're at home.'

The baron snorted. 'A pretty speech, but ineffective. Rupert, would you like to feel the weight of these love balls? They're new ones to me. Cassandra, go round the table, my darling. Stand by Rupert's chair and let him feel the weight of your sex.'

Cassandra stood up and walked demurely round to Rupert. She knew that Katya was furious, while Françoise seemed intrigued by all that was going on. Her eyes darted round all the faces and her top teeth caught on her bottom lip as she watched the young English-woman walk to her husband's side.

Rupert slid an expert hand up the girl's bare leg,

letting his fingers drift casually along the delicate skin of the inner thighs until his hand could cup her beneath her sex. He pressed the palm of his hand against the tight material of the panties the baron had given her and rocked it backwards and forwards to move the balls inside her.

The baron leant forward with his elbows on the table and he watched Cassandra's eyes widen as her outer sex lips tried to open under Rupert's expert handling. If they opened too much the first of the love balls would fall out, and then she would be in great trouble, but as she clenched her pelvic muscles tightly in order to stop that happening she increased the pressure of the balls against the sensitised vaginal walls and nearly triggered an orgasm.

Rupert, aware of what was happening and sympathetic to her plight, suddenly stopped moving his hand, the clitoris which had started to pulse gradually quietened and after what seemed an eternity to Cassandra all the sensations died away and she was at last able to breathe normally again. Rupert carefully removed his hand, this time letting the fingers stray only against the inside of the knees, but she still jumped and he couldn't wait until he could have a turn with her himself.

'They're certainly a good weight,' he said with a grin.

The baron watched Cassandra return to her seat and then raised his glass to her. 'Bravo, my dear! How well you progress.'

'We must get together one night,' Françoise said eagerly. 'My maid is well trained, we could have a wonderful time the three of us.'

'I decide where Cassandra goes,' the baron reminded her sharply.

Françoise glanced at Katya. Katya had survived a long time with Dieter. Rupert said it was because she was clever enough to seem cold while at the same time being driven by sexual urges that equalled her lover's, but now Françoise wondered if Dieter had tired of coldness. Men did; even jaded ones like Dieter wanted something more than the mechanics. The trick was to get the balance right, and she had always thought that Katya's increasing love of sado-masochistic sex was not quite to Dieter's taste. He liked to temper pain with pleasure, but pain alone was enough for Katya, either inflicted by her or on her. Cassandra didn't look as though her abilities lay in that particular direction and she had the feeling that there was a competition going on here, one that would be fascinating to see through to its conclusion.

When the meal was over, Françoise stood up. 'I think poor Clara will be ready to burst if we don't go up and see her soon. Are you interested, Dieter, or do you want Rupert to do it?'

He laughed. 'Of course I'm interested. Not many people bring virgins to my front door, even overweight virgins.'

'I didn't think you liked them,' Katya said harshly.

Dieter shrugged. 'We all change, my dear. Besides, knowing how hard virgins are to find, how could I possibly let Rupert have this one!'

As they all left the room, the baron caught hold of Cassandra's arm and pulled her round to face him. 'Do they feel good? Did you like it when Rupert touched you?' he asked her urgently.

Cassandra wanted to say that she'd have preferred it if he'd touched her, but she didn't. Instead she looked steadily into his eyes and smiled. 'Yes, they feel good and yes I liked it when he touched me, although I nearly . . .'

'But of course, that was why I got him to do it! However, you kept control and I am proud of you. Does the girl upstairs excite you?'

Cassandra hesitated. 'Not the girl, no, but seeing her the way she was before dinner, yes that excited me.' The last part of her sentence was barely audible as her voice dropped through shame.

'It's good!' the baron told her. 'That is how you should find it. Of course it is exciting to watch someone in a state of sexual arousal. Enjoy everything that happens during the coming days, and do not ever be ashamed. Above all, keep hold of your courage.'

Cassandra stared at him. 'Why? What's going to happen?'

Katya had come back to see what was keeping her lover. 'Dieter, they're waiting for you,' she murmured, slipping her arm through his and pulling him away from Cassandra. He bent his head nearer to hers and bit her sharply on her earlobe. She gave a muffled scream and a flush of excitement rose on her cheekbones. Turning her towards him he bent his head and kissed her savagely, biting on her bottom lip until it bled and thrusting his tongue up against the roof of her mouth until she almost gagged, then he suddenly released her and hurried up the stairs.

Katya turned to Cassandra who was wide-eyed and silent. 'You'll never get him,' she said softly. 'He's fascinated at the moment, but it won't last. You aren't brave enough for Dieter.'

Courage. That was what the baron had told her to keep hold of, and now Cassandra was determined that she would. It was obviously important if she was to stay on here, and she knew that she had to, that her life was bound up with the baron's and she would use every weapon she had to keep her place in the house.

By the time Katya and Cassandra entered the bedroom, Clara's legs had been untied and a bolster placed beneath her hips, pushing her abdomen even higher into the air and stretching the skin tightly across it in order to intensify every sensation.

Her arms were still fastened, mainly Cassandra thought to keep her breasts taut, and it was on these the baron seemed to want to start. He sat himself at the side of the girl and rolled one large nipple between two of his fingers, quite gently at first but then with increasing pressure until she began to flinch. Once she flinched the pressure relaxed, and the rolling began again, followed repeatedly by the pressure, pain and release.

After that, he bent down and sucked the soft undersides of the breasts, then licked upwards towards the nipple and again he took a long time over this, only licking the nipple itself when Clara began trying frantically to pull herself lower on the bed.

After that he let his tongue trail down between her breasts until finally it was on the overstretched skin of the belly, and now when he flicked and licked with his tongue her body jerked so much that Rupert signalled for Françoise to hold her ankles once more.

Cassandra was fascinated by the way the girl's belly seemed to keep expanding under his ministrations, although it didn't look as though that was possible the way the bolster had already pushed it out. She could feel herself getting more and more damp between her legs and the love balls combined with watching the baron working on the young girl were giving her a terrible ache in the pit of her stomach as her pelvic region became engorged with no way of releasing the resulting pressure.

The baron flicked his tongue on Clara's hip bones and she jerked again, then he carefully parted her soft downy pubic hair and pulled the skin up across the pubic bone so that the hood of the clitoris moved and exposed Clara's pulsating need for a climax. But it was still too soon.

At a sign from Dieter, Rupert sat beside the girl and fondled the large breasts while Dieter got Katya to hold Clara's outer lips apart, then he rubbed a finger in the milky fluid his attentions had caused and spread it around the whole vaginal area, rubbing his hand in a circular motion that had her gasping until her legs went rigid with desire, but still he avoided the one sensitive spot that would trigger her release. Then, slowly, he began to insert a finger inside Clara and now she stiffened with fear. 'No!' she cried.

Dieter's hand resumed the circular stroking. 'But why? Isn't this nice? And what follows will be even better.'

'It's wrong,' the wretched girl gasped. 'We aren't married. I shall never find a husband if I'm not a virgin. Please, you mustn't do it.'

All the women except for Cassandra laughed. 'Was your governess a nun?' Dieter asked, not unkindly.

'Maman told me. It's wicked, and so's the pleasure,' she added as his fingers brought forth another groan of desire. 'I'm bad, I know I am. I must be to enjoy it.'

The baron looked at Cassandra. 'You see how a conscience can spoil even the best of life's pleasures for us? What nonsense to teach a girl in this day and age.' His hand was still moving, but at the same time he inserted a finger of the other hand so that Clara didn't realise what he'd done until he started to move it from side to side within her.

Katya was watching the tight belly and the exposed clitoris carefully. 'She's very near,' she warned her lover.

'Good,' Dieter murmured, and he added a second finger to the first although he stopped the manipulation of the whole vulva as he did it, which prevented the climax from coming at that moment. As he moved the fingers round inside her, Rupert began to suck hard on her breasts and then Françoise suddenly released Clara's wrists from the rings. She was so surprised that she didn't even realise what was happening when the two men, assisted by Françoise and Katya, swiftly turned her onto her stomach while Lucy pushed on the girl's ankles until she was kneeling but with her buttocks raised by the bolster and her face buried in the duvet.

Standing where she was, Cassandra could see how the bolster beneath the hips and stomach and the movement of the legs had exposed Clara's sex so that Dieter could easily position himself correctly. He waited a few seconds and then with one swift, hard thrust he was inside her.

There was no doubt that it hurt. Clara screamed but she was being pushed face down into the bolster and there was nowhere she could escape to as the baron withdrew slightly from the tight, newly opened channel and then thrust back inside even harder until his thick cock was buried inside her up to its base.

Once there he rested for a moment, reaching a hand down beneath her to find the clitoris, now trying to shelter beneath its hood, but his fingers pulled the skin up and Rupert's hand joined in so that he could hold the hood back while Dieter, his finger moistened by his own saliva, gently rolled the exposed bud round for a few seconds before moving down to the tiny shaft and once there he heard the telltale catch of breath in her throat and he immediately increased the pressure, found the rhythm that seemed to suit her and finally, after weeks of frustration, Clara's body was almost torn apart by an orgasm that tightened her internal muscles in a spasm so intense that the baron's own orgasm was triggered by it, and he pumped himself into her while her body continued to shake and tremble beneath the blessed sensations of her climax.

At last her muscle spasm passed and the baron withdrew. Sobbing with gratitude, Clara turned and reached up for him. At once an expression of distaste crossed his face. He pushed her away and she fell on her back, thighs spread wide and large breasts flopping to the sides of her body.

'She's far too fat,' he said to Rupert dispassionately, 'but still one can't be too fussy about a virgin, I suppose.'

The men laughed, but Cassandra winced at the cruelty. The baron turned to look at her, and the passion in his gaze took her by surprise. 'Give her another orgasm,' he said harshly.

Cassandra stared at him. 'Me?'

'Yes, go down on her. Do what you did to Peter – Katya will help you find her clitoris if you have any trouble. Do it now. I want to watch.'

She remembered what he'd said to her downstairs and moved towards the bed. If this was what it took, then this was what she'd do, and despite the seepage of the baron's sperm that was still dribbling from Clara's entrance, Cassandra crouched between the trembling thighs and waited while the other woman straightened the now deflowered girl out for the new attention she was about to receive.

When Cassandra positioned herself on the bed the love balls moved heavily inside her, rolling forward towards the mouth of her vagina and emphasising the heavy ache that had already settled just above her pubic bone. It was an ache of need; she needed stimulation and release for herself yet she was having to administer it to a girl who was already exhausted and far from anxious for further attention. Nonetheless, this was what the baron wanted and Cassandra tried to forget her own body's yearnings as she set about her task.

Clara, nerve endings still raw and body finally sated, had objected vigorously to what was going on and Rupert and Katya finally had to retie her wrists and ankles in order to keep her correctly positioned. Tentatively, Cassandra ran her fingers down the creases inside the tops of the thighs, pressing the closed outer lips more firmly together but at the same time stimulating the entire area. Clara groaned, but this time in despair, and tried to pull her legs together but the rings held firm. With the back of her hand, Cassandra brushed against the soft pubic hair, still damp from the baron's sperm and she then reversed the movement so that with palm uppermost her hand travelled back up to the pubic bone with the middle finger gently forcing its way between the lips so that it felt the sticky heat beneath.

Clara's arched abdomen jerked. 'Turn your knees out,' Françoise instructed, and much to Cassandra's surprise Clara obeyed. This had the effect of rounding her belly yet further while at the same time forcing the reluctant outer sex lips to open. The young girl was obviously in physical discomfort with her ankles fastened and her knees twisted out but it had the desired result of leaving Cassandra with an easy target.

Katya, who was shivering with excitement because she knew very well that all Clara would be wanting at the moment was sleep, went to the side of the girl and carefully held the thick outer lips apart as Cassandra's tongue finally began to explore the damp channels and thin inner lips of the fettered girl.

She was well aware of her audience; she knew that the baron was watching her closely from the shadows and that both Rupert and his wife were watching too, but above all she understood that Katya was watching her, hoping to see some signs of rebellion or, better still, revulsion from Cassandra. This was something that Cassandra was determined wouldn't happen, and she was surprised to find that in fact there was pleasure to be had from sliding her tongue over the light pink sensitive tissue beneath her. She discovered that every time Clara groaned or tried to jerk away, her heart would beat loudly in her ears and without conscious thought her hands began to roam upwards over the distended stomach, kneading and pressing firmly against the tenseness that she found there as she blissfully tormented the flesh that was stretched like a drumskin over the plump adolescent body.

Clara's body was slow to be rearoused. She'd been stimulated and kept on the edge of satisfaction for so many days that the final, racking release had utterly exhausted her, but Cassandra persevered and slowly the girl's senses were forced to respond. At one point Cassandra remembered her lesson with Peter and moved up the supine body to let her long hair tease across the breasts and down the sensitive sides of the stomach and hips. At this point Clara actually pleaded with her to stop, begging her not to make her come again, but Cassandra didn't listen, knowing that when the pleasure did come it would be great.

For a long time she licked, nibbled, fingered and body-brushed the girl with her hair until the moment when the reluctant little hub of pleasure began to swell again and the hood of the clitoris slid back, giving

Cassandra access to the source of Clara's ultimate satisfaction.

Even then she waited, remembering what she'd seen when the baron was working on the girl, and she swirled her tongue around the area without touching the clitoris itself. Clara's nipples stiffened until they looked like hard pebbles and her breasts swelled, giving the appearance of balls of white marble, yet still Clara pleaded with Cassandra to leave her alone.

Finally, Cassandra knew that the moment was near and she moved her head so that she could flick the tip of her tongue directly against the exposed red bud, but Clara sensed the movement and her fear of experiencing another racking spasm of pleasure was so great that the hood of the clitoris began to protect the delicate organ again. Luckily, Katya was quick and with two tiny fingers manipulated the skin above the bud itself, pulling back the hood and keeping hold of the skin so that Clara was refused any protection from the invasion of Cassandra's tongue.

With unintentional cruelty, Cassandra hesitated for a second and Clara began to sob as she continued her attempts to pull away. Françoise, fascinated by Cassandra's unexpected skill at the game, slapped the girl's abdomen hard and almost precipitated the pleasure by mistake, but then she pinched one of the distended nipples sharply between her long fingernails and this time the pain silenced the wretched girl.

Katya looked at Cassandra, knowing that the hesitation had really come from within herself and not from any desire to prolong Clara's torture, but although she longed for Cassandra to fail she had no hope because Cassandra's own desperate lust and physical need were now so great that nothing would have stopped her from completing her task.

As Clara's whimpers began again, Cassandra finally let her tongue flick directly onto the swollen red button. Clara gave a yelp of shock, pain and pleasure as the frayed nerves were restimulated. Immediately Cassan-

149

dra flicked again, and then again but this time swirling the tongue round the stem beneath the clitoris and because her bonds stopped her body from arching and swelling as much as it needed to, this second orgasm seemed to last even longer than Clara's first and everyone in the room watched in silent excited fascination as the girl screamed while her muscles rippled and contracted against her bonds and her head thrashed from side to side as her cries echoed endlessly round the room.

It was too much for Rupert, who suddenly pushed Cassandra out of the way, unzipped his flies and threw himself on the heaving girl, forcing his way into her without any warning so that he could feel her internal contractions for himself.

His intrusion almost sent Clara out of her mind because he moved his body firmly up and down hers with his legs flat and every movement reactivated the clitoris so that a third climax overtook her before the second had fully died away. This time there was more pain than pleasure and red lights flashed behind her eyes as tears streamed down her face at the realisation that her body would keep responding for as long as these diabolically knowledgeable people wanted to play with her.

Fortunately for Clara, her tightness and the strength of her orgasm quickly brought Rupert to ejaculation and within a few minutes he had slumped on top of her, his weight adding further to the discomfort of her uplifted abdomen. When Rupert withdrew and stepped back from the bed, Clara closed her eyes against the onlookers but her tear-stained cheeks and exhausted body were so exciting to Katya that she couldn't resist staying beside the bed for a few more minutes, pinching and nipping at the large, excruciatingly tender nipples and her breathing grew more and more ragged as the nipples reluctantly hardened despite their increasing redness.

'Leave her,' the baron said suddenly. 'It's enough. She was my present, not yours.'

Katya's eyes glittered as she looked at her lover. 'What shall we do now?' she asked eagerly.

He shrugged, but there was a hint of excitement in his eyes too and Katya felt sure that he had something wonderful in store for her. The boyish enthusiasm that often heralded some of his most outrageous suggestions was back on his face and she found she could hardly breathe for excitement.

'You like to be hurt best of all, don't you my darling?' he said softly. There was no point in lying to him and she nodded hungrily. 'Then I shall have to hurt you in the best or perhaps I should say the worst way possible, yes?' Katya nodded, while everyone else in the room waited silently. 'Very well; you may now go to bed on your own. No one is to visit you and we will all meet again at breakfast. Lucy, attend to Clara and see that she has an undisturbed night's sleep.'

Katya's eyes had narrowed into mere slits and she looked as though she would have liked to strike the baron. 'You can't do that to me!' she hissed furiously. 'I need you. I need . . .'

'By depriving you of what you need I'm inflicting the ultimate pain. That surely is what you want? We all heard you say how much you enjoy being hurt, so go to bed and enjoy!'

Cassandra was standing on the opposite side of the room from Katya, and she could see how the other woman was trembling with suppressed fury, but even she was surprised when Katya suddenly launched herself at her lover, fingernails outstretched as she went for his face. Both Rupert and Françoise gave exclamations of surprise, but the baron merely caught hold of her wrists and pushed her away, hard enough to make her fall to the floor but not hard enough to really hurt her. 'Control yourself, Katya. You are boring me.'

The words were the ultimate disgrace, and Katya knew it. Without another word she got up and walked out of the room, not even glancing at the rest of the group. Abruptly the baron turned and walked across to Cassandra. 'Come with me, Cassandra. Tonight I shall stay in your room.'

She stared at him, half expecting that if she showed any pleasure he would laugh and tell her it had only been a joke. Her steady gaze obviously wasn't what he'd anticipated, but he raised his eyebrows for a moment and then gave a half-smile. 'Such enthusiasm! Come, the night is young. We will see our guests in the morning. Goodnight, Rupert and thank you for the present. It made for a most entertaining evening.'

'My pleasure!' Rupert responded, disguising the fact that he was as surprised as Katya at the way the evening had ended. He compensated by taking Lucy along to bed with him and Françoise but he spared a thought for Katya.

# *Chapter Eight*

$O$nce they were inside her bedroom, Cassandra felt totally at a loss. She hadn't expected the baron's company and had no idea what he expected from her, but she had the feeling that he'd acted on an impulse and if that was true she knew that everything must go right so that he didn't regret it. The trouble was, it was almost impossible to know with him what was right and what was wrong.

He sat on the side of her bed in total silence, watching the play of emotions on her face and drinking in the outline of her body through the transparent silk of the dress. He could imagine how tight and heavy her stomach must feel after the hours of stimulation by the love balls and the scene that had been played out with Clara. It was all so new to her, and just as he'd heard people say that having children made them see life through new eyes, so he was finding that through Cassandra he was rediscovering his earlier enjoyment of sexual pleasure, an enjoyment which recently had been deserting him.

There was something special about her that he hadn't yet managed to analyse. Innocence alone couldn't explain it; he and Katya had destroyed innocence far too many times now for that alone to affect him. No, it was more than that. Sometimes he thought it was the combination of her rapidly developing sexuality contrasting with an inner core of serenity that he found attractive. For many years now he had lived his life at an ever increasing pace, surrounded by people who were all as frantic for pleasure as he was. He needed companions like that, but Cassandra needed pleasure – that was obvious tonight – yet still kept an inner part of herself placid. He wondered if it would be possible to destroy the serenity, to push her beyond her natural inclinations until sheer shame made future peace of mind impossible. He knew that he'd try to find out, but he wasn't certain he wanted to succeed. He also knew what he wanted tonight, and it was such a rare desire he was excited by its very mundaneness. He wanted to make ordinary love to Cassandra.

Suddenly realising that Cassandra was still standing uncertainly in the middle of her bedroom floor, he quickly stood up and went over to her, turning her round to unfasten the tiny buttons at the back of her dress and then sliding it down her body to the floor. Once that was done he took her hand, helped her step out of it and then brought her round to face him, dressed only in the thin, tight panties that were part of the delicious torment of the love balls.

Keeping his eyes on hers he reached down and felt the material between her thighs. It was very damp and when he pressed upwards she pressed down, trying for greater pressure. 'Wait!' he whispered, leading her across to the bed and getting her to lie on her back while he removed the panties and searched for the tiny thread of the balls, now sticky with her secretions and hidden within the folds of her sex. Finally he found it and began to pull very slowly, stopping when her eyes widened and only beginning again when she managed to relax.

For Cassandra the sensations were delicious. The soft tug on the thread, the way the balls moved gently and heavily through her sensitive channel, and even the way he kept stopping and starting the exercise, were all intensely sensuous experiences.

The baron made the exercise last as long as possible, and each time one of the balls was tugged out of the moist opening, Cassandra's breath would catch and her body would tremble like a leaf in the wind.

When they were finally removed he took off his own clothes and lay on his side next to her, propping himself up on one elbow so that he could look into her face. 'Tell me how you felt tonight,' he said quietly. 'Describe what the love balls did to you. I want to know; I want to share the experience with you.'

She didn't know what to say. How could she tell him about the delicious heavy weight that seemed to fill her belly and thighs? How could she make him understand about the small shocks of pleasure that would ripple across her without warning? She couldn't, and yet he had to be answered.

'It was like being poised at the top of a big dipper all the evening,' she said with a smile. 'I felt as though everything had tightened in anticipation but there was nothing I could do to start the ride.'

He nodded. 'And when you saw the girl, Clara? What did that do to you?'

Cassandra thought back to her first glimpse of the girl as the two other women were arousing her before dinner. 'At first I felt sorry for her. I thought what they were doing was cruel, even though she wasn't really in pain, but then I began to feel excited. When they touched her breasts and they actually began to swell in front of me, I could feel my own breasts swelling too and . . .' She stopped.

'Go on,' said the baron, putting out a hand and lightly stroking the inside of her elbow.

'And I could feel it between my thighs. It made the love balls more obvious because I was tightening there. I knew it was wrong, but I couldn't help it.'

His fingers moved up her arm and into her armpit, playing with the soft dark curls there and stroking the tender flesh at the side of the breast. 'What about after dinner?' he asked.

Cassandra swallowed hard. 'I was afraid,' she admitted.

'Afraid of what?'

'Of what I was going to see, and of how I'd react. I didn't want to disgrace myself in front of you.'

Her nipple was hardening as his fingers brushed the underside of her breast and he bent his head and began to run his tongue down her side in long sweeps. Her legs twitched and she tried to turn on her side to face him but he pushed her back flat. 'How could you have done that, Cassandra?'

'By running away, or not doing what you expected of me.'

'You should be more afraid of Katya.'

'Why? What does she matter to me?' Cassandra asked, finding it difficult to speak while his tongue was trailing so languorously across her waist and hipbone.

'She hates you, and she's quite capable of hurting you very badly physically. I can't save you from that you know. You have to save yourself.'

'She doesn't frighten me. I know she hates me, but you must have known she would or you wouldn't have chosen me, would you?' Cassandra said calmly.

The baron laughed. 'What a clever girl you are! No, of course I wouldn't have done. I wanted someone for Katya to hate.'

Slowly his hand wandered between her thighs and she was so over-excited by the events of the evening that she nearly had a climax there and then. 'No!' he said quickly. 'Wait, breathe slowly. Even when it's just for pleasure you should be slow. Only amateurs rush things, Cassandra!'

She blushed scarlet. 'I can't help it. Everything's so sensitive there.'

He played with her pubic curls for a time, running his fingers through them and tugging now and again so that her whole vulva was softly stimulated. She wriggled, wanting to reach out and touch him but not sure if it was allowed.

He seemed to read her mind because a moment later he moved up the bed a little so that his erection brushed her hip. 'Touch me, Cassandra, but carefully. Get to know me as well as I know you.'

She let her fingers close round the thick stem. Paul hadn't been circumcised, but both the Baron and Peter had, and she preferred this. It made everything much easier, and she was able to move her hand up and down the shaft before allowing her fingertips to run beneath the edge of the sensitive ridge beneath the swollen, plum-coloured head.

The baron smiled at her careful attentions, and while she was occupied with him he inserted three fingers into her and once inside he pressed against the upper wall of the vagina and then rubbed delicately until he saw her belly begin to contract and felt her legs shaking. He increased the pressure and her fingers stopped what they were doing to him as her body began to tighten. He was pleased. Not all women were sensitive there, but he'd found that for most highly sexed women the G-spot gave great pleasure. Probably because of the hours of containing the love balls, Cassandra's vaginal walls were already unusually responsive to his touch, and within moments he'd brought her to her first climax of the evening.

It was a different kind of sensation for Cassandra. A deeper, yet less shattering kind of release, but the pleasure was glorious. After that the baron used his tongue on her, keeping her thighs apart with his hands as he teased and titillated her so that her body was shaken by contraction after contraction until she begged him to stop.

He obeyed, and came back to lie beside her, his hungry mouth now concentrating on her breasts and neck. Then he turned her over and licked all down her spine, his tongue lingering in the hollow at the base. The feeling was so beautiful that Cassandra cried out, her whole body seeming to glow but she was also aware of an increasing pressure on her bladder and tried to turn onto her back again.

This time the baron not only knew what was happening but had the chance to take advantage of it. 'No, stay there,' he murmured and quickly fetched a small cushion, similar to the one Katya had put beneath Lucy, which he then slid under Cassandra's hips, spreading her outer sex lips wide as he did so which meant that her protruding clitoris was forced against the material and so continually stimulated.

'This is one of the best ways to have a climax, Cassandra,' he promised her, licking between the small bones at the bottom of her back. 'Everything is intensified.' His tongue made her need the bathroom even more, but she could also feel the burgeoning tightness within her and her whole body was becoming heavy and swollen.

His clever, knowing hand rose up beneath her, between the cushion and the base of her stomach, and he pressed gently on the flesh so that the bladder felt even more full and sent tingling signals to Cassandra.

Unlike poor Lucy however, this night was purely for pleasure and so the baron didn't delay until it became painful, instead his fingers moved on and found the clitoris, still stiff from the stimulation of the small cushion. He caressed it with a finger moistened by his own saliva while the heel of his hand kept up the pressure on the nerve endings from the bladder and Cassandra felt her stomach swelling and the moisture seeping from her secret opening as her excitement mounted until it was unbearable and she began to buck frantically, trying to bring about the great pleasure he'd promised her.

Deftly the baron continued to increase all the pressure and at the last moment he swirled his tongue in circles at the very base of her spine. This incredibly delicate stimulation was the signal for everything to explode, and Cassandra's slim body bucked off the cushion as the ecstasy reached its wonderful, pulsating crescendo.

As she reared up, the baron grasped her buttocks, pulled the jerking body nearer to him and entered her from behind, sliding into the pulsating warmth of her with a groan of satisfaction and making sure his cunning fingers continued their manipulation of her clitoris until finally her contractiions were sharp enough to start his second ejaculation of the evening, only this time his whole body was suffused with the orgasm right down to his toes and he heard himself moan with the force of his own contractions until at last they both collapsed in a heap on the bed.

After a few minutes, the baron rolled off Cassandra and pulled her onto her back so that he could look into her face and see for himself the smile of satisfaction in her eyes, the parted lips and the beads of sweat on her temples and top lip.

Gently he bent down and kissed her on the mouth, letting his tongue trace the outline of her top lip before drawing away. Then he put a hand on each side of her face in a rare gesture of intimacy for him. 'There, you see, wasn't it as good as I promised?'

'Yes,' gasped Cassandra, who had scarcely got her breath back. 'It was incredible. I've never felt anything so . . .' Words failed her, and she simply smiled up at him with a look of such gratitude that he could hardly bear it.

'Why were you so reluctant?' he asked curiously. Cassandra told him about Lucy and he nodded. 'Well Lucy probably enjoyed the day more than you thought. People have strange needs, Cassandra, but Katya's needs sometimes do involve more pain than the other participants enjoy. That's what I want you to understand.'

Cassandra sighed and stretched. 'I do,' she assured him.

'Tomorrow,' said the baron, finding himself strangely reluctant to leave the contented young woman's bedroom, 'we'll all get to know each other better.' He felt her body stiffen, as though she was drawing away from him, but there was no point in hiding the truth; he felt that making love to her tonight had been an indulgence on his part that shouldn't be allowed to mislead her.

'You mean we all have sex together,' she said at last, her voice carefully controlled.

'Yes, in various permutations. Some you'll enjoy more than others, of course, but I believe it's important to try everything at least once.'

'Everything?'

He heard a note of panic behind the query. 'Was there something in particular that you didn't want to try?'

Cassandra hesitated. If she told him then she was putting herself at his mercy; if she didn't tell him then she couldn't complain if he put her in a position where refusal would mean banishment for her. She decided to trust him and opened her mouth, but he quickly put a large hand across it, muffling her words. 'The walls have ears, Cassandra. Always remember that. Perhaps I can keep a secret and perhaps I can't, but that may not matter. There are some things it's better to keep to yourself.'

'Then why did you ask me?' she demanded.

'To see if you would actually tell of course.'

She looked into his face, studying the mixture of features that made him so unusual; the round face was at odds with the sharply defined high cheekbones and arched brows, the boyish smile in marked contrast to the look of world-weary experience in the eyes, and then there was his voice. It was so soft, so deceptively quiet, that when it hardened or was raised the shock was great. He was as enigmatic in outward ways as inward ones, but it didn't matter; Cassandra knew that she was fatally drawn to him and that if she ever had to leave his house there would never be any other man for her.

'What are you thinking?' he queried, sitting up and groping for his watch.

'I was wondering what Rupert and Françoise were doing,' she lied.

He laughed. 'Driving Lucy insane, I imagine. She'll be useless tomorrow; asleep on her feet no doubt. It's always the same when they're here.'

'What will happen to Clara now?'

The baron pulled on his shirt and frowned. 'Clara?'

'Yes, the girl you deflowered tonight.'

'What a wonderful expression deflowered is. Yes of course, I remember her name now. As to what will happen to her, why the same as happens to all Rupert's little toys. She'll be played with for a few more weeks and then abandoned when something new catches his eye.'

'Don't you think that's cruel?'

His eyes twinkled. 'Yes, it probably is, but in this life there are always victims. Clara is a born victim. No doubt her stepfather will take over her education once he returns from his honeymoon. Knowing Claud's particular tastes the mother must only have been the passport to the daughter, but he wouldn't have wanted her totally inexperienced, hence the loan to Rupert.'

Cassandra fell silent.

'Nothing more to say?' he asked. 'Then I must get some sleep, and so must you. Sleep well, *liebling*.' With this brief, unexpected endearment he left her satisfied in body but deeply disturbed in her mind.

Everyone in the household rose late the next day. It was past ten before Cassandra woke, but she was still the first one down to breakfast. As the baron had guessed, Lucy was pale and heavy-eyed as she served breakfast yet she still smiled cheerfully at Cassandra with no hint of the knowledge they shared in her pretty, open face.

While Cassandra was eating toast and marmalade, Françoise came in wearing a tiny pair of white shorts which emphasised her long, tanned legs and a scarlet bikini top that only just covered her nipples. She gave Cassandra a strange look but didn't greet her.

'Did you sleep well?' Cassandra asked politely.

There was a wonderfully Gallic shrug from the former child of the Brazilian slums. 'I suppose yes, probably not as well as you but undoubtedly better than Katya.' This time there was no possible doubt that the expression in her eyes was one of surprise. It was clear that Cassandra wasn't turning out at all as Françoise had expected, and she looked as though this intrigued rather than annoyed her.

'I wouldn't know.'

Françoise smiled. 'Of course you know. Katya was expecting Dieter to spend the rest of the night with her. She was probably hoping that the four of us would go to the gym and play with the equipment. You spoilt all that for her. She'll be furious with you today.'

'I think the baron decides for himself what he'll do,' Cassandra responded, but she sounded far more calm than she felt.

Just then, Katya came in. Her summer dress was short and fitted like a second skin, emphasising every soft curve and her hair had been carefully dressed and teased to a tousled, come-to-bed style. She kissed Françoise on both cheeks while ignoring Cassandra.

'Dieter's promised me we can work out in the gym this afternoon,' she told Françoise. 'He and Rupert are going to the shooting range this afternoon and I thought we three girls could use the time for a workout. He said we must be careful not to exhaust ourselves as tonight will be busy, but a light workout should refresh us all – blow the night's cobwebs away.'

Françoise nodded. 'That sounds perfect. Cassandra?'

'I'd enjoy that,' Cassandra said, knowing very well that she wouldn't but that it had to be faced and she preferred it to be sooner rather than later.

'Wonderful!' Katya enthused, and after that she contented herself with drinking endless cups of coffee and lying out on a sunbed totally nude while Peter regularly covered her in sun oil and massaged her already taut limbs.

The baron and Rupert appeared briefly around midday, promised to be back by six in the evening and then left for the shooting. As he passed Cassandra, the baron gave her a brief, warning glance but whether it was to caution her against talking about the previous night or warning her about the dangers of the gym she didn't know. However, she knew that even that one intimate look would help her through whatever Katya had planned in the gym.

The gym was spacious and air-conditioned with wall bars, rowing machines, bicycles, weights and numerous other pieces of apparatus that meant nothing to Cassandra who'd only ever been to group keep-fit at her local village hall. To begin with the two other women did some skipping while Cassandra tested out the treadmill, which she privately felt was a poor substitute for a walk in the fresh air.

'I'm going to let the machine exercise me now,' Katya declared when she'd finished skipping. 'Help me get it adjusted, Françoise. Then you can have a go.'

Françoise helped Katya onto a raised couch covered by a soft cushion and then adjusted the hand and leg fastenings to suit her friend's body length before pressing a button set at the side. Very gently the couch began to vibrate, the bottom half back and forth so that Katya's spine was carefully stretched, easing out any knots of tension.

'It's a wonderful feeling,' Françoise told the watching Cassandra. 'You should try it some time. You look rather tense today!'

'I feel perfectly relaxed, but I wouldn't mind a go later on.'

Françoise smiled, then peeled off her shocking pink leotard and sat in the rowing machine without a trace of self-consciousness. 'I get far too hot wearing that,' she explained. Cassandra couldn't help noticing that the Brazilian woman's breasts were surprisingly large for her slender frame, with amazing coffee-coloured, cone-shaped nipples.

Françoise saw her looking and laughed. 'Do you like them? They cost Rupert a fortune but he thinks they're worth every penny. Feel them; you won't be able to tell they're not real.'

On the moving couch, Katya lifted her head. 'She won't want to touch them. Wait for me to do that, Françoise. You know how I adore your breasts.'

Françoise ignored her. 'Touch them!' she encouraged Cassandra. 'If you really like them Dieter might buy you a pair as well.'

Slowly Cassandra reached out and let her fingers close round the soft tissue. Françoise was right, she would never have guessed that they were implants. There was no suggestion of unnatural hardness, but as her fingers explored more carefully the nipples hardened and Françoise smiled lazily. 'I think they like you; you've got a very erotic touch, as I'm sure Dieter's told you.'

There was a hiss of irritation from Katya, and Cassandra knew perfectly well that Françoise was deliberately annoying her friend. When she withdrew her hand, Françoise began to row, her slim arms unexpectedly strong.

'Did the babies make much difference to your body?' Cassandra asked, sitting on one of the cycling machines and settling into the comfort of the sheepskin saddle.

'Ugh, yes. I became hideously bloated. I shall never have any more, but Rupert needed an heir and luckily I gave him two in one go. What is it your aristocracy say? "An heir and a spare"?'

'I wouldn't know!' Cassandra laughed.

'I shan't ever have any children, thank God,' Katya announced. 'After Marietta had Christina she was plunged into one of those dreary depressions women get and Dieter was so fed up with her he had a vasectomy. I think he regrets it now, after all most men

164

want a boy, but at least I don't have to worry about taking precautions.'

Françoise looked across to where Cassandra was cycling. 'Did you know that?' she asked mischievously.

'No, but why should it interest me?'

'I thought perhaps you had hoped to give him children yourself.'

'She's just an employee!' Katya snapped. 'I've had enough of this now. Let me out, Françoise.'

Françoise obliged and swapped places with her friend, so that it was now Katya's turn to row. She too pulled off her leotard, displaying her small neatly rounded body with obvious pride in front of Cassandra. 'Why don't you take your clothes off?' she asked. 'Can't you stand the competition or are you still shy?'

'No, I just hadn't thought about it.'

'Then take it off,' Katya ordered.

Realising this was some kind of challenge Cassandra climbed down from the bike, stripped off her leotard and then climbed back on. This time she was acutely aware of the feel of the sheepskin against her unprotected vulva, and the gentle tickling sensation was highly arousing. She felt her neck and chest begin to flush with the stimulation, and bent her head to try and conceal it from Katya, but the other woman's eyes were too experienced to miss the signs she'd been hoping for.

'I think Cassandra should have a turn on the relaxer now, Françoise,' she suggested, and Cassandra was quite grateful for the chance to get off the saddle. Françoise smiled to herself as Cassandra climbed on top of the couch, innocently stretching up her arms and spreading her legs so that her wrists and ankles could be put in the straps.

When the machine began she found it wondefully relaxing and thought that if this was exercise she could probably become addicted, but after only a very few minutes she realised that the other two women were standing on either side of her and she watched Katya put out a hand to press the stop button while Françoise swiftly and expertly pulled the thick protective cushion away from under Cassandra's body.

She gasped as her bare flesh met the cold metal of the table top, but even worse was the realisation that it wasn't a solid table. In the top half there were two round holes, and even while she was trying to work out what they were for, Katya pulled a heavy strap tight across her shoulder blades, forcing her chest down hard against the holes while Françoise slid beneath the table so that she could reach up and caress Cassandra's nipples through the holes.

'Don't do that!' Cassandra exclaimed furiously. 'I want to get off.'

'We'll get you off!' Katya laughed harshly. 'That's the whole idea of this afternoon. Dieter's obviously been teaching your body how to enjoy itself, so I thought we'd join in the lessons.'

Françoise was touching the nipples very lightly, and licking at them with the tip of her tongue so that they quickly became erect. She then grasped them together with the surrounding flesh and pulled hard, which hurt Cassandra and forced her down on the table so that her breasts went as far through the holes as possible.

She knew that they were now totally vulnerable to whatever the two women chose to do to them and she began to panic, but even as her fear grew, she heard Françoise move beneath the table, and suddenly the long, brown fingers were reaching up through another hole further down the table, just at the same time as Katya pulled hard on the final piece of strapping which thrust Cassandra's hips painfully down and enabled the Brazilian woman to burrow upwards between Cassandra's outer sex lips, searching for the entrance.

Her fingers were no longer soft and it hurt. Cassandra struggled to draw away, but the strapping was broad and strong and she couldn't move at all. With a laugh, Katya disappeared from sight and a few seconds later her tiny teeth were busy nibbling on Cassandra's breasts while Françoise's fingers kept up their insistent probing until at last she was able to force two of them inside their hapless victim.

Fear and tension had dried up the juices that the sheepskin saddle had drawn forth, and tears filled Cassandra's eyes as the fingers moved roughly around, pushing upwards as though trying to reach back to the entrance to the cervix and making no attempt to give her any pleasure.

'She's still very tight,' Françoise said at last. 'Perhaps that's what Dieter likes.'

'Her breasts are awfully small,' Katya commented, and then the fingers were withdrawn from within Cassandra and the two women sat whispering together under the table while Cassandra trembled in fear and wondered what they intended to do to her in the time they had before the men returned. She realised that the baron must have known that something like this would happen, he might even have gone out in order to let it happen, and for a moment she hated him.

Suddenly, the two women reappeared beside her. 'We have to fetch some things,' Katya said, her voice sugar-sweet. 'While we're gone, we'll let you have some more relaxation.' Before Cassandra could grasp the implications of this the 'On' button was pressed, and the machine began to move again, only this time her breasts were cruelly imprisoned in the holes of the metal and every movement wrenched them, shooting pain through her breasts like red hot flames. The tugging sensation was enormous and on the downward pull Cassandra feared her breasts would be dragged out, the nipples tearing on the edge of the metal holes, but the women knew the equipment well and it was impossible for the breasts to come free. All Cassandra could do was lie there and feel her soft flesh moving about within the restrictions while the continuing motion rubbed her sex lips over the lower hole forcing her other lips apart and opening her up more for the women when they returned. She lifted her head as they came back through the door. They were both carrying things in their arms but she couldn't make out what they were because everything was covered by towels.

'I hoped that helped calm you down,' Katya said sweetly, switching off the machine. 'Now, we've got some surprises for you.' Cassandra tensed, her breath coming in nervous gasps that made the breasts swing tantalisingly in front of Françoise and Katya as they sat beneath the couch. They looked at the tiny pink petals of her nipples and smiled at each other, then Katya took the lid off a round jar and as steam rose from it she quickly dipped in a piece of flannel and then with a swift flick of the wrist wrapped the heated material round Cassandra's right nipple, moulding it carefully round the ultra-sensitive tip and on round the small, softly curved breast.

Cassandra, totally unprepared, went rigid with shock as a terrible burning heat spread through her tender breast tissue, and she had to bite her lip against the initial pain. Katya waited a few moments, watching how the other breast had puckered in fear and enjoying the sight of her rival's vulnerable feminine curves dangling in her power.

As the material began to cool, and Cassandra began to breathe more easily, Katya quickly removed it and immediately Françoise grasped a handful of ice cubes from the ice bucket she'd brought with her and cupped her two hands round the blotched, red skin of the tiny breast.

The shock was so great that for a moment Cassandra couldn't breathe. When she finally got her breath back it came in gasping pants, but the extremes of temperature had actually aroused her cleverly tortured flesh, and her nipple had hardened dramatically so that when Françoise finally opened her hands and let the melting cubes fall to the ground, she saw for herself the way the originally pink bud was now a rock-hard red point. Reaching up she licked away the water the ice cubes had left behind knowing from Cassandra's increasingly rapid breathing that her body was responding.

The two women then waited for a time, chatting quietly to one another while Cassandra waited tensely above them, knowing that it would eventually happen to her other breast and dreading the terrible heat and yet longing for the coolness of the ice and the kind tongue that would follow.

When the heat did come, it seemed even greater than before; she assumed this was because the first breast was now ice cold and shrinking, and once again the globe glowed and swelled, but the pain didn't seem as obvious this time because she was anticipating the next stage. It was Katya's turn to apply the ice, and she pressed more firmly than Françoise against the glowing skin, but even so currents of pleasure shot through the nipple and when Katya's tongue touched it, Cassandra gave a sigh of gratitude. This was a mistake because Katya promptly closed her teeth and bit sharply on the tiny, abused bud causing pain to jolt through it as though she'd been stabbed with a burning needle. Again tears filled her eyes, but at the borders of the pain there was still pleasure; pleasure that shamed her.

After that the women moved lower, and now it was easy for Françoise to insert her fingers into Cassandra's opening, and she moved them quickly from side to side, a movement that didn't exactly hurt but didn't give pleasure either. However, it opened her wider and made her moist, ready for Katya's next little toy.

This Katya wanted Cassandra to see, and while Françoise's fingers remained steadily busy she stood up and put a hand beneath Cassandra's chin, lifting her head until she could see what her tormentor held in her hand. It was a large, marble replica of a penis, smooth, cold and incredibly thick, so wide that even the thought of it entering her made Cassandra shudder.

'Perhaps after this you won't feel quite so tight for Dieter any more,' Katya said with an unpleasant smile. She stroked the cool marble against Cassandra's hot cheeks, and saw the smears where her earlier tears had fallen. 'I hope you won't cry this time. Crying isn't allowed in this house, you know.'

Cassandra didn't answer her, she was too busy trying to close her mind against the intrusion that was to come. Katya let the marble penis roll across the back of Cassandra's neck and then with a smile disappeared beneath the table again as Cassandra's hips tried despairingly to pull away from the couch and remove her opening from the women's reach.

'She's as ready as she's going to be,' Françoise said, craning her neck and letting her tongue flick inside the hole where her fingers had just been so busy. Cassandra's muscles jerked and she laughed. 'She certainly likes tongues, but then Dieter's an expert at that, isn't he!'

Angrily, Katya pushed her friend out of the way and carefully lined up the head of the imitation phallus with the exposed opening, then she brushed aside the surrounding curls of dark pubic hair and let her cool hand rest against the nervously flinching opening. 'Are you ready, Cassie?' she asked sweetly.

Above her, Cassandra was rigid with fear. Her abdomen refused to relax, and she knew she was making it worse for herself, but letting her see the thickness of the implement had been a clever move and she was incapable of assisting her body to accept it. With agonising slowness, Katya edged the rounded head in, letting it slide steadily but making sure the entrance was gradual to maximise her opponent's mental as well as physical agony.

As Katya had known would happen, for a second or two Cassandra thought that her eyes had deceived her and the marble penis wasn't as thick as she'd feared, but just as she began to let herself believe this, Katya pushed sharply so that the thick dildo forced its way in another inch. This time Cassandra did cry out because the width in her relatively unaroused state was too much and she felt as though she must tear if the insertion continued.

Katya, however, knew better than to damage Cassandra physically although she'd calculated that psychologically this would certainly limit the other girl's responses to any penetration by the men that evening. She'd be slightly sore physically, but mentally she'd be terrified of being entered again so soon.

With Machiavellian cunning, she slowly turned the marble inside Cassandra's frantically stretching inner passage, then pressed steadily so that it moved another half inch deeper, only to be turned and held steady. Then Cassandra would be given a respite, so that she thought it was over, until it would all begin again.

The dildo was some six inches in length, and Katya managed to take half an hour over inserting its full length and all the time, Françoise continued to play her own games with the dangling, irresistible little breasts. Sometimes she used the flannel and the ice, sometimes she sucked on ice herself and then suckled the nipples and from time to time she'd slap the distended breasts lightly with her fingers, watching them move from side to side and enjoying the way they burgeoned despite what Katya was doing to Cassandra elsewhere.

As for Cassandra, all she could do was endure. Françoise's attentions were a welcome distraction from the discomfort of the thick marble dildo, but at times she wished that she could pass out and spoil Katya's game. However, Katya was far too clever for that. Finally, when the mock penis was fully inserted, Katya got Françoise to hold it in place while she stood up and pressed a release button by the machine that made the lower half of the table drop down. Cassandra cried out in alarm as her lower body moved and the muscles of her arms screamed in protest as they were extended to their limits. Now she was almost standing on the floor, her legs still fastened at the ankles, while her upper torso was stretched out parallel with the ground, her breasts continuing to hang down through the holes, and Françoise was gripping the thick marble stem of the dildo so that there was no ease from the pressure there.

Katya was about to finish off her little game. She moved across the gym and returned with a thick leather strap which she showed to her terrified, bewildered victim. 'You'll enjoy this, Cassie. I don't think you've been allowed the pleasures of the strap before, but most girls find it irresistible, particularly when their love channel is already full, and yours is very full, isn't it?' At that moment Françoise pressed slightly on the marble stem and Cassandra gasped. 'Yes, I thought it was,' Katya murmured, letting one hand slide over the gap down Cassandra's spine where it was exposed between the two straps that were holding her. 'What a tender spine you have. Dieter loves it, doesn't he?'

Cassandra remembered the tender way the baron had licked her there the night before and hot tears filled her eyes. 'Remember, no more tears,' Katya cautioned, and then she walked away to stand behind the tautly stretched girl, taking pleasure in the way the feet could hardly touch the ground, forcing her up onto her toes and making the leg muscles tremble with tension. She was thrilled by the way Cassandra's body was bent sharply at the waist where the table divided, which meant the cheeks of her bottom were slightly parted and fully exposed.

For a moment she stood and studied the lean body, then she raised her arm and brought the leather down hard on the back of Cassandra's thighs.

Cassandra screamed, her head snapped up and her hips tried unsuccessfully to press further into the table, but it was hopeless and Katya was free to take her time. She used the strap with infinite skill and cunning until the backs of Cassandra's legs, thighs and buttocks were covered in pink stripes that never quite overlaid each other. Every blow caused a burning pain that made her want to scream, but as they continued the burning started to merge into one and the whole area felt heated and sensitised. Slowly the muscles of her rectum began contracting with each blow, and the contractions built their own tension, a tension that was magnified by the relentless pressure of the marble dildo being held firmly in place by Françoise.

Cassandra had never experienced feelings like it. Every part of her seemed either burning hot or heavy and full. Slowly she forgot the pain because it wasn't pain, it was a strange, dark pleasure that had her moaning in a different way, a plea not for mercy but for sexual release. Katya heard the change in the cries and she quickly called for Lucy, who had been waiting outside the gym all the time in case she was needed. She ran swiftly across the room and at a sign from Katya, pulled Cassandra's small, hard buttocks apart so that the dark inner ring was revealed.

For a moment, Katya turned the leather strap and let the side of it trail down the gap the maid had exposed. Cassandra let out a gasp and both Katya and Lucy saw how the tight mouth of her bottom was pulsing with excitement. Beneath the table, Françoise heard the gasp. She gripped the marble dildo more firmly and slid a finger of her other hand up through the couch hole and along the now widened channel between the inner lips so that she was poised over the previously untouched clitoris.

The moment had finally come for Katya. She swung back her arm and brought the leather strap down between the parted cheeks of the bottom, leaving a burning mark through the centre of the tiny throbbing dark hole between them, and at that final lash of pain Cassandra's abused but pulsating body expanded until she thought she would split open like an overripe plum if she didn't find some kind of release. Françoise knew what was happening and swiftly flicked at the exposed clitoris with one of her long fingernails as she turned the thick stem of the dildo, sliding its marble across the over-stretched vaginal walls.

With an ear-splitting scream, Cassandra's body burst. Every part of her seemed to turn to liquid fire and the dreadful aching pressure that had been building within her, the mixture of pain and pleasure that she had never before experienced, was finally released dissolving into sweetness as her racked body collapsed against the cold top of the couch. She sobbed with a terrible shamed ecstasy, accepting that after this there was no going back. Katya and Françoise had taken her down a path she would never have chosen, but along with pain and mortification she had discovered blissful pleasure and a bitter-sweet glimpse of a dark side of herself that from now on would always need feeding.

In total silence Françoise and Katya picked up their belongings and vanished leaving Lucy to release Cassandra. She handed her a towelling robe and guided her towards the hot shower where she could try to wash away the worst of the afternoon's excesses, but there were some things that couldn't be washed away; the new knowledge she'd gained about herself, and the fear that Katya had hoped to instil but which Cassandra did not yet understand. A fear that would only reveal itself that night, at the worst possible moment in the baron's game.

# Chapter Nine

The baron lay on his narrow single bed in the room that only he ever used and watched the proceedings in the gym in silence. He'd never intended to go shooting. Rupert had an appointment with an ex-girlfriend and the baron had wanted to see how Katya chose to punish Cassandra for the night he'd spent with her.

When it was all over and Cassandra finally left the shower and walked with her head down towards her own room, he switched off his television set and stared thoughtfully into the distance. Katya had been clever. There had been pain and punishment, but not enough to anger him, and there had been pleasure for Cassandra, a new kind of pleasure that would confuse her. But he was also very well aware of the effect the afternoon would have had on her when it came to the night, and her introduction to sex with Rupert and Françoise as well as himself and Katya. She'd be afraid of the men, afraid of them causing her pain in those delicate secret places which would still be sore from Katya's marble toy.

Crossing to the window he stared out into the garden. Françoise was already lying in the sun again, letting Lucy rub suntan cream into her as she sipped from a tall glass of Bacardi and coke, but there was no sign of Katya. Rupert wouldn't be back for another hour or so, and the baron knew that he must soon join his long-term mistress in their room.

He'd never found Rupert's wife particularly attractive, but her undisguised sexuality always excited him. Katya had once attracted him; he'd enjoyed the unexpected curves of her apparently small frame, and the fierce passion that he knew she harboured for him but kept so tightly in check. Now she was beginning to bore him. If she won the game he'd be most disappointed, but he'd accept it, otherwise there was no point in playing. On the other hand, the rules were his and it might well be that he would load the dice in Cassandra's favour occasionally. He'd always cheated at bridge and poker, and this was no different as long as it didn't occur too often.

His mind made easier by this decision, he quietly closed his bedroom door and walked along to the room he shared with Katya. She was coming out of the sauna, a towel wrapped round her hair like a turban which emphasised her cat-like eyes that dominated the triangular face. When she saw him she smiled contentedly.

'You're just in time to see a wonderful video, darling. Françoise and I have had such a lovely afternoon in the gym, but I'm afraid Cassandra wasn't too well behaved. She cried several times.'

He didn't tell her that he'd been watching it all as it happened, knowing that she would probably have doctored the tape that he was to see and interested to find out what she omitted.

'How interesting,' he drawled, taking off his jacket and lying face down across the bed.

'Was the shooting good? Did you win?' Katya wasn't interested in shooting, but she knew that Dieter always liked to win.

'We didn't shoot. Rupert met an old friend and I wandered round London looking at all the pretty girls in their skimpy summer dresses.' He smiled at her.

Katya's eyes narrowed. She didn't believe him for a moment. If he hadn't gone shooting then he'd probably been with another woman, and although it was most likely only an old flame, or a friend of the thankfully dead Marietta, she was still jealous. 'Aren't you a little old to be eyeing the girls in the park?' she teased.

His gaze swept over her. 'Men don't age as quickly as women,' he said shortly. She flushed. 'So, where is the tape?' he continued. 'I am very interested in seeing Cassandra cry.'

Katya inserted a video tape and then went away to choose an outfit for dinner. When she returned he was lying just as she'd left him, with his elbows on the bed and his chin resting on his hand.

'Has she cried yet?' Katya asked eagerly, snuggling down next to him and feeling a sense of relief when he put an arm casually round her bare waist.

'Yes, for the first time. The hot cloth seems to have surprised her!'

'Her breasts are tiny,' Katya said.

The baron laughed and slid a hand over hers. 'I don't think these are enormous, my darling!'

'At least they're like a woman's breasts. Hers are more like a child's.'

'I know.' He sounded pleased, but his fingers were working busily on Katya's nipples and she wriggled nearer to him. When she pressed herself down the length of his side he turned and let his hand sweep across her stomach and flanks, but his eyes never left the screen and she knew she only had half his attention.

When it came to the marble dildo, Katya had decided to remove the section where she showed it to Cassandra because she thought her lover might be annoyed at the width of it. As a result, all the film showed was Cassandra's tears as the insertion began below the table, out of sight of the camera.

'There you are, she's crying again!' Katya gloated. 'Hardly the way for a governess to behave. It isn't as though we were really hurting her.'

'What were you using?' Dieter asked lazily, his hand still wandering over Katya's bare body.

'The blue vibrator.'

'She doesn't seem to be vibrating very much!'

Katya cursed herself for her stupidity. 'No, not the vibrator, the blue dildo. I think she was just too tense. Women don't seem to be quite to her taste yet. She definitely prefers men.'

'So I should hope. Do you prefer women then?' Abruptly he turned and stared at her, his brown eyes distinctly unfriendly.

'Of course not!' Katya exclaimed. 'I only like them as a change, or when you're not here.'

'You like them young and untried, and you enjoy hurting them. That's something you can't get with men. I shall soon feel redundant,' the baron said.

Before Katya could answer the film moved on to where the bottom half of the table top dropped, bending Cassandra down from her waist and her shocked cry drew the baron's eyes back to the film. He watched what followed in total silence, but Katya could see the pulse in his neck beating rapidly and knew that he was excited by it all.

'There, wasn't that a nice present before dinner?' she asked teasingly.

'For me or for Cassandra?'

'I don't give employees presents.'

He laughed. 'Yes you do; you're always making a fuss of Lucy and she's an employee.'

'But not a participant in the game,' Katya said in a hard voice. 'I'm not stupid enough to give an opponent a present.'

'I'd have thought the blue dildo qualified as a present,' the baron said dryly, and watched his mistress's face tighten as she realised that he knew she'd been lying.

'I'm going to wear the red trouser suit tonight!' she exclaimed, jumping off the bed and sitting down in front of the make-up mirror. 'I shall get Lucy to put my hair up to make me look taller as well; I think trousers look better on tall women.'

The baron flicked off the video and turned to the live camera, switching to Cassandra's room. She was lying face down on her bed, apparently resting, but he had the feeling she was crying silently. He gave a small sigh and switched to Rupert's room. His friend had still not returned, and Françoise was crouched in front of a chair where Clara was sitting naked from the waist up as her employer used the hot flannel and ice routine that had just been demonstrated on the film, on the young girl's large breasts.

Clara's eyes were wide open. She didn't appear to be enjoying either the pain of the hot cloth or the contrasting ice cubes and once or twice she tried to get out of the chair but Françoise simply pushed her back, slapping the raw breasts sharply at the same time.

After she'd tired of the treatment she took two pieces of cord from a sewing box and tied them in loops that ran under Clara's breasts. At the top they clipped on to the end of what looked like a tiny dog lead that in turn was attached to a small collar which she fastened round the girl's neck. The result was two very red and swollen globes thrusting out of tight bands and held up and away from the ribcage to make an easier target for Françoise.

The baron could see that when Françoise began to delicately brush the wretched Clara's nipples with a sable brush the breasts swelled even more, the cords tightened and Clara tried to bend her head forward to ease the tension. Françoise told her sharply to sit up straight, and then continued with the brushing until Clara began moaning with pleasure, at which point Rupert came into the room. Immediately Françoise dropped the brush and ran to her husband, kissing him deeply on the mouth and moulding her hips against his while Clara's breasts stood out proudly waiting for further attention.

It seemed though that they weren't going to get it,

179

because Rupert was already thrusting his hands beneath his wife's skirt and as he started to unfasten his belt, Dieter switched off the set. He wondered how Clara would enjoy the swift, raw coupling she was undoubtedly about to witness. Probably not much in her aroused state. He smiled.

It was eight-thirty before they all sat down to dinner, including Clara who looked so sullen that the baron assumed her breasts had never received any further attention. Françoise wasn't really as cruel as Katya; she simply had a short attention span, and if Rupert had proved more interesting at that moment she'd probably forgotten Clara until it was time for them to dress for dinner.

The young girl's dress was a bad choice he thought. Far too tight and flowery for her shape, but at least he could see her large breasts through the material, and they were naked beneath it. He remembered the sable brush and smiled at her. Clara, her nipples still tingling and aroused, unsatisfied and yet further tantalised by the feel of the dress against them, looked at him with a pleading expression in her eyes. He'd given her such pleasure the night before she couldn't help but hope he'd do so again tonight, but although the baron smiled back he knew that Clara wouldn't be joining them later.

Cassandra, wearing a cream dress with large scarlet poppies on it, looked calm and composed. Her dark hair was drawn back in a chignon again, and he couldn't wait to take out the pins and watch it fall to her shoulders. She was wearing make-up, but it was subtle, whereas Katya's was heavy tonight and she positively glittered with rings and bracelets while her red silk trouser suit dominated the table, outshining even Françoise who for once had forsaken her multi-coloured outfits for a coffee-coloured shift with a plunging neckline and side buttons which were only fastened half way down her thigh.

'How did you spend your afternoon, Cassandra?' the

baron asked when a short silence had fallen round the table.

Cassandra glanced up at him. 'I worked out in the gym with Katya and Françoise.'

'And did you enjoy it?'

'Yes, it was . . .' She paused, and he waited as did the other two women. 'It was a new routine for me,' she concluded. 'I think I actually prefer swimming.'

The baron remembered the night he and Katya had played with her in the pool and he smiled at her clever reply. 'Then you must swim more often. Katya prefers the gym I think, but for myself the pool is always an attraction.'

Rupert, well aware that there were undercurrents beneath these seemingly innocuous words, decided to join in. 'I like swimming too. We must have a three-some. Françoise can only paddle, can't you, *chérie*?'

'I hate the water,' Françoise responded with an exaggerated shiver. 'So damp and cold.'

'Of course it's damp, it's water!' her husband laughed, and even Clara smiled.

After coffee and brandy, Clara was sent up to the third floor to look after the babies while the Scottish nanny had a break. The five adults moved to the drawing room where they all talked for a time about apparently famous people that Cassandra had never even heard of, let alone met.

Eventually, the baron glanced at his watch. 'I think we should all go upstairs. Tonight is just a friendly get-together. Tomorrow night I've decided there must be a competition but I'm not yet sure exactly what it will be.'

'Knowing you, I can hardly wait to hear,' Françoise laughed, slipping an arm through his. 'Anyway, a friendly get-together sounds wonderful, doesn't it, Rupert?'

Rupert couldn't have agreed more. He was longing to possess the slim, withdrawn girl who was obviously fascinating Dieter as well. 'I'm a naturally sociable person!' he laughed; Katya giggled.

'He certainly is,' she told the silent Cassandra. 'Once, when we were staying at the château in the Loire, Rupert was "sociable" with seven girls in one night. Of course, he was younger then!'

'I don't remember that,' Françoise said.

'We hadn't met, *chérie*, otherwise how could I have had the strength?' Rupert grinned. 'It was the last big party we ever had at Dieter's château.'

'Wasn't it for Marietta's birthday?' Katya asked.

Cassandra was surprised to see the baron's eyes cloud over, as though he was blocking out something too painful to recall. 'I believe so. Shall we go then? Lucy will tidy up down here.'

They all hurried up the stairs to the large suite of rooms shared by Katya and Dieter. They entered through the baron's dressing room, and Cassandra hesitated in the doorway through to the large bedroom. The baron put a firm hand in the middle of her back and silently urged her through.

Françoise looked about her. 'You've got a new bed! It's even bigger than the last one. Does it still have all the rings round?' She checked, and squealed with pleasure when she located them. 'Yes! How exciting. Do you remember that maid – Suzanne was it? – and how we kept her imprisoned for three days with only Rupert to see to her needs. Do you still have that tape? It was one of the best weekends we've spent here.'

'Perhaps we can make this one even better,' the baron said, quickly starting to take off his clothes and signalling for Cassandra to do the same. She obeyed automatically, but although she'd drunk plenty of wine with her meal and brandy after, she was still afraid.

There was an ache between her thighs that nothing could erase, and as she stripped off her clothes she knew that the outlines of the stripes from the leather strap must still be visible to the other four in the room. Françoise was too busy performing a slow, erotic striptease to notice, but Katya saw and smiled to herself while Rupert noticed and wondered if it was Dieter who'd inflicted the marks the night before. If so he'd take extra pleasure in kissing them slowly during the night, in contrast to his friend's crueller attentions.

When Katya took off her silk trouser suit she was naked beneath it, and ran her hands down her body letting them linger just above her pubic bone while she moved her hips suggestively against them.

Rupert always enjoyed Katya's body. Her round curves sat so unexpectedly on the otherwise lean frame, and there was nothing soft in her nature, which made the feminine physical traits all the more arousing. The other good thing about Katya was that you could never hurt her too much. Françoise hated to be marked or really hurt, although she was quite willing to do it to other people. With Katya he could release all his pent-up desires to inflict pain and not have to worry about her feelings.

Not that pain was the first thing on his mind tonight. Tonight he wanted to get to know Cassandra. To enjoy for himself her relatively inexperienced body, and to teach her some new experiences so that she always remembered him.

Once they were all naked they fell onto the bed in a group, but Cassandra had to be pulled on by the other two women because her instinct was to hang back. This only inflamed Rupert all the more, while the baron's intelligent eyes watched, assessed and made their judgements.

For Cassandra it was an appalling moment. She'd managed to get through the experience of being given sexual pleasure while people looked on, and of having more than one person to pleasure her at once, but this was the first time she'd had to actively join in with group sex and it was hard.

The baron didn't help. He let the other women start caressing her, watching as their hands and mouths went to work on Cassandra while Rupert began kneading Katya's buttocks with his strong hands, pausing now and again to insert a finger into her rectum, pushing it in without warning but she was always aware of what he was doing and bore down at the same time so that entry was made easy. That was the trouble with sophisticated women, he thought, they knew all the tricks.

After a time, the three women separated and now the baron and Rupert played a more active part in the general fondling. The baron knew that Françoise liked to be bitten, and he was soon busy with the soft flesh below her ears and at the base of her throat, nibbling delicately most of the time but now and again giving her a sudden sharp bite that left teeth marks on her skin. Like Rupert he knew that she hated to be marked, but her body's jerks of pleasure told him that she'd only be annoyed in the morning when it was too late to do anything about it.

At last, Rupert found that he was able to reach out for Cassandra. Dieter was keeping Françoise busy, and Katya was sucking on her lover's penis and testicles, taking each one into her mouth and licking it until it swelled and drew up towards his body. This meant that Rupert and Cassandra were free, and he quickly pulled her towards him and almost before she knew what was happening he'd sprinkled a little powder from a tiny box onto her nipples.

She didn't know what the white powder was, but it made her nipples itch and tingle, and the blood began to course through them so that they felt unbearably sensitive even before Rupert had touched them. He watched the swell of the small buds, watched the tissue stiffen until the nipples were rigid and then brushed against them with the inside of his wrist. They were so hard that they seemed inflexibile, unyielding to his skin, and Cassandra moaned with the indescribable sensations his touch had triggered.

Rupert watched her eyes glaze with the pleasure of it, and as her mouth relaxed and opened he bent his head and covered it with his own, letting his tongue move gently inside her lips, lightly roaming around the inside of her upper lip before sliding over her teeth and thrusting more urgently inside her mouth where her tongue met his with equal enthusiasm.

Her drug-inflamed nipples were still over-sensitised, and the throbbing in them began to grow until she felt certain that she could hear it in her ears. Knowing how they must be swelling, Rupert reluctantly removed his mouth from hers and moved it to her breasts where he licked greedily at his favourite drug, sucking at her breasts quite tenderly, but she was so over-aroused that it felt as though he were using all his force. Her groans increased as the breasts swelled yet further, the sensations increased and then, much to her surprise, her whole body arched in an orgasm and she felt small drops of moisture trickle onto her pubic hairs.

Rupert continued to suck at the cocaine powder, enjoying the way his tongue began to tingle, and he then trailed his tongue on down the undersides of her breasts even while she was still shuddering from her climax, and her skin tasted musky and feminine to him.

Cassandra floated in the pleasure of it all. Around them she could hear the moans and cries of the others, Françoise was particularly loud in her moments of release, but none of it troubled her, it all seemed to add to her own excitement. Then, just as she was wondering why she'd felt so nervous, Rupert's hand began to insinuate itself between her thighs and with a jolt she came back to her senses, her body remembered the cruel width of the marble dildo it had been forced to receive that very afternoon and she closed her legs against him.

Rupert was surprised. At first he thought it was part of a game, a kind of token resistance to make surrender all the more sweet, but when her thighs refused to open he pushed at them roughly, his already hard erection increasing as he began to use force.

Cassandra knew that she mustn't annoy him, mustn't refuse to let him do what everyone else was doing and what she herself had done with the baron, but her body refused to obey her attempts to relax and as his hand forced its way between the tight thighs and began to probe her tender sex lips, she heard herself give a small cry of protest.

The baron heard it too, and he quickly but casually rolled off Françoise, at the same time pushing Katya's head away from him as he reached across the circular bed for Cassandra. 'All change!' he said firmly, and although Françoise protested Rupert wasn't displeased.

'She's not much fun at the moment,' he muttered, pushing her towards his friend.

'Try again later,' the baron murmured, amused to see that Katya had already got her head between Françoise's thighs. 'You might need this, too.' He passed across the tiny snuff box.

'Not for this pair surely!' Rupert laughed, his good humour restored, and then he was busy with Katya, parting her knees as she crouched over Françoise and inserting a vibrator into her without any warning so that her body shook with surprise.

Cassandra felt the baron's broad arms around her and wished that she could stop trembling. She knew that he'd be angry, that this wasn't the way she was supposed to behave, and yet she couldn't tell him about the afternoon because then Katya would have scored over her.

'Be still,' he soothed, letting his strong hands move down her spine and feeling her breasts rubbing against the thick hairs on his chest, but she continued to shake until his hands moved sideways across the bottom of her back, the fingers trailing softly across her from one hipbone to the other while he continued to press the length of her naked body against his so that she could feel the full size of his erection pressing up between their stomachs.

When she was finally still he laid her back flat on the bed and pulled a large jar from beneath one of the pillows. Cassandra watched him, her eyes dark and anxious as he dipped his fingers into it and then he held them up for her inspection. 'See, it's only cold cream, to facilitate things for you a little.'

She knew that he was going to touch her where Rupert's hands had been, but even in her fear she didn't dare close her thighs against him, and anyway somehow, miraculously he seemed to understand her terror, and when his fingers carefully parted her outer sex lips the feel of the cold cream was wonderfully soothing to her flesh, which had been burning ever since the women had left her fettered to the gym table.

His right hand massaged the cream carefully over the entire area, into all the tiny crevices and up to where the clitoris was hiding beneath its sheath, and as his fingers worked he kept his tongue busy, darting it round her belly button, and then across her narrow ribcage and down the sides of her body where he knew she was highly sensitive.

It was only when he felt the tiny bud of the clitoris begin to swell and emerge from its hood that he let his fingers go lower again, but he dipped back into the jar before easing his little finger against the entrance to her vagina. Instantly she tried to recoil, the entrance contracted against him and he had to smother her cry with his mouth so that the others didn't realise what was happening.

'Let go, Cassandra,' he whispered in her ear. 'Bear down, press out your sex to me, then I can make the entry easier.'

She swallowed hard, and he could feel the pulse in the side of her neck beating frantically as though she were a trapped animal. He was surprised at how protective he felt, especially when she struggled to obey him and his hand felt her vulva expand into it as she obediently bore down. Now he could spread the cream even more liberally, exciting the tissue and so causing the vaginal entrance to widen instinctively.

Now his little finger could ease in without Cassandra even realising it, and he began to kiss her mouth again. Normally he didn't care for kissing in that way, but

187

although he began it in order to stop her from realising what else he was doing, he continued because her mouth was sweet and when their saliva mingled and his teeth nipped at her bottom lip, his own arousal intensified so much that he had to lift his body slightly from hers to ease the pressure.

By the time he'd finished kissing her he had managed to insert three fingers and the cream had been spread as liberally inside as out, and then very quickly indeed he moved on top of her, his legs inside hers, and slid his erection into the soft, tender passage that had been damaged that afternoon. The cream had been inserted for her benefit, but he found its coldness an exhilarating contrast to the pulsating warmth he would normally have found, and when Cassandra suddenly became aware that he was inside her and tightened in protest his climax began to build at tremendous speed.

'Wrap your legs round my hips,' he instructed her. Cassandra whimpered, but there was no pain, only a strange coolness mixed with the feel of his throbbing stem and she did as he said, enabling him to thrust deeper into this new and arousing combination of heat and cold, softness and tightening muscle, and after only a few thrusts he felt his testicles give one final contraction and then he was exploding into her, his hands gripping her shoulders as he shuddered in his moment of pleasure.

He knew that she hadn't climaxed, but at least she had now crossed the barrier of fear caused by Katya in the gym, and as he withdrew and slid off her he saw that Rupert was ready to take his turn, and Rupert was plainly determined to make sure she climaxed.

He had slipped a latex ring around his penis so that it rested just behind the glans and all round the ring were an assortment of soft knobs and projections that would stimulate and titillate Cassandra's clitoris once Rupert let the bulging head of his erection slip inside her.

Françoise, who enjoyed this device herself, helped a

startled Cassandra to sit up and then waited for Rupert to lie on his back before getting the apprehensive girl to position herself on top of him.

'It's better if you're on top,' Françoise explained. 'That way you can decide how much stimulation you want. If Rupert gets too carried away it becomes more irritating than anything else!'

Cassandra didn't like the look of the sex aid, but the baron had turned his attention to Katya, and she had no choice but to be guided by Rupert and his wife. It was the first time she'd found herself on top of a man, and much to Françoise's amusement she had some trouble in positioning herself correctly. In the end the Brazilian girl had to reach under her and help her husband's erection into the other girl's opening. The touch of her fingers on Cassandra's belly was exciting, and she felt her stomach muscles tighten. Françoise smiled and decided to wait and lend a hand.

Rupert began to lift his body, thrusting upwards hard and then rotating his hips so that the protrusions from the ring moved the whole clitoral area pulling at the stem of the clitoris itself while one of the soft projections actually touched the highly sensitive bud making Cassandra's nerve endings leap with exquisite excitement.

The cold cream inside her had taken Rupert by surprise and although he wasn't sure at first if he liked it, it meant that Cassandra wasn't quite as tight as he'd expected, and it enabled him to control his own climax better.

For a long time he played with the girl above him. He got her to lift herself so that only the very tip of his penis was inside her, then lower and gyrate herself to force the clitoris and inner lips into close contact with the projections. When her breathing began to quicken and her colour rose in her cheeks he'd make her lift again, ordering her to remain still until the last embers of quickening excitement died away. Only then would he let her lower herself again, and sometimes she'd have to sit motionless on him, waiting for him to move his hips which he'd delay until she wanted to scream for some kind of stimulation.

Because his hands were free, Rupert was able to play with her breasts, and also to press the palm of his hand firmly against her stomach, testing the tightness of the muscles and enjoying the first ripples of pleasure that his stimulating ring would arouse.

As he continued to play her like a fisherman plays a catch, Françoise began her own game. She trailed her hair down Cassandra's back, swinging her head from side to side so that it felt to Cassandra as though she were being stroked with a brush. Then she let small strands of her hair trail down over the girl's buttocks and onto Rupert's thighs, gently separating the round tight cheeks and flicking between them with her tongue, often at a time when Rupert had ordered her to sit still.

When this happened, Cassandra couldn't obey him and her body would jerk so that he would reach up and pull her down hard against him, and the rubber knobs would press into the vibrating flesh nearly toppling her over the edge before it was time.

But finally Rupert knew that his own control was vanishing. He put his hands on each side of Cassandra's waist and began to move her up and down on his shaft with ever increasing speed so that her flesh lips were pulled, her clitoris stimulated. Finally Françoise reached round and let her nimble fingers press into the very bottom of Cassandra's stomach, right above the pubic bone, rotating them in tiny circles to increase the all pervasive tightness that Rupert's ministrations had caused until Cassandra suddenly threw back her head as her spine arched in a frenzied spasm of pleasure and the aching tightness that had been so carefully built by the experienced husband and wife escaped into a wonderful release that toppled Rupert over the edge at the same time. He shouted aloud as he spilt his seed into this fascinating girl for the first time.

Exhausted, Cassandra felt herself lifted off him, but

they hadn't finished with her yet, because now Katya, who had been enjoying the baron's undivided attention, suddenly sat up and pushed her opponent onto her back again. She bent her head and began to tongue between Cassandra's thighs, carefully licking off the cold cream that the baron had applied and then letting her tongue snake higher so that she was dipping it in Rupert's sperm as it slowly seeped out of Cassandra.

It was more than Cassandra's body wanted, but she knew that they were all expected to carry on and it wasn't until Katya's fingers moved higher that she began to feel nervous. Her body was still jumpy from the excesses of the climax she'd just experienced, and when Katya held her outer lips apart the others could see the still pulsing flesh and the way the clitoris had hidden from sight to recover.

This didn't bother Katya, who looked to Françoise for assistance. Obediently, Françoise positioned her hand in Cassandra's pubic hair and then let her fingers trail down so that at the vital moment she could pull up on the skin and the hood of the clitoris would slide back with it. The two men watched in silence, knowing what was about to happen but keeping their distance.

The baron reached down to his bedside drawer and quietly extracted a small ampoule. Then he watched Cassandra's body carefully, taking note of the tiny tremors that shook her from time to time as the women's fingers caused too much re-arousal, but they would always cease immediately and between them gradually lulled her into a false sense of security.

Rupert, who had often seen this particular trick of theirs before and always enjoyed it, was surprised to find his manhood stirring again. He wondered why Cassandra excited him so much, but a quick glance at his friend showed that she had the same effect on Dieter.

At last, when Cassandra's weary eyes closed, Katya nodded at Françoise. Her slow, rhythmic pulling movements through the pubic hair didn't change but she pressed her fingers more firmly to make sure that this time the protective hood of the clitoris was pulled back as well.

For one glorious second, Katya stared at the exposed nub of pleasure that now longed only for a chance to recover from the day's stimulation, and then she dipped her head and let her tongue hover above the vulnerable nerve centre which was trying to withdraw but had no place to hide.

The baron's hand rested on the bed, the ampoule between his fingers, and at the exact moment that Katya's wicked tongue flicked down onto the painfully over-used clitoris, he reached across and broke the ampoule under Cassandra's nose.

She gasped with the shock of the tongue on her raw nerve endings, and as she gasped she inhaled the amyl nitrite and immediately all the pain vanished as her whole body was overcome by wave after wave of orgasmic shocks that continued to shake her body for several minutes before the effects of the drug began to wane and her heartbeat gradually slowed to normal.

Katya looked at her long-term lover with something dangerously close to hatred in her eyes. 'You let her enjoy that. You spoilt it for me. It was meant to be my pleasure, not hers.'

'I'm tiring of your cruelty,' he said lazily, stroking some of Cassandra's hair off her damp forehead. Cassandra moaned with pleasure, the drug still making her desperately over-sensitive to every touch.

He didn't want a scene, and the day had gone well as far as he was concerned, so he reached out for Katya, turned her on her stomach and got her to kneel with her head down on the pillow so that Françoise could suckle at her breasts while he fetched a large dildo with a hollow bulb in the artificial testicles and a channel up the centre of the imitation penis. He carefully filled the hollow bulb with warm soapy water, and then spread a little vaseline round the head to make penetration easier.

He knew that Katya loved to have the dildo inserted into her rectum, particularly if a woman was playing with her clitoris and breasts at the same time, but he wanted to see how much she'd enjoy the soapy water when it entered her back passage.

Françoise was busy doing all the things she and Katya enjoyed, and very soon Katya was urging the baron to hurry up with the dildo. 'Patience, my dear. Pleasure is better when prolonged,' he reminded her. Rupert, who had watched the preparations with interest, wondered how long Katya would be able to prolong the pleasure once the soapy water entered her lower bowel.

The head of the dildo was inserted carefully into her rectum as she bore down to make entry easier, then she tightened around it, and the sensations were wonderful especially when Françoise's clever teasing of her clitoris enhanced the full tight feeling within.

Then Françoise inserted three fingers into Katya's vagina, and the baron began to move the dildo gently in and out, slowly at first but then faster as Katya's hips tried to force the pace. He knew that she was close to coming, could tell from the way her toes were beginning to curl on the bed beneath him, and at the last moment before she came he squeezed the bulb firmly between his fingers.

Katya's body, gathering itself together for a blissfully familiar orgasm, was startled by the sudden gushing wetness that flooded into her. At first she rather liked it, it was similar to having a man ejaculate there although there was more liquid, but then the soapiness began to have its effect and as she shuddered and tightened, her bowel went into a terrible cramping spasm and she knew that if she didn't get out of the room she'd lose control and disgrace herself in front of everyone, but the baron still had hold of the dildo and was refusing to let her go as he continued to squeeze the last of the liquid up through the inner tube.

'Prolong it, my dear,' he said silkily. 'Show your self-control. Let the ecstasy last.'

193

Françoise, unaware of what was happening, continued to let her fingers trail over Katya's heaving stomach but suddenly Katya wrenched herself away from the woman's touch and she flung herself sideways, off the bed and then dashed for the bathroom, crying because as she'd moved the baron had pulled the dildo out of her and only her own muscles could prevent the disaster she feared.

As she sat sobbing silently on the toilet, Katya knew that this time it was a very different game the baron had devised. This time, she was the one who was meant to lose, but she had no intention of letting that happen. She'd be more careful in future, and wouldn't attempt to hurt Cassandra again, but she'd use every other weapon she had to defeat this intruder who had spoilt everything since her arrival.

As Katya wept and plotted, the other three showered and dressed, agreeing that the evening had gone well while Cassandra slept the sleep of exhaustion, never knowing that it was the baron who carried her to her own bed and pulled the duvet up over her to keep her warm.

He was looking forward to the competition the next day.

# Chapter Ten

'I hate that girl,' Katya confessed quietly to Françoise as they watched Cassandra through the French windows. She was wandering round the garden chatting to a workman about the new rockery the baron was having built. 'He's changed since she arrived. Nothing's the same any more.'

Françoise smiled. 'Nothing ever remains the same; isn't that why we're with the men we are? Neither of us could survive a routine life.'

'That's not what I meant,' Katya retorted impatiently. 'Of course I'm not pining for domesticity and sex every Wednesday and Saturday night, but I sometimes think Dieter is. He's got the same look in his eyes that he had when he met Marietta.'

'Well she didn't last long!' Françoise laughed.

Katya, trying to suppress a dark memory that had to remain hidden if she was to keep sane, turned to her friend. 'This one would, Françoise. She's made of sterner stuff than Marietta, and there'll never be children to distract her either. I can't afford to have her remain here much longer.'

Françoise watched with interest as her own husband joined Cassandra by the rockery. She saw him put an arm round the girl's waist as they spoke, and noticed

195

how Cassandra moved away at the first opportunity, by bending down to point to some plants she cleverly disguised her rejection.

'She certainly has something special about her. I confess to finding her very attractive myself. Not like Clara, of course, she's just a wonderful toy, whereas Cassandra would be a challenge.'

Katya scowled, then remembered what her beautician had said and quickly erased the lines from her forehead. 'I don't need you to admire her, too. What I want to know is what can I do about her? Dieter would never have humiliated me the way he did last night before Cassandra came.'

'For myself,' Françoise said with a smile, 'I enjoy the enemas. They are an acquired taste, but most pleasurable in moderation.'

'Last night wasn't at all pleasurable because I wasn't expecting it, and he had no right to do it to me.'

Françoise looked at Katya in surprise. 'He has the right to do anything he likes to you. It isn't as though you've ever persuaded him into marriage; you're only here because he lets you stay.'

Katya moved closer to the tall Brazilian girl. 'Help me, Françoise. How can I make sure she loses?'

'Loses what?'

Katya knew that the game was a secret and tried to cover her mistake. 'Loses out to me, of course.'

'I think all you can do is wait. Eventually Dieter will push her too far, and she will make a scene or irritate him. Rupert always says that Dieter's tolerance level is the lowest of any man he's met! Also, as a friend, I think I should give you a word of warning.'

'What is it?' Katya asked shortly; she hated taking advice even when she'd requested it.

'Your desire to inflict pain is not to Dieter's liking.'

'Of course it is! He's always been more than happy to accommodate me in that direction,' Katya said smugly.

'Yes, because you choose it; he does not care very much to inflict real pain on those who do not take pleasure from it, and when you hurt others he is not entertained.'

Katya knew that her friend was right, but it only irritated her all the more. 'What am I meant to do then? Give her nothing but orgasms? The whole idea of having her here was to teach her self-discipline.'

'There are limits surely,' Françoise murmured, surprised to see that Rupert was still following Cassandra round the garden.

'If there are, it's for the first time.'

'My advice to you,' Françoise said, deciding to go into the garden herself, 'is to bide your time. I have no doubt that Dieter has plenty of ideas up his sleeve to test Cassandra's true worth, and I would have thought it would take more than a withdrawn Englishwoman to hold his attention for any length of time. One can scarcely imagine her at one of his magnificent parties!'

'I suppose you're right, but it isn't easy,' Katya muttered, wishing for once that there weren't so many cameras and microphones dotted round the house.

'Where's the fun if life's easy? Compared to my childhood, any problems Rupert and I encounter are nothing at all. Now I shall go and talk to my husband and then join Clara for a little more instruction in the joys of the flesh. She has a passion for Dieter that is really touching. I must try and persuade him to take her again before we leave.'

The conversation did nothing to soothe Katya's ruffled temper. She realised that she had to be sensible, and that Françoise was almost certainly right when she said Cassandra wouldn't last for long, and yet at the back of her mind there was always the spectre of Marietta. If Dieter's wife hadn't become so clinging and feeble after the birth of Christina, then she would have lasted and no one could have called Marietta adventurous. When she had joined in her husband's parties, it was always with the greatest of reluctance and he used to accept her token appearances with apparent equanimity. Once she was dead he reverted, hurling himself

197

hedonistically into every possible sexual challenge, but there had been that moment of danger when Katya had sensed the possibility of an end to their relationship, and this was another such moment. Somehow she had to make sure that Cassandra lost without physically harming her herself.

In the middle of the afternoon, when they were all lying around in the garden enjoying the heat of the sun, the baron stood up and clapped his hands. 'I'm bored,' he announced. 'I think it's time for our competition.'

'What competition?' asked Françoise, who had Clara stretched out beside her and was continually fondling the girl's large breasts while making her eat pieces of truffle from her own mouth and ensuring that every time she did, it ended in a warm fusion of their lips and tongues, a fusion that excited Clara as much as it shamed her.

'You will see,' the baron said with his most boyish grin.

Cassandra, who was sitting in the swing seat reading a book, glanced up and saw the dimple in his cheek. As always it was irresistible to her, and she felt an instant tug of physical attraction. To her delight he looked directly at her. 'Cassandra, come with me. You are to take a leading role in the contest. Katya, bring Françoise, Rupert, Clara and Peter up to the top floor in fifteen minutes.'

'What about Lucy?' asked Rupert, who always enjoyed the little maid's company.

'Lucy has the other leading role. She will be with us. Come, Cassandra.' Holding out a hand he pulled her to her feet. She stood, but reluctantly, suddenly aware of the predatory way the others were eyeing her and beginning to suspect that the competition might not be to her liking.

The baron clicked his tongue impatiently. 'What's the matter with you? Are you already tired of us?'

She shook her head, managed to flash a smile at him, and put her hand in his. His fingers closed tightly round hers, but for once Katya didn't look in the least put out, in fact she smiled at Cassandra and this worried the younger girl even more.

Inside, the house seemed dark after the bright sunlight of the garden and she almost stumbled over the second flight of stairs. The baron's hands caught her round the waist and he could feel her tension. He smiled to himself.

Cassandra had been terrified that he was taking her to the room where Lucy had been disciplined, but this one was far larger and just as luxurious as those on the first floor.

It seemed to be some kind of a bedroom, but two beds were set in the middle of the large room, and they weren't normal beds but the kind of couches found in Victorian drawing rooms with a rounded curve at one end where the head could rest.

Lucy was already waiting in the room, standing by the window in her uniform. She smiled and bobbed a curtsy to the baron. He didn't smile back, but pointed towards one of the couches. 'Take off your clothes, except for your stockings and suspender belt, and then lie there. Cassandra, do the same and lie on the other couch.'

'I'm not wearing stockings,' Cassandra said nervously.

He pointed to a nearby stool. 'All that you need is there. Hurry, the others will be here soon and you must both be ready.'

'What's going to happen?' Cassandra asked.

'We are going to see how well you have learnt to control yourself since you joined us. See that clock on the wall there?' Both girls looked up to where a large clock had been fixed to the wall opposite their heads. 'Once the game begins the clock will be started. It will run for an hour. During that time we will all take turns to try and bring you both to as many climaxes as possible, but I shall be extremely disappointed if either of you has more than two and I am hoping that one of you will manage to last through the hour without having even one.' He glanced at their faces and allowed himself a small smile. 'But perhaps I am over-optimistic, yes?'

Cassandra was beginning to feel hot with embarrassed anticipation. 'What if we have more than two?' she whispered.

'It will show me how much more training you need. I shall make an allowance insofar as Lucy has been with us nearly a year, and her body has had longer to learn the ways of postponing her pleasure.'

'Is there a prize for the winner?' Lucy asked, climbing onto the couch.

'No, only a punishment for the loser.'

'What kind of punishment?' Cassandra asked, keeping her eyes fixed on his and searching for some suggestion of emotion or feeling in them.

'I have yet to decide! Ah, here are the others at last. I have just been telling the girls about the competition, now I will explain the rules to you.' He did, and Katya began to feel much happier. Lucy was well trained. She had suffered a great deal during her early weeks in the house, and her body was used to obeying whatever strictures either Katya or the baron placed on it. Cassandra had hardly been trained at all, except in pleasure, and her body would rush to welcome the sensations it had so quickly learnt to enjoy. She was quite certain that Lucy would win easily.

'Can we do anything we want to bring them to a climax?' Rupert asked, his eyes already on Cassandra as he remembered the previous night.

'No drugs,' his friend replied. 'Cocaine and amyl nitrite are out, but anything else is acceptable. The only rules are that you have to start slowly, and each of us can only spend ten minutes at a time on the same person.

'Peter, you, Françoise and I will start on Lucy while Rupert, Katya and Clara begin with Cassandra. After ten minutes we will change round. Does everyone understand?'

They did, and for once even Clara's eyes were bright. She knew only too well what it was like to be continually stimulated and here at last was a chance to do it to someone else. She could hardly wait to begin. The baron looked at all their faces, flushed with anticipation, and he was delighted with his little idea. With a quick movement of his hand he started the clock and the competition began.

Cassandra watched as Rupert, Clara and Katya approached her and her insides seemed to curl up with terror. They were all so skilled, and had seen her in the throes of excitement often enough to know how to bring about the release she now had to delay indefinitely.

Rupert, remembering that they had to start slowly, gently unfastened the suspenders and began to peel off the black stockings Cassandra had just put on. He rolled the first one down her leg inch by inch, his fingers lingering at each turn. Then he told her to lift her leg so that he could roll it off her foot, and his fingers brushed the soft pads of flesh at the base of her toes, tickling very gently and making her catch her breath. Then he repeated the process with the other leg, and this time she knew what was coming and her slim foot arched in advance so that his fingers had to stretch further to touch the soft flesh pads. This time he chose to rotate them and shivers of delight ran up her leg.

Once her stockings had been removed, Rupert sat at the foot of the couch and put her left foot in his lap, letting it brush against the tight bulge in his trousers so that she was aware of his excitement. Then he began to suck and lick at each of the toes in turn, and she gave little moans of pleasure at the delicious feelings that ran the entire length of her leg and up higher, into the join of her thighs.

As Rupert worked, Katya took a bolster from one of

the cupboards in the room and slid this beneath Cassandra's hips, so that her stomach was pushed up, tight extended flesh was always more susceptible to even the lightest pressure and anyway she wanted to see the frantic ripples of the stomach muscles when Cassandra began to fight off her first orgasm.

Clara, who at first had found herself unable to touch the pale, slim body lying on the couch, finally found the courage to take a long carefully pointed feather from a table at the head of the couch and she stroked this over Cassandra's small breasts, watching with fascination as the tightly puckered nipples began to swell and rise from the surrounding areola. Intrigued, she held the feather point down and let the tip rest in the tiny hollow at the crest of the nipple, in the place where milk would flow if Cassandra should ever give birth, and this touch by the inexperienced Clara made Cassandra groan through clenched teeth as waves of pleasure flooded through her breasts.

With her belly raised by the bolster, Katya couldn't help but let her hand reach out and draw the backs of her fingers across the susceptible flesh, moving her hand down towards the pubic hair and then back up again to the narrow waist. Cassandra's body trembled, and all at once Katya remembered seeing Dieter's hands on the sides of the girl's body and she let her fingers drift to the hollows at each side of her waist and on down over the clearly visible hipbones. This time Cassandra's stomach leapt and her breath caught in her throat.

Rupert regretfully ceased his attentions to her toes and began to flick his tongue up her legs, paying particular attention to the insides of her knees before reaching the silken skin of her thighs. Once there he couldn't resist nipping lightly with his teeth, and while he was doing that, Clara was swirling the feather in the crest of her nipples and Katya was teasing the stretched skin over her hips so that Cassandra could feel herself becoming moist, and Rupert saw the first drops of liquid gleaming on her thick pubic hair.

Cassandra was going mad with the delicious torment they were inflicting on her. She knew that not even ten minutes could have passed because there had been no changeover in the people tormenting her, but already her body felt close to explosion and she could hear her own smothered moans and cries whereas there had been no sound from Lucy, who was only three feet away from her.

She felt Rupert's hands tenderly grasp her outer sex lips. Very slowly he began to part them and her legs went rigid as she tried to steel herself against his touch. He lowered his head and his long dark hair brushed against her lower stomach and upper thighs, a sensation entirely new to her body and highly stimulating. With amazing delicacy he continued to part her sex lips higher up so that he could see for himself her rapidly swelling clitoris and the damp moistness of the surrounding tissue that was such indisputable evidence of her excitement.

He bent his head lower, Katya's fingers rubbed almost as lightly over her hips as the fiendish feather was moving over her tumescent breasts, but just before Rupert's tongue could begin its explorations, the baron's voice interrupted him.

'Time to change!' he called firmly. Rupert was tempted to let his tongue have just one stab at the frantic flesh beneath it, but he knew it wouldn't be fair to the girl and reluctantly stood up while Katya had to grab the feather from Clara's hand and push her over to where Lucy's shaking body was trying to recover from the manipulations of the other three participants.

As soon as Rupert moved, Cassandra let her knees fall apart and breathed through her mouth. She knew that she must not press her legs together or the pressure could trigger the climax she had to repress and breathing through her mouth seemed to calm the thrills of leaping pleasure in her breasts and belly.

The baron looked at Cassandra's upthrust abdomen, noted the swelling tightness of the flesh and the rigid nipples on the tiny breasts and knew that she was already struggling to survive. He wasn't surprised. This was an area of weakness that was to be expected so early on. Pleasure had become a part of her life; delaying it was new to her. She was bound to lose the game, what he wanted to know was by how much she would lose and how many more lessons she needed before her control was good enough to satisfy him and let her become an instructor of others.

Françoise immediately turned Cassandra across the bed and then made her turn over, so that she was lying with her stomach pressed against the bolster which was near the side of the couch, forcing her head and breasts to hang down towards the floor.

She felt the baron's tongue begin to lick the arch of her foot, and his tongue moved more slowly than Rupert's had, in long, lazy lines that followed the nerve paths with unerring accuracy until her toes curled with coiled pleasure. Just when the pleasure was becoming painful through repetition, he removed his tongue, and instead his mouth edged its way up the back of her legs, sucking on her flesh as it went and leaving tiny red marks of passion in its wake.

Cassandra wriggled against the bolster with the excitement, but quickly desisted as the pressure only increased the stimulation and blood coursed even more quickly through her hanging breasts. It was those breasts that were interesting Peter, who had taken a tiny piece of cotton thread, licked it and then shaped it into a loop which he eased over the already swollen nipple, moving it firmly down onto the surface of the breast. He repeated this exercise with another piece of thread until both Cassandra's nipples were encircled, and then began to suck steadily on the dangling tips which promptly swelled even more until the tight, moist thread began to cut into the incredibly tender flesh and further expansion became impossible. Yet still

Peter continued to suck and Cassandra groaned at the streaks of pain that began to mix with the pleasure, arousing the red-hot heat of pain-edged flames to which Katya and Françoise had introduced her, and reminding her body of the flood of shuddering release such sensations could trigger.

Cassandra's breath quickened and she lifted her head, hoping to catch a glimpse of the clock and see how far into her second ten minutes she was, but Peter was in her way and now Françoise was busy pushing and pulling at Cassandra's body again until she was once more lying lengthways on the couch and the bolster was pushed up against her distended breasts so that the baron and Françoise could concentrate their attentions on the lower half of her body.

The baron spread her thighs wide and slid his hand up beneath her, feeling the slick of moisture between her thighs. He turned his hand, palm uppermost, and inserted the top of his thumb into the entrance to her vagina and let his other fingers beat out a rhythmic tattoo on the surrounding flesh, which was rapidly becoming slippery with her own secretions.

The cotton threads were tight round her fiery nipples, her swollen breasts were pressing into the feathers of the bolster and now at last someone was attending to the diabolically aching flesh between her thighs. Cassandra's hips twitched as the clever fingers danced across the leaping tissue and it felt as though something was sending currents of electricity through her body as the sensations flashed in jagged lines up from her thighs to her breasts.

Cassandra's legs began to stiffen, and then she felt Françoise's tongue licking the tender cleft at the base of her spine, in that special place where the baron had aroused her to such heights, and for a moment she thought that she was going to spasm immediately because the pleasure was simply uncontainable.

'Not yet!' the baron said harshly, and whilst his fingers didn't pause in their tantalising arousal, his words broke through the thick curtain of sensuality and reminded her of the penalty she would pay if she lost out to Lucy. She groaned with frustration, trying to lift her swollen breasts from the bolster to ease their arousal, but Peter pushed her firmly back, at the same time letting his hands go beneath her and pinching the nipples firmly to keep them rigid.

Her whole body was swelling with the sensations, and the knowledge that she mustn't climax made it all worse. Suddenly she heard a groan from Lucy, and the maid's voice cried out, 'No! Please, don't! Not yet, please!' There was such despair in her voice that it gave Cassandra a boost of confidence. At least Lucy was finding it difficult too.

'Time to change!' the baron repeated, abruptly removing his fingers, and Cassandra collapsed in relief, pressing up on her knees so that there was a gap between her pulsating vulva and the couch.

Katya and Rupert were with her in seconds, though, their hands still warm and moist from inflicting the bittersweet torture on Lucy. Again Cassandra was turned, now onto her back with the bolster beneath her hips once more putting her in the position that Katya knew was the most arousing for what was to follow.

Carefully, Rupert parted the outer sex lips of the trembling, passion-filled body, and the lips were so sticky they were reluctant to separate. Once they had, he held them spread wide while Katya pressed a long thin plastic rod along the exposed crease, making sure that as it moulded to Cassandra's innermost delicate places the tip of it pressed lightly against the tight little bud that was pulsating with its need for attention.

Cassandra gasped at the feel of the thin cool plastic against her, and then had to bite her lip to stop herself from crying out when she felt Rupert closing her outer lips around the rod so that there was now continual, relentless pressure against the whole length of her vulva, and then he made her cross her legs at the knees so that the rod pressed even more firmly against her, causing a constant steady stimulation that made her body almost cramp with the throbbing ache of thwarted need which aroused her sufficiently to engorge her entire pelvic area with blood without giving her enough stimulation to climax. But she knew that she would now explode instantly if that stimulation were to be applied.

Clara had returned to her favourite feather, only this time she tickled Cassandra lightly beneath the armpits and down the sides of her neck where the pulse of passion was throbbing wildly. She also ran it down between the breasts, the nipples still ringed by Peter's threads, and then round in the hollow of the belly button. This last movement made the distended belly leap and the plastic rod was pulled against her more tightly by her own contraction.

Katya looked down into the eyes of her hated rival. 'How does it feel, Cassandra? Isn't it wonderful? Don't you long for that one final touch to let the pleasure come? How much longer can you hold back? Lucy is still well in control, you know, but you're very near. Look at her Rupert, it won't take much now.'

Rupert knew that Katya was right. Cassandra's stomach muscles were so tight it looked painful, her breasts more swollen with passion than he'd ever seen them and between her wickedly closed thighs the plastic rod had to be exciting her unbearably. 'Then make her come,' he said lightly.

'No, not yet!' Cassandra pleaded. 'It's too soon.'

'Of course it's too soon,' Katya laughed, 'but then you're only a beginner in this game. Your body still has a lot to learn.'

She leant down, and let one tiny hand begin to massage the distended stomach, pressing her outspread fingers as wide as she could so that the skin was pulled in all directions, and the gentle tugging motion could be felt between Cassandra's thighs as the rod moved with every tug.

It was almost beyond bearing, and Cassandra knew

that she couldn't control herself against such experts.
When Rupert finally let her uncross her knees and her
legs fell apart she knew better than to expect any
lessening of their excited experiments on her, and she
was proved right when Rupert pressed his strong hand
between her thighs and then moved it round and
round, not opening the outer lips but knowing that
with each of his movements her clitoris was being
rotated as well, and that the pressure of the plastic rod
combined with the pressure of his hand should force
Cassandra into her first climax.

She felt the bunching sensation in the pit of her
stomach that always signalled the beginning of her
release. Her toes curled in an involuntary movement
and a pink flush covered her breasts and throat as her
arousal reached its peak, and then Katya's busy little
hand moved a fraction lower so that it was over the
pubic bone and it seemed that her hand and Rupert's
were one as the whole area of Cassandra's sex was so
cleverly manipulated, rolled and rotated that the plastic
rod's pressure grew and grew and without meaning to
Cassandra actually pushed up against Katya's hand to
hurry the explosion that she could no longer deny
herself.

Katya laughed, the rod moved one final time against
the delicate stem of the clitoris, Clara's feather dipped
into the tiny belly button and there was a huge explosion of white light inside Cassandra's head as her entire
body leapt upwards off the bed and she screamed with
a mixture of ecstatic relief and an agonised sense of
failure.

Next to her, Lucy heard Cassandra's scream and
strained to keep her sweating body from following suit.
The baron was being diabolically clever with his tongue
while Françoise was busy between her parted buttocks,
and Lucy too was hideously near the edge but hearing
Cassandra distracted her at the vital moment and she
managed to slow her breathing while out of the corner

of her eye she could see the other girl's slim body still thrashing around on the bed.

'Time to change,' the baron called, apparently unperturbed by the sounds of Cassandra's failure, although he did pause long enough to make a note against her chart which was beneath the clock.

Now that she'd actually climaxed, Cassandra thought that it should be easier to hold out against another orgasm for some time. Half an hour had already passed, and she thought it unlikely she would be forced into another failure before the hour was up. Lucy's breathing had become quite audible now, and if they both had one climax in the hour there would be no loser. She would have shown the baron that she had gained more control over her body than he'd expected.

However, the baron knew that once fully aroused, Cassandra would be easy to bring to further peaks of passion, although different methods would be necessary. He and Françoise left her on her back at first, watching as Peter carefully sat between her carelessly spread thighs and began to insert the smaller set of Japanese loveballs into her opening. Cassandra was still coming down from her orgasmic glow and much to her relief the insertion irritated rather than stimulated her, but the baron knew that soon she would begin to feel the pressure in a more constructive way.

After they'd been inserted she was turned on her stomach, but first Françoise removed the pieces of thread from the now detumescent nipples, removing them with her teeth so that her saliva covered the tips of the breasts and the skin began to rise as the moisture cooled in the air.

This time the bolster was left below Cassandra's hips and she was quite surprised when Françoise came to the head of the couch and began to play with her long dark hair, letting her fingers run through it and carefully massaging round her temples and hair line so that Cassandra's body relaxed even more.

As she relaxed, the baron and Peter were busy lower

down her body. To begin with, the baron ran his strong hands round the tight buttocks, cupping them carefully and enjoying the feel of the smooth flesh. He was careful not to alarm her, his hands wandering up and down her spine and straying down the backs of her legs as well so that she didn't realise where his attention was really concentrated.

Then, when she was thoroughly disarmed, he got Peter to separate the warm globes of flesh and very carefully eased a pointed nozzle into the tight dark hole which immediately contracted against the invasion. Quickly he kissed the erogenous spot at the base of her spine which was her weakness, and automatically her body opened more to him, even there, where she was still unhappy with any intrusion. Once the nozzle was inside he pressed on a button and released a thick jet of mousse inside her. 'Don't try and push it out, contain it,' he instructed her. Françoise was still stroking her hair and head, and it didn't really hurt, so Cassandra obeyed, partly because she felt quite certain that whatever he was doing there it wouldn't give her an orgasm, and this was now her one objective.

The baron waited until her protesting muscles had accepted the mousse, and then Peter, whose erection had been paining him ever since he'd first set eyes on Cassandra's naked body, climbed onto the couch and slowly slid the swollen head of his penis into the tight opening which was now so well lubricated by the mousse he caused no pain at all. Once he was inside he nearly came himself at the unaccustomed sensation of the foam around him, but such a look of fury crossed the baron's face that fear made the imminent climax swiftly fade leaving him able to gyrate his hips, moving his throbbing glans around inside Cassandra and pressing through the mousse to touch the thin walls of her rectum.

Every time that he touched them, Cassandra's muscles tightened reflexively, he would then be lost to her again in the sea of foam, and she would relax until the next touch until eventually the continuing sequence of contractions began to trigger off a pulsing need in her that she'd never experienced before. She ached deep inside her stomach, not at the pit of her belly where desire usually grew in her, but higher up and so deep down that it was almost as though it was against her spine. She didn't understand the ache, didn't know how to end it, but she began to thrust her buttocks out against Peter's shaft, quickly learning that as she increased the friction the ache grew more pleasurable and assumed a sharper edge.

Françoise moved Cassandra until she was crouched on all fours, resting on elbows and knees, and then the baron stood in front of Cassandra and unzipped his trousers, letting his own erection thrust free and putting out a hand he traced a line round her already parting lips. She was greedy for him, he could see it in her eyes, and when he thrust forward she encircled him hungrily with her velvet lips, letting her tongue flick at the ridge of his glans while she sucked carefully and steadily.

Cassandra saw the excitement and pleasure in the baron's eyes and her own excitement grew. Peter's skilled movements between her buttocks were having more effect than she realised, and the deep ache was spreading dangerously now but Cassandra was too busy licking and sucking on the baron's erection to really appreciate it. Then, as Peter's cock touched a particularly sensitive spot inside her back passage her abdominal muscles contracted sharply and the Japanese loveballs, which she'd completely forgotten about, moved within her. At the same moment the baron thrust his hips forward forcefully and she had to relax the muscles of her throat to accommodate him as the first drops of his semen began to trickle out of the tiny split at the end of the glans. She could visualise it all, and went almost wild with excitement as he moaned softly. It was his moan of pleasure that was her undoing. The thrill of pleasing him so much combined with

211

the unexpectedly arousing feel of Peter in that forbidden part of her body and the rolling loveballs gave her only a split second's moment of tightness that served as an insufficient warning to allow her any chance of preventing the second climax that crashed down on her, and her body bucked so violently that the baron was very grateful he managed to withdraw safely. Peter was held tight by the spasms of her second orgasm, her muscles tightened around him so that he couldn't withdraw and couldn't control himself but instead spilled his seed into the highly erotic mixture of her tightness and the dissolving mousse.

Finally both Peter and Cassandra were still. Peter, somewhat shamefaced, withdrew and carefully mopped at her with a towel to remove the now melted foam that was trickling from her while Cassandra collapsed onto her arms in exhausted despair.

'Two climaxes,' the baron said in a level voice. 'I hope there won't be any more. You still have twenty minutes to go.'

'I couldn't help it,' Cassandra gasped. 'I hadn't realised . . .' He turned away, totally disinterested in her explanation, and marked her chart for a second time.

'Ten minutes,' he called, and just as he did so, Lucy gave a shrill scream and then wailed with distress as her legs thrashed wildly in the air where they were imprisoned over Rupert's shoulders while Katya worked between the exposed thighs. 'One for Lucy,' the baron added, but Cassandra didn't feel any the better for the knowledge.

Although Katya, Rupert and Clara worked as skilfully as they could on her for their next ten minute session, they were unable to arouse her to anywhere near the level needed for another orgasm, and when they changed over Cassandra hoped they would be all the more determined to force one from Lucy while she herself battled one final time against the baron and his accomplices.

212

At first there seemed little danger of her failing again. The baron and Françoise simply caressed her body in a gentle way with their hands and tongues while Rupert concentrated on her breasts, but then they all stopped their attentions at the same time and Cassandra looked at the clock, wondering if the time could possibly be up. In the brief moment of silence she could hear Lucy's ragged breathing and knew that the maid was very close to a second orgasm. Her spirits lifted.

'Sit up, Cassandra,' the baron said quietly. She moved up the couch, obediently lifting her upper torso from its previously reclining position. Peter removed the bolster and threw it to the floor. 'Now lick your middle finger,' continued the baron. Her mouth went suddenly dry and although she tried to force some moisture into it she couldn't. He smiled, and let Françoise bend down and suck on Cassandra's finger for her, swirling her tongue round it in such a suggestive way that to her horror Cassandra felt her legs twitch.

The baron saw the movement. He'd been certain that Cassandra wouldn't be able to avoid having three orgasms and this confirmed his suspicion. 'Now touch your nipples with it,' he said. Tentatively she let the fingertip rest against each pink shell. 'Harder than that, my darling! Françoise, lick her finger again. It seems to be rather too dry.' Again Françoise swirled her tongue round the digit and again Cassandra's legs twitched. This time Cassandra touched her nipples more firmly, moving the finger round so that the shells began to open and swell.

The baron smiled. 'Good. Now touch yourself between your legs. Did the others remove the love-balls?' She nodded. 'Excellent, then we can go all the way. Hurry now, we're waiting.' Trembling with a mixture of shame and desire, Cassandra moved her hand between her thighs and then hesitated. Peter quickly parted her outer lips to enable her easy access to the part the baron was determined she should arouse herself.

The baron thought that the joy of making her give herself the final climax would be immense. She would want to cry and yet not dare to show her feelings, and once again he would see the delicious confusion in her eyes that so entranced him as she tried to come to terms with all the different facets of herself he was forcing into the open.

'Now slide your finger around, my darling,' he whispered. 'Let me see you giving yourself pleasure. Run it up and down between the inner lips, dip it into the entrance and spread your own moistness around. It will feel wonderful, Cassandra, and I shall be able to see the rising desire in your eyes. Do it, Cassandra. You know you want to do it for me.'

And she did. She wanted to please him more than anything else, but she didn't want to lose the contest. She stared at him, her eyes pleading, but it was a fatal mistake because his eyes could drown her and she became hypnotised by them so that almost in a trance her finger began to slide over the hot damp flesh and she obeyed his instructions to the letter, until her clitoris emerged from its protective hood and rose up proudly, waiting for the finger to touch it and bring the sensations to a peak; but Cassandra didn't touch it. Instead her finger strayed round it, teasing the inner lips, entering the vagina and even moving around inside but never quite touching the tight bud of nerve endings that gave her body such ecstasy.

The baron watched her shining pink flesh and the way it darkened as her finger made the blood rush in and suffuse the tissue so that it swelled and expanded beneath her. His own breathing quickened and he wrenched his gaze away to see what Françoise was doing. She was licking round Cassandra's ears, dipping her tongue inside to swirl patterns inside the delicate entrance, adding further stimulation to that caused by Cassandra's own finger.

Cassandra's eyes flicked to the clock and she saw that she only had three more minutes to endure. Three more

214

minutes, in which Lucy must climax again and she must not.

'Now touch your core,' the baron murmured huskily. 'Touch yourself there, where you ache to be touched, where I can see you throbbing with need. Touch it, Cassandra, and very lightly. Just flick it as you pass.'

Cassandra swallowed hard as she obeyed him. For a moment she thought her body would betray her, but although her breasts and stomach tightened and darts of passion lanced her body, the wrenching spasm was avoided.

The baron was surprised, and his eyebrows arched. 'Again, my love,' he whispered, glancing at the clock himself. There were two minutes left. 'This time touch it on the stem, beneath the very tip.' Cassandra wanted to refuse, although then she would have forfeited the game, but she knew that what he was telling her to do was fiendish because it always triggered an orgasm for her and her body was now so finely tuned that it would instantly respond. He looked steadily into her eyes, and almost crying with despair and the knowledge of defeat Cassandra finally let her finger do as he had intended right from the start, but at the same time she opened her mouth and exhaled, thereby releasing some of her pent-up tension.

He realised what she'd done and knew that it would probably work and although disappointed he was impressed by her control, but at the very last moment Lucy cried out 'Yes! Oh, please yes!' as her own tormented nerve endings were triggered into such pleasure that she actually welcomed it after all the frustration, and ironically this orgasmic cry of pleasure coming at the same time as Cassandra's final touch, forced her third climax from her when she had only needed to last three more seconds in order to force a tie.

The baron's eyes remained locked onto hers as she gasped, her pert little breasts shuddering while her belly heaved and rippled for the last time and sweat trickled slowly down it from between the breasts.

'Three.' The baron's voice was totally dispassionate, but his eyes were soft and Cassandra was certain she could see a kind of amused sympathy in them as he marked her chart again, and also put Lucy's second release below her name. 'A close contest,' he remarked with satisfaction.

'But one which Lucy won,' Katya pointed out.

'Yes indeed. As I would have expected considering the hours of tuition she's had from you, Katya. In fact, it should not have been such a close-run thing.'

'A brilliant game!' Rupert said with satisfaction, watching Lucy begin to dress while Cassandra remained slumped on the couch, her head hanging down so that her hair hid her face from them all. 'You've got a great imagination, Dieter. We'll need that tomorrow, when Clara's stepfather pays us a visit.'

At that, Clara gave a cry of dismay while Françoise too looked far from happy. 'Does he have to interfere already?'

'It's just a quick visit, Françoise. To make sure she's learning something from us.'

'I will certainly try to make his visit agreeable,' the baron said with a thin smile. 'For Clara also of course. Now, let us all get ready for dinner and then I think some bridge. A quiet evening will probably suit us all.'

He lingered behind as the others left until only he and Cassandra were in the room. She lifted an exhausted, tear-stained face to his. 'I lost,' she said brokenly. 'If Lucy hadn't come, then I could have lasted.'

'You'd still have lost,' he pointed out. 'She had to come while you could not in order to draw. Besides, while you lost this little competition, in the overall game I think this could be considered a win.'

'What overall game?' Cassandra asked.

'Now that, my dear girl, would be telling,' he said softly, and then ran a hand gently through her tousled hair before leaving her to dress and return to her room to prepare for dinner.

216

# Chapter Eleven

'*B*ut why isn't Clara's mother coming too?' Cassandra asked Françoise as they ate a light lunch the following day. 'Surely she's the one who should be most concerned. After all, until she remarried she'd kept Clara at home the whole time.'

Françoise, who was looking almost as sulky as Clara at the prospect of the forthcoming visit, laughed shortly. 'She doesn't know Claud's coming here. She thinks he's in America on a business trip.'

'Why won't he let her see her own daughter?'

'Because, you stupid girl, Claud only married Clara's mother to get at her daughter. He's always liked young girls, and Clara's a very young eighteen. He must have realised he could only get to her through Elizabeth, hence the marriage.'

'In that case why send her to you to gain experience? Didn't he want to teach her everything himself? I'd have thought that was the main attraction to a man like that.'

'He didn't want any trouble. Clara was very vocal in her protests when I first started educating her; he could hardly have had that kind of scene under her mother's roof.'

'Well I think it's perfectly horrible,' Cassandra said

with a shudder. 'And I'm surprised the baron doesn't object to him coming here to check up on her progress.'

Françoise smiled. 'I can't imagine why Katya worries about you. Basically you haven't changed at all; you're just another of Dieter's victims, so obsessed with him that you're willing to do anything he wants. Underneath you haven't changed one bit. You're still incredibly conventional and very dreary, in a sexual way I mean. I suppose your personality's attractive enough and you're certainly intelligent.'

'Does the baron know Claud?' Cassandra persisted, ignoring the other woman's personal comments but registering the mention of Katya's fear.

'They were at the same school, although Claud must have been a few years ahead of Dieter. You'll learn that most of the men who come to this house have known Dieter from his early days; he no longer bothers to cultivate new male friends. He used to, but very often they didn't understand his way of life and he hated the continual disappointment and boredom. Women are a different matter; they come and go all the time!'

'What happened to his wife?' Cassandra queried, hoping that Françoise might explain the secrecy surrounding the death of the children's mother.

Françoise seemed uneasy. 'No one's quite sure. Dieter had gone to Austria for a couple of days. On the first night he was away, Marietta either went for a swim when she'd had too much to drink or deliberately drowned herself. There was no note, so in the end it was decided it was an accident but she and Dieter had been quarrelling furiously the previous week and I think he believes she killed herself.'

'Was he very upset?' Cassandra asked.

'No, not so very much. He'd grown tired of her, and she was always in tears about something or other. But, he had loved her once and probably it upset him more than he showed. The girls still miss her, although he never lets them talk about her in his presence.'

'Did Katya meet him soon after that?'

Françoise shook her head. 'No, Katya had known him long before he met Marietta. They go back a long way together.'

'Yet he never married her,' Cassandra mused.

'What is this about marriage?' the baron asked, who had walked up silently behind them.

Françoise jumped with surprise. 'We were only talking about Marietta and how the girls still miss her.'

He looked surprised. 'Indeed? Have they told you this, Cassandra?'

'Not exactly, but they bring her into conversation a lot.'

'Christina cannot have any memories of her, but doubtless Helena has shown her photographs and told her stories about their beautiful, fragile mother!' His tone was scornful, and Cassandra couldn't help thinking that Françoise had been overkind in attributing deeper feelings about her death to him.

'Is Clara ready?' Françoise asked him, anxious to change the subject.

He smiled. 'I think so. Claud should be very pleased with her; you have worked wonders in the short time she's been with you. Rupert showed me a tape of your first session with her. Getting her ready today demonstrated very clearly how fast she's come on.'

At that moment there was the sound of a car drawing up in front of the house, and a few minutes later Katya and a tall, distinguished man with greying brown hair came in through the open French windows.

'Darling, you're up at last!' Katya crooned, going on tiptoe to kiss the baron. 'I went with Peter to collect Claud from the airport. He's only got a couple of hours but I told him that you were already preparing Clara for his inspection.'

The baron embraced the older man briefly. 'It's good to see you again, Claud. How was the honeymoon?'

Claud sighed. 'Elizabeth took more satisfying than I'd anticipated. Marriage to a Frenchman for so many years had obviously removed all traces of the renowned

English reserve. I had to keep thinking of the daughter in order to survive!'

The baron laughed. 'How sad! May I introduce you to Cassandra. She is the new chaperone for my daughters when they are here, and also the epitome of the sexually reserved Englishwoman, but we are working on her, isn't that so my darling?'

The older man's eyes were such a light blue they were almost transparent and when he stared fixedly at her, Cassandra felt hot and uncomfortable. 'I suppose so,' she murmured, dropping her eyes.

The baron chuckled and slid an arm round her waist. 'You see how easily she's discomfited! Come, we will go into the garden. Françoise will fetch Clara down from her room and bring her out to us. I think we will have tea on the top terrace. I have some men working on a rockery there but they will merely provide an additional audience. Katya, ask Lucy to bring us tea please.'

When Rupert, Claud, Cassandra, Katya and the baron were finally seated in various garden chairs on the upper terrace, Lucy brought out the tray of tea and then waited beside the baron. 'You can go,' he said curtly. Lucy bobbed the requisite curtsy but her disappointment was plain.

A few moments later, Françoise came out of the house and crossed the lower lawn closely followed by Clara. As they climbed the three steps to the terrace Cassandra realised that Clara was being led by a short lead attached to a wide collar round her neck. Suspended from the collar were two more circles of leather. These had been tightly wound round the young girl's large breasts and every time Françoise jerked on the lead, Clara's head was forced up and back so that her breasts rose higher into the air, the large dark brown areoles smoothing out as they expanded at the touch of the summer air.

She was naked, but there was a slim belt round her waist with loops at the back and front, and threaded

220

through the loops was a wide length of very soft hide covered on the inside by fur, and this was notched tightly so that it pressed firmly between her thighs, tickling the delicate flesh and pressing on the vulnerable nerve endings.

Cassandra glanced across to Clara's stepfather. He was sitting very still, his breathing slow and even, but his hands shook slightly on the arms of the chairs and his cold eyes were fastened onto the uplifted breasts. 'You dressed her beautifully, Dieter,' Françoise complimented him as she led the girl past his chair. He reached out and ran a hand over her ribcage, letting the tips of his fingers just brush against the undersides of the heavy breasts so tightly upheld. 'I thought you'd approve!'

Françoise led Clara on past the watching adults and the two men busy working on the rockery until she was standing in front of her stepfather. 'Good afternoon, Clara,' he said politely. 'I trust you've been behaving well since I last saw you?'

Clara's body shook and she tried to drop her head but Françoise pulled on the lead to prevent her. 'She's been quite good,' the Brazilian girl told him. 'A little slow to learn, but you did warn us about that.'

'Excellent.' He reached up a hand and carefully cupped one of the ripe breasts. Clara took a step backwards and nearly tripped over Françoise's foot. As she struggled to keep her balance the belt round her waist pulled on the strip of hide and the fur pressed closer to her sex lips, making her gasp. Rupert laughed while Cassandra shifted uneasily in her seat, feeling the beginnings of desire stirring in her abdomen.

'Shall I show you how well she responds to us?' Françoise asked.

Claud nodded, still unable to tear his gaze away from his stepdaughter's bound breasts for which he'd been lusting so long.

With a smile, Françoise reached into the large pocket of her flowing skirt and produced a sable brush. Clara's eyes widened and her breasts rose higher of their own accord, so well did they know the delicious sensations that would follow. Carefully, slowly, Françoise drew the brush across the leather encircled breasts, making sure that it covered the tender undersides as well as the tops before finally running it back and forth across the nipples as they engorged and hardened while the breast tissue swelled with excitement until they expanded so much that the leather circles, unable to expand with the breasts, began to tighten painfully and Clara bit on her lip.

Claud licked his lips and took the brush from Françoise, encircling the breasts himself with its soft sable, then paying particular attention to the large, swollen nipples which he teased with the very tips of the brush hairs making sure that the touch was so light it couldn't trigger a spasm of pleasure.

Clara's mouth opened and her eyes grew heavy. 'I've often played with her like this for hours,' Françoise said in a matter-of-fact voice. 'Really I don't think Clara needs that many orgasms. She prefers the build-up to the release.'

'No!' said Clara despairingly. 'That's not true.'

'I hope you're not calling my friends liars,' her stepfather said sternly. Miserably Clara shook her head, wondering why everyone took such delight in arousing her but cared so little for her ultimate pleasure.

Claud looked at his stepdaughter and knew that his marriage had been worthwhile. This slightly overweight eighteen-year-old could be trained into the perfect companion. Once she'd slimmed down and acquired poise she'd be the one at his side on all the important occasions. Elizabeth would simply have to step aside in due course.

'Would you like me to suck on them for you, Clara?' he asked his stepdaughter. Her nipples were bright red now, standing upright and so rigid they could have been made of stone. She nodded, straining against the lead to get nearer to him. It didn't matter that she hated him, all that mattered was the pulsating need centred in her throbbing breasts.

'Say "yes please step-papa",' he ordered her.

The baron raised an eyebrow and glanced at Cassandra. She was staring at the scene with flushed cheeks, her thighs pressed closely together on the chair, while next to her Katya too was watching greedily but her eyes gleamed with satisfaction at Clara's humiliation in front of her new stepfather.

Once Clara had said the words, Claud closed his mouth around the thrusting conical tips of her breasts and began to suck hard on them. There was no subtlety in the sucking, no gentle pressure gradually increasing, instead he sucked harshly and greedily, and at every tug of his lips Clara's upper torso was pulled forward and thrills of pleasure lanced through her, building higher and higher until all at once her stepfather closed his teeth round the swollen tip of her nipple and she climaxed immediately, gasping with relief and excitement.

'Ask him to do the same with the other breast,' Rupert said lazily. He was quite enjoying the scene, although he didn't find Clara particularly attractive because she still carried too much weight. However, like Claud, he could see her potential, and it was always enjoyable to watch young flesh being tutored by experts.

Clara didn't want to ask him, but the neglected breast was now being quietly stroked by the sable brush again, and as it was in Françoise's hand she knew that she wouldn't get any release from the newly building pressure unless she obeyed and so she acquiesced. 'Please suck my other breast, step-papa,' she said nervously.

'Of course, my dear,' responded Claud, delighted to find that his manhood, which had nearly let him down on several occasions during his honeymoon, was already stirring. He repeated the routine on the second breast, but this time he grasped her nipple between his lips and pulled on it, extending it out like a teat until

Clara was afraid it was going to be pulled off. He also kept her waiting longer, and she was moaning with need before he let his teeth fasten around her and again she was finally allowed to spasm with pleasure.

'Has she been penetrated yet?' Claud asked Rupert, sitting back in his chair while Françoise kept the still trembling girl upright with the lead and the two workmen watched covertly, their eyes round with excitement.

'Yes, of course. You said you didn't want a virgin so I got Dieter to do the deed, and very well he managed it too, isn't that so Clara?'

Clara nodded, and the movement made her still swollen breasts jiggle so tantalisingly that Claud began to lean forward once more but with great self-restraint he forced himself back into the chair. 'Would you like Dieter to make love to you again?' Rupert continued.

Katya turned her head sharply to look at her lover, who shrugged as though the conversation had nothing to do with him.

'Would you, Clara?' Rupert pressed.

'Yes,' whispered the girl, unwilling to nod again.

Rupert stood up and came across to her. 'Bend your knees and crouch down,' he told her. Bewildered she complied, and then Rupert crouched down as well and slid a hand inside the tightly pressed band of hide. His fingers felt the dampness where the fur had been pressed against Clara's opening and he moved them absent-mindedly against her already taut flesh until he could feel the moisture coming out of her. He then withdrew his hand and held it out for her inspection. 'Look at that, Clara! When you first came to us you were punished for being too slow in your arousal. We can hardly complain any more, can we!'

'It's probably the thought of Dieter taking her again,' said Françoise, running her long nails down the girl's bent and exposed neck.

'Tighten the strapping between her thighs,' the baron

said suddenly. 'Then keep her crouching, but with her knees closer together than they are now.'

Rupert did as his friend suggested while Claud watched with interest. It left Clara in a very uncomfortable position, with her legs bent nearly double until the muscles in her thighs ached, and the tightening of the strap sent insidious flutters of pleasure shooting up from her moist crevices through her lower belly but it was still insufficient stimulation to allow the flutters to reach a peak.

'Now watch me, Clara,' the baron said kindly. At once the plump girl's eyes turned gratefully to him. She'd been longing for him to enter her again ever since he'd taken her virginity, and she felt certain that in a moment he'd remove the strapping and let his thrusting manhood trigger her climax. Her round stomach strained with excitement, so much so that her stepfather saw it and couldn't resist reaching down to let his hands wander over the silky flesh.

'Not too much stimulation yet,' the baron cautioned. Claud smiled an apology and waited. 'Watch carefully, Clara,' repeated the baron, and then he stood up and reached out for Katya.

Katya was wearing a tiny bikini top and high-waisted shorts and when she stood beside her lover it only took him a couple of seconds to unfasten the strap of the bikini and she leant forward and let it fall to the grass, leaving her breasts free. Then he hooked his thumbs in the sides of her shorts and eased them down her legs, putting his head between them as he did so, nuzzling against her sex lips until she parted her legs, thrusting her pelvis up as much as she could to increase the contact between them.

Clara watched helplessly, her own excitement increasing unbearably as the fur caressed her opening sex while the tight pressure was maintained. She tried to wriggle her hips, but Françoise jerked hard on the lead snapping the girl's head back and forcing the breasts up so high that they hurt. 'Keep still you stupid girl. Haven't we taught you anything!' she hissed angrily. Clara whimpered; her need was great and she didn't want to watch the baron making love to another woman, she wanted him inside her.

The baron took his time with Katya. He ran his hands all over her as though she were a garden statue, lingering here and there before letting the hands continue their exploration. The two workmen, who'd heard tales of the baron's exploits but never expected to be allowed to witness any of them, stopped pretending to work and watched the girl so uncomfortably hunched on the grass, and the increasing tempo of the baron's lovemaking with his mistress.

Katya gloried in the exposure. She loved it when Dieter took her in front of an audience, it increased her excitement tenfold, and this time the knowledge that Clara was so aroused while she watched added yet another thrill to the experience.

At last the baron lowered Katya to the grass, lifted her legs high until they were resting on his shoulders, and then he entered her. He entered slowly, easing the throbbing head of his penis in a little way, then withdrawing it more quickly and each time he did it, Katya's body jerked with the excitement as the skin around her clitoris was pulled and her centre of pleasure indirectly stimulated.

The baron knew Katya's body so well that he could make love to her for an hour if he wanted to, letting her have one climax after another before he finally had his own, but this time he didn't want to wait that long and after ten minutes he increased the tempo of his movements until her gasping laboured breathing and the frantic movements of her fingernails against his chest told him she was almost there.

Smoothly he thrust in and out, slowing for a few moments and then he began to thrust hard, slamming into her in the way she liked best until her tiny cries increased, her heels drummed against his shoulders and then her buttocks lifted higher into the air and he had to pull her down so that he was able to stay inside her as she obtained her release. He was surprised how detached he felt, and equally surprised to realise that even while her muscles were contracting round him he didn't climax himself.

When he withdrew he looked across at Clara. Her whole body was swollen with desire, her eyes heavy with need and her poor tortured thighs were tightly knotted with the tension of the position that had been forced on her. Crossing the lawn he eased the tension on the strip of hide, then reached inside as Rupert had done and found the fur soaked with the proof of her arousal. Her eyes darkened with desire as he touched her, but he knew that he wouldn't take her ever again. She held no attraction for him at all.

'She's ready for someone,' he commented wryly, and Clara squirmed with embarrassment. She was horribly aware of the damp fur between her thighs but she hadn't been able to help herself, and now the ache in her was such that she didn't care who penetrated her as long as it was someone who could ease the pressure aned let her enjoy the satisfaction Katya had just received.

Claud realised that his moment had come. He stood up and went over to his stepdaughter, taking the lead from Françoise's hand. 'Ask me, Clara,' was all he said, but she understood instantly.

'Please, make love to me step-papa,' she begged him, and there was no longer any reluctance in her voice. She had been reduced to nothing more than screaming, pulsating flesh and its overriding need for satisfaction was the only thing of importance. She no longer cared about what was right and wrong. She didn't even spare a thought for her mother and the way in which she was being betrayed. This tall, distinguished man standing in front of her could give her body what it had to have, and Clara was determined to make sure he did.

She reached out a hand to him. 'Please, please, step-papa,' she repeated, and with a groan of joy Claud began to unfasten all the clips and bindings that were round her plump body so that he could finally bury himself in her innocent, yielding flesh. What he failed to realise was that by allowing Françoise, Rupert and Dieter to tutor her so cleverly the flesh was no longer as innocent as when he had first seen it. Clara was sharp enough, though, to understand that he must never know this and when he began lunging vigorously into her, his hands grasping her breasts with hard, knowing hands, she swore to herself that once she was back home she would make sure she kept him enslaved so that her body would never again lack either stimulation or satisfaction.

As Claud and Clara thrashed around on the grass, both of them crying out and moaning in their ecstasy, the baron turned away. Katya had dressed and gone into the house to shower and Françoise was sitting on Rupert's lap and whispering in his ear. The baron sat down next to the silent Cassandra.

'Claud's a fool,' he said quietly. 'She'll probably lose all that puppy fat and be quite attractive, but she'll never be an innocent again.'

'I thought that's what he wanted,' said Cassandra quietly, her voice so calm that he wondered if he'd imagined the earlier restless signs of her own arousal.

'It's what he thought he wanted, but then aren't all men supposed to destroy the thing they love the most?'

'I've no idea. And even if they do, they have to be capable of loving before that can apply and Claud doesn't seem capable of loving, only lusting.'

'How very perceptive of you, my dear. What about me?'

'You told me yourself there was no such thing as love,' she responded.

'Then I needn't worry about destroying anything?' he queried with a smile.

'No.'

'What if I need to destroy something but find that I can't?'

228

Cassandra looked sideways at him. He seemed to be serious. 'I suppose you'll just have to accept that no one can have everything they want. I'm forever telling your daughters that.'

'And does it apply to you, Cassandra?'

'Yes,' she said honestly. 'I haven't been able to have lots of things I wanted, but I survived – and so will you. It might even do you good. It seems to me that you and your friends always have instant gratification. That can't be character building.'

'There speaks the governess! How strange to hear you say such things when only last night you were convulsing time and again with orgasms in front of an audience, thereby gratifying us in the very way you now insist is so wrong!'

Cassandra closed her eyes. 'I couldn't help it!'

'You could always leave,' he whispered. 'Why not go now, before I ask too much of you?'

She shook her head. 'I don't want to leave. I promised the girls I'd be here when they returned.'

His eyes sparkled. 'Yes, of course, the girls! Then I can relax, safe in the knowledge that you will never leave until they return, yes?'

She knew she was committing herself too far, but in reality she couldn't leave him, and so she nodded. 'Yes, I shall stay until they return.'

'Excellent. Tonight, when Claud has departed, we will introduce you to the joys of enemas.'

Cassandra stiffened. 'I don't think . . .'

He put a finger across her mouth. 'Be quiet, Cassandra. You have just told me that I can never ask too much of you. Enemas are very popular with many people; I think you may be surprised at the pleasure they will give you. After that, I have something very special planned. A large party for the end of the week, before Rupert and Françoise leave. I shall tell you the details after tonight.'

'Why do you like humiliating people?' she asked quietly.

'Because humiliation, like pain, can add to the pleasure. Besides, I want to see you lose control, Cassandra. Even now I don't feel that you have totally given yourself over to me at any time. You have to do this in order to remain here.'

'I have!' she protested.

'No,' he suddenly sounded annoyed. 'You have not, and I am aware of it.'

He strode away into the house and Cassandra shivered. She wondered just how far he was prepared to go in order to totally subjugate her, and if she was strong enough to withstand him.

Cassandra looked out of her bedroom window and saw Claud being chauffeured away from the isolated Hampstead house. As his car disappeared from view she remembered the baron's words in the garden earlier that day and her stomach knotted with nerves. She knew that what lay ahead for her was intended to test her courage to the limit and for a moment she actually contemplated packing her things and leaving now before it began, but she couldn't. Each challenge, and each triumph, brought her closer to this enigmatic man that she knew she loved, and she felt certain that by growing closer to him she could help him rediscover a softer, more affectionate side of his nature, a side that Katya was systematically destroying. What Cassandra did not know was that Marietta had believed the same thing, and so Marietta had died.

The bedside phone rang, and she jumped to answer it. It was the baron. 'Claud has left now. Please come to the gymnasium in fifteen minutes. You need only wear a two-piece swimming costume.'

Exactly fifteen minutes later, her mouth dry and her legs weak with tension, Cassandra opened the door to the gym, the site of her previous humiliation, and she had to make a physical effort to force herself across the threshold into the room where the other four were waiting for her.

Rupert, Françoise and Katya were totally naked, but the baron by contrast was fully dressed, and they all watched her with varying degrees of amusement or interest as she moved towards them. Rupert thought she had almost perfect legs, and his penis began to stir, while Katya revelled in the young woman's obvious distress.

The baron smiled at her. 'A nice bikini, Cassandra. Is it new?'

She felt utterly ridiculous discussing her skimpy costume at such a time but tried hard to match his everyday tone. 'Yes, Françoise helped me choose it.'

'It suits you; however, I must regretfully ask you to remove it now and then climb up onto the couch.' She hesitated and his eyes widened. 'Come, come, Cassandra; this is no time for second thoughts.'

She didn't think she'd ever get used to removing her clothes in front of a group of people, but by keeping her eyes on the baron's face she managed to unfasten her bikini top and slip it off without any fumbling. The bottom half was more of a problem, and as she stepped out of it she caught her foot in the opening and nearly stumbled. At last she was naked, and Françoise gave a murmur of appreciation. 'I think you're putting on a little weight at last, Cassandra. It suits you.'

The baron eyed the rounded breasts and his gaze skimmed on down her body taking in the fact that her abdomen was now very gently rounded rather than totally flat. He nodded. 'I agree, Françoise. Life here must suit her! Climb up on the couch. We are all anxious to begin.'

Once Cassandra was on the couch she lay flat on her back, staring at the ceiling and trying to pretend she was in her own room and entirely on her own. 'Turn on your side,' the baron said briskly. 'Then draw your knees up to your chest and put your arms round them.' She obeyed, and when the baron moved behind her, fear brought her out into a sweat.

He ran a hand down her back, feeling the stickiness

of her skin and the heat burning off it. 'There's nothing to be afraid of; Françoise would love to be in your place, wouldn't she Rupert?'

His friend laughed. 'She certainly would; this is one of my wife's favourite activities.' But Cassandra was not reassured. She'd witnessed Katya's desperate rush from the room after her enema, and there had been no sign of enjoyment on her contorted features.

Rupert walked round to stand in front of Cassandra, and his fingers started playing with her breasts, tenderly squeezing and releasing them while his thumbs moved over the nipples, teasing them into erection.

It was a good feeling, but she was horribly aware of the baron parting her tight buttocks and inserting a carefully greased finger into her tightly puckered anus. She stiffened against the intrusion which only made the insertion painful.

'Relax, Cassandra.' He sounded more than a little irritated, and she wished she could do as he wanted, but her fear was turning to terror and it was impossible to relax even a little. She heard him sigh, and then move away and tried to turn her head to see what was happening, but Rupert grasped her chin. 'Keep looking at me, Cassandra. Look at the effect you're having on me. Doesn't that excite you?'

His erection was now complete, his penis standing up almost flat against his abdomen, and the glans was purple and angry looking with a tiny drop of clear fluid leaking from the top. Cassandra wanted to be excited by his arousal, but she was shaking from head to foot and it was impossible to think of anything but what was to come.

'Lower your knees a little,' the baron said from behind her. 'Put your arms across your abdomen and bend your left knee back.' Grateful for a brief respite Cassandra quickly did as she was told, and Françoise promptly slid a hand between the now open thighs and carefully moved a vibrator over them, slowly letting it play across the labia until the outer lips began to open and she could apply the slowly pulsating head to the more sensitive inner lips, although she was careful to avoid the clitoris.

Pleasure swept up Cassandra's body, especially as Rupert continued to play with her breasts while his wife worked on her sex, and quite quickly she felt the excitement rise to a crescendo until her by now finely tuned body shuddered in a swift orgasm. The vibrator was then removed, and Françoise pushed the long, slim legs back together and thrust the knees up against Cassandra's chest. 'Put your arms round them again,' she instructed her. Reluctantly Cassandra acquiesced, but this time her body was more relaxed, and it was easier for the baron to part the cheeks of her bottom, especially as Rupert was licking and nibbling on the nipples that his thumbs had aroused. Cassandra couldn't help but enjoy the shafts of pleasure his mouth engendered.

Watched by Katya, the baron inserted the end of a piece of thin rubber tubing in the opening where his finger had been and he pushed steadily until it reached the white line marked on it. By then, the pressure of the intrusion had overriden the sensations in Cassandra's breasts, and she had an increasing desire to have a bowel motion.

'Please, stop it!' she begged the baron, struggling to get up from her prone position, but Rupert pressed her torso down, at the same time as Françoise locked her arms tightly round Cassandra's knees so that she couldn't move her legs.

'Really Cassandra, I haven't started yet,' the baron said. 'Breathe through your mouth and relax, the feeling will quickly pass.' Almost weeping with fear, she carried out his instructions and slowly the desire eased. Carefully the baron reached round her and let his hand test the tension of her stomach muscles. Once they had slackened he allowed himself to press on the bulb and let the first gush of warm, soapy liquid flow into Cassandra's back passage.

Rupert felt her frantically heaving beneath his hands, and heard her gasps of discomfort and fear as her bowel began to cramp. 'I don't want to do this!' she cried, sobbing with terror. 'Please, don't make me.'

'No one's making you do anything, Cassandra. If you want to leave the house then you have only to say,' the baron replied coldly. There was a silence, and Katya waited breathlessly, certain that this time Cassandra would leave, but her opponent closed her eyes, gritted her teeth and didn't speak.

The baron smiled to himself. 'Excellent! Now, hold on for a few minutes, with muscles tightly clenched to keep the liquid in.' She did, trying not to think about what would follow. The cramps increased, but just when she thought she couldn't bear it any longer she was bundled off the couch and hustled into the tiny closet a few feet away where the door was closed on her and she could finally sit on the round toilet seat and allow her tortured muscles to relax and expel the soapy infusion.

When it had all been released she knew that she had to go back, that this time she would be expected to learn to take pleasure from the sensations, and it was only the thought of Katya that gave her the courage to progress to the next stage. When she came out of the door, pale and shaking but with her head held high, the baron's lips parted and he actually reached out to touch her softly on the side of her face. 'This time it will be good for you, my darling,' he promised. 'Your body learns so quickly to take satisfaction from stimulation, don't be afraid. The worst is over.'

Cassandra relaxed. He was pleased with her, and Katya's previously gloating face had turned sour with disappointment. She climbed back onto the couch, and lifted her breasts up towards Rupert's waiting hands as the baron began the process again.

This time he let the liquid enter her more slowly, and as she was filled by the warmth of it she felt a heaviness in her whole abdomen, a sweet, aching heaviness that rose up towards her breasts and filtered down between her tight thighs. She gave a small moan of desire, a moan that grew in intensity when the baron let his free hand play over the tight belly, his clever fingers skimming the highly sensitised surface and sending ripples of delight across it.

Katya was furious, furious with Cassandra for having the courage to survive the first part of her ordeal and furious with her lover because this second time there was no soap in the enema, it was only warm water, and she knew what a difference this made to the urgency of the need to expel the liquid, but she also knew she had to keep her rage to herself.

The wonderful, liquid pressure spread through Cassandra's body even as her stomach muscles began to protest against the amount of liquid that had now been inserted into her back passage, but this time when the bowel muscles started to cramp she could feel the excitement the baron had promised her, an excitement that came from knowing she was on the edge of pain, and she kept her muscles tightly contracted so that the pain could gradually intrude more into the pleasure.

The baron watched her body heave and contract and he let her decide for herself how long she wanted to hold on to the water he'd measured so carefully. He saw her mouth go slack as his fingers tickled and tantalised the twisting abdomen, and then her eyes widened as the pleasure and pain rushed together in one indescribable moment of dark forbidden ecstasy and then she lost control as she was swept by a rackingly intense orgasm that first tightened the muscles of her rectum and then released them causing the warm water to gush out of her while she writhed and arched with the shockingly harsh contractions of satisfaction until finally she slumped back against the couch, her body limp and exhausted.

The baron looked across her at Rupert, and was both surprised and amused to see that Cassandra's climax had proved too much for his friend who had lost control and ejaculated over her breasts as they'd pulsated beneath his hands. The baron's amusement was increased by the fact that Rupert was the one who was going to make love to Cassandra if she survived the test, but his lack of control had now taken that reward away from him.

Rupert sighed. 'She's just so incredible! The expression in her eyes when she realised what was happening to her was fantastic. To actually see her having to accept her body's shameless delight in what was to her such an act of perversion proved my undoing!'

'Then I must reluctantly take your place,' the baron laughed.

'What about me?' Katya demanded, putting a restraining hand on the baron's arm. 'I need you, Dieter. I want you inside me, now.'

'I'm sure Peter will oblige, my dear. Perhaps you should call him up to your room. I think I'll take Cassandra into the shower.'

Françoise watched the baron help Cassandra to her feet and lead her across the gymnasium and through into the glass panelled shower room. She hardly dared look at Katya, whose rage was almost murderous at times; instead she decided to go upstairs and play with Clara until Rupert had recovered sufficiently to attend to her himself.

White with fury, Katya left the gym, but she didn't intend to use Peter for her pleasure. Only the thought of inflicting some kind of pain could ease the rejection she'd just suffered, and it would be Lucy who would receive the benefit of her frustrated anger. Fortunately she still had enough sense left to have Peter there as well. He would act as the restraining influence she'd need after what had happened.

Cassandra hardly knew where she was and when the warm water from the shower began to cascade down over her she jumped with alarm. The baron smiled and put his hands on her shoulders. 'It's only the shower, little one. Relax, and I'll attend to the soaping for you.' As his hands slid over her, spreading the lather carefully across her sweat-soaked skin and into all the folds of her body, she allowed herself to be lost in the joy of having him actually caring for her. When his hands moved between her thighs and soaped her there she thought she might faint at the contrast of the gentle pleasure he was giving her now compared to the sharp, jolting spasms of pain-streaked ecstasy he had given her earlier.

She closed her eyes, letting his hands take over entirely, marvelling at the way her body expanded beneath his touch. He covered her in sweet-scented lather and then took a sponge and washed the lather away by constantly squeezing it across her flesh, until finally the water that ran down her body was clear. Then he turned, threw the sponge away and pressed his own damp and naked body against hers, moulding himself into her as he edged her into the corner of the shower before easing her feet off the ground and up the backs of his legs.

With the water still cascading down on them she wrapped her arms round his neck and felt the tip of his penis nudging at the entrance to her vagina moving almost blindly around for a few moments before forcing her sex lips apart and then he was thrusting into her, and she felt his hands brush the wet strands of hair off her face.

'Look at me,' he whispered urgently. 'I want you to look at me while I fuck you. Open your eyes, my darling. Let me see into your soul.'

She opened her eyes, and he was able to see the ecstasy in them as he moved slowly and carefully within her, but even when the pleasure started to peak and her pelvic muscles tightened making her inner walls contract around him, he still couldn't see into her soul. Despite everything that had happened that day there was still a barrier there. She'd passed through shame and humiliation into a new world of previously unimaginable eroticism but her eyes showed nothing of this new knowledge. They were still clear and pure, and he had to see her new self-awareness reflected in them before he could be content.

His movements increased, his hips began to move faster and their soaking bodies met and parted at a frantic pace until Cassandra's eyes finally widened with the onset of her sexual release. Then the baron grasped her hips, bringing her against him with tremendous force so that she cried out as he too joined her in a spine-tingling orgasm.

For a few, infinitely precious seconds, Cassandra felt the baron's arms close round her and he held her protectively against him, but all too soon the arms were removed, the shower turned off and he was once again as remote and detached as the first day she'd set eyes on him.

'You did well, my darling,' he congratulated her, as they wrapped themselves in the soft warm towels that had been left outside the shower cabinet by a servant. 'Didn't I tell you that it would be good?'

Cassandra nodded, not wanting to admit just how good it had felt, nor how much this widening range of sensual experiences was feeding her appetite for yet further stimulation.

'Do you remember that I mentioned a party?' he continued, rubbing himself briskly dry and quickly pulling on his clothes while Cassandra lingered in the soft warmth of the towel.

'Yes,' she admitted.

'I thought it would have a grandiose theme. I shall invite a lot of friends, seventy or eighty perhaps, and it will be based on a Roman orgy. What do you think?' His eyes were amused as he waited for her response.

'I think it would be very exciting,' she replied carefully.

'Yes, but especially since I shall arrange for an extra touch, something special to start the party off well. Shall I tell you what that is to be?' Cassandra nodded.

'A slave auction, and I shall invite volunteers to be the slaves. What do you think?'

She wrapped the towel more tightly round her. 'I imagine you'll have plenty of volunteers.'

'But will you be one, Cassandra?'

Cassandra shook her head. 'No, I don't think so.'

He smiled kindly at her. 'I rather thought that would be your answer, but it isn't the one I wanted, so I shall just have to change your mind before the night of the party.'

'By force? That's hardly the way to get genuine volunteers,' she replied with a calmness that was contradicted by her quickening heartbeat.

'Not by force, Cassandra, but by kindness. In the end I usually get my own way by one means or another. This time, since as you rightly point out the victims are to be volunteers, it will have to be by kindness! Now, time to rest. You look totally exhausted. I will make your excuses at dinner tonight and you must sleep.'

With a final disarming smile he turned and left her, still wrapped in the towel and totally unsettled by the images he'd implanted in her mind. But despite her unease she slept deeply and peacefully, while unknown to her the other participants in the afternoon's game watched the entire episode again on the large television set in the corner of the drawing room.

As he watched Cassandra's final spasms of pleasure on the couch, the baron knew that he had to get her to volunteer for the slave auction, and he also knew exactly how he would bring about her capitulation. The thought of what he would do so excited him that he took the already exhausted and abused Lucy to bed with him and Katya for the rest of the night, and surprised even his mistress by the violence of his excesses on both the servant girl and Katya herself.

When the three of them awoke in the tangled heap late the next morning, the baron could hardly wait for his siege on Cassandra to begin.

# Chapter Twelve

Cassandra was surprised to find that for most of the following day she was alone in the house except for the servants. Rupert, Françoise, Clara and the twins went out sightseeing, while Katya and the baron visited some friends who were in London en route to America.

It was strange to have time to herself, and as she wandered from room to room, memories flooded back of some of the extraordinary things that had happened to her since her arrival. She had difficulty in remembering the person she'd been when she applied for the job, but she knew that she could never revert to the person she'd been then and this disturbed her.

In the middle of the afternoon she took a telephone call from Helena and Christina. The little girls both sounded highly excited, and Helena chattered on about their skiing and the various friends they'd played with. It sounded a far more normal and suitable life than the one they lived in their father's house, but they were still anxious to see him again.

'Tell Papa we're coming home on Sunday afternoon,' shouted Helena, apparently imagining that her voice had to be loud enough to cover the distance between Austria and England. 'He will be there waiting for us, won't he?'

'Yes, I'm sure he will,' Cassandra replied diplomatically.

'Are you lonely without us?' asked her charge.

Cassandra smiled. 'Of course I am.'

'Is it boring?'

She was glad that the child couldn't see how she blushed at the question. 'A little bit,' she lied, 'but I've been making the most of the sunshine and having rather a lazy time so I'm quite spoilt really.'

'We'll see you soon,' Helena yelled, and then hung up. Cassandra had only just replaced the receiver when Katya and the baron returned.

'Helena telephoned,' Cassandra informed him, trying not to remember how his hands had felt as they'd soaped her so intimately the previous night.

'When are they coming back?' he asked.

'Sunday afternoon, and she was very anxious that you were going to be here.'

'Sunday? In that case, the party must be Friday night. Katya, start telephoning the invitations around. I know it's short notice, but most of them will come.'

'What day is it today?' asked Cassandra, for whom time in the real world had ceased to have much meaning.

'Tuesday, so I have little time to find my volunteers!' the baron laughed. Katya gave him a small, intimate smile and Cassandra shivered. She'd forgotten his promise to persuade her into volunteering to be a slave at the party, and although he'd stressed he'd get her to change her mind by kindness, the look he'd exchanged with Katya made her very nervous.

Again she was surprised when the baron and his mistress disappeared upstairs, and even when the others returned from their sightseeing they didn't linger to talk but went off to their rooms. It was as though they were all trying to isolate her, but without any unkind word being spoken or any indication given of how she might have offended them.

At dinner that night the conversation was muted.

241

Rupert and the baron spoke of old school friends and discussed the skiing scene, while the women kept mainly silent, even the normally irrepressible Françoise. When Cassandra attempted to talk about what the children had been doing in Austria she was met with a wall of silence.

'I don't really think any of us are very interested in the children,' Katya said at last. 'As long as they're happy that's all that matters.'

Cassandra was annoyed. 'I think it's important that someone takes an interest in them. Children need to know they're special to someone.'

'Well, that's why you're here isn't it, Cassie dear,' Katya responded, and Cassandra fell silent.

When the meal was over she was again excluded as the baron and Katya challenged Rupert and Françoise to a game of bridge, but when she decided to go to her room, the baron was quick to stop her. 'We won't be long, Cassandra. Why not read a book down here. There are plenty in the bookcase over there.' He pointed to a glass-fronted cupboard, stacked with books, but the only time Cassandra had ever tried to look inside it, it had been locked.

Since it was clear she was expected to remain downstairs she did as he'd suggested. This time it was open. All the volumes were leather bound, and she quite expected to find first editions of rare works, but instead every one she opened was a work of erotica. Some of the books were of eastern origin, others from South America or Scandinavia, but they were all startlingly explicit. She chose one at random, quickly closed the bookcase again, then returned to her seat. When she bent her head to read, she knew that they were all aware of the contents of the book, and she was glad that her hair was long and concealed her expression from the watching eyes.

Rupert, whose turn it was to sit out, watched her with interest as she leafed through the pages, stopping now and again to read some of the passages or study

242

one of the more incredible photographs or drawings. He wished that Clara had been more like Cassandra. Françoise had enjoyed the girl, and he was grateful for anything that kept his wife happily occupied for a time, but she had never been to his taste; he would have been as eager as Françoise if he'd been given the opportunity to tutor someone like the young woman opposite him.

The more Cassandra read the more uncomfortable she felt. She was no longer an innocent, capable of being shocked by the perversions within the covers of the book, but instead a young woman whose body was now stimulated by such material, and when she studied the photos of couples engaged in various stages of bizarre but arousing copulation she imagined herself and the baron in their places.

After a time she forgot the others in the room, forgot all about the game of bridge being played out so sedately in front of her, and became lost in the imagined delights her mind conjured up from the reading material. At last the game was over. The baron and Katya had won and he stretched happily. 'A good game! Rupert, Katya tells me that she will be joining you two tonight so I think Cassandra shall come in with me. What do you think, Cassandra?'

They all turned to her, but she hadn't heard a word he'd said. Françoise laughed. 'Not quite the kind of bookworm I originally mistook her for! Cassandra, Dieter was speaking to you.'

At the sound of their collective laughter, Cassandra came out of her trance and looked up. 'I'm sorry?'

'Katya is joining Rupert and Françoise for the night, my dear. I wish you to join me,' the baron said patiently. He could see from her flushed cheeks and over-bright eyes that the book had already begun its work on her, which was exactly what he had intended.

Cassandra couldn't believe that she was actually to spend a night on her own in the huge circular bed he normally shared with Katya, and she waited for a testing condition to be added, but nothing else was said and with a rising sense of exhilaration she followed him up to the bedroom. Once there he threw himself fully clothed onto the bed and reached for the TV handset. 'Let's see what the others get up to, shall we?' he suggested.

In amazement, Cassandra saw Rupert and Françoise's room come to life on the television screen, and she gasped as their conversation echoed clearly round the room. 'Do they know you can see them?' she asked in amazement.

'Katya knows. As for the other two, well they might have guessed. Rupert knows how I have to be in control, and he'd probably see the camera although it's as well concealed as possible.'

'Are all the bedrooms bugged?' she asked, her dismay obvious.

'Except for this room, every room in the house is covered by my security system. I have a video-tape of your first initiation, we must watch it some time. I think you'd find it interesting.'

Cassandra was horrified. 'What about the gym? Did the camera see what happened there the first time, when I was with Katya and Françoise?'

He smiled. 'Of course. In fact, I watched most of that live.'

'So that's how you've always known everything about me! I think that's vile. How would you like your privacy invaded all the time?'

'I wouldn't, but this is my house, and as for privacy I think that once you agree to enter into the area of group sex and knowingly perform in front of an audience, you yourself forfeit your right to privacy.'

'But I didn't at first! I didn't know anything at the start, and you were already filming me.'

He sighed. 'I do hope you're not going to make a scene, my darling. We have the whole night in front of us, with nothing but pleasure and excitement in store. Why spoil it with an argument?'

Cassandra wondered how she could explain to him

that she felt betrayed. That even when she'd been with him and his friends it had only been for him, and that the thought of her actions being video-taped so that people could amuse themselves watching it at a later date was almost unbearable because it brought her face to face with her own moral decline.

'I don't want to see what you've done to me, and I don't want other people to see,' she protested.

He reached up a hand and pulled her down beside him. 'I haven't "done" anything to you that you didn't want done, Cassandra. I knew the moment I saw you that you'd enjoy being part of this household, and your enjoyment has grown with every new experience. At the moment you still seem to be experiencing some kind of shame about what's happened to you, but that too will pass. It has to pass if you're to remain here with me. You're nearly there, Cassandra. You've nearly played the game to the full. Don't start backing out now. I want you to succeed.'

His dark eyes looked almost black with intensity and she trembled, trapped by their magnetic power. 'I won't be a slave for you,' she whispered. 'I can't degrade myself like that, not even for you.'

He pretended not to have heard. 'Look, my darling. Don't you want to see how Katya gets her thrills?'

Against her will, Cassandra's eyes were drawn to the screen. Katya was standing upright against one of the bedposts, her hands bound round the post behind her. A piece of black velvet ribbon was wound round her neck and the bedpost, preventing her from lowering her head at all.

'She loves pain,' the baron explained in a bored tone. 'It's quite common for both sexes to enjoy a mixture of pain and pleasure, as you yourself have learnt, but Katya's desires have moved ever onwards. She can take incredible pain, so much in fact that I no longer wish to inflict it. Unfortunately she also desires to inflict as much pain on other, less masochistically minded people. There is naturally amusement to be found from

245

such incidents, but always within strict controls, and Katya no longer wishes to accept the controls necessary for safety and mutual satisfaction. In other words, she is becoming a danger.

'I enjoy my life. I am happy with the entertainments I can arrange to fulfil my desires, but I need the right companion for life to be complete. Katya no longer seems the right companion, yet until I find a replacement she must stay. Volunteer to be one of the slaves, Cassandra. Take part in the final entertainment, play the role well, and you will be the one to remain while Katya goes.'

He pressed a hand tenderly into the nape of her neck and let his fingers massage the muscles there. 'Say yes, Cassandra. Tell me you'll volunteer.'

'No,' Cassandra said firmly. 'If Katya's like you say, I'd be at her mercy for an entire evening, because you wouldn't intervene to save me, would you?'

'Perhaps not,' he conceded.

'I can't do it. I can't face a room full of strangers, chained up and then treated like some chattel because I've no doubt that's what it will be like until I've no shred of dignity or self-respect left. I simply can't.'

He looked at her out of the corner of his eye and saw how close to tears she was. 'Never mind that for now, let's watch,' he said urgently, and she felt his arm go across her back as Françoise came into view of the camera.

She too was naked, and she knelt on the floor in front of Katya, closing her mouth around the other woman's sex and working her tongue frantically round the inner crevices while Katya's hips thrust forward as much as her restraints would allow. The baron pressed another button and the picture moved into close-up, showing them clearly how Françoise was thrusting her tongue inside Katya, then bringing it out and swirling the juices around the whole area until the fastened woman's thighs were trembling with delight and her little cries of excitement rang loudly in Cassandra's ears.

246

In the meantime, Rupert was kneading Katya's breasts, his hands rough as he pushed them up and together, pinching at the nipples from time to time until they were swollen and red. Then he produced a small flexible cane and drew it across the heaving breasts, letting it linger across the nipples while Katya's breathing quickened and she moaned with delight.

Cassandra watched the visible signs of Katya's arousal and felt her own excitement beginning again. The book she'd read earlier had made her breasts feel heavy and her stomach tighten, now the same thing was happening again only more obviously and the sight of Katya's heaving breasts and slack mouth was incredibly arousing.

'Rupert's making her wait a long time!' the baron laughed, pulling Cassandra's blouse out of the waistband of her skirt and then reaching for the buttons. Cassandra quickly unfastened the buttons herself, and when she unclipped her bra and her breasts were finally free, she almost gasped with relief.

The baron enclosed a breast in his right hand, but continued to watch the screen. Suddenly, Rupert raised his arm and brought the cane down sharply across the top of Katya's breasts, right through the middle of the already engorged nipples. Katya screamed in delight, her body jerked convulsively against its bonds and then as the tremors began to die away Françoise let her teeth nip at the tender flesh of Katya's inner lips and this brought forth a second scream of pain-filled satisfaction from Katya, whose body heaved so violently that Cassandra wondered if the bonds would hold.

While she was still shuddering from the climaxes, Rupert pushed his wife out of the way and stood in front of the bound woman. Then he pulled a rubber sheath on over his erection. The sheath was thick, with large, protruding nodules all down the shaft, and Cassandra shivered at the thought of having it pushed inside her. Although the velvet ribbon round her neck prevented Katya from seeing exactly what Rupert was doing, Françoise was whispering in her ear, obviously describing the sheath in detail, and she was whimpering frantically for him, again trying to thrust her pelvis forward.

Rupert roughly pressed her back against the bedpost, slapping at her abdomen with his hands until she obeyed, and only when she managed to make herself stand still, did he force his way into her. Cassandra could imagine the feeling of its initial intrusion only too well, yet Katya's eyes were enormous with excitement, and his hard, ruthless thrusting made her scream with a mixture of pain and passion that fascinated the baron who tightened his grip on Cassandra's breast without even realising it.

For several minutes Rupert continued his brutal thrusting, and Katya continued to scream more and more loudly, further excited by Françoise who was hitting her slowly and rhythmically across the belly with the cane causing red weals to appear on the carefully nurtured blemish-free skin.

Finally it was all too much, and yet again Katya's body jerked and shook as she was racked by a final, glorious climax that triggered Rupert's, and Cassandra watched as he bucked and shuddered against the fastened body of his best friend's mistress.

As Françoise began to unfasten Katya, the baron turned off the set. 'They look as though they're going to have a good night! Let's hope we can enjoy ourselves without the pain, my darling.'

Cassandra was unbearably excited by what she'd witnessed. Although it wasn't the way she would choose to gain sexual satisfaction, seeing Katya so out of control, utterly lost in a world of blissful sensuality, had made her own keenly-honed body hunger for the same sensations. Within minutes both she and the baron were naked and lying in the middle of the huge bed as she waited for him to begin to satisfy her craving.

The baron knew from the flush on Cassandra's cheeks and the darkness of her eyes that she was already highly aroused, and that he had to be careful not to go too fast or his plan would fail even before it had begun. He turned her onto her stomach so that she was resting face down on the soft bed and then knelt across her to massage her back and shoulders, letting his testicles brush against the back of her thighs as he moved to and fro.

His hands were exerting exactly the right amount of pressure, and Cassandra's muscles revelled in the deep massage. After a few minutes her skin flinched in surprise as he let a few drops of scented oil fall onto her spine, drops that he then spread around the whole of her back, paying particular attention to the sensitive base of her spine and round the buttocks and the hips.

His movements pressed her down into the softness of the bed, and she wriggled luxuriously against the silk sheets, savouring the texture of the material against her slowly parting outer lips. Tiny currents of electricity began to spark deep inside her and she sighed with delight.

'Turn over, let me do your front,' the baron said quietly, and she rolled over, her skin anticipating the feel of those knowing fingers as they spread the oil across her aching breasts and slowly tightening belly.

His touch was feather-light, almost too light and she pushed her breasts up against his hand for stronger stimulation but he ignored her and moved his fingers away until she lay still again.

When his hands finally reached the join at the top of her thighs, his fingers began to move in the outer creases, pressing on nerves concealed deep inside her labia without actually opening her at all. She felt as though her inner tissue was tightening, drawing up towards the middle of her body, and she gave a whimper of excitement.

Carefully he teased the outer lips apart, then put the fingers of his right hand up to her mouth so that she could moisten them with her own saliva before he began to caress the silky smoothness of her opened sex.

She loved the sensation of his fingers, damp from her own mouth, moving up and down her inner channels and when it circled the throbbing entrance to her vagina she pushed her body down, eager for him to touch her in that special place he'd found just inside the vaginal walls but he only laughed and drew the finger away again. 'Slowly, my darling,' he said huskily.

She felt as though she were melting inside. Every muscle was tight while blood coursed through her veins and the heat of desire spread through every nerve ending until all her wanton longing was centred on one tiny spot, the tight little clitoris aching with need, which impinged on her awareness as never before.

Very slowly the baron's finger slid up towards it, hesitated, then circled it carefully, and he watched how it continued to expand until it was standing more erect than he had ever seen it while her whole body quivered with frustrated longing.

He flicked his finger with deadly precision, allowing it to brush the side of the taut bud for only a fleeting moment, enough to make Cassandra gasp and start to arch, but not quite enough to topple her over the edge and into her orgasm, and then as her own frantic hip movements threatened to complete the pleasure he placed the palm of his other hand firmly against her pubic bone and used two fingers to draw back the hood of the clitoris and ensure her immobility until the climax-threatening pulsations ceased and the moment of danger was over.

'I think we should try something different,' he said pleasantly, releasing her from his grip.

Cassandra lifted her head from the pillow in heavy-eyed astonishment. 'I was just about to come!' she exclaimed. 'Why did you stop?'

He looked at her in apparent surprise. 'Were you? I'm sorry, I thought you'd lost it. I know it happens sometimes, that's why I thought we'd better try something else.'

She couldn't believe what he'd done to her. Her

breasts were still painfully tight and there was a heavy ache in the pit of her stomach, the ache of unsatisfied arousal. 'I didn't need anything else!'

He sighed in regret. 'My dear Cassandra, what can I say? We all make mistakes, even me! Never mind, the pleasure will be all the greater in a moment. Just let me show you what I had in mind.'

She propped herself up on one elbow to see what he was doing, but then he switched on the television set and she suddenly saw herself lying on a rug in the room next to the swimming pool. Katya was holding her sex lips apart while the baron brushed against her clitoris with a long pointed feather, and Cassandra watched her own body writhing as it tried to control its movements, and saw herself struggling to remain silent with incredulous fascination.

She was so caught up in the scene being replayed in front of her that she was taken totally unawares when the baron suddenly seized her by the shoulders, pressing her down flat on the bed, only now there was no pillow beneath her head. The pillow had been removed and with dexterity born of years of practice he pulled her hands up above her head and fastened her wrists in the holes of a spreader board that had previously been hidden beneath the pillow. The board was fastened securely to the bed, and the top of her body now resembled the figure 'Y'.

'Stop it! I thought I was meant to enjoy tonight!' she protested.

'You will,' he assured her, but his smile was not altogether kind. 'Now I'm going to do the same with your legs, Cassandra. Your thighs will be fastened to a similar board beneath your legs, and then you'll be open to me all the time. That way I can be sure of controlling all the stimulation myself. In any case, I've noticed that you find it easier to take your pleasure when some of the responsibility is taken away from you. That way you feel less guilt over your sensual

251

excesses, and I don't want guilt to spoil our night together.'

Cassandra didn't believe a word he was saying, but although she kicked out furiously he was far too strong for her, and a hard wooden board was inserted beneath her legs with steel bracelets set on each side, which he locked round her lower thighs.

He examined her carefully, then propped an oval cushion beneath her neck so that her head was elevated sufficiently for her to see the television screen again if he chose to show her more footage of herself at a later date.

He wasn't surprised to find that she had started to tremble, but he was quick to take pains to reassure her, talking soothingly as he tenderly stroked the still swollen breasts.

'There's no need to be afraid of me, my darling. I promised you nothing but pleasure, and that's all you'll get. The only thing I forgot to mention is that until you agree to volunteer to be a slave your fulfilment will be withheld.

'It's an interesting sight for a man to watch, but knowing how much your body has come to depend on sexual satisfaction I don't think this little game will last too long. If it does, I shall admire your strength of character even more than I do already, but you will experience considerable discomfort from time to time.

'It isn't painful, nor damaging, to arouse a woman and leave her unsatisfied but it does have certain unfortunate side effects. Your breasts for example will ache and feel uncomfortably full, while your vulva,' here he paused to cup his hand round her pubic area, 'will also feel heavy and remain enlarged for several hours before it begins to accept its fate and return to normal. Then of course I shall excite it again, and so we will go on for as long as necessary.

'I should remind you that we have several days at our disposal, so this is a contest that you really cannot win,

252

but prolong it if you wish. The choice is yours entirely. Now, where exactly were we when I stopped?'

Cassandra knew that she was utterly helpless. She wanted to bring her legs together, to lock her thighs against him so that he couldn't touch her vulnerable, sensitive flesh but the spreader board held her thighs in its iron grip, while her hands were stretched out above her head so that her breasts were pushed upwards, emphasising their fullness and making it impossible for her to disguise the excitement he'd already caused.

'Yes, I remember,' he said softly, and then to her horror, his fingers once again parted the lips of her sex only now he lifted her buttocks off the bed as far as the spreader would allow and his tongue slid along the thin membrane between her rectum and vagina, where the nerve endings were right at the very surface, and her body's response was startling in its violence. The walls of her vagina tightened, her buttocks contracted increasing the internal pressure and she felt a tight hard knot of aching desire deep inside her abdomen.

The baron knew how unimaginably arousing this particular caress could be and watched the pupils of her eyes dilate while a flush of excitement covered her chest and spread up her throat to her ear lobes. When he judged she was dangerously close to losing control he stopped, eased her back onto the bed and then picked up a tiny brush taken from one of his daughter's paint boxes. He put the tiny tip in his mouth, sucking it into a fiendishly small point and then showed it to Cassandra.

'Look at this, my darling. Imagine how it will feel when this brush is allowed to sweep across your bud of pleasure. Think of the sensations when your aching clitoris is touched by this delicate tip. Won't that be good? Doesn't the thought of it excite you?'

Cassandra groaned aloud, squirming against her bonds and trying to kick at him with her feet, but although free they were kept apart by the thigh fetters and she couldn't reach him. His words inflamed her even more than his mouth had done moments earlier, and she could feel moisture seeping from her opening as he talked, while the need for his touch grew and grew inside her.

He laughed at the expression on her face, then reached up and let the backs of his fingers rub against her nipples, which hardened even more at the feel of his slightly roughened skin against them. He spread his knuckles wider, letting the surface area of her breasts feel their movements until she was gasping for some relief from the throbbing pressure, whereupon he left her breasts and returned to the spread thighs.

As he began his diabolical application of the tiny brush he restarted the video of Cassandra's pool-side arousal, and she was forced to watch herself receiving stimulation while he cleverly applied further, even more erotic stimulation to her body and poor Cassandra thought she'd go mad as wave after wave of excitement swept over her. Her cries from the video mingled with her pleas for him not to stop as the brush prolonged her torture beyond the point she would have thought possible.

Her whole body felt so swollen she thought her skin would split, and the dreadful aching in her breasts and the pit of her stomach spread to every part of her, even the thigh muscles held so rigidly in place; yet still the brush continued to play on her skin.

The baron watched her carefully from beneath lowered lids. He was an expert at this particular game, though it was usually played with the consent of the woman, and he knew that he could let her go so far she would believe she'd passed the point of no return, and then when he stopped, her heartbreak would be wonderful to see.

Cassandra continued to tighten and her flesh continued to leap, until at last she felt the strange inward sensation of strings being drawn up inside her that always meant she was about to climax. The brush was so close to her clitoris now that she couldn't help but plead with the baron, even though she thought she could climax without its help, but desire for its touch drove her to beg while her body continued on its final contraction prior to release.

'Touch me there, please,' she cried, and remembering an early lesson with him she even bore down so that her clitoris was more exposed and presented an easier target for the brush. 'Let me come!' She was almost screaming at him now, all reserve gone as her body's needs drove her on. 'I'm nearly there, you have to let me come now. Please! Please!'

He let the brush come to rest at the base of the stem of the clitoris and moved it a fraction up the tiny shaft so that her breath caught in her throat and her toes began to curl. 'Will you be a slave for me?' he whispered. 'Say yes and it will all be over, my darling. Just that one little word is all I need to hear.'

Her head thrashed from side to side as the brush moved fractionally again, and the tingling between her stretched thighs deepened into a pulsing that was climbing to a crescendo. 'No!' she muttered through clenched teeth. 'I won't! I won't!'

Once more the brush moved. Cassandra's body knew that it was almost there and began to rise up, her abdomen tightened into a rock-hard swelling and her nipples hurt they were so congested but she knew that she was there, she'd beaten him. Then, as the tightly coiled spring of aroused desire got ready to burst, the brush was removed. His hand pushed the protective hood away from her tormented clitoris and he held her lower body captive between his hands, making all movement impossible so that once more the pulsations were forced to die down; the stomach very slowly softened again and the wonderful, electrifying tingles that had heralded her release vanished, leaving her aching, tense and cruelly thwarted.

It was too much. Cassandra burst into tears. The baron watched her and said nothing. He'd known how it would be for her, and understood how desperately she'd craved the final peak of excitement he and the others had taught her to need, but this was the only weapon he was willing to use against her and he always got his own way. It wasn't his fault if she chose to be unnecessarily stubborn; one word from her and she could even now be writhing with satisfaction instead of sobbing with frustration.

At last the tears stopped. She glared at him, and he knew that at that moment she hated him. 'Poor Cassandra,' he said softly. 'Try and sleep now. I'll be back later to see how you're going.'

To her disbelief he then snapped out the light, leaving her alone in the darkness with her swollen aching body and as an added torture he'd left the video playing so that even when she closed her eyes she could hear her own cries of sexual satisfaction; a satisfaction she could no longer obtain. Eventually her body began to calm down. She still ached, but not as intensely, and although her sex lips felt swollen they were no longer tingling and irritated so that an hour or so later she finally fell asleep.

Her dreams were full of confused erotic images. Her body tried to toss and turn, but was thwarted by the spreader boards, and her head moved restlessly as she cried out in her sleep. Then, after what seemed a very short time, her eyes opened again.

She was still in the dark, but the baron had returned, and now he was rubbing a silk covered hand across her body, letting it slide over her slim figure, down the tender sides and up the middle of her breasts to glide round her neck and down the soft flesh beneath her ears.

He heard her breathing quicken and knew she was awake. 'I thought you'd rested sufficiently, my darling. After all, I did promise you a full night of pleasuring. I'm going to turn the boards now, it will be easier if you help me. If you try and fight I shall have to get Peter in to help.'

Cassandra didn't resist, in fact she welcomed being

moved onto her stomach because then she could press down against the bed again and possibly trigger her own climax. However, the baron had thought of that and he pushed a thick bolster widthways across the bed beneath her waist so that her sex was lifted clear of the bed and there was no pressure on it at all.

Now the silk-covered hand glided up and down her spine, and along her arms to the fastened wrists. Then it covered her back in tiny circles that made her whole body start to come alive before it reached the highly erogenous backs of her knees. There the hand rested, playing first with one and then the other, inflaming the nerve endings until the pleasure turned close to pain, reminding her of a dull toothache, but just the same it had her panting with excitement.

After that he removed the silk covering and used both hands to part her buttocks, carefully licking the skin at the entrance to her anus, flicking at it so that she jerked reflexively. Eventually he opened her wider and let his tongue go deeper, reaching inside the dark hole until she began to moan with excitement. Now he sat back a little on the bed and surveyed her sex, partially opened to him by the bolster, and the parted legs tightened against the spreader board. She was very moist; she was trying frantically to press down even though there was nothing for her to press against.

When he reached up beneath her, Cassandra cried out with relief. The whole area between her thighs felt heavy and swollen again, and the dreadful aching had returned so that she felt she'd go mad if she didn't get some form of more direct stimulation leading to release.

The baron knew very well that by now she'd be even more sensitive to his every move. Her bladder would be quite full, it was several hours since she'd been to the bathroom and they'd all drunk strong coffee during the evening, and her earlier arousal wouldn't yet have completely vanished. He let his fingers wander up her outer lips until they reached the place where her pubic hair began to grow at the base of her stomach.

257

Once there he spread his fingers outwards and up then pressed them firmly down against her unusually tight belly, and her groan told him that he was right. Already those sparks of pleasure would be manifesting themselves, and he let his fingers continue to play against her while he positioned himself close enough to allow the head of his cock to rest lightly against her entrance.

Since it was all taking place in the dark, Cassandra had no idea of what was going to happen to her from one moment to the next. When his wicked fingers began their measured dance of torment on her body, she'd tried desperately to climax at once, but the touch was too light. However, once she felt the head of his cock against her she thrust down, determined to force him inside her. What she forgot was the spreader board holding her thighs apart, and her imprisoned muscles screamed in agony as she attempted to force them beyond their capabilities.

'Naughty!' the baron reproved with a laugh, giving her a light slap on her buttocks. 'If you want me inside you, you know what you have to do. Just tell me you'll be a slave girl, Cassandra, and I'll slip into you now, I'll move myself inside so that you can't stop coming. Imagine it, Cassandra. Imagine how it will feel.'

Cassandra sobbed her frustration aloud. She could imagine it only too well, and her body had been taught to need it, but she couldn't, wouldn't, give in to him. The thought of being a slave, humiliated and passed around amidst a party of strangers was more than she could stand. 'No!' she cried, and then moaned as he slid the tip of his cock into her entrance for a moment, knowing full well that this was the most sensitive part of her, and that by letting her feel him there he could easily drive her insane without fully penetrating her.

For what seemed like hours that was what he did. He rotated his hips, withdrew and re-entered her and then rubbed his whole penis along her open channels, letting the head touch briefly against the engorged clitoris before pulling it away and back down to the entrance.

Cassandra's stomach, pelvis and thighs all felt hard and painfully swollen. She heard herself crying out at every movement, every touch, and she was so over-stimulated that several times she thought she'd pass out if the sensations didn't either ease or let her have her release, but the baron was far too clever to let her escape through unconsciousness, and he kept talking to her while he worked, forcing her to think about what her body was already telling her.

At last he decided that it was time for another break. Still in the dark she was turned onto her back again, but this time one of the tiny flexible rods was pressed between her outer lips which were then closed round it so that even when she was alone she had to endure the constant pressure that promised so much and delivered nothing.

Because of this constant pressure her body found it much harder to come down from its state of arousal, and she had only just managed to drift into a light sleep when the baron returned again. He put on the light and stroked a hand over Cassandra's hot forehead. She opened her eyes and groaned when she realised her arousal was going to begin again already.

'Say yes,' he whispered in her ear, his hand brushing through her hair in a tender gesture that was in total contrast to the way he was tormenting her. 'Give in now, Cassandra.' But she shook her head, and her refusal excited him.

He'd brought a small vibrator with him for this visit, and the first thing he did was let it play across her already over-stimulated breasts, watching as the recently detumescent nipples immediately stiffened again, the blood rushing through them and forcing them into painfully hard peaks that he then laved with his tongue, forcing a cry of pleasure from deep inside Cassandra's throat.

He watched her, his eyes holding hers as he let the

vibrator move to her ear lobes and he saw the amazement in her eyes as sensations coursed through them as well. After a time, when she slowly became accustomed to the new shafts of pleasure, he trailed the vibrator down through the valley between her swollen breasts and then around her navel until at last it touched on the nerve endings from her bladder and she jerked, her eyes growing huge in her face and her cheeks glowing with the wonderful rising heat and pressure that was tightening the coil inside her yet again.

Her body didn't want to respond, but the baron knew how to play it so that it had no choice, and he cunningly let the vibrator travel around the creases inside the tops of her thighs, stimulating the rod that was still encased there, trapped by her own moisture and held by the outer lips and the gentle tremors of growing excitement were the most piquant moments of delight her body had ever known.

The baron saw the effect he was having, and continued to hold the vibrator in the same place. He knew that the soft flexible rod wouldn't give sufficient stimulation to trigger her climax, knew that she was helpless to gain her release and that all he had to do was keep her arousal at the same level from now on and her resistance would finally have to crumble.

Cassandra knew it too. The insidiously delicate movements of the rod had her moaning aloud, because it had been so carefully positioned that no matter what happened her clitoris couldn't be touched and as the pleasure grew so too did the hideous mind-destroying ache in that starved core of her, until she was utterly consumed by her need for just one touch on the tightly gathered collection of nerve endings that was now the centre of her world.

She cried out, she threw her head from one side to the other, her feet kicked and she twisted at the waist in her terrible craving, but the vibrator was held steady and the plateau of ecstasy stayed steady, refusing to rise to the peak she had to have if she was to stay sane.

She had never known such desperation. Every inch of her was consumed by wanting. She was on fire with her need for release, and she could feel sweat dripping from her breasts every time the baron suckled all too briefly on them. His mouth was as cunning as his hands, and when his tongue outlined every one of her ribs as well as dipping into her tiny belly button she screamed at him frantically.

'Please, please, stop! It's hurting me.'

'No it isn't, it's arousing you, Cassandra. There's no pain, except in your lack of release, and that's in your own hands. I enjoy giving you pleasure, and I can't possibly stop now when you're looking so deliciously flushed and stimulated.'

'I can't bear it!' she sobbed as his mouth returned to enclose the entire areola of her right breast and suck tenderly on it. 'It has to stop or I'll go mad.'

But it didn't have to stop, and his hands and mouth continued to play her until she was nothing but a mass of stimulated nerve endings and pulsating need that finally forced everything from her mind except this over-riding craving for satisfaction. 'Perhaps I'll take another little break now,' he said suddenly, and at the thought of the blissful torture being stopped and then restarted she finally snapped.

'No!' she cried, and it was the loudest he'd ever heard her scream. 'Please, don't go. I'll volunteer, I promise. I'll be a slave for you, only don't go. It hurts so much when you stop and leave me like this. I'll do anything you want as long as you let me come.'

She heard his sigh of satisfaction, and then his face was close to hers and he put his lips against her mouth. 'You won't regret it,' he promised her. 'The party will be the most wonderful experience of your life, I promise.' She didn't care any more. She didn't want to hear about the party, or the slave auction, or anything at all except that he was finally going to let her have her release. 'Let me come,' she whimpered. Very carefully he parted her sticky outer lips, removed the cruel but wonderful pressure of the plastic rod and then bent his head and swirled his tongue round the incredibly swollen clitoris that had been pulsating in vain all through the long night.

As she felt the roughness of his tongue encase the wickedly neglected centre of her pleasure, Cassandra's mind exploded and her whole body flooded with a liquid warmth while her hips arched up off the bed and her heels pressed down into the bed trying to lift the imprisoned thighs.

She was still crying out and thrashing around as the baron unfastened the spreader bar round her thighs and thrust himself into her, at the same time inserting the tiny vibrator into her back passage so that her muscles contracted fiercely again and the walls of her vagina enclosed about him until he was held in a velvet grip that throbbed with repeated wrenching spasms so that he felt his seed being milked from him by the force of her climax. Even when he was spent he kept the vibrator inside her rectum so that she continued to spasm round him for several minutes, all the time crying out with the bliss of final satisfaction.

Eventually even she was sated, and he withdrew the vibrator, eased himself out of her and let himself rest against the entire length of her body, feeling her now soft nipples tangle in the hairs of his chest.

After a time he released her wrists and rolled onto his side, keeping his arms round her so that she was still caught against the length of him, and wrapping his legs round hers as further binding. 'There!' he laughed. 'Didn't I promise you a night to remember?'

She kept her face hidden against his chest. She was utterly exhausted by the night, and now that her body was finally satisfied all she could think about was the promise she'd made him, and the fact that she would be open to Katya's most inventive perversions.

'You mustn't be afraid,' he murmured as she pressed closer to him. 'I won't let them hurt you, you know that.'

'I didn't want to say yes,' she whispered, wishing that he would keep her in his arms for ever.

'I know, but right from the start we both knew that you were going to, didn't we?'

'No, I really thought . . .' She tailed off, aware now of how ridiculous she'd been to think she could outwit him in any of his games.

'You were magnificent, my darling girl,' he told her tenderly, and then – as though afraid he'd said too much – he abruptly removed his arms and rolled away from her. 'I hope the other three had as good a time as we did. We must look at their video sometime. And you do have the consolation of knowing they can never see what went on here tonight.'

Cassandra pushed herself into a sitting position. 'How many slaves will there be at the party?' she asked nervously.

'Ten or twelve, I imagine. Enough for each group of guests to have one or two to themselves. Naturally you'll belong to our group, and I shall try and "buy" a male slave to go with you. It makes for better entertainment.'

Cassandra rubbed at her wrists. For a moment she felt like crying again. A few seconds earlier they'd really seemed close, as though there was an emotional bond between them, and yet now he was talking about her as entertainment at the forthcoming party.

'We must get some sleep,' he continued, ignoring the pain in her eyes. 'You might as well stay here. I dislike sleeping alone after sex.' It was a lie, normally he preferred to sleep alone, but Cassandra didn't know that, and so when he flung an arm over her back and fell almost instantly asleep, she didn't realise what a compliment he'd paid her. However, Katya who was keeping a watch on the comings and goings from the main bedroom knew, and it fuelled her already all-consuming hatred of the girl who would very soon belong to her and her friends for a whole evening.

As Cassandra and the baron slept, Katya and Françoise plotted while Rupert listened and mentally placed a bet on the final outcome of the party that promised to be one of the best the baron had ever held.

# Chapter Thirteen

'How do I look?' Katya asked, spinning round in front of the baron as he dressed for the party. He turned round on his stool in front of the mirror and studied her with gratifying interest. She knew that the purple and black dress which clung tightly over her breasts and then hung in draped folds to her ankles was both striking and flattering.

'You look most attractive,' he assured her, but there was a note of amusement in his voice that she didn't care for.

'Is there something funny about it?' she demanded.

'Not at all. I take it that you chose purple because of its connections with Rome rather than because it suited you!'

'Françoise and I both thought it suited me. Anyway, you've never had any idea about fashion. It's only after a woman's taken her clothes off that you can call yourself a connoisseur,' she retorted.

He laughed. 'That's probably true. At least you'll make an impact, which I'm sure was the intention. How many are here?'

'Sixty-three at the last count. When does the slave auction begin?'

'Not until after we've dined. Are you looking forward to the grand finale?'

Katya hesitated. Normally she would have said yes. It was exactly the kind of entertainment that amused her and, with her particular sexual preferences and skills, a confrontation at which she would excel, but she knew better than to imagine it would be an easy victory. She had never expected Cassandra to get this far. The very fact that the girl was still there was worrying, and Katya knew that after tonight either she or her rival would leave his house for ever.

'Yes, I am,' she told him, hoping he hadn't noticed the pause. 'I'd like to see Cassandra totally lose control and give herself over to the pleasures we've taught her, but unfortunately I don't think that's going to happen. Mind you, it will be great fun trying to break through the last barriers!'

'You don't think it's going to happen?' The baron sounded thoughtful. 'If I were a betting man I'd say it was, but we will see. If I'm wrong and you're right, then we'll be looking for a new governess for the children from next week. I shall have no further use for her.'

'What if I'm wrong?' asked Katya, finally daring to voice the question she and Françoise had discussed endlessly over the past forty-eight hours. He rose from the stool and walked over to her, putting his hands on each side of her face and kissing her very lightly on the tip of her nose. 'In that case, you will be looking for a new benefactor and lover, my darling. So, as you can tell, the stakes are high. Now, I must finish dressing and then we will go down to dinner.'

As his hands released her, Katya's legs gave way and she sat down on the bed. She had never expected him to be so blunt. Their relationship went back many years, and she'd imagined she was as necessary to him as he was to her. With those few words he'd destroyed all her self-confidence, but he'd also made her even more determined to succeed.

As they went down to dinner together she concentrated her mind on what lay ahead. Cassandra would be the slave, forced to do anything the baron and his friends chose, and Katya would be one of his group. She would be in control of the situation, not Cassandra. Given that advantage she couldn't believe she'd fail. She dared not believe it because if Dieter cast her adrift she didn't know where in the world she would go.

Katya was a survivor. By the time she and Dieter entered the dining room her head was erect, her eyes shining and she held her lover's hand tightly in her own. No one there would have guessed that there was anything amiss in her world, and all through the meal she chattered and laughed with the other guests, occasionally catching the baron's eye and smiling at him across the table. He admired her for that.

Cassandra was not looking nearly as cheerful as her antagonist in the forthcoming confrontation. While Katya was laughing and talking with the other guests, Cassandra had been herded into a large attic at the top of the house where, along with a dozen or so other volunteers she was waiting to be fitted into her slave costume.

Peter was there as well, but to her surprise there was no sign of Lucy. Instead Clara was there, having presumably elected to be a slave for the night, although she was now looking as though she was regretting her decision as a tall, forbidding slave master fitted her into a complicated harness. This covered her sex with a leather shield which was attached to a chain round her waist while the top half, made entirely of black rubber, fitted her like a glove, covering everything except for her large breasts which stuck out in front of her for everyone to see.

Not all the slave girls wore the same costumes. Some were in short, satin tunics with matching satin panties which fitted snugly into their crotches, but in these cases their hands were fastened behind their backs so that they couldn't loosen the costume in any way.

The men, of whom there were only four, were all dressed the same. Their penises were covered in leather sheaths which were held against the sides of their legs by attached thongs, and they all had their wrists hand-cuffed; a light shackle round their left ankle prevented them from moving with any speed.

Cassandra, still in her own cotton skirt and blouse, shivered with apprehension as the slave master approached her. She assumed that he was a friend of the baron's but his eyes were a terrifying chill grey, like the sea in winter, and when he caught hold of her upper arms, his hands were rough.

'Name?' he demanded, tearing off her blouse before she had time to unfasten the buttons herself. She was so nervous that for a moment she couldn't find her voice and he pinched her right ear lobe hard until she gave a yelp of pain. 'Name?' he repeated.

'Cassandra,' she said softly. He gave her a more searching glance, as though the name meant something to him, and then pulled her bra straps from her shoulders. 'Hurry up and get your clothes off, girl,' he ordered. 'This is no time to start acting coy.'

Ridiculously considering what lay ahead of her, Cassandra wanted to protect her breasts from his gaze; however she had no choice but to take off all her clothes until she was standing naked in front of him. He ran a cold hand over her. 'A harness, I think,' he remarked, signalling for an assistant to bring him one.

Cassandra had been hoping for a tunic and panties; she didn't want to go out onto a stage or platform with her breasts wantonly displayed like Clara's, but she was relieved to find that this harness wasn't the same as the other girl's. Rings were slid up her legs supporting two pieces of webbed material held together in the middle by a chain with a padlock fitted in the centre of her sex lips. Her breasts were supported by a similar construction that lifted them without revealing anything and a small padlock covered the ends, resting lightly on her nipples. A slim chain was put round her waist and her hands were fastened at the front of this.

They were all ready over an hour before the guests had finished their meal, and this added to the general air of tension in the claustrophobic room. Cassandra was grateful when Peter, accompanied by another youth with fair hair and gentle blue eyes, came over to her.

'May I join you?' he queried apologetically.

'Of course! Are you as nervous as I am?' she asked.

He glanced at the slave master who was busy conversing with his assistant. 'Better keep your voice down or he'll separate us. To be honest, I'm more excited than nervous, but I had to get away from Clara. The sight of her tits when I'm wearing this hideous contraption is painfully arousing.'

For the first time, Cassandra took in the full significance of the leather sheath strapped firmly down, and she shivered in sympathy. 'Why did you volunteer?' she asked curiously.

'I like anything that's different. We had a wonderful masked ball in Venice once, but I think this is going to be even better. The baron's so inventive. What about you? I imagined you'd be one of the guests.'

Cassandra shrugged lightly. 'I suppose I thought I'd like to try something different too, but I'm beginning to regret it. I don't like this atmosphere much.'

'It's all meant to add to the authenticity. By the way, this is Anton. He's come over from Austria with a group of the baron's friends, and they drew lots to see which of them got to be the slave.'

Cassandra smiled at Anton in sympathy. 'And you lost!'

He shook his head. 'No, I won.'

She would never understand them all, she thought to herself. 'Why isn't Lucy here?' she asked Peter.

'The baron thinks she's had too much fun lately! Besides, Clara wanted her last night here to be special. After this she returns to her mother and stepfather, and then who knows what her life holds.' Remembering Claud, Cassandra didn't think there would be many pleasant surprises in it.

As time passed, some of the girls in tunics would slip out of the room to use the nearby bathroom and Cassandra realised this was probably a good idea. However, when she came to pass through the door the slave master stopped her.

'Where are you off to?'

'The bathroom.' She wished she didn't sound so nervous.

He smiled unpleasantly. 'Not much point is there? I haven't got a key for your chastity belt.'

'Who has?' she asked.

'It will be given to your new master. Now get out of the way, there are others who need to go there before the auction starts and time's getting short.'

Flushed with distress, Cassandra returned to Peter and Anton, who both sympathised. 'It's the same for us,' Peter pointed out. 'Don't worry. You'll be unlocked as soon as you're bought, and the baron's bound to be the one who buys you. I wish I knew who I was going to. I just hope it's not Claud. He can be vicious.'

'You mean Clara's stepfather's here tonight?' Cassandra asked in surprise.

'Of course. He's flown in specially to take her back with him.'

Before they could talk any further a gong sounded somewhere in the house, and at once the slave master called for silence. Then they were herded into groups of four, driven out of the room and down three flights of stairs then along a hallway to the large ballroom that ran the width of the back of the house. Cassandra had never been in there; as far as she knew it was normally kept locked. They weren't led straight in, but instead taken into a small ante-room which scarcely had space for them all and Cassandra quickly became aware of the odour of nervously perspiring bodies along with the sharper, musky scent of sexual arousal.

270

They could hear the murmur of voices through the small door leading out into the ballroom, and the murmur grew steadily louder the longer they waited. Just when Cassandra felt ready to scream with impatience, the gong was struck again, and immediately the four young men were led out. For a moment the voices came unhindered through the open door, and they all sounded high-pitched with excitement.

The slave master gripped Cassandra by the arm and pushed her towards the door, along with Clara and a tall brunette who was in the tunic costume. At the last moment, the slave master's assistant joined him and the two men swiftly blindfolded the three female slaves. As everything went dark, Cassandra wished with all her heart that she hadn't let herself be put in this position. Her pulse was racing wildly with fear, and as the door swung open and the voices in the ballroom rose to a crescendo she instinctively backed away from the ordeal that lay ahead.

The slave master had expected as much. He pushed her roughly in the back and she stumbled out into the ballroom, her hands chained in front of her, her skimpy webbed costume emphasising her slender form, and her nipples, now rigid with fear, pressed against the tiny silver padlocks.

The baron was seated at the front of the room, and as she came into view his throat went dry with excitement. She looked wonderfully vulnerable with her hands in chains and her eyes covered, while her parted lips and hesitant steps revealed the fear she was experiencing.

Katya stood next to him and watched as the three girls were pushed up the hastily erected ramp and onto the platform where orchestras had once played for the balls that Dieter and Marietta had held when they first moved into the house. As Clara tripped over the top step her breasts bounced and there was a collective sigh of appreciation from the men.

Then the bidding started. For Cassandra, facing the front but unable to see anything, it was the worst moment so far. Clara was sold first, and the sale was quickly completed. Cassandra recognised the voice of the purchaser as belonging to Claud. Next it was the brunette's turn, and this time the sale took longer. Many of the men came up on to the platform to feel the young woman's body, touch her through her satin panties and comment loudly on what their probing fingers discovered, while all the time Cassandra stood in shivering silence awaiting her turn.

Finally the brunette was taken away by a group of men and women and now Cassandra knew that she was standing alone in front of everyone. She didn't know what currency they were bidding in, but the first sum called out was a five figure one and it increased rapidly without her once hearing the baron's voice. At one stage a man came on to the platform and ran his hands over her, letting his fingers linger round her bare waist, and then he moved them up over the web-covered breasts and ran his fingertip in a circle round the silver padlocks. She shivered with a mixture of pleasure and nerves, and then he must have knelt down, because suddenly his hands were parting her legs and she could feel his breath between her thighs as his hands skimmed across the webbing that covered her sex. Finally he cupped her buttocks thoughtfully in both hands and increased the bid considerably as he left the platform.

After his offer there was a long silence. Cassandra wanted to open her mouth and call out for the baron to better the bid. She suddenly realised that if he went back on his word now, there was nothing she could do about it, and her bottom lip began to tremble.

The baron had been watching her closely, and when he finally saw that her natural fear was being over-whelmed by genuine terror he negligently raised his hand and made his own offer. It was a formality. There was no one there who could afford to bid higher, even if they had wanted to run the risk of offending him, and so a few minutes later Cassandra was being led down from the platform by Katya and as she was pulled through the crowd who were eagerly awaiting the next batch of slaves, hands reached out to touch and fondle her, and their laughter held a chilling note of cruelty.

'Well, Cassandra, here you are then,' the baron's voice said in her ear. She came to an abrupt halt as Katya handed the chain over to her lover. 'I hope you weren't too uncomfortable while you were waiting upstairs. Let's have that blindfold off now, then you can have a good look at us all.'

When the black band was removed, her eyes found it difficult to adjust, and she blinked at the blurred figures gathered round her, while gold spots danced in front of her eyes. Slowly her vision corrected itself, and she was able to make out the baron, whose eyes were wide and amused, and Katya, Françoise, Rupert and three couples she'd never seen before who were all staring at her with greedy intensity.

They were in a corner of the ballroom, and there were comfortable velvet-covered chairs for those who wished to sit, all set around a long brocaded couch, the width of a double bed, on which a male slave was already kneeling.

Cassandra realised it was Anton from upstairs but neither of them dared show any sign of recognition and despite his previous excitement over the evening, he now looked almost as apprehensive as Cassandra felt. The noise around them was still deafening as bidding for the new batch of girls began, but Cassandra tried not to think about anyone else in the room. She had to pretend that this was just another group sex session and she could only do that by blotting out the rest of the party in the ballroom.

Slowly the baron held out his hand, and in its palm lay two small silver keys. He took one and unfastened her wrists with it, then used the other to remove the padlocks from her breasts, but he still left her fastened between her thighs.

One of the new women in their group drew close to

Cassandra and caressed her breasts, her fingers making the webbing cling even more firmly to them as she watched the nipples rise instantly at her touch. 'She is lovely,' she said to the baron with a smile. 'No wonder you wanted her so badly.'

He smiled at Cassandra, then pulled the webbing apart where the padlocks had previously secured it until her nipples were fully exposed, their pink hardness accentuating the pallor of the small amount of her breasts that could be seen.

The ballroom was hot, and bodies pressed against her from surrounding groups who were still bidding for their own slaves. Cassandra felt dizzy and wished that she could sit on the couch, but for the moment she seemed destined to stand in front of them all while they took enjoyment merely from looking.

Françoise handed her a tall glass of colourless liquid with ice cubes in it. 'Drink this, Cassandra. It will cool you down,' she promised, feeling the warmth of the younger woman's skin beneath her touch as she pressed a hand against Cassandra's spine. Cassandra drank gratefully, but when her thirst was eased and she tried to stop, Françoise insisted that she drain it all.

When she'd finally complied, Katya came round behind her to unfasten the buckle at her back that held the webbing around her breasts in place, but the material stayed put, stuck there by her nervous perspiration. Rupert was the one who stepped forward and peeled it off her, and as he did so there was a groan from the kneeling Anton.

Cassandra looked down at him, and realised that his penis was still covered by the leather sheath and strapped firmly in place so that although she was arousing him, he was unable to have the erection his body was demanding.

'Be silent!' the baron ordered sharply, and to Cassandra's surprise he flicked the luckless young man's lower belly hard with a tiny whip. The leather sheath visibly strained against the thongs, but they held firm and this time he bit his lip to prevent himself from making another sound.

'Get on the couch, Cassandra, and lie on your back so that Anton's between your legs,' the baron said. She felt very sorry for the young male slave but quickly obeyed. 'Now, Anton, you may lick her breasts,' the baron continued smoothly. 'She likes to have them sucked hard.'

Cassandra's belly contracted with fear as Anton bent over her. There were so many faces round them, so many people watching with visible excitement that she wanted to die from shame, and yet once his tongue began to move across her nipples she felt the pulse in the side of her neck start to quicken and the by now familiar tension began to grow inside her.

Although his penis was encased in the sheath, the rest of Anton's body was totally nude, and when he leant over her to lave her breasts, his testicles brushed against her lower abdomen, adding to her excitement. Her legs began to move restlessly on the couch, and seeing this the baron swiftly unfastened the final padlock so that now they could all see how the fine webbing had been drawn into her increasingly moist flesh moulding against her vulva and he couldn't resist drawing a finger lightly up the middle of her outer lips, feeling her moisture spreading through the material as he did so.

Above Cassandra, Anton was sucking hard on her breasts, moving his head slowly back to extend the tiny nipples to their limit and then letting them ease back into place. This, coupled with the feel of the baron's finger against her tightly confined sex, caused her flesh to quicken in response and with shaming speed her body abruptly bunched and then arched in a quick climax.

Cassandra heard Katya laugh. 'How shameless, Cassandra, and in front of all these strangers as well!' She pressed the palm of her hand between the girl's parted thighs and heard the quick intake of breath. 'Never

275

mind, I'm sure there are plenty more where that came from. We paid enough for you, the very least you can do is display stamina in return.'

'What about Anton?' a woman's voice asked.

Cassandra stared up at the blond young man still crouched above her, his face a twisted mask of excitement and discomfort. 'I hope they take that thing off me soon,' he muttered to her.

Almost before he'd spoken he gave a genuine cry of pain as the baron's whip came down on his naked buttocks. 'I don't remember telling you to speak,' he commented with deceptive gentleness. 'What do the rest of you think? Should we release him?'

'I think we'd better,' Rupert commented with wry amusement. 'He might suffer irreparable damage if we don't, and somehow I can't see his wife being very pleased if that were to happen.'

'Keep still then,' cautioned the baron, and then hands were fumbling with the thongs, the sheath was removed and at last Anton's erection was allowed to spring free. He shut his eyes in relief as it straightened from its tight imprisonment, then flinched as he felt women's hands fondling his testicles and the delicate flesh of the perineum. His penis hardened painfully, but he still hadn't been given permission to move from where he was crouched above Cassandra.

'Let's take bets on how long he'll last before he comes,' a man's voice suggested, and there followed a quick exchange of times, and wagers were placed.

'Sit up, Cassandra,' the baron said. 'The result will all depend on your skill and his self control. I've placed my money on a quick ejaculation, so please remember that when you're working on him!'

Cassandra sat upright, and at once the full ignominy of her position was brought home to her. Everyone in the baron's group was now partly unclothed and in varying degrees of arousal, but their eyes were all fixed on her and Anton and the expressions in those eyes

276

were both excited and malicious, making her wonder what lay ahead of her before the night was finally over.

'Use your mouth on him,' the baron said. 'No hands, nothing at all except your mouth. Incidentally, Anton quite likes a little pain to spur him towards his release.'

A stopwatch was produced, and Cassandra quickly began. Anton was still on all fours and so hard and engorged that she felt certain it would only be a matter of a minute or two before he came. What she hadn't bargained on was Katya whispering to Anton that she'd bet on a longer time than the baron, and Anton was obsessed with Katya so he was now determined to last as long as possible.

Cassandra began as she'd been taught, sliding her tongue beneath the sensitive skin below the glans, then flicking it more firmly up and down the shaft before sucking on the tip and letting her tongue swirl along the slit at the top.

His body grew tense and his chest heaved, but to her amazement he managed to withhold his climax so long that she heard the baron click his tongue with irritation. Then she remembered his final words and all at once she changed her approach. Instead of the softly sliding, gentle pressure of lips and tongue, the head of Anton's penis was abruptly nipped with unbelievable delicacy between Cassandra's teeth, and a white streak of pain shot through the bliss he was experiencing. His hips thrust forward until he touched the back of her throat, and as she instinctively gagged and fought to find her rhythm again, the delicate underside of his glans slipped backwards against the top of her bottom teeth, and this final edge of pain brought the sperm rushing up through his shaft and he ejaculated violently into her mouth, hips pumping furiously until every last drop had been expelled.

'Excellent!' the baron applauded. 'I win, I believe. Well done, Cassandra. You may both change into more comfortable positions for a moment.' Cassandra opened her mouth to speak but then stopped, uncertain if it was allowed. He raised an eyebrow. 'You have a question?'

'I need to use the bathroom,' she murmured. 'No one had the key before.'

'Of course not, the key was in my possession all along. You may use it, Cassandra, but not until you've managed to coax another climax from our young friend here. That should add a spur to your efforts, I imagine. He must of course have a brief rest first, so while he does we will turn our attention to you. In view of what you've just told us, I think you should lie on your front this time.'

As Cassandra hesitated, members of the group surged forward, their hands reaching out hungrily for her and she was bundled onto her stomach until she was lying spread-eagled across the width of the couch with four people holding on to her wrists and ankles. In the meantime, Anton was made to stand at the foot of the couch to watch.

'Such lovely skin,' commented Rupert, his hands gliding down Cassandra's spine. 'I've always wanted a pleasure slave. Pass me some of the oil, Françoise.' Cassandra heard the sound of a stopper being removed, and then Rupert's hands were back on her skin and he was massaging the oil in. His fingers were lighter than the baron's had been when he'd massaged her, and more tantalising because her muscles longed for a deep massage rather than the soft, insidious touching that merely kindled the beginnings of desire.

While he worked, the people holding her wrists and ankles let their hands roam over her limbs. Some touched her lightly, stroking her as though she were a baby while others used their hands more roughly, kneading the calves of her legs and squeezing and stretching her fingers and toes. The entire surface area of the back of her body was soon alive with the different sensations, and she couldn't help but wriggle against the brocade of the couch, trying to press down and ease the deepening ache in her lower abdomen.

Her breasts tingled as well, and the nipples stayed tightly erect because of the friction of her movements against the couch. Now and again someone would slide a hand beneath her armpits and fondle her breasts, but never for long enough to satisfy the need the constant touching was arousing in her.

Eventually, Rupert's hands ceased their ministrations and then everyone else stopped touching her too, but they maintained their grip on her wrists and ankles. She tried to lift her head to see what was going to happen next, but the baron ordered her curtly to keep her head face down on the couch.

The seconds grew into minutes and still her outstretched body waited. There was a soft murmur of voices, but the words were indistinguishable and she grew tense with anticipation. Every fibre of her body was knotted with nervous expectation, and the group looked down on her body, which was trembling with fear, and their own excitement increased.

Carefully, the baron positioned a glass bottle with a long slim neck about two feet above Cassandra's back and then he gradually tilted it, watching the ice-cold water flow along the opening until at last it met the glass stopper in the end. This had a small hole which allowed only a single drop to pass through at a time. In absolute silence his party watched the first clear ice-cold drop pass through the stopper and fall onto the slave girl's unsuspecting back.

As the freezing liquid hit her oiled and over-heated skin, Cassandra gasped with shock and her body bowed inwards, pressing her into the couch even more deeply. 'Keep your face down,' the baron reminded her, and then she knew that more drops would follow. They did, but at first the intervals between them were long and she lay in a turmoil of expectation, wanting the feel of the cool liquid yet dreading the shock at the moment it hit her.

As she became more accustomed to the waiting, the drops were allowed to fall more frequently, and then hands spread her tightly clenched buttocks apart and her legs were stretched more widely to enable the water to be dropped into the revealed crevice, making the flesh pucker and the small round opening contract against the sensation.

Her whole body leapt with each droplet that was poured into this shamingly exposed crease, and her desire grew and grew until she began to whimper with need. As soon as they heard her muted cries, the hands turned her on her back, but immediately the blindfold was replaced so that she still couldn't see where or when the water would touch her.

Now the droplets fell on her hot, tight breasts, trickling down the gentle swell of them and wandering over her ribcage and along the sides of her waist onto the couch below. Then the bottle was moved and with great accuracy the baron let a drop spill into the dip of her navel. Her whole stomach contracted sharply as it landed, and her abdominal muscles continued to ripple uneasily as her body waited for a second drop to follow, but instead he let several drops fall across the gentle swell of her stomach, watching them run in tiny rivers towards the join in her outstretched thighs.

By preventing Cassandra from seeing what was happening, the baron knew that Cassandra's other senses would become more sharply tuned and she chewed on her lip as his blissful torture continued. When the water actually reached her pubic curls, she let out a moan of relief and her hips writhed to try and get the water to move onto her vulva, that was swollen with excitement.

All at once she felt fingers parting her outer lips and then tiny fingers that felt like Katya's eased back the small hood of skin beneath which her clitoris was hiding and held it firm. Cassandra could feel the air on her exposed bud and even the shame of knowing so many people could see her wantonly displayed couldn't dampen her need to feel a drop of the cold moisture on her most intimate secret spot.

The baron waited, watching her restless attempts to

move her lower body. Finally he signalled for Anton to step forward and one of the women pressed Anton's right hand, palm down, against Cassandra's stomach so that now she was reminded of her full bladder. The pressure of this made her try to twist enough to move the hand, but it was impossible, and the tingling of those nerve endings continued to grow while every part of her tensed waiting for the final drop of water to fall.

Still the baron waited until Cassandra began to moan aloud. Her need for release was so great she didn't care about the audience, didn't care what anyone thought of her, she simply wanted her flesh to be satisfied and so she appealed to them all. 'Please, please,' she whimpered, arching her back as much as possible. Anton's hand was pressed into her more firmly and the terrible dark aching need expanded until she thought it would utterly consume her.

'Help me!' she begged them all. 'Please, please!'

'How sweet she sounds,' Françoise laughed. 'And how lovely to see her lose control like this. Even Anton's beginning to get interested again.' They all looked at the male slave whose previously limp penis was now starting to stir. Katya smiled at the young man and her tongue flicked across her top lip.

On the couch Cassandra continued to plead with them to end the water torture, but they kept her waiting still longer. Her toes were licked and sucked, the backs of her knees softly caressed with a piece of silk drawn steadily to and fro across them, while her pubic area was held firmly motionless with the clitoris standing out totally exposed and unable to withdraw because the hood was still drawn back. Finally the baron tired of the game. He lowered his hand a little, tipped the bottle and let two drops fall in quick succession onto the throbbing little bud that was driving Cassandra to distraction.

As the first drop hit her, her body tried to rise from the couch and she screamed in relief but the hood was still held back and when the second drop followed she became almost delirious with the overstimulation and her head thrashed wildly from side to side as she cried out in gratitude while the shock waves of pleasure flowed over her body in a blissful blanket of release.

She was given no time to savour the full pleasure of the moment though because almost before the final spasm had ceased her blindfold was removed and she was pulled into a sitting position. At once her need to empty her bladder made itself strongly felt, but then she remembered that first she had to coax another climax from Anton.

Katya, who understood the other woman's discomfort very well, pushed the reluctant Anton onto the couch beside the sitting girl. 'Here you are, Cassie. Luckily for you Anton seems to be a virile young man, but arousal's one thing, a climax is quite another. After all, it can be quite painful for a man to be forced into a second ejaculation too soon so you can't expect him to cooperate with you.'

Anton's hands had now been fastened behind his back and he sat uncertainly beside Cassandra, waiting her instructions. Everyone in the group watched with interest as she looked down at his penis, realising that despite all he'd witnessed since his own climax, there was only the faintest suggestion of an erection.

She felt quite frantic. Her bladder was full to bursting thanks to the drink Françoise had forced down her, and now that the afterglow of her own climax had died down she needed the bathroom more than ever, and yet this young man stood between her and the urgently needed opportunity to relieve herself.

She reached out and took his limp organ in her hand, closing her fingers round it and letting them slide up and down the stem. He was uncircumcised and Cassandra hoped it didn't mean he could take more stimulation. Her grip tightened as she moved her hand right down the root to the anus and she was rewarded with a slow, unfolding movement between his thighs.

Now she decided to pull back the foreskin and then

she bent forward and let her long dark hair tickle his belly, swinging her head from side to side to increase the sensation. His penis continued to swell and she moved her hand up the shaft to the sensitive fraenum below the head, where her fingers swirled softly round, but this didn't seem to increase his erection any further.

Suddenly remembering what she had enjoyed, she looked up at the baron who was watching with keen interest. 'May I have some of the massaging oil?' she asked politely. He nodded, and one of his male friends quickly handed her a small bottle. She carefully lubricated her fingers with it and then returned to the highly sensitive ridge of skin. This time it had the desired effect as Anton's breathing became more rapid and the penis started to straighten fully.

Cassandra was surprised how much his growing arousal excited her. She enjoyed being in control of him, of being in a position where she could force him into a state of sexual excitement even against his will and she knelt back on her heels for a moment to study his body. For some reason, the very fact that she was watching him increased Anton's excitement and his penis was now almost fully erect.

There was a wonderful musky odour coming from him that made Cassandra dip her head again, only this time she let her tongue trail across the top of the glans, waiting for the first tell-tale drop of clear fluid to appear in the slit, but to her disappointment that didn't happen. Her whole pelvic area was now tight with excitement and pressure from her bladder and she rocked herself to and fro as she worked on him, totally unaware of what she was doing because she was utterly lost in a world where only sensuality counted.

The baron's party of friends watched her stimulating herself and some of them began to fondle each other, unable to watch any more without taking some kind of action themselves, but the baron and Katya stayed apart both watching the unfolding scene carefully.

Anton stared at the wide-eyed young woman with

the wonderful long dark hair and struggled to slow his arousal down. He knew his own capabilities, and he wasn't yet ready to have another climax, but her skill was going to force one from him if he wasn't careful. She saw the fear in his eyes and it only spurred her on. She moved a hand and ran one long fingernail across his scrotum before carefully cupping his balls in the palm of her hand and applying very light pressure that she slowly increased as she continued to stare directly into his eyes.

Anton felt the tightness at the root of his shaft and his testicles drew up against his body in preparation for a climax. 'Yes,' whispered Cassandra, her mouth warm against his belly. 'That's right, come for me. Let me see you come again.'

Her words were as erotic as her touch and he gave a sigh of despair as the tightness grew and the tip of his penis became suffused with blood and turned an angry purple. He was desperately near now and Cassandra knew it. She drew back for a moment before applying the final touch, and Katya seized her moment. Reaching between the two slaves she pinched the top of Anton's penis hard between her fingers. Anton could have wept with relief. He knew that this would delay his climax and give his body more time to recuperate from his last one, but Cassandra was furious and without realising what she was doing she launched herself at the other woman with her fingers outstretched.

'No!' she shouted. 'That's not fair. He was about to come.'

Immediately two of the men in the party gripped her by the shoulders and pulled her back, while the baron stared at her in displeasure. 'You both belong to us,' he reminded her in cold tones. 'We can do what we wish with either of you. Apologise to Katya immediately.'

Cassandra wanted to sob with frustration. She desperately needed to use the bathroom and now despite all her efforts, Anton's erection was visibly decreasing

284

in front of her, but with the baron's dark eyes fixed on her face she forced out an apology.

'I'm sorry,' she said quietly. 'I apologise. I forgot my place.'

Katya, her aim achieved, could afford to be magnanimous. 'Just a quick application of the whip, I think, Dieter,' she said casually. He nodded, and as Rupert and Françoise pulled her arms back behind her, Katya produced a thin whip which she then used to strike her cowering opponent's breasts. Her aim was good, and she caught the nipples two stinging blows so that they burned and stung bringing tears into Cassandra's eyes, but through the tears the baron could still see simmering hatred and he was pleased.

By the time she'd been released, Anton's penis had nearly retreated out of sight, and for a moment Cassandra was in utter despair, but then she thought of the one thing she hadn't tried and she ordered him to crouch on all fours with his head away from her.

Reluctantly, already guessing what she was about to do, he obeyed and now she was the one to part tight buttocks with her hands and once again she carefully lubricated a finger in the aromatic oil before swirling it round the entrance to his anus.

Even at this lightest suggestion of a caress, Anton's penis came to life again, and as her finger pushed steadily against the opening he knew that he would be finished if he let her succeed so he tightened against her. 'Bear down,' she said shortly, no longer caring about his pleasure only about her own unbearable need. He didn't obey her and the baron put a hand on his shoulder.

'Do as she says, Anton, or we will make you suffer a great deal more than she can.'

Immediately Anton obeyed, bearing down until the entrance to his anus opened enough for Cassandra's finger to slide in. Her searching finger soon found his prostate gland which she massaged in a firm, circular movement that brought his penis sharply upright, tight and hard in total arousal. Still massaging him internally, Cassandra reached round his shaking body with her free hand and positioned her fingers above the purple head, then quickly squeezed and released the glans in continuous movements that combined with the glorious sensations coming from his stimulated prostate made Anton lose all control of himself so that his body spasmed furiously, his hips jerked back and forth into her cruelly soft encompassing fingers and he finally climaxed.

Cassandra was so excited by her success and the surge of power that swept over her that she didn't at first realise his cries were more of pain than joy, but when he'd finished she found that her hand which had held him was almost dry, and then she knew that for him the climax had come too fast upon the heels of the first and so his moment of release had racked him more with pain than pleasure.

Anton collapsed onto the couch, sobbing with pain and humilation, wishing now that he'd never volunteered to be a slave, but it was too late to go back and he simply had to wait until the night was over. All round the room others were discovering the same thing, but Cassandra was almost revelling in her role, and she found that the young man's heaving body moved her hardly at all except to emphasise her success.

She looked up at the baron waiting for his permission to leave the room for a moment, but to her surprise he signalled for her to wait. After a few moments Françoise came into view carrying a large copper bowl. She pushed the still sobbing Anton off the couch and placed the bowl on it.

'There,' the baron said with a smile. 'You may now use that to relieve yourself, Cassandra.'

Her cheeks flamed as she stared up at him incredulously. 'You mean now, in front of you all?'

'Of course. Slaves aren't entitled to any privacy.'

'I can't,' she whispered, her voice almost vanishing with the shock.

'Come, come, Cassandra. If you can have orgasms and manually and orally masturbate a total stranger then I fail to see why you can't relieve yourself in the bowl. However, if your need is not as pressing as you led us to believe, Françoise can take it away again.'

'It is!' she cried. 'I have to go, but not here. Not with you all watching.'

'I'm afraid there's no choice,' Katya said with satisfaction. 'Of course, you can always ask to leave the party. That would be allowed, but you couldn't ever come back.'

That changed Cassandra's mind. She could feel their hot eyes upon her, but she wasn't going to give in to Katya at this late stage. She crouched naked above the bowl and tried to relax her muscles sufficiently to allow her bladder to empty. At first the muscles refused to obey, but she had learnt a lot about self-discipline since she first came to the house in Hampstead, and by slowing her breathing and pressing down her internal muscles she finally managed to conquer her shame and once the hot liquid began to splash into the bowl she even found a strange excitement in the bliss of the easing pressure mixed with the knowledge that this was another victory over the now silent Katya.

As soon as she'd finished the bowl was removed, and then the group all surged towards the couch, so that both she and Anton were caught up in a tangle of arms and legs as the men and women started to take their own particular kinds of pleasure from their unresisting bodies. After a time she no longer knew whether the hands on her were male or female, all that she was conscious of was the constant stimulation of her flesh as she was penetrated in all her orifices. Men came between her breasts and thighs, while women crouched above her and she licked and sucked at their hungry, moist pussies until they screamed their release and made way for the next person to take their place.

She had no idea how much time had passed when she heard the baron's quiet voice calling them all to order. As everyone withdrew she lay, sweat-covered and exhausted gazing up with vacant eyes and slack mouth at the ornately decorated high ceiling of the ballroom.

He looked down at her and smiled, then touched her on her cheek with two fingers. 'You're doing very well, Cassandra. We've come to the last part of your test, and after what I've seen I have no doubt that it will give you as much pleasure as Rupert. You see, tonight, Rupert's ambition to see if the snake trick he witnessed was an illusion or not will be realised. I bought this especially for him.' Cassandra's mouth went dry as he held aloft a small, rust-coloured corn snake.

# Chapter Fourteen

When the baron had held the snake aloft, Cassandra's eyes grew enormous with terror, while there was a soft murmur of anticipation from the group. After pausing briefly for effect, he passed the snake to Rupert and then sat down on the couch next to Cassandra.

He hadn't taken part in the group sex himself, being far more interested in watching the behaviour of his friends and also Cassandra's responses to their various methods of stimulation. Even he had been surprised by the way her appetite for sex had grown during her weeks of tutorage, and at one moment he had felt sure that she'd finally cast aside the last veil of reticence so that he had nothing left to learn about her; but then on closer examination of her expression he'd decided he'd been wrong. She was lost in the sensations, but still managed to retain the inner core of privacy he wanted to destroy.

Cassandra had succeeded by shutting herself away from them all. Instead of abandoning herself to their expertise, she had used them for her pleasure while remaining apart. He had never seen this before in a woman. Normally they longed to belong and he wondered if Cassandra's childhood had made her emotionally self-reliant. If so it was contradictory to his original assessment when he had thought her to be emotionally immature and in need of a surrogate family.

What the baron had failed to understand was the intensity of Cassandra's feelings for him. It was easy for her to ignore the group because they were of no importance to her. He was the only person who interested her, and it was because of the mental as well as physical attraction she felt for him that she was capable of doing almost anything that would enable her to become his permanent partner rather than Katya.

Now he fondled her with his strong hands, totally untroubled by the fact that they were being watched. He knew that he must arouse her sufficiently for Rupert to have his fun without harm coming to either Cassandra or the tiny snake and so he brought her breasts close together in his hands, rubbing them against each other and then pushing them upwards where he ran his tongue round the areoles in the way he knew she liked.

Although Cassandra had thought herself utterly satiated, the physical closeness of this totally compelling man, and the knowledge that Katya and Françoise were having to watch him caress her in such a wonderfully tender and arousing way, reawakened her body and she felt her nipples rising again to peaks of hardness.

Some of the men in the group moved forward at the sight, wanting to touch her once more themselves, but no one dared interrupt the baron. In the meantime the women watched her vulnerable young body begin to squirm, the limbs to twitch, and they reached for the equally exhausted Anton, dragging his hands to their breasts or pressing their sex up against his mouth, tugging his head up by his hair until he carried out their orders.

Cassandra was conscious of the movements going on around her, and conscious too of the various cries and groans coming from all parts of the ballroom, but what mattered most was the way the baron's hands were now gliding down her, pressing on vital nerve spots as they moved, and sliding beneath her buttocks to massage the small tight cheeks with strong fingers until she was twisting and turning in his grip as the liquid heat began to form once again in her breasts and between her legs.

He wanted her to watch another slave's arousal at the same time as he coaxed hers on, but Anton didn't look in any condition to do more than please the women with his hands and mouth so the baron glanced round the room and then sent Rupert to find Claud and Clara. Moments later they all returned, and he knew from the vibrations of Clara's still imprisoned breasts and the despairing appeal in her eyes that she at least wasn't totally satiated.

Quickly he had her laid face down over her stepfather's knees, and then he pulled Cassandra up against him, still fondling her constantly and letting her rest her head against his shoulder. 'Watch this, Cassandra,' he urged her.

She watched as Claud separated the scarlet cheeks of Clara's bottom, only recently whipped with a leather strap, wielded by one of the most expert female hands in Europe, and while Clara moaned a protest at the feel of fingers on her tender flesh, Rupert lubricated the entrance between her cheeks with cold cream and then lifted up a thin piece of rubber tubing with a tiny bulb at one end and a larger bulb at the other. After a few clever movements with his fingers he was able with Claud's assistance to slide the smaller bulb into Clara's rectum, and then Claud released her scarlet buttocks and they closed tightly about the intruder leaving the tube and larger bulb protruding.

Now she was pulled to her feet, and then Françoise pushed forward a rocking chair with a soft cushion in the seat. Claud led his stepdaughter to the chair and then sat her firmly down on it. 'Sit quite still, Clara,' said the baron, his hands massaging Cassandra's belly and thighs. 'You can have a rest while Françoise rocks the chair.'

Cassandra watched as the chair began to rock, and she was puzzled to see that very soon, Clara's expression changed from one of passive acceptance to bewildered discomfort. She tried to stand up but Claud slapped her across her breasts and ordered her to stay as the baron had commanded.

'What's happening?' whispered Cassandra, fascinated by what she was seeing and almost drowning in the pleasant sensation caused by the baron's hands.

'Each time the chair moves, the larger bulb at the end of the tubing pushes air through the tube and into the bulb at the other end, causing it to gradually expand. In a few minutes it will touch the walls of her rectum and she'll experience a lot of very interesting sensations.'

Cassandra could imagine them only too well, and when Clara suddenly cried out her mouth opening in surprise and bewilderment, Cassandra's arousal grew. She could imagine the heavy tightness making Clara's bowel muscles cramp, and remembered the delicious warmth that followed the initial discomfort.

Now Clara's eyes were filling with tears, and the baron signalled for the rocking to be stopped. They left the girl sitting in it and she remained very still, obviously afraid that any movement would increase her discomfort. Claud then knelt between her legs and parted them, before tipping the rocking chair back, making Clara cry out a little, and then he began to probe her front entrance with his tongue.

Cassandra's breathing was shallow and rapid. She could almost feel the heavy weight of the inflated bulb in Clara's rectum, and the matching fullness in her vagina as Claud's tongue moved inside it while he sucked carefully at the surrounding flesh.

Obviously the feelings excited Clara as well because her body began to jerk of its own accord and her spread legs were lifted into the air by Rupert until they were round Claud's neck which pressed her firmly backwards and inflated the bulb a fraction more.

Now Clara was moaning aloud. Her body was

obviously on the brink of a climax, but she was terrified of the effect it would have on her already painfully distended rectum.

'She doesn't dare come,' whispered the baron, his hands going between Cassandra's legs and seeking out her moistness. 'What delicious torment for her, my darling. I wonder what she'll do?'

Cassandra moaned, unable to speak because her body was so aroused by the mental and physical stimulation it was receiving. Her eyes couldn't leave the hapless Clara's struggles with her own flesh, and when the young girl was finally forced to spasm by the skill of the older man's mouth and tongue her screams of ecstasy were indistinguishable from her cries of pain as she heaved her body off the seat of the rocking chair in an attempt to spare herself more pain.

'There,' whispered the baron. 'Now Clara's satisfied, and it's your turn again. Lie back, Cassandra. It's time for Rupert's little pet to take an outing.'

Cassandra's legs were weak and shaking from the baron's caresses and she didn't resist when he put a pillow beneath her hips to expose her sex more fully. Now everyone gathered close, but as Rupert approached with the corn snake and Cassandra started to close her eyes the baron bent down and put his mouth to her ear.

'Eyes open, my precious. I want to watch your expression while this is going on. I want to see into your soul.'

Rupert looked down at her. 'There's nothing to worry about, Cassandra. He's perfectly harmless, and I won't let go of his tail! Look, he isn't even very big.' She stared at the already writhing snake. It was probably no more than eighteen inches long, but its tongue was darting out as its head moved from side to side searching for a place to hide and the thought of it making those movements inside her caused her stomach to tighten and churn and her body closed against the expected intrusion.

Rupert sat down beside her and got Françoise to open the outer lips and run a moistened finger over the shrinking sex beneath. Cassandra was already very damp from the baron's attentions and Clara's experience, and Françoise quickly spread the slick of escaped moisture around the light pink tissue while Rupert set the snake down on Cassandra's left thigh.

It slid along the smooth flesh in rapid S-shaped movements. Totally deaf, it was guided only by vibrations, and Cassandra's legs were trembling so violently it was looking for cover.

Cassandra could feel every movement as it travelled up her thigh, and several times its tongue flicked against her flesh, now exposed due to Françoise holding her so firmly open. She knew that she could just leap up and run from the room; that she didn't have to stay and endure this final perversion, but the baron was still sitting at her head staring down at her and his nearness, his almost visible desire for her to succeed, gave her the necessary courage.

It took a long time before the snake started to slither down the inside of her thigh and when it did its head brushed against her inner lips. Cassandra gasped at the unimaginable eroticism of the touch. Rupert then took hold of the snake round its middle and moved it up and down her sex himself, knowing that it wouldn't be able to find a grip on such a moist surface. Its head twisted and turned, the underside brushing against her constantly, and when her clitoris was touched, she gasped aloud and nearly climaxed with a shocking mixture of fear and excitement.

Now Rupert decided it was the moment for him to see for himself how far into her it would go, and he nodded for his wife to open Cassandra up so that he could thread the head of the snake into her vagina. The feeling was so delicate, the movements so unpredictable and constantly shifting that the entrance to the vagina, the most sensitive part of the whole canal, was stimulated far more than by a thicker or rougher penetration and Cassandra groaned at the glorious sensations that were setting her body alight.

Rupert paused, wondering whether he should stop now or let the snake continue escaping into the warm dark moistness of Cassandra's love channel. 'Don't stop!' she moaned, trying to open herself more fully to the intruder. 'Please, don't stop!'

Katya gazed down at the naked, pulsating figure revelling in this, the greatest perversion the baron had ever devised and she knew that she was lost. Even if she was given the chance to do the same thing she wouldn't be able to. She had always feared snakes and even the sight of this small, harmless specimen before the auction had made her feel sick. As Cassandra continued to moan and Rupert gradually let more of the snake slip inside her, Katya glanced up the girl's body to where her lover was sitting at her head.

Their eyes met, and she was shocked to find that instead of compassion, or even the amusement she had expected to find there, he was staring at her with hatred. Stunned she blinked and took a step towards him, but his frown froze her in her tracks.

'Isn't she wonderful, Katya?' he said, and there was such joy in his voice she could hardly recognise it. 'Didn't I tell you she'd triumph? To think I could have searched all my life and never found such a woman.'

Cassandra was continuing to moan as the snake wriggled within her, while her eyes remained fixed unseeingly on the baron's face. She was utterly lost to lust. Her world was nothing but incredible sensations and she revelled in it without shame. When Rupert finally withdrew the snake, she felt it slither out in a warm moist rush, so that it felt as though it were taking her own entrails out with it and her body jackknifed on itself with the intensity of a climax that was almost beyond bearing. The baron looked deep into her eyes and he realised with unexpected joy that he still didn't really know her, that she had retained her inner core of strength and serenity that he had thought he wanted to destroy, and so she wasn't spoilt for him but instead could remain by his side, the perfect lover and a continuing enigma.

As Cassandra's now exhausted body finished shuddering and she drew herself up into the foetal position that the baron found extraordinarily touching, Katya gazed at him. 'Why do you hate me so?' she asked.

'Because you persuaded Marietta to kill herself,' he replied. There was a gasp from their friends, and everyone drew away from Katya.

There was no point in denying it, but she had to find out how he knew. 'Did she leave a note then?' she asked almost inaudibly.

His right hand was smoothing Cassandra's brow with a tenderness he'd never shown Katya. 'No, however you forgot that when I'm away I leave a camera running in the main bedroom. Ironically it was really to check up on Marietta that night, in case she'd found herself a lover. When I finally got round to running the tape, you can imagine my shock at seeing you with her, pouring your poison into her ear like a female Iago. You were clever, I'll admit that. It was true she was irritating me, and that I blamed the children for coming between us, but unfortunately for you, Katya, I still cared for her. In time I might have tired of her, but you couldn't wait long enough for that to happen could you? Well, it's of no significance now. Cassandra here is a far better companion for me than either you or Marietta could ever have been, and that is why I hate you.'

'I only did it because I loved you,' Katya protested.

He laughed. 'Come now, neither of us know the meaning of that particular word. Your possessions are already packed. Peter will drive you to the airport within the hour. You are to travel with Claud and Clara. There may well be a place for you in that household, but if not I have no doubt one or other of my friends will take you in.'

Stunned, Katya turned to look at the others in their group, but they were all busy avoiding her eyes. The baron was their friend; she had only been accepted because she was his mistress. Without his protection she was nothing, and in that split second she both knew and accepted that. With her head held high she walked away from them all, but deep inside her she was already beginning to plan her future revenge on the dark-haired girl now lying so still on the couch while the baron continued to stroke her face and neck with tender, intimate caresses.

When Cassandra awoke the ballroom was deserted. She was still lying curled up in a ball on the brocaded couch, but no one else was around and she rose in a panic, stumbling to the doorway with her heart pounding.

Out in the hall, everything was quiet. Not even a servant's footstep disturbed the silence, and Cassandra was suddenly certain that she was the only person in the house. It had all been a trick, she thought in terror. The baron had merely wanted to see how far she was prepared to go in her efforts to stay with him, and having watched her take that terrible final perverse pleasure from Rupert's snake, he and Katya had departed, their entertainment complete. She choked back a sob, her exhausted body aching after the night's excesses and her legs reluctant to support her because they were so tired. Slowly she sank down onto the carpeted floor and wondered what would become of her now.

She was sitting with her arms round her knees, still naked and vulnerable when the baron found her. He watched her unnoticed for a few moments, admiring the slender curve of her neck and the softly swelling breasts that had matured during her sexual education. Then he called her name, and she swung round to face him, her eyes alight with relief.

'I thought you'd gone!' she exclaimed.

'Gone where?'

'I don't know. I thought you and Katya might have left for Austria, to join the children.'

'No, but Katya has left. She will never return to this house or enter any of my homes again. It's over, Cassandra, and you have won. How does it feel to be the victor?'

Cassandra lifted her head, growing in confidence at the look of reluctant admiration in his eyes. 'It feels good, although I never really knew what the rules of the contest were.'

This time he smiled. 'Of course not. The rules are always mine, and they remain my secret. We must get packed. I have decided we will fly to the Loire and join the children there.'

Cassandra stood up, totally unselfconscious despite her nakedness. 'I had to win, because I'd promised them I'd be there when their holiday was over.'

'Of course,' he replied gravely. 'I knew that was your motive all along. But before we go, I must make love to you just once, to make sure you know you're now mine.'

She let him lead her by the hand up the stairs to the bedroom where Katya had dressed herself in the purple and black gown only a few hours earlier, and then he laid her on the bed and covered her body with kisses while he removed his own clothes.

After that he lay down next to her pulling her across until she was lying on top of him, her breasts squashed against his chest, her stomach pressed to his. He reached above her and then round, his fingers going beneath her and massaging her whole vulva until moisture seeped from between the outer lips. Then he slid one finger up the damp channel until it located the slippery clitoris, already swelling with excitement.

As she rotated her hips against him his fingers matched her rhythm and she felt the tiny bud expanding and growing hot with excitement, while his mouth fastened on to one of her breasts hanging so invitingly above his face. The tugging of his lips along with the expert swirling of his finger made her insides grow tighter and tighter until she was moving more and more quickly against him, uttering little mewing sounds of excitement.

At last the tiny electric currents began to pulse through her, her toes curled and the baron slid his finger down to the underside of the clitoris so that he could caress the tiny stem on which it stood. It was the touch that always triggered her climax and this time was no exception. She bucked with the force of the explosion, an explosion made so much sweeter because for the first time he was really making love to her rather than experimenting with her sexuality.

He found her tiny mewing sounds unbearably exciting, and before the last ripples of her excitement had died away he pulled her down against his straining erection, driving into her and then moving her by her hips up and down to a rhythm of his own choosing, slowing when his climax threatened to come too soon but speeding up again when her mouth and eyes opened reproachfully. At this moment he could refuse her nothing, not even if it meant his own satisfaction came sooner than he would have chosen.

To his delight and her amazed wonder, they climaxed simultaneously, wrapping their arms around each other as they rolled across the huge bed, caught in the contractions of their union as lovers of equal standing.

Cassandra fell instantly asleep again but the baron didn't. He kept his arms round her, listened to her steady, gentle breathing and wondered what the future would hold for them both and how long their relationship would last given his never-ending search for constantly fresh and original stimulation.

At last, knowing that eventually the balance of power would change yet again, he regretfully woke her. 'Cassandra, open your eyes. It's time to pack. My jet is standing by.'

She looked at him sleepily, wishing she could tell him how much she loved him, but wise enough to know that she must never ever even say the word or their relationship would be finished.

299

'Did you say we're going to France?' she asked when they were finally sitting in the back of the sleek black Daimler, its windows darkened against the intrusive eyes of the outside world.

'Yes, I have a chateau in the Loire that I intend to re-open. You can help me get it into shape again, and then we can start having parties there. The neighbouring people are all very friendly. I'm sure you'll quickly feel at home.'

'I'm sure I will too,' she said placidly.

He put a finger under her chin and tipped her face up so that he could look into those tranquil eyes that darkened so gloriously in moments of passion. 'The game is on again, darling girl,' he whispered, and despite herself, a shiver of excitement ran down her spine.

*Already published*

# NO LADY
## Saskia Hope

30 year-old Kate dumps her boyfriend, walks out of her job and sets off in search of sexual adventure. Set against the rugged terrain of the Pyrenees, the love-making is as rough as the landscape. Only a sense of danger can satisfy her longing for erotic encounters beyond the boundaries of ordinary experience.

ISBN 0 352 32857 6

# WEB OF DESIRE
## Sophie Danson

High-flying executive Marcie is gradually drawn away from the normality of her married life. Strange messages begin to appear on her computer, summoning her to sinister and fetishistic sexual liaisons with strangers whose identity remains secret. She's given glimpses of the world of The Omega Network, where her every desire is known and fulfilled.

ISBN 0 352 32856 8

# BLUE HOTEL
## Cherri Pickford

Hotelier Ramon can't understand why best-selling author Floy Pennington has come to stay at his quiet hotel in the rural idyll of the English countryside. Her exhibitionist tendencies are driving him crazy, as are her increasingly wanton encounters with the hotel's other guests.

ISBN 0 352 32858 4

# CASSANDRA'S CONFLICT
## Fredrica Alleyn

Behind the respectable facade of a house in present-day Hampstead lies a world of decadent indulgence and darkly bizarre eroticism. The sternly attractive Baron and his beautiful but cruel wife are playing games with the young Cassandra, employed as a nanny in their sumptuous household. Games where only the Baron knows the rules, and where there can only be one winner.

ISBN 0 352 32859 2

# THE CAPTIVE FLESH
## Cleo Cordell

Marietta and Claudine, French aristocrats saved from pirates, learn their invitation to stay at the opulent Algerian mansion of their rescuer, Kasim, requires something in return; their complete surrender to the ecstasy of pleasure in pain. Kasim's decadent orgies also require the services of the handsome blonde slave, Gabriel – perfect in his male beauty. Together in their slavery, they savour delights at the depths of shame.

ISBN 0 352 32872 X

# PLEASURE HUNT
## Sophie Danson

Sexual adventurer Olympia Deschamps is determined to become a member of the Legion D' Amour – the most exclusive society of French libertines who pride themselves on their capacity for limitless erotic pleasure. Set in Paris – Europe's most romantic city – Olympia's sense of unbridled hedonism finds release in an extraordinary variety of libidinous challenges.

ISBN 0 352 32880 0

# OUTLANDIA
## Georgia Angelis

At first, Iona Stanley longs for her temperate home of nineteenth century England. Shipwrecked on the remote South Sea island of Wahwu, she finds the exotic customs of the inhabitants alarmingly licentious. But her natural sensuality blossoms as she is crowned living goddess of the island. Her days are spent luxuriating in the tropical splendour, being worshipped by a host of virile young men. Suddenly, things don't seem so bad after all.

ISBN 0 352 32883 5

# BLACK ORCHID
## Roxanne Carr

The Black Orchid is a women's health club which provides a specialised service for its high-powered clients; women who don't have the time to spend building complex relationships, but who enjoy the pleasures of the flesh. One woman, having savoured the erotic delights on offer at this spa of sensuality, embarks on a quest for the ultimate voyage of self-discovery through her sexuality. A quest which will test the unique talents of the exquisitely proportioned male staff.

ISBN 0 352 32888 6

*WE NEED YOUR HELP . . .*
*to plan the future of women's erotic fiction –*

*– and no stamp required!*

Yours are the only opinions that matter.
Black Lace is a new and exciting venture: the first series
of books devoted to erotic fiction by women for women.

We're going to do our best to provide the brightest,
best-written, bonk-filled books you can buy. And we'd
like your help in these early stages. Tell us what you
want to read.

---

# THE BLACK LACE QUESTIONNAIRE

## SECTION ONE: ABOUT YOU

1.1  Sex (*we presume you are female, but so as not to discriminate*)
     are you?
     Male                    ☐    Female                    ☐

1.2  Age
     under 21               ☐    21–30                     ☐
     31–40                  ☐    41–50                     ☐
     51–60                  ☐    over 60                   ☐

1.3  At what age did you leave full-time education?
     still in education     ☐    16 or younger            ☐
     17–19                  ☐    20 or older              ☐

1.4  Occupation _____

1.5  Annual household income

    under £10,000          ☐      £10–£20,000          ☐
    £20–£30,000            ☐      £30–£40,000          ☐
    over £40,000           ☐

1.6  We are perfectly happy for you to remain anonymous;
     but if you would like us to send you a free booklist of
     Nexus books for men and Black Lace books for Women,
     please insert your name and address

     _____

     _____

     _____

     _____

## SECTION TWO: ABOUT BUYING BLACK LACE BOOKS

2.1  How did you acquire this copy of *Cassandra's Conflict*
     I bought it myself        ☐    My partner bought it   ☐
     I borrowed/found it       ☐

2.2  How did you find out about Black Lace books?
     I saw them in a shop                                  ☐
     I saw them advertised in a magazine                   ☐
     I saw the London Underground posters                  ☐
     I read about them in _____
     Other _____

2.3  Please tick the following statements you agree with:
     I would be less embarrassed about buying Black
     Lace books if the cover pictures were less explicit   ☐
     I think that in general the pictures on Black
     Lace books are about right                            ☐
     I think Black Lace cover pictures should be as
     explicit as possible                                  ☐

2.4  Would you read a Black Lace book in a public place – on
     a train for instance?
     Yes              ☐      No              ☐

# SECTION THREE: ABOUT THIS BLACK LACE BOOK

3.1 Do you think the sex content in this book is:
Too much ☐ About right ☐
Not enough ☐

3.2 Do you think the writing style in this book is:
Too unreal/escapist ☐ About right ☐
Too down to earth ☐

3.3 Do you think the story in this book is:
Too complicated ☐ About right ☐
Too boring/simple ☐

3.4 Do you think the cover of this book is:
Too explicit ☐ About right ☐
Not explicit enough ☐

Here's a space for any other comments:


# SECTION FOUR: ABOUT OTHER BLACK LACE BOOKS

4.1 How many Black Lace books have you read? ☐

4.2 If more than one, which one did you prefer?

4.3 Why?

# SECTION FIVE: ABOUT YOUR IDEAL EROTIC NOVEL

We want to publish the books you want to read – so this is your chance to tell us exactly what your ideal erotic novel would be like.

5.1   Using a scale of 1 to 5 (1 = no interest at all, 5 = your ideal), please rate the following possible settings for an erotic novel:

Medieval/barbarian/sword 'n' sorcery ☐
Renaissance/Elizabethan/Restoration ☐
Victorian/Edwardian ☐
1920s & 1930s – the Jazz Age ☐
Present day ☐
Future/Science Fiction ☐

5.2   Using the same scale of 1 to 5, please rate the following themes you may find in an erotic novel:

Submissive male/dominant female ☐
Submissive female/dominant male ☐
Lesbianism ☐
Bondage/fetishism ☐
Romantic love ☐
Experimental sex e.g. anal/watersports/sex toys ☐
Gay male sex ☐
Group sex ☐

Using the same scale of 1 to 5, please rate the following styles in which an erotic novel could be written:

Realistic, down to earth, set in real life ☐
Escapist fantasy, but just about believable ☐
Completely unreal, impressionistic, dreamlike ☐

5.3   Would you prefer your ideal erotic novel to be written from the viewpoint of the main male characters or the main female characters?

Male ☐          Female ☐
Both ☐

5.4 What would your ideal Black Lace heroine be like? Tick as many as you like:

| | | | |
|---|---|---|---|
| Dominant | ☐ | Glamorous | ☐ |
| Extroverted | ☐ | Contemporary | ☐ |
| Independent | ☐ | Bisexual | ☐ |
| Adventurous | ☐ | Naive | ☐ |
| Intellectual | ☐ | Introverted | ☐ |
| Professional | ☐ | Kinky | ☐ |
| Submissive | ☐ | Anything else? | ☐ |
| Ordinary | ☐ | _____ | |

5.5 What would your ideal male lead character be like? Again, tick as many as you like:

| | | | |
|---|---|---|---|
| Rugged | ☐ | | |
| Athletic | ☐ | Caring | ☐ |
| Sophisticated | ☐ | Cruel | ☐ |
| Retiring | ☐ | Debonair | ☐ |
| Outdoor-type | ☐ | Naive | ☐ |
| Executive-type | ☐ | Intellectual | ☐ |
| Ordinary | ☐ | Professional | ☐ |
| Kinky | ☐ | Romantic | ☐ |
| Hunky | ☐ | | |
| Sexually dominant | ☐ | Anything else? | ☐ |
| Sexually submissive | ☐ | _____ | |

5.6 Is there one particular setting or subject matter that your ideal erotic novel would contain?

_____

## SECTION SIX: LAST WORDS

6.1 What do you like best about Black Lace books?

_____

6.2 What do you most dislike about Black Lace books?

_____

6.3 In what way, if any, would you like to change Black Lace covers?

_____

6.4  Here's a space for any other comments!

_____
_____
_____
_____

---

*Thank you for completing this questionnaire. Now tear it out of the book – carefully! – put it in an envelope and send it to:*

**Black Lace**
**FREEPOST**
**London**
**W10 5BR**

*No stamp is required!*